Gripping Novels of
Crime and Detection

**SIGNET
DOUBLE
MYSTERIES:**

Face to Face

AND

*The House
of Brass*

SIGNET Mysteries You'll Enjoy

Face to Face

AND

The House of Brass

By
Ellery Queen

A SIGNET BOOK
NEW AMERICAN LIBRARY
TIMES MIRROR

Face to Face: Copyright © 1967 by Ellery Queen
The House of Brass: Copyright © 1968 by Ellery Queen

All rights reserved. For information address
Scott Meredith Literary Agency, 845 Third Avenue,
New York, New York 10022.

Published by arrangement with Frederic Dannay and the late Manfred B. Lee. *Face to Face* and *The House of Brass* appeared in paperback as separate volumes published by The New American Library.

 SIGNET TRADEMARK REG. U.S. PAT. OFF. AND FOREIGN COUNTRIES
REGISTERED TRADEMARK—MARCA REGISTRADA
HECHO EN CHICAGO, U.S.A.

SIGNET, SIGNET CLASSICS, MENTOR, PLUME, MERIDIAN AND NAL BOOKS are published by The New American Library, Inc., 1633 Broadway, New York, New York 10019

First Printing (Double Ellery Queen Edition), April, 1982

1 2 3 4 5 6 7 8 9

PRINTED IN THE UNITED STATES OF AMERICA

Face to Face

CONTENTS

1 PROFILE

There is in every human countenance
either a history or a prophecy.

S. T. COLERIDGE

ONE

~~~~~~~~~~~~~~~~~~~~~~~~~~

On the penultimate lap of his round-the-planet tour, pumping police chiefs in odd cities for usable stories, Ellery had planned an overnight stop in London. But on flying in from Orly he ran into an Interpol man in Commissioner Vail's office at New Scotland Yard. The Interpol man was *muy simpático,* one good yarn led to another in a procession of pubs, and before he knew it several days and nights had blinked by, putting the New Year just around the corner.

The next morning, spurred by conscience and a head, Ellery stopped in at the airline office to pick up his ticket. And that was how and when he met Harry Burke. Burke was negotiating passage on the same jet to New York.

The Interpol man introduced Burke as a private inquiry agent— "one of the best, Queen, which of course means he doesn't pad his expense account by more than ten percent." Burke laughed; he was a short sandy-haired man with the neck of a wrestler who looked like a good companion for a fight. He had very light, almost transparent, eyes and they had a trick of disappearing, as if they were not there at all. He looked like a Teuton, the "Burke" said he should have talked with a brogue, but his speech came out on the burry side, and before leaving them together Interpol cheerfully identified him as a renegade Scot.

Over a pint and a much sucked-on pipe in the nearest pub, Burke said: "So you're Queen the Younger. This is fantastic."

"It is?" Ellery said.

"Meeting you this way, I mean. I was with your father not fifteen hours ago."

"*My* father?"

"Inspector Richard Queen of the New York police department," Burke said solemnly.

"You've just flown in?"

The Scot nodded.

"But I saw you buy a plane ticket back to New York a few minutes ago."

"I found a cable from Inspector Queen waiting for me when I got off the plane. Seems there's been a development in the case that originally took me to the States. He wants me to turn right around and fly back."

"That's my daddy," said Ellery. "Does he mention why?"

"No, but the cable contains that salty word, 'pronto.'"

"It must be important." Ellery fondly accepted another ale from the barmaid, who looked as if she could have fetched the entire keg on one palm. "This case, Burke. Could it be the sort of thing I have no strength to resist?"

"I don't know your capacity for punishment." Burke smiled at the vast barmaid, too, and buried his Caledonian nose in the mug. He was a handsome man.

They made the westward crossing shoulder to shoulder. For all the good Ellery's hinting did, the Scotsman might have been from the CIA. On subjects unrelated to his case, however, he was talkative enough. Harry Burke was an ex-Yard man who had recently resigned his detective inspectorship to form an agency of his own. Business was picking up, he said wryly.

"In the beginning it was touch and go. If not for my connections at the Yard, I'd be scratching like a Bantu. Commissioner Vail has been very kind." Ellery gathered that Burke's current professional preoccupation was a result of Vail's latest kindness. The inquiry had come into the Yard and the Commissioner, finding it not proper Yard business, had privately recommended Burke for the job. It was not, Ellery suspected, Vail's first kindness of the sort. Burke was kept hopping now.

"But I'm a bachelor," the sandy-haired man said, "and I don't have to make a ruddy accounting to some whining female for my hours. No, there's no one on the agenda, thank you. I don't stay in one place long enough to form an attachment."

"You," quoth Ellery, speaking strictly from hearsay, "are the sort who gets hooked in one fell jerk."

"The angler hasn't been born who can hook me."

"Watch out for the ones on my side of the puddle. Catching the hard ones comes naturally to American women."

"They seem to have missed you, Queen."

"Oh, but I'm the original Artful Dodger."

"Then we have a great deal in common."

And so they proved to have, including a penchant for small disagreements. By the time they set down in Gander they were on a first-name basis and arguing amiably over the comparative merits of serving Scotch kippers with and without sautéed onions. They almost forgot to mark the passage of the old year, which took place between heaven and earth after the flight resumed.

They landed at Kennedy International Airport early New Year's morning in a fog only slightly less gothic than the one that had grounded them in Gander.

"There's no point in your groping about for a hotel room at this hour," Ellery said. "Come on home with me, Harry."

"Oh, no. I couldn't put you and the Inspector out."

"Rubbish, there's a daybed in my study. Besides, it will give you a jump on whatever my father's brought you back to New York for." But this delicate feeler brought forth from Harry Burke no more than a good-natured nod. "Taxi?"

Their cab drove uptown through Times Square, which looked like a ghost town invaded by tumbleweed. "People are a mucky lot, aren't they?" Burke remarked, pointing his pipe stem at the litter. "Every time I see a thing like this I think of that last scene in *On the Beach*."

"Maybe that's what they were thinking of, too."

They achieved the Queen apartment and found the Inspector not in his bed, or anywhere. "Out celebrating?" Burke ventured.

"Not a chance. Not my daddy. It's a case. What's this?"

This was a message for Ellery propped against the typewriter in his study, inscribed in the old man's squibby hand.

Dear Son:

A Miss Roberta West of East 73rd St. wants you to call her. No matter what time you get in, she says. Me, I'm up to my ears in something. I'll be phoning you. Oh, yes. Happy New Year!

It was signed "Dad" and there was a telephone number.

"Is this a sample of the Queens' home life?" asked the Scotsman.

"Only when interrupted by mayhem. Dad and I usually spend New Year's Eve dozing at the telly." Ellery dialed the number. "Dump your bags in my bedroom,

11

Harry—it's in there. Oh, and there's a bar in the living room if you'd like an eye-opener. Hello?"

"Ellery Queen?" asked a deeply anxious voice.

"Yes. I have a message to call a Miss West."

"I'm Miss West. It's wonderful of you to call me so early. Whoever answered said you were flying in from England. Did you just get in, Mr. Queen?"

"Just. What's this about, Miss West?"

"Are you calling from your home?"

"Yes?"

"I'd like to come over."

"Now?" asked Ellery, astonished. "I need a shave, I haven't had breakfast, and sleeping on transatlantic planes isn't one of my accomplishments. Can't this wait?"

"I haven't slept, either, waiting for your call. Please?"

She sounded like a pretty girl. So he sighed and said, "Do you know the address?"

TWO

~~~~~~~~~~~~~~~~~~~~~~~~~~~~~

Roberta West proved even prettier than she sounded. The moment Ellery set eyes on her he labeled her "theater," with "little?" in parentheses. She was dainty of body and fair of skin, with true sorrel hair, luminous eyes that were underscored with late hours or trouble, and an enchanting birthmark on her upper right cheek that looked remarkably like a little butterfly. Ellery's dramatic deduction derived from a number of small observations—the way she walked and cocked her head, a certain tension in her posture, an impression of newly acquired muscle-discipline, and above all the studied diction, as if even its slight occasional slurring had been carefully rehearsed. She was dressed in skirt and sweater-blouse of some angoralike material, with a Parisian-looking coat flung over her shoulders, a scarf wound about her neck that might have been designed by Picasso, and gauntlet gloves. Her tiny feet were expensively shod in stylish flats, with butterfly bows—a touch, Ellery noted, that balanced the birthmark on her cheek; he was sure the bows had been chosen for just that reason.

The whole woman was an artful study in casualness—so much so, in fact, that Ellery was tempted to doubt his own conclusions. When they looked as if they had

12

just stepped out of the pages of *Vogue*, he had found, they were almost always somebody's office help.

"You're in the theater," he said.

Her brilliant, nearly fevered, eyes widened. "How did you know, Mr. Queen?"

"I have my methods," he grinned, seeing her into the living room. "Oh, this is Mr. Burke. Miss West."

The girl murmured something, and Harry Burke said, "D'ye do," in a startled way, as if he had just stumbled over something. He moved over toward the doorway to Ellery's study and said with plain reluctance, "I'll wash up, Ellery. Or something."

"Maybe Miss West won't mind your sitting in on this," Ellery said. "Mr. Burke is a private detective, in from London on business."

"Oh, in that case," the girl said quickly; and for some reason she lowered her head. As for Burke, his glance at Ellery was positively canine. He slithered over to one of the windows and stood there, out of the way, staring.

"Now," Ellery said when he had the girl seated, had offered her breakfast and been refused, and lit a cigaret for her, "shall we get down to cases, Miss West?"

She was quiet for a moment. Then she said, "I hardly know where to start," looking confused; but suddenly she leaned over and rapped her cigaret ash into a tray. "I suppose you remember Glory Guild?"

Ellery remembered Glory Guild. He would have had to be deficient in all senses to profess amnesia. He not only remembered Glory Guild, he had listened to her with both enraptured ears in his youth, he had had wishful dreams about her—an international trauma—and even the memory of her voice sufficed to tickle his giblets. Memories were all that were left to those whom the press agent in her heyday had, with unfortunate failure to refer to the dictionary, termed her "myrmidons" of admirers.

Oh, yes, he had heard of GeeGee, as her intimates were said to call her (he had never been one of them, alas, alas); he still occasionally spun one of her old 78s on a moonlit night when he was feeling his years. He was surprised to have her name thrust at him so abruptly. It was as if the girl with the sorrel hair had recalled Helen Morgan, or Galli-Curci, or the little girl with the palpitant throat in *The Wizard of Oz*.

"What about Glory Guild?" Ellery asked. A movement by Harry Burke, swiftly stilled, had told him that Burke was surprised, too; surprised, and something more. Ellery slavered to know what it was. But then he compelled his attention to revert to Roberta West.

"I'm in love with Glory Guild's husband," the girl said and the way she said it brought Ellery to the point. "I mean, I ought to say I *was* in love with Carlos." It seemed to Ellery that she shuddered, something he had found very few people did in actuality, regardless of authors. Then she said, "How can women be such fools? Such blind fools?" She really said "blind fools."

She began to cry.

Crying women were no novelty in the Queen living room, and the obvious cause of these tears was one of the commonest; still, Ellery was touched, and he let her cry it quite out. She stopped at last, sniffing like a child, groped in her bag for a handkerchief, and pawed at her little nose. "I'm sorry," the girl said. "I hadn't meant to do that. I'd made up my mind I *wouldn't*. Anyway, it was all over seven months ago. Or I thought it was. But now something's happened . . ."

THREE

~~~~~~~~~~~~~~~~~~~~~~

Roberta West's story came out episodic and random, a mosaic tumbled to fragments that had to be put together by the bit. As Ellery reconstructed it, it began with a sketch of Glory Guild, her life and works.

She had been born Gloria Guldenstern in 1914, in Sinclair Lewis country; and in the 30s she had come out of the Midwest with Lewisite fidelity to take New York by storm and, inevitably, the wide country. She had never had a music lesson in her life; she was completely self-taught—voice, musicology, piano. She played her own accompaniments.

It was said of Glory Guild that she also played her voice. Certainly her singing technique was as calculated as the notes on her music paper. There was a throb of passion, almost of grief, in her projection that swayed audiences like the fakir's reed—faint and faraway, something not quite lost. In nightclubs it silenced even drunks. The critics called it an *intime* voice, fit for bistros; and yet, so pervasive was her magic, it affected multitudes. By the end of the 30s she was singing weekly on her own radio show to tens of millions of listeners. She was America's radio darling.

She came on the air to the strains of "Battle Hymn of the Republic," a signature played sweet and slow by her 42-piece orchestra; in the nature of things in those simpler days, a columnist nicknamed her Glory-Glory. Glory-Glory was otherwise a shrewd, practical woman. Her smartest act was to place her fortunes in the stringy hands of Selma Pilter, the theatrical agent, who quickly became her business manager as well as booker. Mrs. Pilter (there had been a Mr. Pilter, but he had vanished in the mists of some antique divorce court) managed Glory's affairs so astutely that, at the time of her loss of voice and retirement in 1949, the singer was said to be a millionaire.

In her limited way Glory had a questing mind; retirement threw her back not merely upon music but on puzzles, her other passion. She was a hifi fanatic long before the pursuit of the perfect tweeter became a national aberration; her library of contemporary music was a collector's dream. The motivation for her absorption in puzzles was less clear. She had come from a rural Minnesota family whose interest in such pastimes had never risen above the ancient copy of Sam Lloyd in the farmhouse parlor. Nevertheless, Glory spent many hours with crosswords, Double-Crostics, anagrams, and detective stories (the classic bafflers of the field—she had no use for the sex-and-violence or psychological mysteries that began to clog the paperback racks after World War II). Both her New York apartment and her hideaway cottage—nestled in a stand of packed pines on a lakefront near Newtown, Connecticut—were cluttered with players, discs, FM radios, electronic recording equipment (she could not bear to part with it), musical instruments, mountains of mystery stories and puzzle books and gadgets; and on her own open terrace such gimmickry as a set of *buinho* chairs, handwoven in Portugal of wet reeds, whose marvelous secret was that each time they were rained on their weave tightened.

Glory had remained single during her singing career, although she was a deep-breasted, handsome blonde much (if gingerly) pursued. When her voice went back on her at the age of 35, the senseless trick of fate sent her into Garbo-like seclusion, and (as in Garbo's case) it was assumed, in the media where such speculations are of earth-shaking concern, that she would never marry. And she did hold out for nine years. But then in 1958, when she was 44 and he was 33, she met Count Carlos Armando. Within three months they were man and wife.

The "Count" Armando was a self-conferred title which no one, least of all Carlos, took seriously. His origin had a floating base; not even his name could be taken for granted. He was altogether charming about it. He claimed Spanish, Roman, Portuguese, and mixed Greek-and-Romanian descent as the fancy took him; once he even said his mother had been an Egyptian. One of his friends of the international set (a real count) laughed, "In direct descent from Cleopatra, obviously," and Carlos, showing his brilliant teeth, laughed back, "Of course, *caro*. By way of Romeo." Those who claimed the worthiest information asserted that his parents had been gypsies and that he had been born in a caravan by the side of some squalid Albanian road. It might well have been so.

None of this seemed to make any difference to the women in his life. Like obedient tin soldiers, they fell to his amorous fire in ranks. He kept his ammunition dry as a matter of working principle, careful not to allow it to sputter away because of an honest emotion. Women were his profession. He had never worked an otherwise gainful day in his life.

Carlos's first marriage, when he was 19, had been to an oil dowager from Oklahoma. She was exactly three times his age, with a greed for male youth that amused him. She cast him adrift well within two years, having barged into a beautiful boy from Athens. His severance pay was considerable, and Carlos spent a mad year throwing it away.

His second wife was a wealthy Danish baroness, with the features of a cathedral gargoyle, whose chief delight was to dress his curly black hair as if he were a doll. Four months of lying on couches with those terrible fingers creeping about his head were enough for Carlos; he seduced his wife's bedazzled secretary, contrived to be caught at it, and gallantly insisted on being paid off.

Another year of high life, and Carlos began to look around again.

He discovered a United States senator's juicy little 16-year-old daughter summering in the Alps; the resulting scandal involved a highly paid Swiss abortionist (from whom Carlos collected 15 percent) and a very large senatorial check, conditional upon his silence, with the threat of prosecution to enforce it.

The years marched by, and with them a grand parade

of wives, all rich and silly and old enough to be his mother: a New York socialite who divorced her banker husband in order to marry him (this union broke up after a $100,000 brawl at an all-night party in his wife's Newport villa that made tabloid history); an alcoholic Back Bay spinster whose simple escutcheon was first plotted at Plymouth Rock; a Hungarian countess dying of tuberculosis (she left him nothing but a castle surrounded by a stagnant moat and debts—with easy foresight he had run through her fortune before her death); an aging Eurasian ex-beauty he quite literally sold to a rich Turk whose real objective was her nubile daughter (as she had been Carlos's); a Chicago meatpacker's widow who, accompanied by a photographer, surprised him in her maid's bed and booted him out without a penny's salve, even producing the photographs in court— to Carlos's smarting surprise—with unsporting disdain for the press.

This debacle left him in financial extremis. He was in great need when he met GeeGee Guild.

Not that Glory was so hard to take; she was still attractive, and younger at their meeting than any of his ex-wives had been. Still, to Carlos the prime question was: Is she rich enough? He had led a cowboy's life herding idleness, and it was beginning to leave its brand on his dark athletic flesh, or so he fancied from increasing self-study in his mirror. The middle-aged and old ones who, like his first wife, sought to lap thirstily from the waterhole of male youth might soon notice the flattening taste of Count Armando. When that day came, the bogus count assured himself glumly, the bellowing kine would turn to greener pasture.

So at this stage of his life, Armando decided, he could not afford to make a mistake. Undercover he made a financial survey of Glory Guild that would not have shamed an ace credit agent. What he found out heartened him, and he stripped down for the conquest.

It was not easy, even though Glory was receptive. She had become lonely and restless, and what she was seeing daily in *her* mirror dismayed her. Between her need for companionship and attention and the hurrying truths revealed by her glass, a young man like Carlos Armando was inevitable. Because she had heard stories about him and glimpsed him for what he was, she hired a reliable agency to check his background. It confirmed what she suspected, and she was determined not to go the way of all the female fools in his life.

17

"I like having you around," she told Carlos at his proposal of marriage, "and you want my money, or as much of it as you can lay your hands on. Right? Well, I'll marry you on one condition."

"Must we speak of technicalities at a time like this, my darling?" asked Carlos, kissing her hands.

"The condition is this: You will sign a premarital agreement renouncing in advance any share of my estate."

"Ah," said Carlos.

"Even the one-third dower share ordinarily guaranteed by law," said Glory dryly, "the gleam of which I can see in your eye. I've consulted my attorney and, properly drawn up, such a contract would be perfectly legal in this state—I mean in case you have an idea you could break it later."

"What you must think of me, *bonita*," mourned Carlos, "to make such an unfair condition. I am proposing to give you all of myself."

"And quite a hunk it is," said Glory Guild fondly, ruffling his hair (he caught himself in time to keep from flinching). "So I've worked out what the lawyers call a *quid pro quo*."

"And what is that, my enchantment?" asked Carlos, as if he did not know what a *quid pro quo* was.

"A tit for my tat."

"I see. . . . Time?" Carlos said suddenly. He was intuitive in all matters relating to women.

"That's it, baby. Give me a minimum of five happy years of married life and I'll tear up the contract. I've had you investigated, Carlos, and the longest you've ever stuck to one woman was less than two years. Five are my terms, then zip! goes the contract, and you come into your normal legal rights as my husband."

They looked each other in the eye, and both smiled.

"I love you madly," murmured Carlos, "but love is not all. Agreed."

"Love, shove," said Glory.

And so it was arranged; and he signed the prenuptial agreement, and they were bound in not so holy matrimony.

FOUR

〰〰〰〰〰〰〰〰〰〰

"I met Carlos in Easthampton," continued Roberta West, "while I was doing summer stock. It was at the tail end of the season, and he and Glory came backstage. The director was an old man who made a great to-do over Glory, but she was no more than a name to me—I was a little girl when she retired—and all I could see was an overweight woman with stupidly dyed hair looking like some aging Brünnehilde out of a second-rate opera company and clinging to the arm of a man who seemed young enough to be her son.

"But I thought Carlos was cute, and I suppose I was flattered by the fuss he made over my performance. There's something in Carlos's voice," she added gloomily, "that gets through to women. You know he's a fake, but it doesn't matter. It's not so much what he says as how he says it . . . I suppose I sound like a gullible idiot."

Neither man, being a man, said anything.

"When the stock engagement was over, I hadn't been back in town twenty-four hours—I don't know how he got my phone number, because it was a new one and still wasn't in the book—before he called me. He handed me some transparent story about being awfully impressed by my talent, and how he knew he could pull some strings for me, and wouldn't I like to talk it over? And I fell for it—the oldest line in show business!—knowing all the time that I was letting myself in for trouble. . . . The funny part of it was that he did manage to get me an audition—and the part—in an off-Broadway play. To this day I don't know how, except that the producer was a woman. Men have nothing but contempt for him —or jealousy—but women can't seem to resist his charm. I suppose this producer was one of them, although she's an old bag with a personality like a buzz saw. Anyway, he sweet-talked her into it. The way he did me."

The girl with the sorrel hair half shut her eyes. Then she picked a cigaret out of her bag, and Harry Burke leaped with a lighter. She smiled up at him over the flame, but not as if she saw him.

"He kept turning up . . . Carlos has a persistence that batters you down. No matter how careful you are. . . .

19

I fell in love with him. In a raunchy sort of way he's beautiful. Certainly when he pays attention to a woman she feels that she's the only woman in the world. It becomes total involvement—I don't know—as if you're the absolute center of the universe. And all the time you know he hasn't an honest bone in his body, that he's pulled the same line on hundreds of women. And you don't care. You just *don't*. . . . I fell in love with him, and he told me the only thing in the world that would make him happy was to marry me."

Ellery stirred. "How well-heeled are you, Miss West?"

She laughed. "I have a small income from a trust, and with what I can earn here and there I just manage to get by. That's what fooled me," said the girl bitterly. "He's never married except for money. Being poor, I began to think that in my case his protestations of love might be, for once in his life, the real thing. How naive can you get! I didn't know what he really had in mind. Until one night, a little more than seven months ago..."

For some reason Glory had gone up to her Newtown cottage, and Carlos had seized the opportunity to see Roberta. It was on this occasion that he had finally shown his hand.

Roberta had known about his premarital agreement with his wife, and that the five-year mark had been passed—by that date he and Glory had been married five and a half years. According to Carlos, Glory had torn up their agreement at the expiration of the five years, as she had promised; so that now, if anything were to happen to her, he would inherit at least one-third of her estate under his ordinary dower rights; more, if she had named him in her will, about which he seemed uncertain.

At first, the West girl said, she had not seen what he was driving at. "How could it occur to any normal person? I told him truthfully that I had no idea what he was talking about." Was there something wrong with his wife? Was she incurably ill? Cancer? What?

Carlos had said easily, "She is as healthy as a cow. *Dios!* She will outlive both of us."

"Then do you mean a divorce settlement?" Roberta had asked, confused.

"Settlement? She would not give me a lira if I were to suggest a divorce."

"Carlos, I don't understand."

"Of course you do not, *palomilla mia*. So like a child! But you will listen to me, and I shall tell you how we can be rid of this cow, and marry and enjoy the milk from her udders."

And, calmly, as if he were relating the plot of a novel, Carlos had disclosed his plan to Roberta. Glory stood in the way; she had to be knocked aside. But as her husband he would be the first to be suspected. Unless he had what was called an alibi. But for an alibi to stand up, it had to be unshakable; that is, he, Carlos, truly had to be elsewhere when the thing was done. This was simply arranged, in any of a thousand ways. Who, then, was to do it? Who but she, Roberta, the co-beneficiary of Glory's death? Did she now see?

"I now saw," Roberta told the two silent men. "Oh, how I now saw! In that mocking voice of his, as if he were talking about taking a walk in the park, he was actually proposing that I murder his wife so that he and I could get married and live on the blood money. I was so stunned, so horrified, that for a minute I couldn't get a word out. I guess he took my silence for consent, because he slithered over and tried to make love to me. It broke the spell with a bang. I pushed him away so hard he staggered. This lovely conversation took place in Glory's and Carlos's apartment, and I ran out of there as if the devil were after me. For all I know, he was— he has the devil's own gall. How could I have thought I loved that monster! My skin was crawling. All I could think of was getting away from him. I cabbed home and walked the floor all night, shaking like a leaf."

Carlos had telephoned her the next day, the girl went on, and she had told him never to call or try to see her again and hung up on him.

"The bloody bastard," muttered Harry Burke. He looked as if he could cheerfully have committed murder himself at that moment.

"You were lucky to get out of it without a beating," Ellery commented. "Sometimes these types, when they're balked, can be awfully rough. But, Miss West, I don't get it. If all this happened more than seven months ago— back in May?—why have you waited so long to tell the story? And, in any event, why the urgency now?"

The girl looked puzzled. "The urgency? What do you mean, Mr. Queen? I would have thought—"

"We obviously have our wires crossed," Ellery said with a smile. "There's more to your story?"

"Of course." She glanced from him to Burke and back again, shaking her head. "Or don't you believe me? I don't understand . . . As for why I didn't tell anyone all

21

this time—I don't know. It was such a shocking experience, as if I'd dreamed it all. The thought of going to the police, or to someone like you, never entered my mind. For one thing, I kept telling myself he couldn't really have meant it. For another"—her delicate skin colored—"it would have meant getting my relationship with him smeared all over the papers. You know the bit. Anyway, I didn't. And when he didn't call or try to see me again, I put the whole thing out of my head, or tried to. Until it was forcibly recalled to me two nights ago. What's today? Yes, the night before last, Wednesday night."

"The night of December thirtieth?" Harry Burke asked sharply. It made Ellery look at him.

"Yes. Carlos phoned me. I hadn't heard from him, as I said, since late spring. Of course I hung up on him—"

"What did the beggar want?" snapped Burke.

"He had to see me, he said. I told him that what I'd said months ago still went, and banged the receiver. Not a half hour later my apartment bell rang, and when I opened the door, there he was. I tried to shut it in his face, but he stuck his foot in the way. He made such a fuss, in such a loud voice, that I was afraid the neighbors might come running out. So I let him in."

"What *did* he want?" Ellery asked.

"At the time I couldn't imagine. He made no attempt to bring up that fantastic proposition again, just talked about trivial things—me, the plays on Broadway, what he and Glory had been doing recently, and so on. I kept asking him to go, and he kept making conversation. He wasn't drunk, or anything like that—Carlos never drinks enough to lose his head; at least I've never seen him sozzled. I kept getting the feeling he was stalling for time, because he would glance at his watch every once in a while."

"Oh," said Ellery in an odd voice. And "Oh," said Harry Burke, in an even odder voice. But while Ellery's "Oh" had a speculative quality, Burke's was deep with foreboding; and again Ellery wondered.

Roberta West leaned forward in an attitude of tense appeal. "I finally got rid of him at midnight. Or rather at midnight, without warning, he suddenly decided to leave. I remember he looked at his watch again and actually said aloud, 'It's midnight, Roberta, I'll have to go.' As if he had a deadline or something. I didn't understand any of it. Until later. That's really why I'm here, Mr. Queen. He used me!"

22

"It sounds like it," Ellery agreed. "But for what?"

"Don't you *know?*"

"Don't I know what, Miss West?"

"That Glory Guild Armando was murdered Wednesday night?"

FIVE

~~~~~~~~~~~~~~~~~~~~~

Ellery had not seen a New York newspaper for a long time, and if GeeGee's murder had been reported in the London *Times,* he had missed the leader in the malty haze of some pub.

As for Harry Burke, the Scot seemed both knowledgeable and appalled. He stalked over to Ellery's bar and poured himself a slug out of the handiest bottle, which happened to be bourbon, and tossed it down neat, with no more awareness of what he was doing than if he had raised his hand to scratch himself.

Ellery kept dividing his attention between the West girl and Burke.

"How dense of me," she was saying. "Of course you don't know about the murder—you've been in Europe. Don't you have this morning's paper?"

"No," Ellery said. "What time did she get it, Miss West, do you know?"

"Not the exact time, no. But I do know, from the news stories, that it was while Carlos was in my apartment Wednesday night. It's perfectly clear now what he was up to. When he couldn't talk me into killing his wife last summer, he started looking around for another patsy. And he must have found her—it has to be a her, Mr. Queen; he wouldn't be able to talk a *man* into giving him the time of day. So Wednesday night, while this woman did the killing—whoever she is—he made it his business to be in my place. Using me as his alibi! Dragging me into this after I thought I was rid of him and his wife and the whole nasty mess!"

She seemed on the edge of hysteria, and Ellery went to some lengths to back her away. Burke was marching like a grenadier before the bar now, evidently struggling with a problem.

"Question," Ellery said to the girl. "Just why have you come to me?"

23

She was twisting the straps of her bag. "It's that— well, I'm so *alone* in this, Mr. Queen. Up to my neck in a horrible situation through no fault of my own— well, perhaps I *was* at fault to fall for Carlos's line, but how could I have known what I was getting into? Certainly I couldn't have dreamed he was scheming to commit murder. . . . Carlos, of course, must have promptly told the police of his alibi, which meant me, because they've already been to my apartment to question me, and I naturally had to tell them the truth, which is that he was with me Wednesday night until midnight."

"Did you tell the officers about Carlos's proposing to you last May that you murder his wife?"

"No. I guess I should have, but I just couldn't bring myself to. I kept thinking how the more I said, the more deeply I'd get involved. So all I did was answer their questions. What do I *do*, Mr. Queen? How do I get out of this?"

"I'm afraid it's too late for that. My advice to you is to tell the police everything, and the sooner the better."

She bit her lip.

"Ellery," said Harry Burke abruptly. "I'd like to talk to you."

"Would you excuse us a moment, Miss West?" When they were in his study, behind the closed door, Ellery said, "You've been bursting with some kind of bombshell since that girl got here, Harry. You're involved in this case, aren't you?"

"I am now," Burke said unhappily. "Until a moment ago I didn't know any more about the murder than you did. But the thing that brought me to New York originally—my first trip here—was tied up with Glory Guild. She'd made a request of the Yard which was outside the Yard's competence, and Vail recommended me to her, as a private agent. It was a routine inquiry—I can't see how it could have anything to do with this, although there's always the possibility." The Scot scowled. "The fact is, Ellery, on Wednesday night I was with the Guild woman in her apartment until a bit after eleven, on the business that brought me overseas. I made my report, and from her place I went directly to the airport. My plane took off a short time later, at 1:00 A.M. I left her alive and well."

"Then she was murdered by someone who got to her place between a few minutes past eleven, when you left her, and midnight, when Armando left Roberta West's apartment."

"It would seem so." Burke seemed troubled about something, but he said nothing more.

Ellery squinted at him. "This matter that brought you to New York—you consulted my father about it?"

"Yes. It required the cooperation of the New York police."

"Then that's why dad cabled you to come back—the hunch that it might have something to do with the killing." Ellery paused, inviting Burke to comment. But Burke did not. "He must have gone on the murder some time after it broke. Apparently when he dashed off this telephone-message note to me he hadn't connected the West girl with the case, or still didn't know any of the facts. These things over here are always handled on the precinct level first. Well, Harry, this puts a different complexion on things. I seem to be in it, too, like it or not."

Burke merely nodded.

They returned to the living room. "All right, Miss West, I'll stick with you," Ellery told the girl. She was staring at them in a frightened way. "At least until we see how it shapes up. The first thing you're going to do is tell the police the whole story. Carlos's alibi notwithstanding, it may well be that he's as guilty of his wife's murder as if he committed it himself. At this point I'd say that it's likelier than not."

"I'll do whatever you say, Mr. Queen." She seemed relieved.

"This Armando character is obviously devious. Whoever the woman is he's snake-charmed into doing his dirty work for him, he's probably been seeing her in secret—as he saw you, I take it?"

He could barely hear her "Yes."

"And now he'll be careful not to see her at all, or one of these days he'll pretend he's meeting her for the first time. He's got to wait for the heat to let up. Well, we'll see. She may be his weakness, too. At any rate, she has to be found, and I have the feeling it won't be easy."

Just then the phone rang in Ellery's study.

"Son?" It was his father's nasal rasp. "So your plane finally landed, did it? What did it do, play skipping stones all the way from London? Ellery, I'm on one beaut of a case—"

"I know," said Ellery. "Glory, Glory Hallelujah."

"So the West girl did get to you. She was questioned by some precinct men, and I didn't put two and two

25

together till after I got the early reports. Is she there now?"

"Yes."

"Well, come on over and join the party, and bring her with you. By the way, you didn't happen to run into a man named Harry Burke on the plane coming over, did you?"

"I did. And he's with me. House guest."

"I'll be damned," said the Inspector. "Another of your magic acts. I've been waiting to hear from Burke—I suppose he's told you I cabled him. Bring him along, too."

"Where are you, dad?"

"At GeeGee's Park Avenue apartment. Do you know the address?"

"No, but Burke and Miss West do."

"That's a fact, isn't it?" The old man cursed and hung up.

SIX

The doorman at the cooperative had a wild look in his eye. There was a patrolman conspicuously on duty in the lobby, and another in the foyer of the Guild-Armando apartment. Several detectives, including Sergeant Velie, were working their way through the penthouse duplex. Ellery left Roberta West in a small drawing room off the foyer, and at Velie's direction he and Harry Burke went up the wrought-iron stairway to the master bedroom, where they found Inspector Queen going through a clothes closet.

"Oh, hello, son," the old man said, barely looking up. "Damn it, where *is* it? Sorry to bring you all the way back across an ocean, Burke, but I had no choice. It's got to be here *somewhere*."

"Before we get down to cases, daddy-o," Ellery said in a pained tone, "may I point out that you haven't seen me for almost two months? I didn't expect the fatted calf, but could you spare a handshake?"

"Oh . . . *booshwa*," said the Inspector crossly, falling back on the slang of his youth. "Help me find it, you two, will you?"

26

"Find what, Inspector?" asked Burke. "What are you looking for?"

"Her diaries. I'm mad for cases where they keep diaries. Her secretary, Jeanne Temple, tells me Glory-Glory kept one ever since her retirement—wrote up the events of the day every night before going to bed. By now it's volumes. A few months ago she started working on a publishing project, an autobiography or book of memoirs or something, with the help of that gigolo husband of hers and Miss Temple, and she's been using the diaries as reference material, where she couldn't trust her memory or had to look up details. And that's great, only where are they? Or it? I'm anxious to see the latest one especially, the current diary—what she wrote in it Wednesday night. If she did, that is. We've been searching for two days."

"They're all missing?" asked Ellery.

"Including the manuscript of the autobiography."

"Inspector," said Harry Burke. "I saw her Wednesday night."

"The hell you did. I was hoping for a break like that! It's one of the reasons I cabled you. What time was it you left her?"

"A few minutes after eleven."

"That's good, that's good," the Inspector said in an absent way. "She wasn't excited or nervous or anything?"

"Not as far as I could tell. Of course I didn't know her very well—just the few conversations we'd had about the matter I was on for her."

"Well, those diaries are tied into this case some way, I'll bet a cookie, or the whole kit and caboodle wouldn't be missing. They've been lifted. The question is, why?"

Ellery was looking over the Hollywood bed, with its bold satin spread and silken bolsters and gold damask draped canopy. The bed had not been slept in.

His father caught the glance and nodded. "She never did get to bed Wednesday night."

"I take it, dad, she wasn't killed in this room."

"No." The Inspector led the way past a vast master bath with a sunken marble tub and gold-plated fixtures, into an untidy den—if it had been human, Ellery would have called it disheveled. "She was shot in here."

Except for the clutter, the room was surprisingly Spartan. One scatter rug on the parquet floor, a knee-hole desk and a leather swivel chair behind it, facing the doorway; a far-out armchair of some black wood, covered with what Ellery could have sworn was elephant

27

hide; one work of art on a pedestal, a carving in ebony of a Watusi warrior, of native African craftsmanship, and not very good, he thought. There was not a painting on the wall, and the lamp beside the armchair had a mica shade that was flaking. High above the Watusi warrior, inset in the wall near the ceiling, was a wood-framed grille of some coarse, potato-sacklike material, with a volume regulator, which Ellery took to conceal a speaker that piped music in from the elaborate player he had noticed in the living room downstairs; he had seen a similar speaker in one of the bedroom walls, and one in the bathroom. And that was all except for the bookcases, which ran around three walls to a height of some eight feet. The shelves were mobbed with books—lying down, leaning both ways, protruding (chiefly detective stories, Ellery noted with interest—he spotted Poe, Gaboriau, Anna Katharine Green, Wilkie Collins, Doyle, Freeman, Christie, Sayers, Van Dine among many others, including a number of his own early books); scrapbooks of all sizes and colors, tricks, puzzles, whatnots . . . the accumulation of what must have been many years. Ellery strolled over to one shelf and plucked a Double-Crostics book at random from a small army of them. He riffled through it; all the puzzles had been completed, in ink. In his experience, there was nothing quite so useless as a filled-in Double-Crostics book, especially one filled in in ink, the mark of the thirty-third degree. Glory Guild Armando had evidently been unable to part with anything relating to her hobbies, even the things that had served their purpose.

The top of the kneehole desk was a mess. The desk blotter, centered before the swivel chair, was considerably stained with dry, oxidized blood.

"Chest wound?" Burke said, studying the bloodstains.

"Two of them," Inspector Queen said. "One bullet through the right lung, the other in the heart. The way we put it together, she'd come in here—some time after you left, Burke—maybe intending to write in her diary, more likely to make some notes for her book of memoirs. Miss Temple says she'd been doing that before she went to bed practically every night for the last few months, and then she'd dictate the notes to Miss Temple the next day, to be typed up. Probably Glory'd just sat down at the desk when her killer showed up and shot her, most likely from the doorway there, Doc Prouty says. The angles of entry of the two bullets fired into her confirm this. The blood got on the blotter when she fell forward on being shot, as you guessed, Burke. It's a cinch she saw who shot her."

"Did she die instantly?" Ellery asked.

"No, she lived a few minutes, Doc says." The Inspector's tone was peculiar.

"Ah me and oh my," Ellery mourned. "Wouldn't it be tidy if she'd left a dying message? But that's too much to expect."

"Ask and ye shall receive," rasped his father in the same nasally mysterious way. "And may it do you a lot more good than it does us. As far as I'm concerned it could be ancient Martian."

"Don't tell me—"

"That's just what I'm doing. She lived long enough, and had enough strength—though where she got it Doc says he can't imagine, with that heart wound—to pick up a pen, or maybe she already had it in her hand, and write something on the nearest piece of paper."

Ellery was aquiver.

"Come over here. You, too, Burke."

They joined the old man behind Glory's desk. One of the objects on the bloodstained blotter was a police photostat of what had clearly been a sheet of ordinary lined pad-paper ("Yellow?" Ellery muttered, as if the color mattered; and his father nodded with a straight face) and roughly on one of the lines, toward the bottom of the otherwise unmarked sheet, a single word had been written.

The writing was tortured and difficult, a scrawl executed under extreme stress. The word was:

f a c e

SEVEN

~~~~~~~~~~~~~~~~~~~~~~~

"Face," Ellery said, as if he were tasting it.

"Face?" Burke said.

"Face," retorted Inspector Queen. "And that's it, gentlemen. Short, sweet, and ridiculous. It's another reason we're looking for those diaries and the manuscript of the autobiography. They might throw some light on whose face."

"Or it could be somebody's name," ventured the Scotsman. "Although I've never run across a name like Face."

29

"You ought to spend more time at our ball parks," Ellery said. "However, Harry, you're wrong on a different count. That f is definitely lowercase. No, it's got to be 'face,' as in 'face the music'—"

"Which is just what I'm going to be doing," said the Inspector, "unless we crack this thing. I've already heard rumblings from upstairs. Can't you make anything out of it, either, son?"

"No." Ellery's own face was squeezed up in a lemon-like scowl.

"Another thing." The Inspector matched the scowl; both scowling, there was a remarkable resemblance. "We still have no answer to how the killer got into the apartment. There are only two keys, it seems, Glory's and her husband's. And this Armando has a real alibi, according to the West girl; also, he produced his key. Glory's apparently hasn't been touched. What's more, the apartment door seems to have been locked—there's all kinds of evidence that Glory was scared to death of burglars. So another question is, how did her killer get in?"

"Perhaps she knew who it was," suggested Burke, "and let him in—or her—herself." Then he shook his head. "No, that doesn't follow. If she'd known her assailant, she'd have written his name before she died."

Ellery was worrying it, shaking his head at Burke's last statement. He kept scowling.

"That West girl," sighed the Inspector. "I'd better talk to her personally." He called down to Sergeant Velie to fetch Roberta West. Harry Burke joined the old man at the door; the two began to whisper.

Ellery glanced at them. "Is that conference top secret," he asked in an annoyed voice, "or can you declassify it?" They paid no attention to him.

The sorrel-haired girl came up the stairs visibly bracing herself. Inspector Queen broke off his palaver with Burke to glare at her. His glare made Burke glare at *him*. The Scot touched the girl's elbow reassuringly. She gave him a pale smile.

"I'm Inspector Queen, in charge of this case, Miss West," the old man said crustily. "I've read the reports of the detectives who questioned you, and I want to know if you have anything to add to your statement. Do you?"

She glanced at Ellery, and he nodded. So she gulped and told the Inspector what she had told Ellery and Harry Burke about Carlos Armando's incredible proposal to her over seven months before.

"He wanted you to kill his wife for him," said the Inspector, perversely pleased. "That's very helpful, Miss West. Would you be willing to testify to it?"

"In court?"

"That's where people usually testify."

"I don't know . . ."

"Now, look, if you're afraid of him—"

"Wouldn't any girl be, Inspector? And then there's the publicity. I'm just getting started on my career, and the wrong kind of publicity—"

"Well, you've got time to think about it," the old man said with sudden kindliness. "I won't press you now. Velie, see that Miss West gets safely home." The girl rose, made an attempt to smile, and left with the mountainous sergeant. Harry Burke watched her slender figure twinkle down the stairs. He watched until she was lost behind the closing front door.

The old man was rubbing his hands. "That's a real development! This Armando is behind it, all right. And whoever this woman is he conned into doing the killing for him, that's the way she got in. Armando had a duplicate of his house key made and provided her with it. And since she's a woman he's undoubtedly been two-timing his wife with, Glory never saw her before. That's why she couldn't leave us a direct clue. She didn't know the woman's name."

"She obviously meant something by that word 'face,'" argued Ellery. "So there must be something about the woman that Glory knew, or spotted—"

"Something about her face?" exclaimed Burke.

"No, no, Harry," Ellery said. "It's not anything like that, or she'd have specified. Face . . ."

"Have you anything on the time she was shot, Inspector?" Burke asked.

"As it happens, we can place it to the minute. There was a small electric clock on her desk there, a leather job her left arm must have knocked off the desk as she slumped forward, because we found it on the floor, to her left, with the plug pulled out. That stopped the clock at 11:50. No, the clock isn't here now, Ellery; it's at the lab, though it won't tell them any more than it's told already. Ten minutes to twelve was the time she stopped those two bullets. Incidentally, Doc Prouty's finding as to the time of death jibes roughly with the clock."

"In connection with that," Burke said, "I just remembered that as I was leaving here Wednesday night, Mrs.

31

Armando remarked to me that she was expecting her husband home a little past midnight."

"That means," said Ellery slowly, "at the time she was shot, Glory knew Armando would be walking into the apartment in a matter of minutes."

"He found her," nodded the Inspector, "between fifteen and twenty minutes past twelve. If he left the West girl's apartment at midnight, by the way, that would just about check out."

"It also clears up one aspect of the clue Glory left," mused Ellery. "Knowing she was dying, knowing her husband would almost certainly be the first to discover her body, she realized that he would also be the first to see any dying message she could leave. If she wrote down something that accused or described his accomplice, or involved him, he would simply destroy it before notifying the police. So—"

"So she had to leave a clue that would trick Armando into thinking it had no bearing on her murder?" Burke had taken out his pipe and was loading it absently from a Scotch-grain pouch.

"That's right, Harry. Something obscure enough to fool Armando into ignoring it—perhaps as the start of one of the word-game puzzles she was eternally doing; after all, why should he figure it was a clue?—and still provocative enough to make the police follow it up."

"I don't know," Burke said, shaking his head.

"It's too damned bad she didn't leave something good and plain," grumbled the Inspector. "Because all her fancy last-minute figuring turned out to be unnecessary. When she did die she fell forward among the papers on the desk, and the word she'd written on the top paper was hidden by her head. Armando probably didn't notice it at all—he'd sure as shooting keep his hands off that body! According to the story he tells, he never even set foot in the den—just stood in the doorway, saw the blood and his wife lying over the desk, and went right to the bedroom phone to call the police. And, you know, I believe him."

"All of which," said Ellery, pulling on his nose, "gets us back to where we started: Just what did she mean by 'face'?"

"That's not where we started," his father retorted. "We started with those missing diaries, and where they are; and while, strictly speaking, it's none of your business, I'm soft-headed enough to ask both of you: Where are they?" He poked his head out the study doorway and bellowed down, "Velie! Anything on those diaries yet?" And when the sergeant's glum negative was bellowed back, the old man pulled his head back in and almost pleaded, "Any suggestions?"

The two younger men were silent.

Finally Harry Burke said, "The killer—or Armando before he phoned the police—could have taken them from the apartment."

"Not Armando—he didn't have time enough. The woman, maybe." Then the old man shook his head. "It wouldn't have made sense, though. *All* the diaries? *All* the biographical material? And don't forget, mere possession would be as dangerous as a fingerprint. Incidentally, talking of fingerprints, there aren't any except Armando's, Glory's, the maid's, and the secretary's, Jeanne Temple's; and the maid and the secretary sleep out."

"Then they're here somewhere." Burke sucked on his pipe quietly, the very figure of a proper British police officer. "Those bookshelves, Inspector. Have the books on them been individually inspected? It occurs to me that the diaries may have false and misleading covers—"

"You mean disguised as a set of my son's books, for instance?" Ellery winced at his father's tone. "Well, they're not. That's the first thing I thought of."

"Has anything been removed from this room?" Ellery asked abruptly.

"Lots of things," said his father. "The body, the clock—"

"That's two. What else?"

"The piece of paper she wrote on."

"And that's three. Go on."

"Go on? Go on where? That's all, Ellery."

"Are you sure?"

"Of course I'm not sure! Velie!" the Inspector shrieked. The sergeant came thundering upstairs. "What's been taken from the study here?"

"The body," began Sergeant Velie, "the clock—"

"No, no, Sergeant," Ellery said. "Something not apparently connected with the crime."

The sergeant scratched his head. "Like what, for instance?"

"Like a three-step ladder," said Ellery. "As I recall her, Glory Guild wasn't more than five foot six. These bookshelves are eight feet tall. She'd need a little ladder to reach the top shelves; I can't see her dragging a very expensive monstrosity like that elephant-hide chair over to the shelves every time she wanted to reach a book

33

over her head, or risking her neck standing on the swivel chair. So, Sergeant, where's the ladder?"

Burke was staring at him. The Inspector's mustache had lifted in a puzzled smile. Velie's mouth hung open.

"Shut the flytrap, Velie, and go get it," said the Inspector mildly; and as the sergeant left, shaking his big head, the old man said, "I forgot about the ladder. There was one in here, all right, but a detective borrowed it yesterday to look over the Dutch shelving in the dining room downstairs and didn't bring it back. Why do you want it, Ellery? We've examined everything on the top shelves."

But all Ellery said was, "We'll see."

Sergeant Velie lumbered back with a library-type ladder of ivory-decorated blackwood, with plastic-covered risers that had been scratched and scored by heavy official shoes. Ellery said, "Sergeant, would you get that pedestal out of the way?" and when Velie had moved the Watusi warrior to one side, Ellery set the ladder down where the pedestal had been standing and mounted to the top step. His hair nearly brushed the ceiling. "The loudspeaker," he explained. "I noticed that the inset of the speaker in the bedroom was screwed into the frame, whereas this one has hinges and a winged nut to hold it closed. Didn't your crew look up here, dad?"

For once the Inspector had nothing to say, although he glanced at Sergeant Velie, who paled.

"I say!" Harry Burke said. "You have a pair of eyes, Ellery. I missed it completely."

Ellery spun the nut parallel to the frame and began to pry at the inset of the loudspeaker. He got a purchase, and the inset swung out on its almost invisible hinges. "Well," Ellery said, pleased. His arm disappeared in the opening. "Just the sort of gimmicky hiding place a puzzle addict like GeeGee would think of." His arm reappeared; he flourished a metal box of the safe-deposit type. "Here you are, dad. I'll be very much surprised if what you're looking for isn't in these boxes."

EIGHT

~~~~~~~~~~~~~~~~~~~~~~~~~~~~~~

There were six identical metal boxes in the hiding place, none of them locked; each was crammed with diaries, manuscripts, and other papers. In one of the boxes lay a kraft paper envelope sealed with wax, with the typed inscription: "My Will. To Be Opened by My Attorney, William Maloney Wasser." This envelope the Queens set aside, hunting through the boxes for the current diary.

Ellery found it, and opened it at once to the December entries. The last entry was under the date of Tuesday, December 29, "11:15 P.M.," the night before Glory Guild Armando's murder. The Inspector pronounced a salty word. She had evidently not got round to penning an entry for the day of the night she was shot; this was confirmed, as Ellery pointed out, by their having found the diary in her loudspeaker cache rather than on her desk.

All the entries were written with a fine-line pen in a tiny, precise script. A peculiarity of the dead woman's chirography was that the script looked more like italic letterprinting than ordinary writing. The individual letters were not only slanted but unjoined, as in the word *f a c e* of her dying message, which Ellery also pointed out. There was very little spacing between lines, so that with the separation of the letters of individual words on the one hand, and the closeness of the lines on the other, the whole effect was at once scattered and crowded-looking. It made for difficult reading.

They skimmed through the diary from the earliest entries, page after page, and found an omission. Except for the pages date-printed *December 30*—the day of her death—and *December 31*, the only page not written on at all was the page for *December 1*.

"December first blank," muttered Ellery. "Now why didn't she write an entry for that day?"

"Why? Why?" the Inspector said, annoyed.

"Did anything unusual happen on December first?" asked Burke. "I mean generally?"

"Not that I recall," the Inspector said. "Anyway, why would that have stopped her? Unless she was sick or something."

"Inveterate diary writers don't let sickness stand in their way," Ellery said. "They almost always go back afterward and fill in. Besides, as far as I can tell"—he riffled the pages of several of the other diaries—"she kept a daily account faithfully for years. No, there's a reason for this blank page, and it hasn't anything to do with illness or oversight." He stopped suddenly. "Of course!" And he fished in his pocket and landed his cigaret lighter.

"What are you going to do, Ellery?" demanded Inspector Queen, alarmed. "Watch that flame!"

Ellery had doubled the diary back on its spine, leaving the blank page dangling, and he was carefully passing the flame of the lighter under the page.

"Invisible ink?" said Burke. "Oh, come, Ellery."

"Considering her tricky mind," Ellery said dryly, "I beg to differ."

Still, even to Ellery's astonishment, something began to appear on the blank page. The entry seemed to consist of a single word; try as he would with the flame, no other writing showed up.

Then they were staring at it:

f a c e

handprinted in the same spidery italic fashion, with spacing between individual letters, as in the case of the dying message, except that this *f a c e* was more surely written.

"Again." Ellery glared at it. "She wrote that same word on December first! In her *diary*. Now why would she have done that—four weeks before she was murdered?"

"Unless she had a premonition of her death," Burke suggested.

"She must have had a lot more than a premonition," Inspector Queen said irritably, "to have written it in invisible ink." Then he threw up his hands. "Why am I always stuck with the nut cases? Magic ink! The next thing, it'll be rabbits out of a hat!"

"Very possible," Ellery said. "It seems to be that kind of rabbity business."

"Isn't it common in the States, talking about show business," murmured Burke, "to nickname theatrical personalities? Bing Crosby, The Voice. Betty Grable, The Legs. And wasn't there a star—what was her name? Marie McDonald—you people called The Body? Has there ever been one called The Face?"

"If there has been, I missed it," Ellery said. "Anyway, Harry, I point out again that in both cases—the dying message and this invisible-ink diary entry—the word is spelled with a lowercase *f*. No, it's nothing like that. Face . . ." Then he said, "Dad."

"What?"

"Was there anything unusual about Glory's face?"

The old man shrugged. "Just a face. They all look the same dead."

"I think I'd like to see this one."

"Be my guest." And they left Inspector Queen seated

36

gloomily behind GeeGee Guild's desk, beginning to leaf through the diaries.

NINE

~~~~~~~~~~~~~~~~~~~~~~~~~~~~~~~~~~~~

In the taxicab on the way to the Morgue, Ellery said, "Now that we're out from under the frosty eye of my father, Harry, how about telling me what you and he were putting your heads together about?"

"Oh, that." Burke seemed abstracted. "I didn't want to mention it before I checked it out with your old man —" he smiled briefly "—I'm in a strange country, remember, and one should learn the protocol of the natives. But he says it's all right."

The Scotsman squirmed back in the cab. "It has to do with the case that brought me here in the first place. Miss—Mrs. Armando's original request to the Yard was to ask if they would find a certain girl, a niece of hers, Lorette Spanier. Since it wasn't either a criminal or a missing-persons case, simply a question of locating a relative whose whereabouts she didn't know, the Yard had no jurisdiction and Commissioner Vail recommended me for the job, as I told you. I made the financial arrangements with Miss Guild—damn it all, I cannot think of her as Mrs. Armando!—with a transatlantic phone call, and went to work."

The background for his search, Burke explained, had been ordinary enough. Glory's family back in Minnesota were dead; her sole surviving relative, a younger sister, had married a British dairy farmer and gone to live in England. Both the sister and her husband had been killed in a plane crash many years before, during a summer holiday; they had left an only child, a daughter, who would now be in her early twenties.

"It seems that Glory was never very close to her sister," Burke said, between spurts of pipe smoke, "according to what she told me—disapproved of the sister's marriage, that sort of thing—and she simply lost track of the sister's daughter. Now she wanted to find the girl."

"Just like that," Ellery murmured. "Sounds as if she were looking for an heir."

Burke took the pipe out of his mouth. "You know,

that never occurred to me. It might have been her reason at that."

"How did Glory communicate with the Yard?"

Burke stared. "By letter. Vail turned it over to me. For heaven's sake, what difference does it make?"

"Airmail?" asked Ellery.

"Of course."

"When did the letter come in, do you recall?"

"It arrived on the fourth of December."

"Even more interesting. Possibly significant. The page with the hidden word 'face' in the last diary is dated December first, and Glory's letter about finding her niece got to the Yard on the fourth. Which means she must have written that word invisibly about the same time she wrote to England."

"You mean there's a connection between 'face' and the niece?"

"I don't mean anything, unfortunately," Ellery said sadly. "I'm just scrounging around among the possibilities. Did you find the girl? I take it you did."

"Oh, yes."

"Where?"

Burke grinned. "In New York. Ironic, what? I traced Lorette Spanier from an orphanage in Leicestershire—in the Midlands—where she'd been brought up after her parents' death, to a flat on your West Side, just a couple of miles from her aunt! And I had to come all the way from England to find her.

"The only difficulty I had was on the home grounds—it took me several weeks to trace her to the orphanage. There they told me where she had gone, although they didn't know her specific address or what she was doing—having reached her majority she was a free agent, and the orphanage people had no further control over her movements.

"When I got to New York I promptly enlisted the aid of Centre Street, which shunted me off to your Missing Persons Bureau, who could do nothing for me because the girl wasn't listed as missing anywhere in the States. And then, somehow, I got to your father. Does Inspector Queen have a finger in *every* New York police pie? He seems more like an omnibus than a man."

"He's a sort of all-purpose vacuum cleaner," Ellery said absently. "Lorette Spanier. Is that spelled with one *n* or two? And is she married?"

"One. And no, she's quite young. I think twenty-one. Or—no. By now she's twenty-two. Old enough to be married, I grant you, but there's something awfully virginal about her. And anti-male, if you know what I mean."

"I don't."

"I mean she has no time for men."

"I see," said Ellery, although he didn't, quite. "What does she do for a living?"

"When she first got to the States she took a secretarial position—there was a vogue in your metropolis about that time, I understand, for pretty young English secretaries. But that was merely to keep body and soul together. What Lorette really wanted was to get into show business, she told me. She has a good voice, by pop standards, with a rather distinctive style."

"Anything like Glory's?" Ellery asked suddenly.

"A good deal like it, I'm told, although I don't qualify as a pop music buff. I'm more of a Handel-Mendelssohn-choral-society-oratorio bloke myself."

"Heredity," Ellery mumbled.

"What?"

"It apparently runs in the blood. That must have pleased Glory no end. Has the girl broken in anywhere?"

"Yes. She managed to get a few wireless commercial jobs. It encouraged her to quit her situation and try to earn her living singing full time. She's had a few third-class nightclub dates—barely scrapes along, from what I gather. She's an independent sort—no complaints, stiff upper lip, smiling through, that sort of bilge. I couldn't help but admire her grit, though."

"Why did she come to the United States?"

"Really, Ellery. Isn't this where the pounds and pence are? Look at the Beatles." ("You look at them," said Ellery. "No, thanks," said Burke.) "She's a most practical young woman."

"Then it wasn't to look up her famous aunt?"

"Heavens, no! She means to do it on her own."

"Didn't she make any attempt at all to find her mother's only sister?"

"She told me she had no idea where Glory Guild was living. It might have been in Pago-Pago, for all she knew. No, this was all apparently coincidence."

"Not so coincidental. Where else would a Glory Guild live? And where else would a stagestruck girl come? Were you present when they were reunited?"

"Oh, yes. But getting them together took a bit of doing. I told Lorette why I'd been hunting for her, and

I found myself with another job on my hands—I mean persuading her to visit Mrs. Armando."

"When did all this take place?"

"I didn't actually locate Lorette until late afternoon of the thirtieth—Wednesday. Took her to dinner and spent most of the evening talking her into coming with me. She has no particular feeling for her aunt—the woman was just a name to her as a child, and when her father and mother died—what with Glory's silence—even the name faded out after a bit. She was very young, you know, when she had to go into the orphanage."

"Bitter?"

"I beg your pardon?"

"Did Lorette seem bitter at her aunt's neglect?"

"Not at all. She's a quite remarkable young person, this Spanier girl. She said she couldn't imagine why her aunt wanted to find her after all these years. All she wanted was to be let alone to make her own way. As I say, it took me the entire evening to talk her into accompanying me. The fact was, I didn't know why Mrs. Armando wanted to see her so suddenly, either, so I had to muster some remarkable arguments."

Ellery laughed. "So that's what you and dad were being cosy about." Then he stopped laughing. "Just when did you and the girl get to Glory's apartment Wednesday night, Harry?"

"About a quarter to eleven." Burke's pipe had gone out, and he looked around the cab for a place to deposit the dottle. But the ashtray was missing, and he stuffed the whole thing in his pocket. "It was awkward. Lorette was no help at all; after all, the woman was a total stranger to her. And Mrs. Armando made a bad job of explaining to the girl why she had never looked for her before, such a bad job that I decided I was in the way, and left. My assignment was finished, anyway. Mrs. Armando saw me to the door—gave me my check, by the way; I'd of course phoned her we were coming, and she had the check ready for me—and I was out of there, as I've told you, at 11:05 or so. Went to the airport, took off at 1:00 A.M.—and turned around and flew back, as you know, when Inspector Queen cabled me to return."

"Then you left the Spanier girl alone with Glory," Ellery said abruptly. "And Glory was shot at 11:50."

"I understand Lorette says she left, too, long before that," Burke replied. "She's been questioned, your father told me, and her story seems to put her in the clear. But

40

she's going to be questioned again later today, I gather, so you can sit in and judge for yourself."

TEN

~~~~~~~~~~~~~~~~~~

"Which one do you want to see today, Mr. Queen?" asked the attendant.

"Glory Guild Armando, Louie."

"That one." The man went straight to one of the drawers and pulled it open. "There's been quite a run on her."

She was unlovely even for a corpse. The body was almost shapeless with fat; the death-darkened, sagging cheeks under the disordered bottle-blond hair were puffy and swollen by overindulgence.

"Sic transit Glory," murmured Ellery. "This was once a sex-pot, inspiring dreams. Would you believe it?"

"With difficulty," said Harry Burke. "I don't see anything remarkable about her face, Ellery, except grossness. No mark or bruise, certainly."

"Then it wasn't her own face she meant."

"Who said it was?"

"You never know. What was it the poet said? 'A face that had a story to tell. How different faces are in this particular!' But he also said, 'Some faces are books in which not a line is written, save perhaps a date.'"

"Which poet?"

"Longfellow."

"Oh."

"*Hyperion. Not* from the fragment by Keats."

"I'm relieved," said Burke gratefully. "Well, nothing is written in this face but obesity."

"I don't know," Ellery said suddenly. "Thanks, Louie. Harry, come along."

As he hurried Burke out, the Scot said, "Where to now?"

"The Medical Examiner's office. I just had another thought."

"Minus poetic quotation, I hope," Burke said.

"I'll try to remember to spare you our native bards."

They found Doc Prouty eating his lunch at his desk. The old-timer had his disreputable cloth hat far back on his bald head, and he was making faces at a sandwich.

41

"Oh, Ellery. Tomato and lettuce again. By God, I've told that woman of mine a thousand times a man in my line of work doesn't necessarily have to be a vegetarian! What's on your mind?"

"The Armando case. By the way. Harry Burke, Dr. Prouty." The Medical Examiner grunted, continuing to masticate. "You've done the p.m. on her, I take it?"

"Yes. Didn't you see the report?"

"No. Anything?"

"Death by gunshot, as advertised. What did you expect?"

"Hope."

" 'That very popular trust in flat things coming round!' " murmured Burke.

"What?" said Ellery.

"Dickens," said Burke. "Charles."

Doc Prouty was gaping at them.

"Did you look into her mouth, Doc?"

"Did I what?"

"Look into her mouth."

Now Burke stared.

"Of course I looked into her mouth. It's primary standard procedure when you're looking for poison. Not that poison was indicated," said Doc Prouty. "But then I'm the very model of a proper thorough M.E. Gilbert, W.S." He grinned like an elf.

"What did you find?"

"What I expected. Nothing."

"No wad of paper?"

"Wad of paper?"

"Wad of paper."

"Of course not!"

"And that's that," Ellery said to Burke as they left.

"I don't understand, Ellery," Burke complained.

"It's simple enough. Face—mouth? I thought perhaps she wrote the word face as a clue to look in her mouth— where, hopefully, she'd secreted a more direct message, like the name of her killer. Only she hadn't."

All the Scotsman could do was shake his head.

ELEVEN

~~~~~~~~~~~~~~~~~~~~

They stopped in at a chophouse haunt of Ellery's, consumed vast T-bone steaks—Burke ordered his well done, to Ellery's horror—and then went back to the Queen apartment for a few hours' nap. Before they flopped Ellery sought the phone and located his father at police headquarters where, the old man said, he had conveyed the diaries and other papers.

"When are you intending to question Lorette Spanier, dad?"

"Five o'clock."

"Where?"

"Why?"

"I want to be present."

"I asked her to come down here to headquarters."

"Have Armando there, too, will you?"

The old man was silent. Then he said, "Any particular reason?"

"Nothing spectacular. I want to watch them together. The presumption is that they've never met."

"The Spanier girl and Armando?" The Inspector seemed startled. "She's hardly dry behind the ears. Fresh out of an English orphanage."

"Armando goes for anything that fills out a sweater, according to Roberta West. Does Lorette fill out a sweater?"

"Oh, yes."

"Then have Armando there."

"All *right*."

"Incidentally, has anything been done yet on the women in Armando's tasty life?"

"I started a check on that," said his father grimly, first thing."

"The reason I ask is that the woman he got to do the job for him might be someone he knew and then—presumably—dropped. He's had platoons of them. Or she might even be one of his ex-wives."

"I'm way ahead of you, son."

But if there was anything between Carlos Armando and Lorette Spanier they concealed it like paid-up members of Equity. Armando seemed puzzled, in an amused way, by his summons to Inspector Queen's office; and Lorette, after one swift look, lifted her unplucked eyebrows and ignored him. Ellery did think that, for a girl as naive as her background made her appear, it was a singularly sophisticated appraisal; but then he half dismissed it as an instinct for character analysis often displayed by the very young female of the species. As for Armando, his glance kept going over her like a dentist's probe. She filled out her sweater—it was actually a

43

sweater—with the greatest of ease.

Lorette had nothing of the pinchy English look that might have been expected from her Midlander father. She was all Norse, busty and blond; she might have come to the Inspector's office directly from a Swedish cruiseboat. (And, like the struggle her deceased aunt had so fulsomely lost, in her middle years she would have to fight the good fight against overweight.) The girl had the face of an angelic child, with a little straight nose, blue blue eyes, red red lips, and a skin as fair as an infant's backside. The pouting set to her lips had been fashionable for a long time; it was the requisite touch of sex in the child-face, and it would remind men of the woman her body said she was. Armando's eyes kept probing her, smiling with pleasure.

Armando was not at all what Ellery had expected. He did not have the lean lizard grace and greasy hair-oil look of the patented gigolo. His body was muscular and even squatty, and it moved with clumsiness. His hair, crisp, curly, and dry, was very nearly Negroid; his skin, pitted and burned black by sunlamps, enhanced the Negro impression. He possessed a pair of extraordinary black eyes, swimming with intelligence, and shaded by feminine lashes. Only his mouth was weak, being pretty and full-lipped and entirely without character. What women saw in him Ellery could not imagine. He loathed the fellow on sight. (And at once realized the source of his loathing: Armando exuded sexual self-confidence from every pore—which was perhaps what women saw in him after all.)

Inspector Queen made the introductions (Armando barely acknowledged the two men with a lazy *"Buon giorn'"* in a deep coo, like a pouter pigeon; Lorette shook Ellery's hand, serious and stiff-armed, a once-up-and-down pump, and then dimpled at Harry Burke, immediately illuminating the dingy headquarters office as if a shade had been raised to the sun), and sat them all down—Ellery took a chair in a corner, from which he could watch them unobserved—and said smoothly, "I've asked you here, Mr. Armando, because this is a matter that evidently concerned your wife, and I think you're entitled to know what's going on. Did you know, by the way, that Mrs. Armando was having her niece searched for?"

"Between GeeGee and me," said Carlos Armando, "there were no secrets. She told me." Secretly, Ellery doubted it. The man was improvising.

44

"How did you feel about it?"

"I?" Armando pulled down his pretty mouth. "I was sad. I have no family, except two uncles behind the Iron Curtain, and they are probably dead." His liquid eyes washed over Lorette gently. "Miss Spanier is much to be condoled. To find such as GeeGee, and to lose her, both in the same night, is an irony so deplorable it is better not discussed."

Lorette glanced at him curiously. His blunt, brilliant teeth shimmered in a smile that dropped at the corners— punctuation marks to the extravagant foreign turn of his phrasing—while his eyes went over her in the universal language; could she be unaware of what he was? Ellery could not decide.

As for Inspector Queen, he dismissed Armando with a grunt and turned to the girl. "Mr. Burke brought you to Mrs. Armando's apartment at a quarter of eleven Wednesday night. She was home alone. Mr. Burke was with the two of you until a few minutes past eleven. Tell me as exactly as you can remember what happened after Burke left."

"Nothing *happened* while I was there, Inspector Queen," Lorette said in a reproving tone.

The old man showed his dentures in a reproved way. "I mean, what did you and your aunt talk about?"

"Oh. Well, she wanted me to come live with her, give up my flat and move in with her and Mr. Armando. I thanked her and said no, thank you, that I valued my independence, although she was very kind to ask me. You see," the English girl said, looking down at the hands in her lap, "I spent the better part of my life living with other people; you don't get much privacy in an orphanage. I tried to explain to Mrs Armando—to Aunt Glory—that for the first time in my life I was enjoying going it *alone*. And that, besides, I didn't know her. Really at all. It would have been like moving in with a stranger. I think she was hurt, but what else could I say? It was true."

"Of course," the Inspector murmured. "And what else did you two talk about, Miss Spanier?"

"She wouldn't let it go at that. She seemed to have some sort of compulsion. It was quite awkward for me." Lorette raised her amazing blue eyes. "She even . . . well, it seemed to me she went rather too far. She kept *pressing* me. She had a great many connections in show business, she said; she could help my theatrical career no end, and so on. I frankly didn't see what that had

45

to do with my living with her—if she wanted to help me, why didn't she just do so? She was offering me a carrot, as if I were some sort of donkey. I didn't like it at all."

"And you told her so?"

"Oh, no, that would have been rude. I don't believe in that sort of tit for tat, do you? People are too self-centeredly unkind to one another as it is. I simply said that I preferred to make my own way, just as I understood she had done in her own career, and anyway I don't believe that people can boost other people in the arts—you either have talent, in which case sooner or later you'll get there, or you simply don't, and that's that. It's truly the way I feel."

"I'm sure it is. And I'm sure you're right," said the Inspector. You're a treacherous old hypocrite, Ellery thought admiringly. He caught Burke's eye; the Englishman was trying not to grin. "And that was the sum and substance of your talk with Mrs. Armando?"

"Yes."

"What time did you leave your aunt's apartment?"

"About 11:30, I should think."

"She saw you out?"

"Yes, to the lift. I mean, elevator."

"Did she say anything about seeing you again?"

"Oh, yes. She asked me to telephone her next week, something about having a spot of lunch together at Sardi's. I didn't promise. I said I would if I could, and I left."

"Left her alone—and alive."

"Certainly!"

"Was there anyone in the lobby when you went down?"

"No."

"Where did you go after you got downstairs?"

"I went home." The implications of Inspector Queen's questioning had begun to make her angry; the pink flushing her cheeks was the color of anger, and the breasts under the sweater had risen noticeably. (Most noticeably by Carlos Armando, whose eyes quivered like mercury seeking a balance, never leaving her chest.) "Where else would I go at that hour, Inspector?"

"Just asking," the Inspector said. "I suppose you took a taxi?"

"I did *not*. I walked. Is there anything wrong with that?"

"Walked?"

"Across Central Park. I live on the West Side—"

"There's something definitely wrong with that," the

46

old man said. "Hasn't anyone told you that it's dangerous for an unaccompanied girl to walk through Central Park at night? Especially near midnight? Dont' you read the newspapers?"

"I suppose that was idiotic of me," Lorette admitted. She has spirit, Ellery thought, and the quick temper that goes with it. Also, surprising in a girl of her age and background, considerable self-control; she was now speaking with great care. "But I was not so much upset as—well—stirred up. I'm afraid I wasn't thinking clearly. I just suddenly felt like walking, across the Park was the direct route, and so I walked across. Inspector, I don't see what any of this has to do with my aunt's death—I mean, how I got home Wednesday night!"

"Did you meet anyone you know on your walk?"

"No—"

"Or in your building?"

"No."

"And, as I understand it, you live alone?"

"That is correct, Inspector Queen." The blue eyes flashed. "As for what I did when I arrived at my flat—I'm sure that's your next question!—I undressed, tubbed, brushed my teeth, said my prayers, and went to bed. Is there anything else I can tell you?"

Ellery grinned at the expression on his father's face. The Inspector liked to keep on top of his opponent during these wrestling matches, and this one wasn't playing the game. The old man's dentures showed in something like respect.

"Did your aunt mention anything to you about her will?"

"Her will? Why should she have?"

"Did she?"

"Certainly not."

"Mr. Burke tells us that, as she was showing him out that night, Mrs. Armando said something about expecting her husband back a little past midnight." Mrs. Armando's husband shifted his attention for an instant from Lorette's sweater to the old man's mustache; then it went back again. "Did you hear her say that, Miss Spanier?"

"No, but she made the same remark to me after Mr. Burke left."

"But you never did see Mr. Armando Wednesday night?"

"I've not laid eyes on Mr. Armando until today." Or vice versa? Ellery wondered. If it was true, Armando was certainly making up for it now. The laying on of

47

eyes was becoming positively obscene. Lorette did not seem to notice. She was concentrating on her inquisitor.

She waited now for Inspector Queen to resume, but she had to swivel her head.

"Question," Ellery said suddenly. "After Harry Burke left the Armando apartment, Miss Spanier—while you were alone with your aunt—did she receive a telephone call, or a message of any kind? Or did anyone ring the apartment bell?"

"We were not interrupted in any way, Mr. Queen. Of course, I can't say what may have happened after I left."

"Can you recall Mrs. Armando's remarking anything —at all—to you, no matter how trivial-sounding, that had to do with somebody's face?"

"Face?"

"Yes, f-a-c-e."

The girl shook her blond head. She seemed genuinely mystified. "I don't remember any such reference."

"Then I think that's all, Miss Spanier," said the Inspector, rising. "By the way, I take it you've heard from your aunt's attorney, William Maloney Wasser, about the reading of her will?"

"Yes. I'm supposed to be at his office directly after the funeral Monday."

He nodded. "Sorry to have broken into your New Year's Day."

Lorette rose and rather haughtily made for the door. Somehow Carlos Armando was there before her, hand on the knob.

"Allow me, Lorette—you will not mind if I call you Lorette? After all, I am your uncle."

The fine brows over the blue eyes drew together a little. "Thank you, Mr. Armando."

"Oh, but not Mr. Armando! Carlos."

She smiled faintly.

"May I drive you home? Or wherever you are going?"

"That's not at all necessary—"

"But we must know each other. Perhaps you will let me give you dinner? There are so many things about GeeGee you must be wishing to learn. Now that she is dead, so soon after finding you, I feel a responsibility . . ."

That was all the three men heard before the door closed.

"Skirt-chasing blighter," Harry Burke said, making a face. "Doesn't waste time, does he?"

"It could be," muttered Ellery, "that someone's being awfully clever."

48

2 HALF FACE

*Physiognomy . . . may also serve us
for conjecture.*

LA BRUYÈRE

TWELVE

Ellery opened his eyes to a creeping gray Saturday morning. His father was gone, and in the study Harry Burke was going through the morning newspaper.

"You were pounding the feathers so hard I hadn't the heart to wake you," Burke said. The Scotsman was dressed and pinkly shaved, he had made the daybed, and the pot of coffee on Ellery's electric plate was bubbling. "I've been up for hours."

"Didn't you sleep well?" Ellery made for the coffee pot like a man dying of thirst. He had slept in fits, dreaming over and over of a faceless face topped by Glory Guild's dyed hair, until, with daylight prying at the venetian blinds, he had fallen asleep from exhaustion.

"Like a side of beef," Burke said cheerfully. "That's a sleeping man's bed. My only complaint is that I couldn't find any tea in the kitchen cupboard."

"I'll pick some up today."

"Oh, no," the Scotsman protested, "one night is imposition enough. I'll put up at a hotel."

"I won't hear of it. You may have to hang around for some time, Harry, and you're no longer on an expense account. New York hotel bills have a way of escalating."

"This is terribly kind of you, Ellery."

"I'm a terribly kind person. What's in the paper?"

"Nothing we don't know. Although there's some background stuff on Armando in one of the columns."

"Whose?"

"Kip Kipley's."

Ellery set his cup down and grabbed the newspaper. He knew the Broadway columnist well; on numerous occasions Kipley had given him valuable tips. This morning's column was devoted almost entirely to the late Glory Guild's count; Ellery could imagine Armando baring his magnificent choppers. "Most of this is pretty much public property, Harry, but I have an idea Kip's

51

holding back the real pay dirt for later developments. It gives me a thought."

He consulted his address book and dialed Kipley's unlisted number. "Kip? Ellery Queen. Did I get you up?"

"Hell, no," said the columnist's famous piping voice. "I'm in the middle of breakfast. I was wondering when you'd get around to me, Charlie. You're in this GeeGee business up to your belly button, aren't you?"

"Just about. Kip, I'd like to see you."

"Any time. I keep open house."

"Privately."

"Sure. One o'clock at my place?"

"You have a date." Ellery hung up. "You never know," he said to Harry Burke. "Kipley's like that wine horn of Thor's, inexhaustible. Give me twenty minutes, Harry, and we'll have brunch and hit Kip for the inside scoop."

THIRTEEN

~~~~~~~~~~~~~~~~~~~~~~~~~~

The columnist was a tiny dark vibrant man with the profile of a doge, dressed in a heavy silk kimono of authentic manufacture. "Excuse the negligee," Kipley said, shaking Ellery's hand limply. "I never get dressed before four o'clock. Who's this?"

Ellery introduced Burke, who submitted to a quick examination by a pair of birdy black eyes. Then he was dismissed with, "Harry Burke? Never heard," and Kipley nodded toward the elaborate bar, where his Puerto Rican houseman was hovering—because of Kipley's column, Felipe was probably the most advertised houseman in Manhattan. The penthouse apartment was almost sterile, unfeminine to the bone; Kipley was a notorious hypochondriac and woman-dodger, with a housewife's passion for order. "What'll you have to drink?" He was also a non-drinker.

"Too early for me, thanks," said Ellery; and Burke, sensing a clue, declined as well, although he eyed the Johnnie Walker Black Label longingly. Kipley nodded to Felipe, and the houseman vanished. It seemed to Burke that the columnist was pleased.

"Park it, gentlemen. What do you want to know?"

"Whatever you've got on Carlos Armando," Ellery

said. "And I don't mean that warmed-over rehash you ran this morning."

The columnist chuckled. "It's all in the timing, Charlie; I don't have to tell *you*. What's in it for me?"

"Nothing I can think of," Ellery said, "at the moment. Because as yet I don't know a thing. If I come up with anything I can let you have, Kip, you'll get your *quid pro quo.*"

Kipley looked at him. "I take it Mr. Burke here is all right?"

"Harry's a private detective from London. He's connected with the case in a peripheral sort of way."

"If you'd rather, Mr. Kipley, I'll leave," Burke said without rancor. He half rose.

"Sit down, Charlie. It's just that when I spill my girlish secrets I like to know who-all's on the bugging end. So this thing has a British tie-in? Who?"

"Who's spilling whose girlish secrets?" Ellery asked, laughing. "Come on, Kip, open up. I told you we have a deal."

"Armando." Kipley pulled his Venetian nose. "The guy is strictly a no-goodnik. A sex-crazy maniac. And greasy as the top of a one-arm short-order cook's stove. The way he slimed up GeeGee's nest for over five years— with that stupid middle-age canary never suspecting a thing, as far as I know—is enough to make even me puke."

"He's been two-timing her?"

"Your arithmetic stinks, Charlie. Two times whatever he can lay his itchy hands on, which is every broad within reach. He even gets nostalgia every once in a while."

"What do you mean?"

"Goes back to one of his rejects. For instance, he's been spotted recently in some night spots with Number Seven on his hit parade—the wife before GeeGee, the Chicago meat-packing dame who got the goods on him while he was giving it to the upstairs maid and kicked him out without a dime, which was a real switch. You know, Mrs. Gertie Hodge Huppenkleimer—she dropped the Armando when she got the divorce. Gertie's living in New York now, in a fifty-thousand-a-year pad on Beekman Place, and somehow he's managed to shinny his way back into her good graces. Don't ask me how he does it. Of course, there isn't a woman who can see beyond the end of her panty-girdle; even so, life isn't

53

all beddy-bye. What do they see in that jock? Unless he's found a way Krafft-Ebing or Kinsey missed."

"The question is, what does Armando see in Mrs. Huppenkleimer?" Harry Burke put in. "While I was still on duty for the Yard, Ellery, I saw her at one of the Queen's garden parties. She has the physique of a Beefeater, topped with three-foot hats. Perhaps it's a matter of professional pride with Armando—I mean, not having succeeded in tapping her the first time round."

"That could be his weakness," Ellery nodded. "Who else, Kip?"

"I'm not through with his ex-wives. He's been seen squiring Numbers Three and Four—Three was Mrs. Ardene Vlietland, the one they call Piggyback, who divorced Hendrix B. Vlietland, the banker, to marry Armando—*that* one broke up after that brawl in Newport where the guests were swinging from the crystal chandeliers and throwing horseshoes at everything breakable, including two Picassos. Four was that Boston dame, the alcoholic with the race horses, Daffy Dingle; she went AA and stayed on the wagon four years, and Armando's been seen in Boston bistros here and there buying her vodka martinis by the quart—just for the hell of it, I guess."

"Nice chap," Burke muttered.

"The best," said Kipley.

"The Huppenkleimer, Piggyback, Daffy," said Ellery. "Three ex-wives. I take it you haven't exhausted the inventory, Kip?"

"Get set for this one," said Kipley.

"I'm quivering all over."

"GeeGee's secretary," said Kipley. "What's-her-name—Jeanne Temple."

"Ah, me," said Burke.

"Oh, my," said Ellery. "This one *is* rancid. And damned dangerous for him. Or is he the complete fool? Under Glory's nose, Kip?"

"No, this he's played cosy. He's got a kind of animal cunning that pops out once in a while. With Jeanne Temple it's been hideaways around town. Not too often. Only a dirt-hound like me would have nosed it out."

"I haven't met the Temple woman. Is she anything to look at?"

"A pair of boobs surrounded by the usual number of arms and legs. With a face like a stepped-on egg. According to my information, he's got her tongue hanging out."

"Our mammary culture," murmured Ellery. "The poor European infected with the American disease. Anyone else?"

The columnist said, "I've hardly started."

"I'd better take notes!" He actually produced his notebook and began writing.

"A two-bit would-be actress named Roberta West." Burke paled slightly. "No money in her, but she's young and pretty—I guess the count needs relief every once in a while from the dogs. But he hasn't been seen with the West number for six, seven months, so that one's probably broken off." Ellery and Harry Burke exchanged glances. "What's the matter, did I say something?"

"No," said Burke.

Kipley's black eyes narrowed unpleasantly. "You two wouldn't be holding out on me, would you?"

"Yes," Ellery said. Burke looked positively unhappy. "But we don't have the right to go into that, Kip. Anyway, the West girl's connection with the case will probably break soon. Who else?"

The columnist jotted something down on a pad at his elbow. "I didn't furnish this joint out of official handouts, Charlie. Thanks for the tip. . . . Well, there's Marta Bellina."

"The opera singer?"

"In person. Bellina was probably GeeGee's best friend. Armando's been crawling all over the best friend, too, and if Marta minds she's been keeping it a deep, dark secret. Women!"

"Incredible," Burke muttered.

"Marta Bellina," Ellery wrote. "Next?"

"Her doctor."

"Whose doctor?" Ellery asked, glancing up.

"GeeGee's."

Ellery looked startled.

Kipley laughed. "If Armando's a faggot he hasn't been caught at it. No, Dr. Merckell is a lady doctor—Susan Merckell, M.D."

"The Park Avenue laryngologist who's so popular with show people?"

"The same. Handsome woman; never married. Made to order for the count. All he has to do is fake a sore throat, go to Dr. Merckell's office, and get into her examining room. My information is that during Armando's visits it's the doctor who gets examined."

"Where do you dredge up all this muck?" asked Harry Burke in a disgusted voice.

55

"Do I ask you where you plant your bugs, Charlie?" the columnist asked amiably. "Then there's the broad with the veil."

"What?" exclaimed Ellery.

"He's been seen in the company of a chick who always wears a violet veil. A thick one, so you can't make out her face."

"Always?"

"Always."

"How old is she?"

"Can you tell a femme's age nowadays when you can't see her puss? If the sun stopped coming up and all the power failed, there'd be one hell of a lot of happy grandmas."

"How about the veiled woman's hair?"

"Sometimes it's blond, sometimes it's red, sometimes it's brunette. But it's the same woman in my book. With wigs . . . I see you two are interested in Madame X. As interested as I am. Basically, Armando is stupid. Letting himself be seen around town with a veiled dame! She might just as well be wearing a topless bathing suit. Don't you ever read my column?"

"Not as often as I'm going to from now on," Ellery said fervently. "By the way, have you any idea when Armando was last seen with the mysterious veiled woman?"

"Before Christmas, I think. You ask like pushy questions, man. What's the date got to do with anything?"

"It's just an idea I'm working on. Is there anyone else?"

Kipley said simply, "I've run out."

Ellery signaled to Burke. "Kip, I can't tell you how grateful I am—"

"You can take your gratitude and you know what. Give me some poop, Charlie, and we're brother Elks."

FOURTEEN

~~~~~~~~~~~~~~~~~~~

They went down to police headquarters and spent the remainder of the day going through page after crammed page of Glory Guild's diaries and memoirs. For the most part the diary entries were inconsequential —guests entertained, parties attended, weekends spent;

reactions to first nights, an occasional acid comment about a pop singer. The diaries were sequined with name-dropping references to the great and notorious of show business, as if the late GeeGee had never entirely out-grown her Middle West clothes. There were surprisingly few allusions to her husband, and not a syllable about Carlos's relationships, real or imagined, with other women. Either Glory Guild had been unaware of his woman-chasing or she had chosen to ignore it, at least for the record.

There was no clue in the entries to what she might have meant by "face." Nor any mention of a veiled woman; nor even of a veil, violet or any other color.

Close examination of her memoirs—the typed parts and the notes on which they were based—proved equally barren of any references that might remotely connect with the singer's death.

A glance at Inspector Queen's reports advanced noth-ing; they told less than both men already knew. The Inspector's detectives had turned over some stones and discovered various crawly things—Armando's renewed alliance with ex-wife Number Three, Ardene Piggyback Vlietland, her of the Newport catastrophe; his affairs with his wife's secretary, Jeanne Temple, and with her physician, Dr. Susan Merckell; his duet with the opera singer, Marta Bellina. But there were no reports on Num-ber Four, the Back Bay alcoholic, Daffy Dingle, or on Number Seven, Gertie Hodge Huppenkleimer, Glory Guild's immediate predecessor.

Or, significantly, on the veiled woman.

"We'll get after *her* first off," the Inspector said, "and I'll give Boston a call about the Dingle woman. I'm most interested in this purple-veil dame—"

"Violet," said Ellery gravely. "It could make all the difference."

"Get off my leg," his father snapped. "I'm not much interested in Mrs. Huppenkleimer. She's the only wife Armando wasn't able to take for anything. I can't see a woman like that committing murder for him."

"Still, according to Kipley, she's been going out with him again. Why?"

"Who knows why women do what they do? Maybe she's been overcome by fond memories. You chase after her if you want."

"Which is exactly," said Ellery, "what Harry and I are going to do."

They tracked Gertie Huppenkleimer that night to a

charity ball at the Americana. She stood out like an atom bomb in the New Mexico desert—a towering mushroom of a woman who dominated most of the thousand glittering people in the ballroom.

"Suppose I make the approach," murmured Burke. "Gertie has a thing for Englishmen."

"You're a Scotsman."

"Believe me, old chap, she won't know the difference."

Ellery watched Burke maneuver his broad shoulders toward the punch table, where Mrs. Huppenkleimer was bellowing into the ear of a captive African diplomat. A few minutes later the Scotsman was dancing with her, fitting neatly under her hat. And a few minutes after that he was back.

"Nothing to it, Ellery. We have a breakfast appointment with her for tomorrow morning. She was charmed."

"By what?"

Burke grinned. "I told her we'd met at the Queen's garden party. I could have had her bra after that. Although, come to think of it, what the hell would I use it for?"

"A hammock," said Ellery glumly, eyeing her awesome proportions.

They were admitted to the Beekman Place duplex at 11:00 o'clock Sunday morning by an English butler who actually sported sideburns. Madam, it appeared, was awaiting them; they followed the butler to a glassed-in terrace, where Mrs. Huppenkleimer was enthroned in an enormous basket chair before a breakfast table set for three.

"Mr. Burke, how very *nice!*" their hostess roared. "And this is your friend. I'm so happy to meet any friend of Mr. Burke's; . . . Ellery Queeg, did you say? . . . *Queen.* How gauche of me! Please sit down, Mr. Queen! And, of course, you, Mr. Burke . . ."

Burke launched into British social chitchat skillfully while the butler served from a king-sized steam table. Mrs. Huppenkleimer ate on the same enormous scale as the rest of her; quantities of wheatcakes, shirred eggs, sausages, kippers, toast, and coffee disappeared down her maw. Ellery, insinuating a phrase or two here and there to keep his oar in, found himself thinking of Moby Dick— she was vastly dressed in billowing white. Was Carlos Armando some sort of Captain Ahab, pursuing her out of complex notions of vengeance—bending her to his will to the ultimate point of slaughter? Or was he more like the Man-Frog Mowgli, riding Hathi the Elephant to their mutual satisfaction?

"Oh, yes," Harry Burke was saying to her. "I've also run into Count Armando. Oh, dear, I suppose I shouldn't have mentioned him, Mrs. Huppenkleimer. Weren't you and the count once married?"

"I was, and as a count he's a phony, and there's no reason why you shouldn't, Mr. Burke," the woman said, reaching for a cigaret with her flipper. Burke hastily snapped his lighter to the ready. She puffed, nodded, belched, and sank back in the basket chair. "Dear Carlos is such a transparent fraud," she laughed, shaking all over. "But one can't stay mad at him. You know? Such a gallant. Though I don't think he's ever quite forgiven me for having a photographer present when I caught him with that maid. I was joking with him about it only the other night."

"Really?" said Burke. "You're seeing him again, Mrs. Huppenkleimer? I think that's awfully decent of you. Letting bygones be bygones, I mean, and all that."

"Why shouldn't I see him again? There's nothing Carlos can get out of me that I'm not willing to give him, is there? Of course," she said thoughtful as a cow, "with this mess he's in I may have to drop him for good. We'll see." She reached for a piece of cinnamon toast that had escaped her earlier and began to masticate it, the cigaret smoldering between the heavily jeweled fingers of her other hand. "I certainly can't afford to become involved."

"You mean in his wife's death?"

"I mean in his wife's murder," the woman said grimly, and flicked the crust to the fat blond cocker waiting for it.

Ellery had a sudden revelation. Gertie Huppenkleimer, in spite of appearances, was nobody's fool. For one thing, she had kept switching her glance on and off him all the while she was talking to Harry Burke—not inquiringly, but as if she had known all along who "Ellery Queeg" was.

He made a decision.

"I'm afraid we've eaten your delicious breakfast under false pretenses, Mrs. Huppenkleimer," Ellery said. "What we're doing here is investigating Mrs. Armando's murder." Burke looked pained.

"Everybody tries to take advantage of poor me," Gertie said calmly. "Go ahead and investigate—Mr. What-Was-It? I haven't a thing to hide."

"Queen," Ellery said. "I'm glad you haven't, Mrs. Huppenkleimer, because that makes it easier for me to ask

59

you where you spent the half hour before midnight of this past Wednesday."

"The night before New Year's Eve. Let me see . . . Oh, yes! I attended a United Nations reception for the new ambassador from whatever-it-is, some Southeast Asian country. Afterwards a group of us went down to one of those places—what do they call them? disco-something— the one on Sheridan Square, in the Village."

"What time did you leave the U.N. reception?"

"About 10:30." The shrewd eyes, imbedded in fat, took Ellery in. "Am I suspected in the Guild murder? That would be too funny."

"What's funny about it, Mrs. Huppenkleimer?"

"Why would I want to shoot Carlos's wife? To marry him again? Once was enough, thank you. He amuses me, and I'm perfectly satisfied with the present arrangement, or I was until this thing came up. The whole idea is ridiculous."

Suddenly, it was.

"You went directly from the reception, in a group of people, to Greenwich Village?"

"That's correct."

"Did you leave the discothèque at any time?"

"No, Mr. Queen." She was smiling a big fat smile.

"And at what time did the Village party break up?"

"After three in the morning. Sorry to disappoint you." The smile was swallowed by abdominal laughter.

"This business is mainly disappointments, Mrs. Huppenkleimer. We'll have you checked out, of course."

"Of course." She was still laughing at him. But when she turned to Harry Burke, it was with a gargantuan baby pout. "As for you, Mr. Burke, shame! I really fell for that Queen's garden-party line, and I don't mean Mr. Queen."

"Oh, I was there," said Burke gallantly. "Keeping an eye on the jewelry."

"And you would have made such a wonderful lord." Mrs. Huppenkleimer sighed. "Hawkins"—what else could her butler he called? Ellery thought—"show these gentlemen out."

They found Jeanne Temple in an apartment building on East 49th Street where, from the card under the bell in the lobby, she shared an apartment with a girl named Virginia Whiting. It consisted of one bedroom, a kitchenette, and a living room; the bedroom and kitchenette were tiny, the living room large. The apartment was nondescriptly furnished and in bachelor-girl disorder. Both girls were dressed in Capri slacks and jersey tops; both were barefoot. The Whiting girl, who was rather pretty, had vivacious gray eyes; but Jeanne Temple was a plain mouse, her only attribute of note being an astonishing bust which taxed the jersey to its limit.

"No, I don't mind Virginia's being present," the Temple girl said. She looked thirty, although Ellery suspected she was younger. There was fear in the muddy brown eyes behind the aluminum-frame glasses. "In fact, I'd rather she . . ."

"Take it easy, Jeannie," said the other girl. "You've got nothing to worry about."

"I know it," Glory Guild's secretary burst out, "but *they* don't seem to. Why can't you people let me alone? I've told everything I know—"

"Not everything, Miss Temple," Ellery said.

The droopy skin yellowed. "I don't know what you mean."

"I'm referring to you and Carlos Armando."

The yellow began to burn. "Me and Carl—Count Armando?"

"Your relationship with him."

"What do you mean?" she asked excitedly. "Did he tell you—?"

"Our information is that you and Armando were having an affair behind Mrs. Armando's back."

"That's not true."

"I'm afraid it is. You've been seen with Armando in hideaway restaurants and bars, Miss Temple, on a number of occasions. Men like Armando don't take their wives' secretaries out secretly in order to give them dictation."

"Miss Temple," said Harry Burke gently. "We're not interested in blackening your reputation. What we're after are the facts."

She was silent, the hands in her lap clutching each other. And then she looked up. "All right, we've been having an affair," she said faintly. "I . . . I don't know, really, how I got into it. It just seemed to happen. I've tried to break it off, but he wouldn't let me. He's kept threatening me, saying he'd see to it I lost my job. I haven't known what to do. I like—liked my job, and Mrs. Armando paid me well, and treated me nicely, well, most of the time . . . I've felt so guilty . . . He wouldn't let me alone after that first time . . ."

"We know what a swine he is," Burke growled.

Ellery frowned at this unprofessional remark. But it seemed to do something to Jeanne Temple, as if she

61

sensed that Burke was an ally. After that she addressed all her answers to him, in a sort of gratitude. Virginia Whiting sat quietly by; of course she had known about the affair—Jeanne could hardly have kept it a secret from her.

Ellery said abruptly, "Did *you* know Carlos Armando, Miss Whiting?"

The gray-eyed girl was surprised. "Me? Hardly! I've seen him in the apartment here—twice, I think. But it was only for just long enough to get out of the way and go to the movies."

He found himself rather liking her.

"Did he ever make a pass at you?"

"Once, while Jeannie was getting her face on in the bathroom," Virginia Whiting said grimly. "I've been taking karate lessons, and I gave him a sample. He didn't try it the second time."

Jeanne Temple's mouth was open. "You never told me that, Virginia."

"There's a lot of things I've never told you, Jeannie. Including what a patsy I thought you were to let that wolf get his paws on you in the first place."

"I know," Jeanne said, "I know what a fool I've been."

"Did Armando ever say anything about marrying you?" Ellery asked her.

"No."

"I mean, if you got rid of his wife for him?"

Her eyes flashed at that. "Certainly not!" she cried. "What do you think I am, Mr. Queen? Is that what the police are thinking?"

"The thought," said Ellery, "has crossed a few minds. He never made such a proposal? Even hinted at it?"

"*No*. And if he had, I'd have—I'd have gone straight to Mrs. Armando and told her everything!" She was trembling. Virginia Whiting took her hand, and she began to cry.

"I'm sorry if I've upset you, Miss Temple. There isn't much more. How did you spend the evening of December thirtieth—last Wednesday?"

"But I've been all through that with the detectives—"

"Let's go through it once more, shall we?"

"I'm Jeannie's alibi," said the Whiting girl calmly. "We had dinner together that evening. Neither of us left the apartment—I'd turned down a date because I had a big one coming up the next night, New Year's Eve. Jeannie and I watched television together all evening. We saw the 11:00 o'clock news, then part of the Johnny Carson show.

It was a few minutes past the 12:00 o'clock break when we turned the set off and went to bed. At the same time. Together."

"Miss Temple didn't leave the premises at any time Wednesday night?"

"She did not. Neither did I, so I'm in a perfect position to know."

"That would seem to be that." Ellery rose, and Burke followed suit. Jeanne Temple was swabbing her eyes. "Oh, one other thing, Miss Temple. Does the word "face" mean anything special to you?"

The girl looked blank. "Face?"

"You know, face? *f-a-c-e?*"

"I can't imagine what you mean."

"Do you recall Glory Guild's ever making a point of anyone's face? Around December first? More recently? Particularly on Wednesday?"

The secretary shook her head. "Mrs. Armando certainly never remarked about anyone's face to me. As a matter of fact, she was always rather vague about people's features; she never knew what color anyone's eyes were, things like that. She was nearsighted, and for some reason couldn't wear contact lenses, and she didn't use her ordinary eye-glasses except for reading or working. She was rather vain, you know. She did notice women's clothes, that sort of thing, but—"

"Thank you, Miss Temple."

"That mucker," Harry Burke muttered in the taxi. "There ought to be special laws for men like Armando. So you could get a court order to have him altered, like a dog."

"He does have a way with women, doesn't he?" said Ellery absently. "If only we could get a lead to what she meant."

"What who meant?"

"GeeGee. By that word she wrote. It might explain everything. It *would* explain everything."

"How can you know that?"

"It's a feeling I have, Harry, in my northernmost bones.

FIFTEEN

Dr. Susan Merckell proved disconcerting. She was entertaining some people in the huge Park Avenue apartment behind her street-level office, and she was openly annoyed at the Sunday interruption. "I can give you only a few minutes," she said in a brusk voice as she led Ellery and Burke to a study. "Please say what you have to say, and let me get back to my guests." She was a small woman with an hourglass figure, blunt unfeminine hands, and very little makeup. But her simply coifed blond hair was natural, and her lips were almost grossly sensual. It was not hard to think of her as a physician; she had the medical stamp of authority. "What is it you want to know today? I've already been questioned."

"Your exact relationship with Carlos Armando," Ellery said.

"I've already answered that one." Her hard green eyes did not change expression. "Count Armando was the husband of one of my patients. He's come to me for treatment himself on several occasions. Next question?"

"I'm not through with the first question, Dr. Merckell. Have you ever had any relationship with Armando that might be called nonprofessional?"

"If you think I'm going to answer that, you're an imbecile."

"Our information is that you have had."

"Does your information include proof?" When Ellery did not reply, Dr. Merckell smiled and rose. "I thought not. Will there be anything else?"

"Please sit down, Doctor. We're not through." She shrugged and sat down. "Do you recall where you were Wednesday night? The night before New Year's Eve?"

"I was at Park Center Hospital."

"Doing what?"

"I was called into an emergency consultation."

"Who was the patient?"

"A man with a laryngeal carcinoma. I don't remember his name."

"Who called you into consultation?"

"A g.p. named Krivitz—Jay Jerome Krivitz. There was also a surgeon present, Dr. Israel Mancetti."

"At what time Wednesday night, Doctor, did this consultation take place?"

"I got to the hospital about 11:00 o'clock. The consultation lasted over an hour."

"You mean it was after midnight when you left?"

"What else can I mean? Over an hour from 11:00 P.M. makes it after midnight, yes. Really, gentlemen, you're wasting my time and making me neglect my guests." Dr. Merckell rose again, and this time it was evident that she had no intention of resuming her chair. "I've been asked these questions before, as I told you."

"But not by me," said Ellery. "Doctor, does the word 'face' convey anything significant to you?"

The green eyes gave him a mineral stare. "I'm a laryngologist, not a dermatologist. Is it supposed to?"

"I don't know, I'm asking. Can you recall Mrs. Armando's ever mentioning anything about someone's face, or faces in general?"

"You're either drunk or irresponsible. Even if she had, how could I possibly remember anything as trivial as that? Good day, gentlemen!"

SIXTEEN

~~~~~~~~~~

Marta Bellina was in Los Angeles, they discovered, giving a concert.

So they went to police headquarters where, not surprisingly and Sunday notwithstanding, they found Inspector Queen floundering in a swamp of reports.

"Nothing," the old man grunted. "Not a blasted thing anyone could call a development! What did you two find out?"

Ellery told him.

"Well, then it all washes out. I've already checked the Huppenkleimer woman's whereabouts on the night of the murder—"

"I thought you weren't interested in Huppenkleimer," Ellery said with a grin.

"—just for exercise," his father snapped, "and it checks with what you say she told you. The Temple girl is given an alibi by her roomie, as you just found out. Boston has cleared ex-wife Number Four, Daffy Dingle—what a name for a grown woman!—who suddenly committed herself to a nursing home in Springfield last Monday to take the cure from all those vodka martinis Armando's been pouring down her guzzle; she hasn't set foot from the premises since she went in. Ex-wife Three, Ardene Vlietland, has been with friends on a yacht cruising the Caribbean since last Saturday; I've had the Coast Guard check on the yacht, and it hasn't put in to a port since it sailed. That takes care of the ex-wives Armando's been diddling around with. And my report on Dr. Merckell confirms her consultation alibi at that hospital."

"What about the opera singer?" asked Harry Burke.

"Marta Bellina is in L.A."

"We know that, Inspector. But where was she last Wednesday night?"

"In San Francisco. She's been on a concert tour for the past three weeks and hasn't been back to New York since. We did an especially careful job on Bellina, because in this jet age how far is New York from anywhere? But, according to the information we've received from the California authorities, her alibi stands up."

"Leaving," mumbled Ellery, "the woman in the violet veil. Dad, what have you got on her?"

"A big fat nothing. Your friend Kipley seems to have it down pat. The last time a woman of that description was seen with Armando was just before Christmas. If he's been out with her since, we can't get a make on it."

"Leaving," Ellery mumbled again, "the woman in the violet veil."

"Stop saying that!"

"I have to. She's the only woman Armando's been seen with who hasn't an alibi for the night of the murder."

"Unless," said Burke, "you find her and she does have."

"Okay, so she's a possibility as his accomplice," growled Inspector Queen. "So are a hundred other women, for all I know. With Armando's magic touch with the more foolish damn fools among the opposite sex, we could be on this case until NASA lands a man on Venus."

Their last interview that day was with the magician himself. They found Armando in his widow's Park Avenue duplex with a weak bourbon and water in his manicured hand, the TV set tuned to the Ed Sullivan show. He did not offer them a drink. He did not even ask them to sit down.

"Alone at the boob tube, Count?" asked Ellery. "I expected to find some lady with a *Playboy* center spread holding your hand, condoling with you."

"Peasant," said Carlos Armando. "Am I never to be rid of you louts? My wife is to be buried tomorrow, and you torment me! What do you want?"

"I could ask you for the secret of your allure, but I'm afraid such secrets aren't transferable. Who's the woman in the violet veil?"

"I beg your pardon?"

"Oh, come, Armando," said Harry Burke. "You're not playing ticky-tack-toe with a lot of gullible females. Among your various other enterprises, you've been squiring some wench in a violet veil. Quite openly, which makes you more stupid than I think you are. We want to know who she is."

"You do."

"You can understand English, can't you?"

"You will never force one word about the lady from my lips," Armando said profoundly. "You are all boors where women are concerned, you Anglo-Saxons." ("Highland Scottish in my case, old chap," Burke murmured.) "That is why your attempts at fornication and adultery are so pitiful compared with the techniques of European men. We Europeans know what women want; you know only what *you* want. And what women want, secondly—I do not have to tell even you what they want firstly—is not to have their names thrown about in delicate affairs. I have heard American men discussing their conquests in locker rooms, clubhouses, and over brandy and cigars as if the women involved were street whores. I spit on your questions." He actually pursed his pretty lips.

"Bully for you," said Ellery. "But, Carlos, this is not an ordinary conversation. Or affair. Your wife is dead by shooting, and not accidentally, either. And you engineered her departure—"

"I of course reject that utterly and absolutely," Armando said hotly. "It is slanderous and insulting. I point out to you that when my wife was shot I was visiting in the apartment of Miss West. I wish I had a non-interested witness here so that I might sue you for defamation of character. Alas, I have no such witness. I can only ask you to leave my premises at once."

Neither Ellery nor Harry Burke moved.

"He's a beauty, isn't he?" said Burke. "Sheer brass, and a yard deep. Tell me, Count, are you as much of a man with your trousers buttoned? I'd like nothing better than to square off with you and find out."

67

"Are you threatening me, Mr. Burke?" Armando asked in an alarmed voice. He glanced quickly at the nearby telephone. "Unless you leave at once, I shall call the police!"

"I'm half tempted to let you find out how much good that would do you," Ellery said. "Was the woman in the veil the love-nest birdie you charmed into shooting your wife for you, Armando? Because we're going to find her, I promise you that."

Armando smiled. "The best of luck to you in your search, my friend," he said softly.

Ellery stared at him, puzzled. Then he said, "Come on, Harry. I need fresh air."

SEVENTEEN

~~~~~~~~~~~~~~~~~~

"Where are we going?" Roberta West asked Harry Burke.

The Scot said shyly, "I had a thought, Miss West. I hope you'll like it."

He had phoned her on impulse late Sunday evening, after parting from Ellery, and had not only found her in but in a mood for company. They had had a late dinner in a hole-in-the-wall Italian place on Second Avenue, candlelit, with Chianti from a wicker bottle with a three-foot neck.

The taxi hit 59th Street and turned west. The streets were beautifully empty. It was a brisk, star-prickled night.

Roberta glanced at him curiously. "You seem awfully excited."

"Perhaps I am."

"By what, may I ask?"

"Oh, something." Even in the dark she could have sworn that he was blushing. He added in a rush, "By you, for example."

The girl laughed. "Is that a sample of the latest British line? Over here it went out with the bustle."

"It's *not* a line, Miss West," Burke said stiffly. "I've been too busy to learn any."

"Oh," Roberta said. And they were silent until the taxi pulled up in the plaza. Burke paid the man off, helped Roberta down, and waited until the taxi drove away. "Now what?" Roberta asked expectantly.

"Now this." He took a delicate hold on her muskrat-covered elbow and steered her to the first of the three horsedrawn cabs waiting at the curb. "An amble around your park. That is . . . if you'd like?"

"What a scrumptious idea!" Roberta squealed, and hopped in, to be enveloped by the wonderful odor of horse, old harness, and oats. "Do you know something?" she exclaimed as the Scot pulled himself up beside her and began fussing with the lap robe. "In all the time I've been in New York, I've never taken a ride in one of these things."

"Do you know something?" Burke mumbled. "In all the time I've been in London, I never have, either."

"You mean you've never been in a hansom cab?"

"Never."

"How wonderful!"

Later, while the carriage was clopping along in Central Park, being whooshed at by passing cars, Harry Burke's hand fumbled under the robe and found Roberta's.

Her hand was correctly cold, but she let him hold it.

Still later, on the return swing of the journey, he leaned over and, in an act of sheer desperation, pecked about for her lips and ultimately located them. They felt like rubber gaskets.

"Can't you do better than that, Miss West?" Burke muttered.

In the dark he heard her giggle. "Under the circumstances, Harry, don't you think the least you could do is call me Roberta?"

Only when he had left her outside her apartment building—she was quite firm about his not escorting her upstairs—did Burke realize that she had failed to demonstrate whether she could or could not do better.

He sighed not unhappily. He rather thought she could, and he rather thought she would.

In time.

EIGHTEEN

It is universal police procedure to stake out detectives at the funeral in a murder case, on the magnetic theory that the murderer will be drawn to his victim for the last possible time. Inspector Queen dutifully had his men at the Long Island cemetery. Ellery passed the departmental rites up; he lacked the traditional police mentality. As far as he was concerned, he knew the murderer —if not in deed, then in inspiration; besides, he had no stomach for Armando's playacting this morning. And it was beyond belief that the woman in the violet veil would put in an appearance. Armando would see to that.

"He might have telephoned to warn her off," Harry Burke said over their late breakfast. "Haven't I heard rumors about an occasional discreet official wiretap in your marvelous country?"

"I see no evil and I hear no evil," proclaimed Ellery from behind a mouthful of scrambled egg and Canadian bacon. "Besides, I doubt Armando would be so careless. If I gauge our boy correctly, Violet Veil has had her orders for a long time. I'm much more interested in today's will reading."

"Who's going to be there?"

"The only one we haven't met is Selma Pilter, Glory's old manager. Which reminds me, Harry. We'd better try to get a make on her."

He reached for the extension phone on the cupboard and dialed a number.

"Felipe? Is there any chance that Mr. Kipley is out of the hay? This is Ellery Queen."

"I go see," said Felipe noncommittally.

"Marvelous country," Burke murmured, glancing at his watch.

The columnist's voice shrilled in Ellery's ear. "God damn it, man, don't you ever sleep? What's with the Guild case? A break?"

"I'm afraid not. I just need some information."

"Some more information, you mean. When do I get my *pro quo?"*

"In time, in time, Kip," Ellery soothed him. "Do you have anything on Glory's manager? Selma Pilter?"

"Do I have anything on the Sphinx? Not a speck of dirt, if that's what you're after. And if you think the count's been tossing Selma around, forget it. Even he draws a line. She's an Egyptian mummy."

"How old is she, Kip?"

"Four thousand, if you've got twenty-twenty. In her sixties, if you're blind. She used to be a singer herself. A long time ago. Never made it, quit, and turned to the percentage racket. Damned good at it, too. She made Glory a millionaire."

70

"I know that. Is there anything else about her I ought to know?"

"Well, she and Glory were a tight twosome. They never had the troubles most temperamental artistes have with their managers. Selma couldn't be a threat to other women, which was one reason; the other was that she's a real cool operator. What else? Aside from agenting, she keeps pretty much to herself. If she has a life of her own, she hides it under her falsies. She's a deep one."

"How do you mean?"

"Deep. Don't you understand English?"

"Thanks, Kip."

"When am I going to have to thank you, Charlie?"

They were a little early for the will-reading appointment. William Maloney Wasser turned out to be a large, portly, outwardly calm man with a polka-dot bow tie and a tic. The tic seemed to fascinate Harry Burke.

"No, I can't say I knew Glory Guild really well," the lawyer said as they waited for the funeral party in his office. "My dealings with her were mainly through Selma Pilter—who, by the way, is one of the smartest businesswomen I've ever had anything to do with. It was Selma who recommended my firm to Glory when Glory was looking around for somebody to handle her affairs. Selma's steered a number of her clients my way."

"Then I take it you haven't been Glory's lawyer long?"

"About fifteen years."

"Oh. Didn't she have a lawyer before you?"

"Willis Fenniman, of Fenniman and Gouch. But old Will died, and Glory didn't like Gouch—she used to say they didn't make music together." Wasser seemed more amused than irritated by the interrogation. "Do I understand, Mr. Queen, that I'm being grilled in a murder case?"

"Habit, Mr. Wasser. Forgive me. Besides, you've already been looked up. The police department has found you and your firm lily-pure and clean-o."

Wasser chuckled, and then his secretary announced the arrival of the funeral party. Before he could instruct her to show the party in, Ellery said hurriedly, "One thing, Mr. Wasser. Does the word 'face' have any special meaning for you?"

The lawyer looked blank. "Is it supposed to?"

"F-a-c-e."

"You mean in the context of this case?"

"That's right."

Wasser shook his head.

71

NINETEEN

~~~~~~~~~~~~~~~~~

Carlos Armando ushered Lorette Spanier into the law office with a deference that none of the onlookers could doubt, least of all the girl. It seemed to Ellery that she was half pleased by it, the other half being annoyance. Armando actually took up a post behind her chair. She was the mystery ingredient in his ointment and, as such, had to be fingered with care. Jeanne Temple he ignored. Whether this was out of the contempt of familiarity or the discretion of broad experience Ellery was unable to decide. In any event, it was clearly a bad situation for the secretary of the dead woman. By the side of the busty child-blonde with the pout and the dimple, the Temple girl faded like an overexposed chromo. She was so aware of it that her muddy brown eyes spattered Armando with loathing before her glance lowered to the gloved hands in her lap, where it remained.

Selma Pilter produced a shock, and a downward revision of Ellery's estimate of Kip Kipley's judgment. The old woman's ugliness approached an esthetic experience, like the ugliness of a Lincoln or a Baronesse Blixen. Her fleshless frame was so fine as to suggest hollow bones, like a bird's; Ellery half expected her to flap her arms and sail to a chair. Her long face narrowed to an almost nonexistent chin; the coarse dark skin was like the bed of an extinct river with the ripple-marks showing. Her nose was a scimitar edge, her lips a multitude of hairline wrinkles, her pendulous lobes further elongated by African earrings of ebony. (Had the elephant-hide chair and the Watusi warrior in Glory Guild's den been gifts from Selma Pilter? The old woman's wrists and fingers were loaded with jewelry of African craftsmanship.) Only a sliver of dye-shiny black hair showed under the tight turban she wore. For the rest of her, her emaciation was covered by a severe suit; her throat was mercifully hidden by a scarf; her birdlike feet perched on stilted heels. But her eyes were beautiful, black and lustrous, like Carlos Armando's, and with a deep intelligence. The whole woman was somehow medieval. Ellery was fascinated by her; so, he noted, was Harry Burke.

Inspector Queen came in last; he shut the door quietly

and stood with his back against it. When Ellery offered his chair in pantomime—the office was two chairs shy—the Inspector shook his head. He evidently wanted to be in a position to study every face.

"We meet here today," began Wasser, "for the reading of Glory Guild Armando's will. Two of the interested parties cannot be present—Marta Bellina, who is on a personal appearance tour on the Coast, and Dr. Susan Merckell, who has been called out of state on a consultation.

"The will," continued the lawyer, unlocking a desk drawer and taking out a kraft envelope sealed with wax, "or rather this copy of it, is a true copy properly witnessed and notarized." He broke the seal and drew out a document backed with blue legal paper. "It is dated December the eighth last."

Ellery recognized the envelope as the one he had found in a metal box in GeeGee Guild's loudspeaker hiding place—the envelope marked "My Will. To Be Opened by My Attorney, William Maloney Wasser." The date of the will struck him as significant. December 8 was only seven days past the date of the blank page in Glory's diary—the page to which he had applied his lighter and brought out the word "face." Something had happened on December 1 that apparently was pivotal in the retired singer's life—some event that immediately caused her to institute a search for her niece Lorette Spanier and within a week to write a new will (it was inconceivable that no previous will had existed).

He was right, for at this moment Wasser, reading from the document, was saying, "This is my last will and testament, revoking any and all wills in existence prior to this date," and so on. Whatever the result, the cause had been sufficiently alarming to prevent Glory Guild from spelling it out in her diary, and to drive her to the cryptic one-word reference in disappearing ink, an act which more and more took on the cast of desperation.

But then Ellery concentrated on the legacies.

Wasser was reading a long list of bequests to individually named charitable organizations—surprisingly picayune bequests; none exceeded $100 and most were for $25 and $50. Considering the extent of the murdered woman's estate, this opened a whole new wing of her character. She had evidently been one of those insecure people who dispense their largess diffusively, Ellery thought, to cover as many good causes as possible with the least hurt to
73

themselves, out of some conflict between social parsimony and a hunger for praise. Armando, hovering over Lorette Spanier's shining head, seemed pleased.

But the will revealed paradoxes. There was a $10,000 bequest to "my faithful secretary, Jeanne Temple." (The faithful secretary's glance leaped from her lap to the lawyer's face and back again, the brief leap accomplished with surprise, delight, and—Ellery was sure of it—shame.) "My dear friend, Marta Bellina" received a like sum (paradox now, since the opera star was rich as Croesus's wife, not only from her professional earnings but from the estates of the two rich husbands she had buried). "My physician and friend, Dr. Susan Merckell" was left $10,000 also. (Another *pourboire* to the well-heeled; Dr. Merckell's practice brought her an income in six figures.)

And Selma Pilter, "my dear friend, to whose brilliant and devoted management over the years I owe everything . . ." Ellery watched the old woman closely. But there was nothing to be seen on the wrinkled little face. Either she had supreme command over herself, or she knew what was coming. ". . . I leave the sum of $100,000." Ellery heard Armando utter something unpleasant-sounding in Italian.

Ellery leaned forward. Wasser was coming to the meat of the will, and he had paused. The lawyer seemed embarrassed, or uneasy.

"To my husband Carlos," Wasser began, and paused again.

Armando's black eyes were staring at Wasser's lips. "Yes?" he said. "Yes!" Ellery thought it unworthy of him.

"To my husband Carlos"—the lawyer paused again, but only for a moment this time—"simply to tide him over until he can find another source of income, I leave the sum of $5,000."

"What!" shrieked Armando. "Did you say $5,000?"

"I'm afraid so, Mr. Armando."

"But this is—this is criminal! There is some mistake!" The widower was waving his arms hysterically. "True, GeeGee and I had an agreement in which I renounced my share in her estate. But I point out to you, Mr. Attorney, that in the contract it said that at the end of five years GeeGee would tear this agreement up. The five years went by, and she did tear it up—before my eyes. That was almost a year ago. So how could she have cut me off with this . . . this bagatelle!"

"I don't know what you saw torn up, Mr. Armando,"

said Wasser uncomfortably, "but your premarital agreement with Glory Guild is still in existence, therefore in force—" he waved a paper "—here is a copy of it, attached to Mrs. Armando's copy of the will. The original of the agreement is attached to the original of the will. Both are already in the hands of the Surrogate's Court."

"I wish to see that!"

"Certainly." Wasser hastily rose, but Armando had already bounded to the lawyer's desk and snatched the paper from his hand. He scanned it unbelievingly.

"But I tell you she ripped the original of this to bits and burned them!" The man was in a panic. He muttered, "I see, I *see*. She did not actually reveal the paper to me. She merely told me it was the one, and I was stupid enough to take her at her word, and then she tore up the dummy paper . . ." A millrace of invective, in some language Ellery did not recognize (could it be Romany, the language of his allegedly gypsy background?) streamed from Armando's lips. "She duped me!" he howled. The hatred and anguish on his pitted face were Glory-directed; what was in all their minds—that GeeGee Guild had known about or suspected his continuous infidelities, so that in her eyes he had flouted their agreement over and over—apparently did not enter his. "I shall sue! I shall take this to your courts!"

"That, of course, Mr. Armando," said Wasser, "is entirely up to you. But I don't see what you hope to gain. You can hardly contest your authentic signature on this agreement; and the mere existence of the agreement past the end of the conditional five-year period is *prima facie* evidence that your wife did not consider you to have fulfilled your end of the bargain. I think you'll find that the physical evidence carries all the weight. It certainly isn't going to be overthrown by your unsupported word that she destroyed the agreement when she clearly didn't."

"I could have had at least one-third of her estate. A million dollars! My dower right! It is not to be borne!"

"In the face of this agreement, Mr. Armando, you'll have to be satisfied with the $5,000 your wife left you."

Armando seized his head and turned away. "I will get it, I will get it," he mumbled. Then he seemed to collect himself, and his pretty mouth tightened. He resumed his position behind the English girl's chair, glaring blackly into space. Ellery divined what he was glaring at. He was glaring at the irony of his act. He had engineered his wife's murder for $5,000, instead of the million he had looked forward to. Now someone else would fall heir . . . Ellery

75

saw Armando's fiercely bitter eyes narrow as his train of thought came to this way station. Who was GeeGee's principal beneficiary?

The lawyer read on: "I leave the whole of my residuary estate, real and personal, to my only close blood-relation, my niece Lorette Spanier, if she should be found . . ." A long paragraph followed, providing for the event that Lorette Spanier should have died prior to testatrix's death, or the alternative event that she should not have been found, alive or dead, within seven years of testatrix's death; in either instance, the residuary estate was to establish a foundation, the purpose of which was to provide scholarships and fellowships for furthering the musical careers of singers and other musicians. The formulation of the foundation was gone into in detail—irrelevant now that Lorette Spanier had been found alive and legally identified.

It was Carlos Armando who spoke first. "Congratulations, Lorette. It is not every orphan who finds herself a millionaire at the age of twenty-two." He did not even sound bitter. The count had regained command over himself. Like a good general, he wasted no time brooding over the failure of his attack. He was already making plans for the battle ahead. (Ellery thought: He must be giving himself a medal for his foresight in establishing a bridgehead to his wife's niece at their first meeting.)

As for the young heiress, she sat stunned. "I don't know what to say. Really I don't! I met my aunt only once, for less than an hour. I don't feel as if I have the right—"

"The feeling will pass, my child," murmured Carlos Armando, stooping over Lorette. "I know of no feelings that can stand up against so much money. Tomorrow, when you have thrown me out of the apartment I have occupied so long—and did you know that it is a condominium, fully paid up?—you will wonder how you could ever have been poor."

"Oh, don't say that, Uncle Carlos! Of course I shan't do any such thing. You may stay in the apartment for as long as you like."

"Do not be so generous," said Armando, shaking his head like a wise old uncle. "I would be tempted to accept, now that it is I who am poor again. Besides, our Mr. Wasser would not allow it—am I correct, Mr. Wasser? I thought so. And we could hardly occupy the same premises; it would cause the kind of talk that is so unfairly associated with my name. No, I shall take my few miserable possessions and move out to some rooming house. Do not

76

concern yourself about my fate, *cara*. I am quite accustomed to privation."

It was a splendid performance, and Lorette Spanier was moved to tears by it.

TWENTY

~~~~~~~~~~~~~~~~~~~

As the group was dispersing, to Ellery's surprise William Maloney Wasser asked Selma Pilter and Lorette to remain. Harry Burke glanced at Ellery, who gave him the nod, and Burke left with Jeanne Temple and Armando. Armando went away reluctantly.

"Do you mind if I hang around, Mr. Wasser?" asked Inspector Queen.

"Well, no," the lawyer said. To Ellery, glancing at his father, it looked like a put-up job. "You don't object, do you, Mrs. Pilter?"

"I want Inspector Queen to sit in on this," said the old woman; she had a voice that seemed to come from her bird's feet, high and clear and sweet. "And Mr. Queen, since he's obviously an interested party."

"That I am," muttered Ellery.

Wasser came around and shut his office door carefully. Then he hurried back to his desk, sat down, and rubbed his heavy chin. Lorette was looking puzzled; whatever was on the lawyer's mind, the girl was ignorant of it.

"I hardly know how to say this, Miss Spanier," Wasser began. "It's an unusual situation—not a black and white matter by any means. I mean . . . I suppose the only thing for me to do is lay the facts before you and let you be the judge."

"Facts?" asked the English girl. "About Mrs. Pilter?"

The old woman simply sat there, silent.

"You know, of course, that Mrs. Pilter was your aunt's trusted manager and booking agent for a great many years. I had it from Glory's own lips—and I know it out of my personal dealings with Mrs. Pilter—how very astute and absolutely scrupulous she has been in her handling of Mrs. Armando's affairs. The fact that your aunt left Mrs. Pilter that handsome legacy in her will is proof enough of her esteem and gratitude. However." He stopped.

It sounded like an ominous conjunction. Lorette glanced over at Selma Pilter in bewilderment.

77

"I think, Mrs. Pilter," said the lawyer, "you had better take it from there."

The ugly old woman rustled as she stirred in her chair. But her beautiful black eyes were fixed on the girl. Whatever lay behind the look, it was deeply tucked away.

"My dear, I am one of those silly, unfortunate people who have an uncontrollable passion for betting on horse races," Selma Pilter said. "Every penny I've ever saved has gone into the pockets of bookmakers. I would be a wealthy woman today if not for my weakness for gambling.

"Late last month I found myself into the bookies for a great deal of money. They're not exactly reasonable people, and I was actually in physical danger. Of course, it was all my own fault; I had no one to blame but myself. I was badly frightened. They gave me forty-eight hours to pay up, and I had not a single legitimate way of raising the money. So . . ." she hesitated; then her withered old chin came up. "So, for the first time in my life, I did something dishonest. I borrowed—I told myself it was 'borrowing'—the money from Glory's funds.

"You see," the old woman went on steadily, "I had the rationalization worked out in my mind. I knew Glory was leaving me $100,000 in her will—she had told me so. So I talked myself into believing that I was only taking an advance against my own money. Of course, it wasn't that at all; for one thing, Glory could have changed her mind about leaving me so much money. It simply wasn't mine to take. But—I did. And then, a few days later, came Glory's sudden death, which was such a shock by itself, and for the other reason that I faced an accounting that would reveal the shortage. And I had no way of replacing it—I'm afraid my credit isn't very good at the banks.

"That's the situation, Miss Spanier. The legacy will more than repay the shortage, but the fact remains that I did take money entrusted to my care, and you would be entirely within your rights to bring charges against me. And that's the story."

She stopped and simply sheathed her claws.

"Not the whole story," Wasser said quickly. "I was completely unaware of the borrowed funds until Mrs. Pilter herself called it to my attention. She phoned me about it last night. And I decided to hold the matter over until after the reading of the will today.

"It's the main reason," he went on, turning to Inspector Queen, "that I called you last night and asked you to be sure to be present, Inspector. Naturally, I don't relish the prospect of possibly being accused of withholding information in a murder case, although I'm positive the information is totally irrelevant to the case. As far as the borrowed funds are concerned, of course, it's Miss Spanier's decision as to whether to press a charge or not. She's the principal legatee."

"Oh, dear," said Lorette. "I don't know you, Mrs. Pilter, but from everything I've heard you practically made Aunt Glory's career. I'm sure that if she put so much trust in you you're a basically trustworthy person. Besides, I can hardly play the role of First Stone-thrower. I saw too much misery in the orphanage—" her dimple showed "—in fact, I caused a great deal of it myself. No, I shouldn't dream of preferring charges."

Selma Pilter drew a wobbly breath. "Thank you, thank you," she said in an unsteady voice. "I'm lucky for your charity, child. I have very little for myself." She rose. "Will there be anything else, Mr. Wasser?"

"Inspector Queen?" The lawyer looked relieved.

"If Miss Spanier won't charge her, that's it as far as I'm concerned," said the Inspector; and the Queens left.

"You know, Ellery," the Inspector said as they taxied downtown, "the Pilter woman's embezzlement could be a motive."

"It could?" Ellery sounded preoccupied.

"Knocking off GeeGee for the hundred grand legacy in order to cover the shortage."

"And telling Wasser all about it before she even collected? You can't have her covering the shortage and uncovering it in the same hypothesis."

"She could be playing this smart. For the very reason you've just given—to make herself look like the original honest woman. Meanwhile, she's off the hook with the defalcation. She knew she couldn't have kept it under wraps indefinitely. Not with a shrewdie like GeeGee Guild to account to. And Wasser doesn't seem to me a lawyer you can fool for very long. I say it's a possible motive."

"I say it's a possible nothing," Ellery said crudely. He was slumped so far down he was almost sitting on his shoulderblades. "That part of it, anyway. But there is something about Selma Pilter that bothers me."

"What's that?"

"Her face. It's certainly the outstanding face of the century—outstandingly, outrageously, superbly ugly. So much so that it may be why Glory wrote the word down as she was dying."

"Do you believe that for one minute?" his father snorted.

"Not for a second," muttered Ellery.

TWENTY-ONE

~~~~~~~~~~~~~~~~~~~~~~~~~~~~~~~~

"You certainly know how to feed a man," said Burke, lying back on the well-worn French provincial sofa.

"You certainly know how to pick out the music that goes with it," said Roberta West, sitting straight up on it.

They were spending the evening in Roberta's apartment on East 73rd Street. It was in an old elaborate building whose gentility was a bit scabbed at the edges, and its rooms had high ceilings with elaborate plasterwork, the kind of curlicued decorations that should have framed mural cupids and dryads with ash-green architectural trees and pale flat brown French horizons for background. But there was nothing in the panels except a few unframed and not very good Dufy and Utrillo reproductions. The tall windows were swoopingly draped in burlap dyed maroon, and there was an ancient Italian fireplace that had been stopped up for a generation. And since Roberta possessed very little furniture, the allover effect was gigantic, dwarfing her petite dimensions further, so that she rather resembled a redheaded Alice caught in the Shrink-Me stage.

Burke thought she looked adorable. He did not, of course, dare to say so.

She had fed him a roast beef and Yorkshire pudding dinner, "to make you feel at home," and the beef was too rare and the pudding too doughy for his taste (or anyone's, he caught himself guiltily thinking); but then a man needn't expect everything in a woman with so many exemplary points (although points wasn't quite the word); therefore the manful lie about her culinary wisdom.

As for the music, that was his contribution (aside from a bottle of undistinguished California burgundy) to the festivities. Roberta had said that she owned a modest hifi, and he had stopped into Liberty's on Madison Avenue on his way uptown and bought an *Elijah*, with the Huddersfield soloists and chorus, not knowing that Roberta's small collection of records consisted mainly of Mancinis, old Glenn Millers and such, her prizes being two or three

80

vintage Whitemans; but Burke was taking such obvious pleasure in the oratorio that Roberta had the extra wisdom to express pleasure in it, too, although most of it either mystified or bored her.

So they both lied gallantly, and it turned out a smashing evening.

Afterward, as they sat side by side on the sofa, he lolling with sternly repressed longings and she properly straight-backed, Burke murmured, "This is so comfortable. It makes a man feel like—well, like taking his shoes off."

"Don't," said Roberta, "give in to the feeling."

"Oh? Why not, Miss—I mean, Roberta?"

"Taking your shoes off could start a trend."

He blushed. This time, in the full light, she was positively bathed in it. "I didn't mean—"

"Of course you didn't, cookie," Roberta crooned. "That was bitchy of me. Take your shoes off, by all means."

"I believe," the Scot said huffily, "I'll leave them on, thank you."

Roberta laughed. "Oh, you're so—so Scotch!"

"Scottish is the preferred term."

"I'm sorry. I've never known a Scotchman—I mean a Scotsman—before."

"I've never known a young American girl before."

"Not so young, Harry. But thanks for the compliment."

"Rot. You can't be more than twenty-one or two."

"Why, thank you! I'll be twenty-seven my next birthday." Considering that she was going to be twenty-eight, Roberta did not think the fib too enormous for her conscience to bear.

"Oh! And when will that be?"

At the conclusion of the evening, as Burke stood in the doorway hat in hand, he suddenly found himself seizing her like a rapist and catching her lips before they could go into their rubber-gasket act. He was astounded by both his lust and their softness.

So it was a smashing evening to the very end.

TWENTY-TWO

〜〜〜〜〜〜〜〜

Into the penthouse apartment moved Lorette Spanier, out of it went Carlos Armando—the suffering but understanding "uncle" to the end—and less than two weeks later Lorette took a companion to share the apartment with her.

Harry Burke was the catalyst.

Ellery had expected him to return to England, but the Scot lingered. It was certainly not the Guild-Armando case that was keeping him in New York; the Inspector had no further need of him, and in any event he would be a mere jet's flight away if he went home. Yet the only move Burke made was from the Queen apartment—"I can't take advantage of your hospitality indefinitely," he said, "like *The Man Who Came to Dinner*"—to a modest midtown hotel.

"It's none of my business, Harry," Ellery said to him, "but my nose is itching. Don't you have to earn a living? Or is something keeping you here that you've been holding out on me?"

"I have an associate in my office in London," Burke retorted, "who can jolly well carry on while I take my first sabbatical in years. That's one thing, chappie. For another, I feel a certain responsibility toward that girl."

"Lorette? Why?"

"A, she's a British subject. B, this is a murder case. C, I was instrumental in bringing her into the case when I located her for Glory Guild. On top of that, she's grown on me. Reminds me of a favorite sister of mine who trapped an Aussie into wedlock fourteen years ago and whom I haven't seen since. But the principal reason—I'm uneasy about her."

"Because of Armando? You needn't be. There's a man on his tail day and night."

"It's not so much Armando, although I don't like the way the mucker looks at her. I don't know, Ellery. Lorette's rattling around alone in that museum of an apartment, she's a very inexperienced twenty-two, and she's suddenly an heiress to millions. She could become the target of all sorts of nastiness."

"Well, congratulations," said Ellery with every appearance of heartiness. "It's mighty decent of you, Harry."

Burke reddened to the roots of his sandy hair. "Oh, I'm a mighty decent bloke."

Ellery did not doubt the verity of Burke's professed reasons for hanging about New York, but he suspected that Burke had another reason he was not professing. The great man's suspicion was soon confirmed. Burke was seeing Roberta West regularly. Remembering how instantly smitten the Scot had been on that New Year's morning, when the West girl had come to the Queen apartment to tell her appalling story about Armando's proposal to her, Ellery was not surprised. He ragged Burke about dissembling.

"Are you checking on me, too?" Burke asked in a hard voice—a very hard voice. It was the first time Ellery had seen him angry.

"Of course not, Harry. But with so many detectives running around in the case, you could hardly keep your meetings with Roberta West a secret."

"It's no secret, old chap! I just don't like making a display of my personal life."

"Are you in love with her?"

"Nothing is sacred to you, is it?" Burke unexpectedly chuckled. Then he said soberly, "I think so. No, I'm pretty damned sure. I've never felt like this about a woman before."

"Does Roberta feel the same way about you?"

"How the hell should I know?" We haven't discussed her feelings—or mine, for that matter. It hasn't reached that stage. Do you know, Ellery, you've the cheek of an overgrown Mod?"

"That opinion of me," Ellery said cheerfully, "is now transatlantic."

It was Harry Burke who got Lorette and Roberta together. He took the two girls to dinner one night, and they liked each other immediately. Afterward, they went back to the penthouse, where the girls spent the rest of the evening in intense exploration. It turned out that they had a great deal in common—their views on men, morality, Viet Nam, the Beatles, *Playboy* Magazine, Martin Luther King, bikinis, Frank Sinatra, Joan Baez, pop art, and the theater generally were in delightful agreement. Best of all, to Lorette at least, Roberta had already achieved a success—in Lorette's eyes—as an actress. The blond girl's windfall fortune, it seemed, had not affected her ambition to follow in her late aunt's footsteps.

"You two were made for each other," Harry Burke said, beaming. "In fact, it gives me an idea."

The blond head and the sorrel top turned to him. In their discovery of each other, they had almost forgotten he was there.

"Lorette, you simply can't live in this huge place alone. Why doesn't Roberta move in with you?"

"Of all the gall!" Roberta gasped. "What a thing to

say, Harry. I thought Englishmen were the soul of reserve."

"They are. I'm a Scot."

He beamed again.

"Why, Roberta, it's a lovely idea!" Lorette cried. "Oh, would you?"

"Lorette, we've only just met—"

"What has that to do with anything? We like each other, we have the same interests, we're both unattached—oh, Harry, that's an inspiration! Please, Roberta!"

"Golly, I don't know," the little actress said. "How does that cornball line go? This is so sudden." She giggled before she said, "Are you sure, Lorette? I'd have to sublet my apartment—my lease isn't up till October —and if we didn't get along or something, I'd have an awful time finding another place to live. A place I could afford."

"Don't worry about *that*. We'll get along, Roberta, I know we will. And another thing. It wouldn't cost you tuppence to live here. Imagine all the rent you'd be saving."

"Oh, I wouldn't dream of such an arrangement!"

"You two battle it out," murmured Harry Burke, "while I wash my hands." He had made the suggestion not hopefully, remembering Lorette's independence, her living alone on the West Side, her shyness with strangers. But apparently the grandeur of the Guild apartment had overawed her. It was an immense place for a lone girl to rattle around in, and his suggestion of a compatible companion had come at the psychological moment. Burke congratulated himself.

When he came back, they were clinging to each other. So that was that.

Burke felt top hole about it.

As for the murder case, it limped. In spite of intensive investigation, Inspector Queen's detectives were unable to turn up a clue to the mysterious woman in the violet veil; as far as they were able to determine, she had not appeared in public again, certainly not in Armando's company. He was cultivating a fresh crop of women these days, pretty young ones for pleasure, aging ones with fat estates behind them for potential investment—all of whom were investigated with reference to Violet Veil, and all of them fruitlessly.

There was nothing to indicate that any of these neweomers to Armando's *liste d'armour* might be women he had previously wooed.

It was exasperating.

Not that the count was neglecting his past. He was also paying court to a few of his ex-wives—notably Gertie Huppenkleimer—and making an occasional phone call to the penthouse "to ask how my little niece is coming along." At such times Roberta found an excuse for leaving the room.

"I can't stand the sound of his voice. It makes me sick," Roberta said when Lorette once asked her why. "Look, darling, I know it's really not my business, but Carlos was behind your aunt's death—how can you bear to talk to him?"

Lorette was distressed. "I don't encourage him to call, Roberta, really I don't . . ."

"You do, too. By answering the phone."

"If I didn't, Carlos would come up here, possibly make a scene. I abhor scenes. Besides, I can't bring myself to believe it."

"Believe what?"

"That he planned Aunt Glory's death. I don't care what Harry Burke, Ellery Queen, and the police say. They'll have to prove it to my satisfaction first."

"Lorette, he proposed it to *me!*"

"Maybe you misunderstood him—"

"The heck I did," Roberta said. "Don't you believe me?"

"Of course I believe you. I mean, I believe you think he did. Oh, I know Carlos is no rose—that he's done a lot of things that aren't very nice—especially where women are concerned—but . . . murder?" The blond head shook in disbelief.

Roberta looked appalled. "Lorette, you're not *falling* for him?"

"What an absurd idea." But the English girl had turned quite pink.

"You *are.*"

"I'm *not*, Roberta. I wish you wouldn't even suggest it."

Roberta kissed her. "Don't you ever let that animal mess around," she said fiercely. "I know."

"Of course not," said Lorette. But she drew away from the other girl, and a little coolness settled between them. It soon lifted, but each made an excuse to go to bed early that night.

It was the first far cloud of the thunderstorm.

TWENTY-THREE

~~~~~~~~~~~~~~~~

One Sunday in mid-February the girls invited Burke and Ellery to brunch. The Scot arrived at the penthouse early, with Ellery only a few minutes behind. The new maid admitted them (Glory Guild's staff had resigned in a body, on various excuses, all of them adding up to the undelivered wish to get as far away as possible from the scene of murder). Lorette and Roberta were still dressing.

When Roberta was finished she wandered into the master bedroom. "You about ready?"

"In arf a mo'," Lorette said; she was applying her lipstick. "Roberta, what a stunning cross. Where did you pick it up?"

"I didn't," Roberta said, fingering it. It was a heavy silver Maltese cross on a silver chain, and it glittered like a star. "It was a birthday gift from Harry."

"And you didn't tell me."

Roberta laughed. "At your age, darlin', you can afford to advertise. Me, I'm up in the late twenties."

"Not so late. Twenty-seven."

"Lorette! How did you know?"

"Harry told me."

"I'll never tell that man another secret as long as I live! Actually, I fibbed a bit. I'm twenty-eight."

"Oh, don't be a ninny. He didn't tell me till yesterday, and I picked something up for you at Saks."

"That wasn't necessary . . ."

"Oh, shut up." Lorette rose from the vanity and went to one of the closets. She opened the door and reached up to a high shelf piled with hatboxes; a Saks box tied with gilt cord was perched on one of them. "I'm sorry I'm late with a gift," she said, rising on tiptoe to reach the Saks box, "but it's your own fault—damn!" In pulling at the gift box she tipped over one of the hatboxes, and both boxes fell off the shelf. The lid of the hatbox came off and something distinctly not a hat came bouncing out and stopped at Lorette's feet.

"What," exclaimed Roberta, pointing, "is that?"

The English girl stared down at it.

It was a revolver.

"It's a revolver," Lorette said childishly. Then she began to stoop.

"I don't think you ought to touch it," Roberta said, and Lorette stopped. "Whose in heaven's name is it?"

"It doesn't belong to *me*. I've never even seen a gun so close."

"Unless . . . Is that your Aunt Glory's hatbox?"

"It's mine. A hat I bought only a fortnight ago. But there certainly wasn't any revolver in the box when I set it on the shelf."

They stared at each other. A disagreeable something settled over the bedroom.

"I think," Roberta said, "I think we'd best let Harry and Ellery handle this."

"Oh, yes . . ."

They went to the door together and called down together. The men came bounding upstairs.

"A gun?" Harry Burke ran into the master bedroom, Ellery at his heels. Neither man touched the weapon. They listened in silence to the girls' story of how it had been found, then simultaneously they made for the closet and examined the tumbled hatbox and the floor around it.

"No ammo," muttered Ellery.

"I wonder," began Burke, and stopped. He looked at Ellery. Ellery did not look back. He was on all fours, rump in air, examining the weapon as best he could without handling it. "What make and caliber is it, Ellery?"

"Colt Detective. A .38 Special, two-inch barrel, six-shot. Looks pretty aged to me—the plastic stock is nicked and cracked, the nickel finish looks worn." Ellery took a ballpoint pen from his pocket, inserted it in the trigger guard, and rose, balancing the revolver on the pen. Burke squinted at the gun.

"Loaded with .38 Special cartridges. Four. That makes two shots fired. Glory Guild stopped two bullets." The Scot's burry voice sounded like a damp firecracker.

"You mean this could be the weapon that killed Mrs. Armando?" Roberta West asked in a smallish voice.

"Yes."

"But how could that be?" cried Lorette. "And even if it is, I don't understand what it's doing in the apartment. Did my aunt own such a weapon?"

"Not legally," said Ellery. "There's no record of a gun permit issued to her."

"Then it undoubtedly belongs to her murderer," the

87

British girl said reasonably. "That follows, doesn't it? But it makes matters more puzzling than ever. He certainly—whoever he was—didn't leave the gun behind. Or . . . is it possible the police didn't search the apartment thoroughly enough?"

"The apartment was gone over like a bloody dog looking for fleas," Harry Burke said. "There was no gun here. That is, directly after the shooting."

Lorette's eyes burned a brighter shade of blue. "What you mean, Harry, is—before I took possession of the apartment. After all, the gun was found in my hatbox. Isn't that what you mean?"

Burke did not reply.

The silence became embarrassing.

Lorette broke it with a toss of her blond locks. "Well, the whole notion is the most silly nonsense. Surely no one would believe—?" But then she stopped. It had evidently occurred to her that there were potential believers within sound of her voice.

Ellery slid the revolver carefully down on Lorette's bed. "I'd better call in," he said.

"Why do you have to?" Roberta burst out. "It *is* nonsense! There's undoubtedly the most innocent explanation—"

"Then nobody will be hurt." He went to the extension. "May I?"

"Be my guest," Lorette said in her bitterest American-ese. She sank onto the other side of the bed from the gun and clasped her hands between her knees, the picture of little-girl helplessness. Roberta ran out of the room. They heard her crying while Ellery waited for his father to answer the phone.

TWENTY-FOUR

The report from Fingerprinting was negative; there were no prints on the .38 Special—the usual result. But Ballistics had news for them. Firing tests and the comparison microscope had established that the bullets dug out of Glory Guild's body and the bullets fired by the Colt Detective found in Lorette Spanier's hatbox had been discharged by the same weapon. The markings were identical.

They had the murder gun.

"It's a break," Inspector Queen chortled to the two silent men in his office. "This is all we need to establish a case against the Spanier girl, as I'm sure the D.A. will agree."

"Let's hear it," muttered Ellery, "out loud."

"The girl claims Glory didn't tell her about the new will naming her principal legatee. Doesn't it stand to reason that Glory did tell her? After all, what had Glory been looking for her for? To make Lorette her heir. Is it reasonable that, after finding her, Glory *didn't* tell her?"

"They had only a few minutes alone together."

"How long does it take?" his father retorted. "Five seconds? Number one."

"That's hardly conclusive, Inspector," Harry Burke protested.

"I'm talking about the weight of the circumstances, Burke, as you very well know. Number One covers motive.

"Number Two: Lorette claims she left her aunt alive that night at around 11:30. But, again, we have only the girl's word for it. By her own admission no one saw her leave, no one saw her during her alleged walk home through Central Park, no one saw her when she got to her apartment house, no one saw her in her apartment afterward. She can't produce a single corroborating witness to any detail of her account of her movements. As far as the provable circumstances show, she could just as well have been in her aunt's place till 11:50, she could just as well have shot Glory and got home—however she did it, whether crossing the park on foot or taking a cab—twenty minutes or half an hour later than she says. So that's opportunity on top of motive."

"That," said Ellery, "is possible opportunity on top of possible motive."

"What are circumstantial cases but possibles and probables, Ellery? But then there's Number Three. You can't deny the evidence of this revolver. And neither can she. It's the gun that shot Glory, and that's a fact. *And* it was found in Lorette's bedroom. *And* in Lorette's closet. *And* in Lorette's hatbox in her closet in her bedroom. And all she can say about the gun is that she never saw it before and doesn't know how it got there. Just her unsupported denial."

"It's true," the Inspector said, "that we haven't been able to establish through the records that she bought the weapon—there's no record of such a gun at all—but

89

she'd hardly buy it through regular channels, anyway, to commit murder with it. You know what a pipe it is to buy an unregistered weapon in this town under the counter. At that, we may be able to tie such an illegal sale to her. If we can, we've got her in spades.

"But even without that," and the Inspector showed his dentures, "we've got her. In my book this all adds up to a case we can get through the grand jury. What does it add up to you, my son? You look droopy."

Ellery was silent.

Harry Burke snapped, "Doesn't it strike you, Inspector Queen, that your argument makes the Spanier girl out all kinds of idiot? Why in hell should she have held onto the revolver if she shot her aunt with it? After—to use your own argument—going to the trouble of getting hold of one that couldn't be traced to her? It seems to me the very first thing she'd have done was throw the bloody thing into one of your rivers."

"That's what you or I'd have done, Burke. But you know as well as I how stupid amateurs can act when they're playing around with murder. Anyway, that's an argument for her lawyers. I can't see the D.A. losing sleep over it. And talking about the D.A., I'd better go over and drop this in his lap."

The old man took the Ballistics report and, cheerily, left.

"What do you think, Ellery?" Burke asked after a long silence.

"If you can call it thinking." Ellery looked as if he had swallowed something with a live bug wiggling in it. "I don't know, Harry. Looked at one way, it's one of those slick circumstantial cases that's all façade, like the camera side of a Hollywood set. Go behind the set and you see nothing more substantial than shoring. Still . . ."

"Well, in my view there's only one way to look at it." The Scotsman got to his feet. "With due respect for age and paternity, anyone who maintains that that girl is capable of murder just doesn't know people. The police mind—and I should know, from my years at the Yard—looks at facts, not human capabilities. Lorette Spanier is as innocent of Glory Guild's murder as I am. I'd stake everything I have on that."

"Where are you going?"

"Over to her apartment. If I judged the Inspector's expression correctly—and if I know prosecutors—she's going to need every friend she can muster. And Roberta would give me the sack if I didn't stand by the poor girl. Coming?"

"No," Ellery said glumly, "I'll hang around here."

He did not have long to wait. Less than two hours later a warrant was issued for the arrest of Lorette Spanier.

TWENTY-FIVE

On hearing the news, Attorney Wasser acted as if his late client's principal heiress had developed bubonic plague. With haste he recommended the services of a criminal lawyer and retreated behind a barricade of an astonishing number of appointments. The criminal lawyer, a veteran of the juridical wars named Uri Frankell, tackled the bail problem first.

It was thorny. Lorette Spanier's only substantial assets, her inheritance—aside from interim funds for maintenance of the apartment and incidental expenses—were tied up in Surrogate's Court. They would remain so trussed until the estate was settled, which might take months. Besides, a criminal could not enjoy the rewards of his crime, so until Lorette's guilt or innocence was legally established her rights to the inheritance dangled in limbo. Where, then, was she to get the collateral without whose negotiable existence bail bondsmen developed zippers on their pockets? All this, provided the arraigning judge was willing to set bail in a Murder One case to begin with.

In the end, Lorette went to jail.

Lorette wept.

Roberta wept.

Harry Burke was heard to mutter something not nice about American jurisprudence. (In fairness, he had often in his day muttered not-nice things about English jurisprudence, too.)

Frankell did not think the People had much of a case. He was confident, he said, that he could cast sufficient reasonable doubt into the minds of a jury to get the girl off. (Ellery began to entertain reasonable doubts about the wisdom of Attorney Wasser's recommendation. He distrusted lawyers who were confident in murder cases;

he had seen too many unreasonable juries. But he kept his mouth shut.)

"In this one," Ellery said unhappily to Harry Burke, "I find myself with crotch trouble." "Crotch trouble?" Harry Burke said, puzzled. "Crotch trouble," Ellery said. "I'm hung up on the fence."

Ellery found himself unable to do much of anything in the weeks before Lorette's trial. He haunted police headquarters waiting for progress reports; he frequently visited the Guild apartment (where Roberta kept flinging herself from top to bottom of the penthouse bemoaning Lorette's fate, and her own—"I have no *right* to be living here while Lorette's in that awful cell! But where can I go?"—once even berating Harry Burke for having "talked" her into giving up her old apartment, a charge the Scot suffered in dignified silence); he went to see Lorette and came away with no improvements in her story but a gripe in his groin.

"I don't know what you're so bothered about," his father said one day. "What's eating you, Ellery?"

"I don't like it."

"You don't like what?"

"This whole case. Something about it . . ."

"Like what, for instance?"

"Like the way things don't hang together," complained Ellery. "Like the way loose ends keep flopping."

"You mean that face business."

"For one thing. It's important, dad, I *know* it. And I've vacuumed my brains and can't come up with a single conceivable cross-reference to Lorette."

"Or to anybody else," the Inspector retorted.

"Yes. That's right. It's a flopper. Keeps flopping. Charging that girl, dad, was premature. You ought at least to have found out what GeeGee meant by 'face' before you made the arrest."

"You find out," the Inspector said. "I've got other things to occupy my time. Anyway, it's all in the hands of the D.A. and the Court now. . . . What else?" he asked suddenly.

"Everything else. We'd been going, for example, on the assumption that the murder was Carlos Armando-inspired, with some woman doing the dirty work for him. Now it seems Lorette was that woman."

"I didn't say that," the old man said cautiously.

"Then you've changed your mind about Armando? He had nothing to do with his wife's murder?" When his father did not reply, Ellery said, "I still maintain he did."

"On what grounds?"

"By the pricking of my thumbs. By his general odor. By everything I've found out about him."

"Take *that* into court," Inspector Queen snorted.

"Granted," Ellery said. "But you see how tangled everything is. Did Lorette know Armando before they supposedly met for the first time here in this office—when you questioned her after the murder? If she did, was she Violet Veil? Armando's willing accomplice? That makes no sense at all. Why should she have consented to act as Armando's tool when, according to you, she knew she was inheriting the bulk of the estate?"

"You know his way with women. Maybe she fell for him, the way the others did."

"*If* she knew him beforehand." Ellery lapsed into brooding.

"Look, son," his father said. "There's a side to this we haven't touched on. Certainly we'll never be able to prove it—"

"What?"

"I'm not sure myself that money was the motive behind the murder."

"How do you mean? Are you conceding—?"

"I'm conceding nothing. But if you want to fish around in theories, how about this one? GeeGee Guild dropped her sister, Lorette's mother, after the sister married that Englishman. When Lorette's parents died in the plane crash, GeeGee let the kid be placed in an English orphanage instead of going over there, taking custody of the child, legally adopting her, or otherwise making herself responsible for the girl's future. That kind of cold-blooded neglect could well have made Lorette grow up hating her aunt. It could have been a festering sore that broke out when Burke took her to the Guild apartment that Wednesday night. It's even possible the girl came to New York in the first place to track down her aunt and let her have it.

"It's a theory," the Inspector went on, "with a built-in advantage. Under it Lorette could have told the truth about not knowing anything of the inheritance."

"It also raises an interesting alternate," Ellery said. "That if Lorette killed Glory Guild out of hatred, and not for the estate, then Carlos Armando could still have been plotting Glory's death through an accomplice, only Lorette beat the accomplice to it."

The Inspector shrugged. "That's certainly possible."

"If it's possible, why insist that it was Lorette who beat Violet Veil in the race to kill? Why couldn't it have been the other way around?"

"Because," his father replied, "we have no evidence that it was Violet Veil, as you call her, and we do have evidence that it was Lorette."

"The .38?"

"The .38."

Ellery fell into reverie. He had been theorizing as pure exercise. The truth was, he did not believe any of the theories. Had his father pressed him, he could not have answered why, beyond the pricking of his thumbs.

"Unless," the Inspector concluded, "Violet Veil *was* Lorette. Two motives—Armando's, for what he thought he was going to inherit, Lorette's for revenge."

Ellery threw up his hands.

TWENTY-SIX

~~~~~~~~~~~~~~~~~~~~~~~~~~

On the day before the Lorette Spanier trial there was a meeting in the law office of Uri Frankell. It was a Tuesday afternoon, with a dirty overcast and a threat of snow.

The lawyer, who looked to Burke remarkably like Winston Churchill, sat Roberta and Harry Burke down, offered Burke a cigar, was refused, and began to suck on a cheroot himself, looking throughtful. His air of confidence seemed a little forced today. He said with a well-these-things-happen sort of smile that his investigators had come up to the proverbial blank wall.

"You haven't found *any* corroboration of Lorette's story?" cried Roberta.

"None, Miss West."

"But somebody must have seen her somewhere along the line—leaving the building, crossing the park, getting home. . . . It's incredible."

"Unless," said the lawyer, squinting at the tip of his cigar, "she hasn't told us or the police the truth. You know, you can't find what never was."

"I don't think that's the answer at all, Mr. Frankell," Burke said. "I tell you again, that girl is innocent. It's the premise you must go on, or she hasn't a chance."

"Oh, of course," said the lawyer. "I merely raised the possibility; the district attorney is certainly going to more than raise it. What I'm counting on is Lorette's ability to communicate her little-girl quality to the jury. She's the only defense we have."

"You're putting her in the witness box?"

"We call it 'stand' over here, Mr. Burke." Frankell shrugged. "I have no choice. It's always risky, because it opens the defendant up to an all-out attack by the D.A. on cross-examination. I've been over it with Lorette a number of times, playing the devil's advocate, so she'll have a good idea of what she's facing. She stands up well. Of course, how she'll handle herself under actual cross remains to be seen. I warned her—"

His secretary came in, shutting the door behind her.

"Miss Hunter, I told you I wasn't to be interrupted!"

"I'm sorry, Mr. Frankell, but I thought this might be important, and I didn't want to talk over the intercom in front of him—"

"In front of whom?"

"A man just came into the office who insists on seeing you right away. Ordinarily I would have said you're out, but he claims it's about the Spanier case. He's very shabbily dressed. In fact—"

"I don't care if he's in his underwear, Miss Hunter. Send him in!"

Even Frankell was startled by the creature his secretary showed in. The man was not shabbily dressed; what he wore was a catastrophe—a ruin of an overcoat which looked as if it had been retrieved from a garbage dump; under it a velveteen smoking jacket of trash-barrel vintage, motheaten, runneled with dregs, spattered with old egg, stewstains, and less identifiable slumgullion; a pair of muddy trousers, evidently cast off by some fat man, held up at the waist by a length of filthy rope; shoes two sizes too big; he wore no socks or shirt. He was skeleton-thin, but his hands and face were puffy, his eyes bloodshot and watering, his nose a purple lump. He had not shaved in days.

He stood before them, shivering as if he had never in his life been warm, and rubbed his palms together. They made a sandpaper sound.

"You asked to see me," Uri Frankell said, staring at him. "Okay, you see me. What's the pitch? Who are you?"

"Name of Spotty," the man said. He had a hoarse, wine-soaked voice. "Name of Spotty," he repeated. He added, with a grin that was almost a leer, "Counselor."

"What do you want?"

"Dough," the derelict said. "Do-re-mi. Lots of it." He stood there grinning; half the teeth in his mouth were missing. "Now ask me what I got to sell, Counselor."

"Look, bum," the lawyer said. "I'm going to give you just ten seconds to spill what's on your mind. And if this is a pitch for a handout, I'll heave you all the way back to the Bowery."

"No, you won't. Not when you hear what I got to sell."

"Well, what?"

"Inf'mation."

"About Lorette Spanier?"

"That's it, Counselor."

"How do you know about Miss Spanier?"

"I read the papers."

"If so, you're the first bum in Bowery history to do it. All right, what's your information?"

"Oh, no," the man said. "I tell you, and what do I get? A boot in the backside is what. On the line, mister."

"Get out of here."

"No, wait," Harry Burke said. He said to the derelict, "You mean you actually expect payment in advance?"

The bleary eyes slid Burke's way. "That's it, mister. And none o' your checks, neither. Cash. On the line."

"How much?" Burke asked.

The purple tip of his tongue appeared. Roberta West watched it, fascinated. It swished across his lips and back, like a rain-wiper.

"A grand."

"A thousand dollars?" the lawyer said incredulously. "You don't want much, do you? What do you think we are, halfwits? Go on, scram."

"Just a moment, Mr. Frankell," the Scot said. "Now see here, Spotty, try being reasonable. You walk in here and ask for a thousand dollars on your unsupported claim that you have information that may help Miss Spanier's defense. You'll have to admit you're not the most reliable-looking bloke in New York. How can you expect a reputable attorney like Mr. Frankell to pay out so much of his client's money for a blind article?"

"Who are you?" the man demanded.

"A friend of Lorette Spanier's. So is this lady."

"I know about *her*—I seen her picture in the paper. How can I expect, mister? Take it or leave it. Them's my terms. From what the paper says," the bum grinned, "he ain't got much of a case." A scarred thumb wavered Frankell's way.

Probably never before in his derelict life, Burke thought, had this wino been in possession of a highly negotiable asset. And he had the natural cynicism of the downtrodden everywhere. Spotty was not going to be budged. Nevertheless, Burke thought he must try.

He put on his most man-to-man expression.

"Can't you give us at least a hint, Spotty? The sort of information it is?"

"How do I know what sort? I ain't no lawyer."

"But you know enough to know that the information is worth a thousand dollars to Miss Spanier's attorney?"

"All I know is it's about the Spanier dame, and it sounds to me like it's mighty important."

"And if it turns out not to be?"

"That's his hard luck. The grand in advance, and the counselor takes his chances." The bony jaws set. "I ain't giving no money-back guarantee." The jaws set harder.

"Let it drop, Mr. Burke," Frankell said wearily. "I know this breed, believe me. It's probably a sheer invention in the first place. If I paid him for it I'd have to hire Pinkerton guards to keep all the rest of the Bowery bums out of my office, once the word got around. But even if it's legitimate . . . I'll tell you what I'll do with you, Spotty. You tell me what the information is, here and now. If I think it can help Miss Spanier's case, I'll pay you for the information—what I think it's worth. That's the only deal I'll make with you. Taking or leaving?"

They could see in the man's watery eyes the struggle between cupidity and suspicion. They also saw suspicion win.

"No grand, no talk."

He shut his broken mouth with finality.

"Okay, bum, you've spoken your piece. Out."

The derelict stared at the lawyer. Then he grinned again, slyly this time. "You change your mind, Counselor, ask around the Bowery for Spotty. I'll get the word."

He shuffled out.

The moment the door closed Roberta burst out, "But we can't let him go this way. Mr. Frankell! Suppose he's telling the truth—has really important information? Look, if you feel you can't go into a deal like this, I mean as Lorette's lawyer, how about my putting the money up?"

"Do you have a thousand dollars to throw away, Miss West?"

"I'll borrow it—take out a personal loan from my bank—"

"That's up to you," the lawyer said, shrugging. "But believe me, Lorette Spanier isn't going to be acquitted through the sherry-colored imagination of some providential Bowery bum."

Roberta caught the man in the hall as he waited for the elevator. "Wait a second, Mr. Spotty," she panted. Burke was with her, watching the derelict closely. "I'll pay you the money!"

The man put his dirty hand out.

"I don't have that much on me. I'll have to arrange to get it."

"Better arrange fast, lady. That trial starts tomorrow."

"Where can I reach you?"

"I'll reach you, lady. When will you have it?"

"Tomorrow, if I can."

"You going to the trial?"

"Of course—"

"I'll get to you there." He winked at her, a rather elaborate process. He stepped into the elevator and the door closed.

Harry Burke made a dive for the fire door.

"Harry! Where are you going?"

"After him."

"Is that wise? It might get him mad—"

"He won't see me."

"Wait! I'll go with you. Does he really know something, do you think?" Roberta panted as they raced down the stairs.

"Frankell's probably right," Harry Burke panted back over his shoulder. "But we can't afford to pass up even a long shot, Bertie, can we?"

TWENTY-SEVEN

~~~~~~~~~~

They tailed the bum on a zigzag course that staggered downtown. Spotty paused now and then to panhandle a passerby, in an absentminded way—not so much for the dime or quarter, they would have sworn, as to keep his hand in. Below Union Square the man's shuffle quickened. At Cooper Square he bore east around Cooper Union and homed into the Bowery like a pigeon.

His destination was a 25¢-a-night "hotel" with a diseased sign over its pimpled door. Harry Burke took up his stand two doors down, in the boarded-up entrance to an empty store. The gray of the sky began to turn slate; snow was palpable in the raw air. Roberta shivered.

"There's really no point in your sticking this with me," Burke said to her. "This may go on and on."

"But what are you planning to do, Harry?"

"I told you—stick it," he said grimly. "Spotty should come out sooner or later, and when he does I want to see where he goes. There may be others involved."

"Well, if you're going to stay here, Harry Burke, so am I," Roberta said. She began to stamp her tiny feet.

"You're shaking." He pulled her to him in the doorway. She looked up at him. For a moment they were silent. Then Burke flushed and released her.

"I'm not really cold." She was wearing a forest green fuzzy-piled coat with a standup collar. "It's these men, Harry. How can the poor things stand it? Most of them don't even have an overcoat."

"If they had, they'd sell it for the price of a pint of wine or a shot of whisky."

"Are you really as heartless as you sound?"

"Facts are facts," Burke said stubbornly. "Although it's true I'm no bleeding heart. I've seen too much misery no one can do anything about." He said suddenly, "You must be getting hungry, Bertie."

"I'm *starved*."

"I noticed a cafeteria a block or so north. Why don't you fetch us a few sandwiches like a good girl, and a couple of cartons of coffee? I'd go, but I can't chance Spotty's slipping out in the meanwhile."

"Well..." Roberta sounded doubtful. She was eying the passing derelicts.

"Don't worry about the bums. If they accost you, Bertie, tell them you're a policewoman. You're safer among men like these than you would be uptown. Sex isn't their problem. Here." Burke pressed a $5 bill on her.

"I can pay for it. Goodness!"

"I'm old-fashioned." To Burke's astonishment, he found himself smacking her round little bottom. She looked startled, but she did not seem to mind. "On your way, wench!"

She was gone fifteen minutes.

"Any trouble?"

"One man stopped me. When he heard the magic word he almost sprained an ankle getting away."

Burke grinned and uncapped the coffee.

Darkness fell. The scarred flophouse door began to do a brisk business. There was no sign of the man who called himself Spotty.

It began to snow.

Two hours dragged by. It was now snowing heavily. Burke, too, stamped his feet.

"I don't understand it . . ."

"He must have gone to bed."

"While it was still daylight?"

"I don't see what we're accomplishing here, Harry," Roberta complained. "Except risking pneumonia."

"There's something wrong," Burke muttered.

"Wrong? How do you mean?"

"I don't know. Except that it makes no sense, his going in before dark and remaining there. He'd have to eat, and there's certainly no dining room in that black hole." Burke seemed suddenly to make up his mind about something. "Roberta."

"Yes, Harry?"

"I'm sending you home." He seized her arm and steered her across the sidewalk to the curb.

"But why? I mean, aren't you going, too?"

"I'm going into that fleatrap, which you obviously can't do. And even if you could, I wouldn't allow you to. And I'd rather not leave you standing out here alone."

He shook off Roberta's protests, managed to commandeer a taxi, and packed her into it. She craned back at him rather forlornly as the cab took off, its chains slapping and clanking and spitting slush. But Harry Burke was already hurrying toward the bums' hotel.

TWENTY-EIGHT

The lobby proved to be a small, poorly varnished desk at the end of a dark hallway, presided over by an old man with a blue-veined nose and acne. The old man wore a heavy sweater; the rusty radiator was hissing, but the place was like the grave. The only illumination came from a 60-watt bulb dangling over the desk under a scratched green glass shade. There was a staircase at one side, with a railing. The steps were worn down in the middle, and the railing reflected a sickish gloss in the murk.

"I'm looking for a man who checked in just before nightfall," Burke said to the old man. "He calls himself Spotty."

"Spotty?" The old man stared suspiciously. "What you want Spotty for?"

"Which room is he in?"

"You a cop?" When Burke said nothing, the old man said, "What's Spotty done?" He had dark brown teeth.

Burke's tone hardened. "Which room is he in?"

"Okay, mister, keep your benny on. We got no private rooms here. Dorms. He's in Dorm A."

"Where is that?"

"Up the stairs and to your right."

"You come with me."

"I got to stay at the desk—"

"Old man, you're wasting my time."

The old man grumbled. But he came out from behind his desk and led the way up the stairs.

Dorm A was like something out of the *Inferno*. It was a long narrow room with cramped ranks of cots on each side, a filthy and cracked linoleum floor that looked like a relief map and a naked red bulb hanging from a cord in the middle of the ceiling which bathed the scene in blood. Half the thirty cots were already occupied. The room was unpleasantly alive—snuffles, mutters, snores, thrashings about; a blended stench of unwashed bodies, dirty clothing, urine, and alcohol fumes. There was no heat, and the two windows at the end of the room looked as if they had not been opened in a century.

"Which bed is he in?" Burke demanded of the old man.

"How in hell should I know? First come, first served."

He went up one side, followed by the old man. Burke stooped over each cot. The dim red light made his eyes water. He found himself holding his breath.

The man called Spotty lay on the other side of the room on the rearmost cot. He had his face to the wall, and he was covered to the neck by the blanket.

"That's him," the old man said. He pushed past Burke

101

and punched the still shoulder. "Spotty! Wake the hell up."

Spotty failed to stir.

"Must of had a bottle," the old man said. He jerked the blanket off. He fell back, all his brown teeth showing.

The handle of a switchblade stuck out of the derelict's overcoated back, on the left side. The only blood Burke could see looked black in the red light. He felt for the carotid artery.

He straightened up. "Do you have a telephone?" he asked the old man.

"He dead?"

"Yes."

The old man cursed. "Downstairs," he said.

"Don't touch anything, and don't wake the other men up."

Burke went downstairs.

TWENTY-NINE

~~~~~~~~~~~~~~~~

Inspector Queen's interrogation took until 3:00 A.M. Twice Burke and Ellery walked over to the all-night cafeteria for coffee; the cold in the flophouse went in to the bone.

"He had something," Burke muttered. "He really did. I knew it. But that damned Frankell had to freeze him out."

"You didn't recognize anyone going into the place, Harry?" Ellery asked him.

"I was concentrating on spotting Spotty, damn it all."

"Too bad."

"Don't rub it in. I'm trying to tell myself that the knifer may have got in and out through the rear. There's a rear door, off an alley, and a back stairs."

Ellery nodded and sipped his coffee, which was horrible but hot. He said no more. Burke seemed to be taking the murder of the derelict personally; for that disease there was no remedy.

"We'll get nothing here," the Inspector said when he had finished upstairs. "The knife is a cheap switchblade, and there are no prints on it. And if these bums know anything, they're not opening their traps."

"Then why are we hanging around here?" Ellery complained. "I can think of better places to be. My sweet clean bed, for instance."

"One thing," his father said. "While you and Burke were out I questioned a man who claims this Spotty had a pal, somebody they call Mugger. The two seem to have been thick as the thieves they are—or at least Mugger is. He got his monicker for good and sufficient reason, Velie tells me."

"Mugging record long as your arm," Sergeant Velie said. "Works the quiet dark spots. Never hurts anybody, far as we know. He likes to pick on the soft touches—old people mostly."

"Have you talked to the man yet?" Burke asked.

"He's not here," the Inspector replied. "That's why I'm waiting. In case he shows up."

The man reeled in at 3:30 A.M., decks awash. It took three cartons of black coffee to heave him to within reasonable sight of sobriety. After that, when Sergeant Velie told him with calculated callousness that his pal Spotty had gone out the hard way, with a shiv in his back, Mugger began to blubber. It was a fascinating sight. He was a wrecked fat brute of a man who looked as if he might once have been a heavyweight prizefighter. He would say absolutely nothing to all questions.

But he underwent a sea change when they drove him up to the Morgue and showed him his friend's body.

"Okay," he growled, *"okay,"* and spat on the floor, hard.

They found him a chair. He overflowed it, glowering at the aseptic walls.

"You going to talk now?" Inspector Queen asked him.

"Depends."

"On what?"

"On what you ask." It was evident that any question involving his nocturnal activities would be out of the answering zone.

"All right," said the Inspector. "Let's try this on for size: You knew what Spotty had to sell, didn't you?"

"Info on that girl up for trial tomorrow on the murder rap."

"You were partners with Spotty? Going to split the take?"

"Spotty didn't know I knew."

"What was the information?"

The man was silent. His bloody eyes roved, as if seeking safe harbor.

"Look, Mugger," the Inspector said. "You may be pretty deep in these woods. Spotty knew something he said would help Miss Spanier. And he was going to collect a thousand dollars for it. You knew what it was all about. That gives you a mighty good motive to want Spotty out of the scene. If Spotty was dead, you could take over and collect the thousand for your own self. Looks as if we're going to have to trace that switchblade to you."

"Me? Shiv Spotty?" Life crept into the devastated eyes. "My buddy?"

"Don't hand me that buddy stuff. There's no such thing as a buddy on your beat. Not where a score is concerned."

"He was," Mugger said earnestly. "Ask anybody."

"I'm telling you. You either stuck that blade into him—and if you did we'll nail you for it—or you were waiting for Spotty to make the score and then you'd step in. It's one or the other. Which?"

Mugger ran the back of his hairy hand across his mashed nose. He looked around and saw nothing but hostile eyes. He sighed deeply. "Okay," he said, "so I was going to let Spotty do it. Then I'd put in for my half. Spotty would split with me. We was pals. I kid you not."

"What was the information Spotty was trying to sell?" Inspector Queen asked again.

It was almost 6:00 A.M. before the man could bring himself to reveal the precious information. And then it was only when Sergeant Velie brought out some precious information of his own. Mugger was a parolee on a mugging rap. One word to his parole officer about his uncooperative attitude, and he would find himself back in the can. Or so Velie alleged. Mugger was not disposed to argue the point. He spilled.

As a matter of routine, the sergeant checked him out for the Spotty killing. He was clean. He had an alibi attested by two bartenders in a Bowery joint. He had not left the bar from midafternoon until past midnight (and what he had been doing between past midnight and 3:30 A.M. they could guess, which was not difficult, considering the vocation that had earned him his monicker).

The alibi that stood up strengthened his story about Lorette Spanier, although Inspector Queen pointed out

104

that a defense based upon the testimony of a witness of Mugger's nature and character was hardly the sort of thing defense attorneys greeted with huzzahs.

The last thing they did in that dawn was to spirit the hulk to an out-of-the-way hotel, where they locked him in under police guard.

As Ellery said, "Whoever killed Spotty has the identical hex against Mugger. Let's keep him alive at least until he can testify."

He and Harry Burke went their respective ways for a few hours' sleep. Ellery found Morpheus slippery. He thought, as he rotated on his axis in bed, that he now saw half the face of the mystery as it rotated on *its* axis. But if the three-quarter face was coming round into focus, it was taking its sweet time.

3 THREE-QUARTER FACE

*The countenance is the portrait of
the mind, the eyes are its informers.*

CICERO

THIRTY

~~~~~~

For a man who had been so cavalierly confident that he could cast doubt on the People's case against his client, Uri Frankell seized the straw handed him by the unexpected defense witness with remarkable alacrity.

"I naturally prefer positive to negative testimony," the defense attorney said, "in a trial by jury."

"Why don't you try to get the D.A. to withdraw the charge?" Ellery asked him. "Then you won't have to go to a jury at all."

"Herman wouldn't buy it," Frankell said. "Not with this character as my witness. In fact, that's what we've got chiefly to worry about. He's going to light into Mugger like a bum into a Salvation Army turkey."

"Then do you think it wise to restrict the menu to the turkey?"

"It's the best we've got."

"I thought you were relying on Lorette. Have you changed your mind about putting her on the stand?"

"We'll see. It all depends on how it goes with Mugger." Frankell looked cautious. "You're sure he wasn't offered a consideration for his testimony? No promise of or actual money payment—anything like that?"

"I'm sure."

"Then why is he so willing to testify? I couldn't get it out of him."

"It was tactfully suggested to him in the original police interrogation that he might wind up back in prison if he was uncooperative. He's a parolee."

"This was a police threat? Not made by someone on our side?"

"That's right."

Frankell looked glad.

The district attorney did his usual workmanlike job without, Ellery noted, his usual *joie d'oeuvrer*. It was not so much the nature of Herman's case, Ellery decided, as the nature of his witnesses. With the exception of officials, like Inspector Queen and Sergeant Velie, those who had to testify to the circumstances were hostile to his case or, at the least, sympathetic to the defendant. Carlos Armando, Harry Burke, Roberta West, Ellery himself, had had to be subpoenaed. They were far more compliant under cross-examination than direct questioning.

Nevertheless, by the time the People rested, the district attorney had blocked out a persuasive case against Lorette Spanier. She was the last person known to have been alone with Glory Guild before the singer's death. Her statement as to the time of her departure from the Guild apartment, her homeward walk across Central Park, and her arrival at her flat was without support of any kind. The .38 Special that had taken Glory's life had been found in the defendant's closet, in a hatbox belonging to her. She was the victim's principal heir to a considerable estate. She had been neglected—the D.A. used the word "abandoned"—by the victim since early childhood, implying that the motive had been either gain or hatred, or both.

The jury seemed impressed. Their multiple eye persistently avoided the blond child-face at the defense table.

Frankell opened and closed his case with Mugger. It was a far different Mugger from the derelict Lorette's friends had last seen. His suit had been dry-cleaned and pressed; he was wearing a clean white shirt, a dark necktie, and a pair of shined shoes; he was blue-shaven; and he was cold if bleary-eyed sober. He looked amazingly like a hardworked plumber dressed for church. ("Sure Herman will bring out that we prettied him up," the defense lawyer murmured to Ellery. "But it's going to take a lot of hammering away to make the jury forget how decent the guy looks. Personally, I think we've got Herman hung up. What's more, Herman knows it. Look at his nose." The district attorney's nostrils were shuttling in and out as if searching for bad odors which, for all their experience, they could not detect.)

It turned out that Mugger's name was a surprising Curtis Perry Hathaway. Frankell promptly elicited from Mr. Hathaway the information that he was "sometimes" known as Mugger. ("Why did you ask that?" Ellery demanded later. "Because," the lawyer replied, "Herman would if I didn't. Took the sting out of it. Or the stink—take your choice.")

"How did you get your nickname, Mr. Hathaway?"

"I broke my nose playing baseball when I was a kid," Mugger said earnestly. "It give me this ugly mug, see, which I would make faces—you know, clown around, the way kids do—because I was ashamed. So they begin to call me Mugger." ("Oh, my ears and whiskers," muttered Harry Burke.)

"Now, Mr. Hathaway," said Uri Frankell, "you're under oath, a witness for the defendant, an important witness, I might say the most important witness, and we've got to be dead certain the Court and the jury understand just who you are and how you stand in all this, so that nobody can come along later and say we tried to conceal something—"

"He means me!" yelled the district attorney. "I object to speeches!"

"Mr. Frankell, do you have another question of this witness?"

"Lots of them, your Honor."

"Then ask them, will you?"

"Mr. Hathaway, you have just told us how you came to get the nickname Mugger. Is there any other reason?"

"For what?"

"For your being called Mugger."

"No, *sir*," said Mugger.

"Mr. Hathaway—" began Frankell.

"Leading the witness!" shouted the district attorney.

"I fail to see how pronouncing the witness's name is leading him," said his Honor. "Go ahead, Mr. Frankell. But don't lead him."

"Mr. Hathwy, do you have a police record?"

Mugger looked crushed. "What kind of a question is that, for gossakes?"

"Never mind what kind it is. Answer it."

"I been pulled in a few times." Mugger's tone said, Isn't everybody?

"On what charge?"

"Mugging, they put it down. Listen, I never mugged nobody in my whole life. You mug, you hurt people. I don't hurt people. Never. Only they tag you with it, it sticks—"

"The witness will answer the question and stop," his Honor said. "Mr. Frankell, I don't want speeches from your witnesses, either."

"Just answer my question, Mr. Hathaway, and stop."

"But they tagged me—"

"Isn't that also why you're sometimes called Mugger,

111

Mr. Hathaway? Because the police collared you on a few alleged mugging raps?"

"I told you. They tagged me—"

"All right, Mr. Hathaway, we understand. But the principal reason you're called Mugger is that you've borne the nickname from childhood because of your nose being broken playing baseball and you clowned about it, made funny faces?"

"Yes, *sir.*"

"I was under the impression that this witness was testifying for the defendant," his Honor remarked to Uri Frankell, "not for himself. Will you please get with it?"

"Yes, your Honor, but we don't wish to conceal anything from the Court and the jury—"

"No speeches, Counselor!"

"Yes, sir. Now, Mr. Hathaway, did you know a man named John Tumelty?"

"Who?" said Mugger.

"Better known as Spotty."

"Oh, Spotty. Sure. He was my pal. Real buddies, we was."

"Where is your pal Spotty now?"

"In the cooler."

"You mean in the city Morgue?"

"That's what I said. Somebody cooled him good the other night. Stuck a shiv in his back while he was grabbing some shuteye." Mugger sounded indignant. It was as if he would have felt better about his friend had Spotty come to an end on the *qui vive* and face to face with the author who was about to write finis to his life.

"Is that why Spotty isn't here today testifying for Miss Spanier?"

"Object!" cried the district attorney, flapping his fat hand.

"Of course," said his Honor nastily. "You know better than that, Mr. Frankell. Strike the question. The jury will disregard it." Mugger opened his mouth. "Witness, don't you answer!" Mugger shut his mouth. "Proceed, Counselor."

"Before we get to the meat of your testimony, Mr. Hathaway," Frankell said, "I wish to clear up something for these good ladies and gentlemen of the jury. I ask you—and remember you're under oath—have you been offered any money or other material consideration for your testimony in this case?"

"Not one dime," said Mugger, not without bitterness.

"You're sure of that?"

"Sure I'm sure."

"Not by the defendant?"

"The who?"

"The lady on trial."

"No, sir."

"Not by me?"

"You? No, sir."

"Not by any of Miss Spanier's friends?"

"Not me."

"Not by—"

"How many times does he have to answer the same question?" inquired the D.A.

"—by anyone connected with the defense?"

"I told you. Not by nobody."

"Then why are you testifying, Mr. Hathaway?"

"The fuzz," said Mugger.

"The fuzz?"

"The fuzz told me if I didn't answer their questions on the up and up they'd tell my parole officer."

"Oh. The police told you that when they were interrogating you? When was that?"

"The night they found Spotty shivved."

"So it's because of police pressure that you're giving your testimony—your truthful testimony—in this case?"

"Object!" howled the district attorney. "Unwarranted inference! The next thing we'll hear is about police brutality in a routine interrogation!"

"Take your seat, Mr. District Attorney," sighed his Honor. "Mr. Frankell, phrase your questions in the proper way. I'm getting tired of telling you. There has been no testimony adduced from this witness as to police pressure."

"I'm sorry, your Honor," said Uri Frankell in a sorry voice. "The point is that this witness's testimony is the result of a police grilling, not from any offer of consideration to the witness by the defense—"

"And don't use the word grilling, Mr. Frankell! Get on, get on!"

"Yes, your Honor. Now, Mr. Hathaway, I want to take you back to certain events that occurred on the night of Wednesday, December the thirtieth last."

There was an immediate and sensible tightening in the courtroom. It was as if everyone present—in the jury-box, among the spectators, in the press section—was telling himself, Here it comes! without knowing just what was on the way, but anticipating, from Frankell's

113

buildup, that it was going to be a real swinger of a blow to the poor public servant at the prosecution table. Even his Honor leaned forward. Among the certain events that had occurred on the night of Wednesday, December the thirtieth last, was GeeGee Guild's push toward eternity.

"Do you recall that night, Mr. Hathaway?"

"I do," said Mugger, as fervently as if he were at the altar.

"That's quite a while ago. What makes you remember that particular night after all this time?"

"'Cause I hit a real score," said Mugger, licking his blasted lips at the recollection. "Nothing like that ever happened to me before. That was some night."

"And what was the unusual event on that memorable night, Mr. Hathaway?"

Mr. Hathaway hesitated, lips moving silently in communion with the glorious past.

"Come, come, Mr. Hathaway, we're waiting," said Frankell in an indulgent way. His eyes were saying, Stop looking as if you're rehearsing your testimony, damn you.

"Oh! Yeah," said Mr. Hathaway. "Well, it's like this, see. It's a cold night, and I'm kind of short. So I goes up to this guy and asks can he help me out. Sure, my man, he says to me. And he pulls out his leather and smooches around in it and finally comes up with a bill and sticks it in my hand. I take a look and almost drop dead. It's a fifty. Fifty bucks! While I'm still wondering am I dreaming he says, ' 'Tis the season to be merry, old friend. But never let us forget that it's later than we think. Here, you take this, too.' And he pulls off his wristwatch and gives me *that*. 'Every man,' he says to me, 'is got to keep an eye on the rear end of Father Time,' or something like that—and off he staggers before I can say a word."

"Staggers? You mean he was intoxicated?" asked Frankell quickly, not looking at the jury.

"I don't mean he was sober," said Mugger. "Higher'n the Empire State Building. Full o' sauce. Nice joe. Nicest I ever met." Ellery would not have been surprised had Mugger added, "God bless him."

"Where did this encounter take place?"

"On Forty-third off Eighth."

This time Frankell did look at the jury. Ellery could only admire his astuteness. Frankell knew that no man or woman in the courtroom believed Mugger's yarn about the manner in which he had come by his windfall. Each mind was thinking, He rolled the poor shnook. Sheer technique demanded a frontal attack on the implausibility of the story.

"Let us get this straight. You say you approached a drunk in the Times Square district and asked him for a handout, and he promptly and voluntarily gave you a fifty-dollar bill and his wristwatch?"

"I don't expect nobody to believe me," said Mugger simply. "I couldn't hardly believe it myself. But that's just what he done, so help me. And I never laid a finger on him."

"And this occurred on the night before New Year's Eve?" Frankell asked hurriedly.

"Yeah. He must have got a head start on the bottle."

The jury was hooked. There had been an astonishment in Mugger's voice, an afterglow of wonder at his incredible luck, that could only recall Cinderella's feelings at the touch of the Fairy Godmother's wand. Frankell was satisfied. He pressed on.

"All right, then. What happened?"

"What happened? Nothing. I mean I had to tell somebody about it—Spotty. I couldn't wait to tell Spotty. So I went on up to Central Park—"

"Why Central Park?"

"That's where Spotty liked to make his scores. I figure I'll find him working his old territory, so I go on up there and sure enough I find him."

"Let's take this step by step, Mr. Hathaway. You could hardly wait to tell your pal John Tumelty, or Spotty as you call him, about your good fortune, so you went to the place where he usually operated, in Central Park, and you did find him. Did you speak to him the moment you found him?"

"How could I? I come up the walk and I spot him stopping this young broad—lady. So I wait behind a bush till he's through."

"He was begging a handout from a young lady. Do you see that young lady, Mr. Hathaway, in this courtroom?"

"Sure I do."

"Oh, you do? Would you point her out to us, please?"

Mugger's cleansed forefinger pointed smack at Lorette Spanier.

"Let the record show," said Frankell briskly, "that the witness indicated Miss Lorette Spanier, the defendant." He was all confidence now. "Now I want you to pay close attention, Mr. Hathaway, and be very sure you answer with the exact truth. Did you, at the time you were in the bushes while Spotty was talking to Miss Spanier in Central Park—did you have occasion to glance at the watch the intoxicated man had given you?"

"You betcha."

"Why did you look at the watch?"

"Why did I look at it? Say, I'd been looking at it all the way uptown to the park. I hadn't had a watch for so long I couldn't hardly believe I wasn't dreaming."

"So when you looked at the watch while your pal Spotty was accosting Miss Spanier, you were doing so simply because of the novelty of it? The novelty of having a watch to look at after so many years?"

"You could say that," said Mugger, nodding. "Yeah, that's it, all right. The novelty."

"By the way, do you happen to know if the watch was set accurately?"

"Come again?"

"Was the watch telling the right time?"

"Was it! I checked it against the street clocks and the clocks in stores must have been a dozen times on my way up. What's the good having a watch if it don't give you the right time?"

"No good at all, Mr. Hathaway, I agree absolutely. So your watch was set to the right time, according to a dozen clocks you consulted on your walk uptown." Frankell asked casually, "And what time did your watch tell you it was when you saw Spotty stop Miss Spanier for a handout."

Mugger said promptly, "Twenty minutes to twelve on the schnozz."

"Twenty minutes to twelve on the schnozz. You're sure of that, Mr. Hathaway?"

"Sure I'm sure. Ain't I just got through telling you? Twenty minutes to twelve."

"This was twenty minutes to midnight?"

"I just said it."

"On the night of Wednesday, December thirtieth last, the night before New Year's Eve—the night Glory Guild was murdered?"

"Yes, sir."

"In Central Park?"

"In Central Park."

Frankell turned and began to walk back toward the defense table. The expression on the district attorney's face seemed to stir his sympathy. He smiled sadly in the D.A.'s direction, as if to say, Sorry, old man, *mais c'est*

la guerre, n'est-ce pas? But then he suddenly turned back
to Mugger.

"Oh, one thing more. Did Miss Spanier—the young
lady sitting over there—did she give Spotty anything
after his pitch?"

"Yeah. After she walked away and I stepped out of
the bushes and went over to Spotty, he showed me the
quarter she give him, like it was a bonanza." Mugger
shook his head. "Poor old Spots. A lousy—a measly
quarter, and me with half a C note in my jeans. I
almost didn't have the heart to show it to him."

"Did you happen to notice in which direction Miss
Spanier walked after she left Spotty?"

"Sure, she walked west. It was on the crosstown
walk, so she had to be headed for the West Side exit."

"Thank *you*, Mr. Hathaway," said Frankell tenderly.
"Your witness," he waved to the district attorney. Who
rose from his chair slightly stooped over, as if he had a
bellyache.

THIRTY-ONE

~~~~~~~~~~~~~~~~~~~~~~

In the innocent orgy celebrating Lorette's acquittal, there was unanimous agreement that she was
indeed the child of fortune. How she had come to forget
about the derelict who had accosted her during her walk
across the Park after leaving her aunt she could not say;
it had simply left no impression on her. As Ellery reminded her, if it had not been for an openhanded drunk,
a thunderstruck mugger, and a panhandling wino, Lorette
would probably have wound up on the unpleasant side of
the verdict. (He did not remind her that someone had
permanently stopped the mouth of the wino to keep it
from wagging in just such a courtroom—the same someone who had planted the Colt Detective in her Saks box.
After all, it was a celebration.)

Even Curtis Perry Hathaway, who was included at
Lorette's insistent invitation, and who was drinking Irish
whisky with both hands, seemed affected. He still bore
the scars of his cross-examination at the hands of the
district attorney, who had swung wildly from both hips.
But Mr. Hathaway had not yielded an inch; Horatius,
Harry Burke had dubbed him. Mugger's pockets were

full of newspaper clippings attesting to his importance; he looked exhausted, dazzled, full of the milk of *simpático* as well as Duggan's Dew, and totally unbelieving. It was the supreme moment of his life.

Too, now that she was forever free of the charge of murder, cracks had become visible in Lorette's British armor. She was laughing immoderately, chattering away with everyone within earshot; but her unplucked brows were drawn together as if she were in pain, or seeing badly, her blue eyes were mere slits, as if the light hurt them, and the cups of her nostrils looked like unglazed china. It would take very little, Ellery thought, to break her down and start those amazing eyes flowing. At the same time there was a new hardness about her mouth. The childish pout was gone. Instant maturity, he thought. She had gone into this an adolescent and come out of it a woman. And he sighed.

"You look as if you've swallowed a bad oyster," Harry Burke remarked to him a little later. "What's the trouble, chum?"

"Face," Ellery grumbled.

"Whose?" asked Burke, looking around.

"I don't know, Harry, *That's* the trouble."

"Oh."

Whose face had GeeGee Guild meant?

THIRTY-TWO

"Something's the matter," Burke said to her.

"It's nothing, Harry," Roberta said. "Really."

"You can't fool me, duck. Not any more. It's Lorette, isn't it?"

'Well . . ."

"You ought to slow up a bit, Bert. On the Armando business, I mean. You can't keep mothering her. Seems dangerously near resenting it."

"Oh, Harry, I don't want to talk about it! The whole thing has me on the verge of throwing up. Please. Put your arms around me."

Lorette had diplomatically gone to bed—at least she had retired to her bedroom—and they were alone in the cathedral vastness of the penthouse living room.

With Roberta in his arms, Burke closed his eyes. She

118

felt so warm and *right*. The whole world had a rightness these days that not even the periodic sight on the premises of Carlos Armando's dark, pitted face could upset. Why had he wasted all these bachelor years?

Roberta settled herself more deeply into his arms, snuggling like a tired child.

"Harry, I didn't know a man could feel so good," she murmured. "I'm so downright grateful."

"Grateful?"

"It's the only word. I wish . . ."

"Yes, Bertie?"

"Nothing."

"You can't begin a sentence like that and leave it dangling! Wish what?"

"Oh, that you'd come along years ago, if you must know."

"You do, luvvie?"

"I wouldn't say it if I didn't mean it. You make me feel—I don't know—the way a woman ought to feel, I suppose. Not . . ."

"Not what?"

"Never mind."

"The way Armando made you feel when you were in love with him?"

She sat up then, fiercely pushing him away. "Don't ever say that to me again, Harry Burke. Ever! I was a ninny. Worse than a ninny. I look back on it now and it seems as if it happened to somebody else. All of it. It did happen to somebody else. I'm not the same person I was then." Her voice trembled. "And you've made the difference, Harry. Don't—see how shameless I am!—don't ever stop making the difference."

"I won't," Burke said, softly; and this time when they kissed there was no nonsense about lust feelings or lips surprised into tenderness. It was the kiss of rightness, ordained by the nature of things, and Burke knew he was hooked. They were both hooked. And it was marvelous.

THIRTY-THREE

"Then it is serious," Ellery said a few days later.

Burke arched his sandy brows across the luncheon table.

119

"You and Roberta West."

The Scotsman looked uncomfortable. "You do keep after a man. What's your line of reasoning this time?"

"Your last excuse for not winging home was that you felt a responsibility for Lorette Spanier. Lorette's out of the woods, and you linger. If it isn't Lorette, it has to be little Robby. Does she know it yet? How long does a thing like this take you Scots?"

"We're a canny tribe," Burke said, pink-cheeked. "A generally monogamous breed. That sort of thing takes time. Yes, it's serious, chappie, and be damned to you."

"Does Roberta know it yet?"

"I think she does."

"You think! What do you two talk about, anyway?"

"There are some things, Horatio, that are simply none of your affair." Burke seemed anxious to change the subject. "Anything new on the case?"

"Nothing."

"Then you've abandoned ship?"

"The hell you say. That face business haunts my bed. By the way, what's this I hear about Lorette and Carlos Armando?" The gossip columns were ripe with hints, and Ellery had not seen Lorette since the night of the celebration.

"It's incredible," Burke said angrily. "The bugger has the gall of a brass monkey, or do I have it mixed up? Women mystify me. You'd think Lorette would see through him. She's a practical girl! But apparently she's as helpless as the rest of the geese when he turns on the charm."

"You have to be born with it," Ellery said. "Well, I'm sorry to hear it. Armando's record should speak for itself."

"To you and me and the rest of male humanity," Burke snapped. "To these women it's a foreign language."

"No way to disillusion her?"

"God knows Roberta's trying. As a matter of fact," and the Scotsman banged the dottle from his pipe, "it's beginning to come between the girls. I've tried to get Bert to take it a bit easy, but Armando is a thing with her. She detests him, and she can't bear to see Lorette getting involved."

Ellery heard from Burke about the blowup between Lorette and Roberta West the following week. Their fight over Armando had reached the moment of truth.

"Look, darling," Roberta had said. "It *is* none of my

business, but I can't stand seeing you sucked in by that—that human quicksand."

"Roberta," Lorette had said, chin up. "I'd rather not discuss Carlos with you any more."

"But someone has to pound some sense into you! Letting him send you flowers, date you, hang around here till all hours—don't you realize what you're getting yourself into?"

"*Roberta*—"

"No, I'm going to say it. Lorette, you're being silly. You've no experience of men, and Carlos's got pelts like yours hanging on his belt by the dozen. He isn't even being clever about it with you. Can't you see that all he wants is the money he didn't get after he married your Aunt Glory?"

Lorette's temper had surged in like surf. But she had made an effort, and half turned away, clenching her little hands. "And can't you stop trying to run my life?"

"But I'm *not,* darling. I'm only trying to keep you out of the clutches of one of the world's ace heels. Who happens to be a murderer, besides."

"Carlos murdered no one!"

"He masterminded it, Lorette. He's guiltier than she is. Whoever she is."

"I don't believe it!"

"Do you think I'd lie about it?"

"Perhaps you would!"

"Why should I? I've told you over and over how Carlos tried to get me to do it for him—"

Lorette had faced her then, her perky nose the color of pearl. "Roberta, I've changed my mind about you. I didn't believe you were that sort, but now I see that you are. You envy me. You're eaten up with it."

"Me? Envious of you?"

"Of the money Aunt Glory left me. And of Carlos's interest in me!"

"You're out of your everloving mind, darling. I'm glad about your good luck. And, as for Carlos's attentions, I'd rather be chased by a shark; I'd be a lot safer. And so would you."

"You *admitted* you were gone on him—"

"That was before I found out what he is. Anyway, that horrible chapter in my life is finished, thank God. If you must know, Lorette, I'm in love with Harry Burke, and I'm sure Harry's in love with me. I couldn't care less about that hand-slobbering monster—"

"That's enough, Roberta." Lorette was shaking. "If you can't keep from slandering Carlos..."

She stopped.

"You were going to say that you want me to leave, weren't you?" Roberta asked quietly.

"I said if you can't keep—"

"I know what you said, Lorette. I'll move out the minute I can find a place. Unless you'd rather I did it today—right now?"

The two girls had glared at each other. Finally Lorette had said in her chilliest British voice, "It isn't necessary to do it today. But, under the circumstances, I do think it would be better if we broke off this arrangement as soon as convenient."

"I'll be out of here by tomorrow morning."

And Roberta was. She moved into a Y, and Harry Burke helped her find an apartment. It was a dark one-and-a-half roomer on York Avenue, in a rundown building, with bars on the street-level window and a bathroom washbowl that had half its procelain chipped off and a crack through which the water dripped. There was a bar on the corner of the block from which men reeled at all hours.

"It's a stinking hole, Bertie," Burke said crossly. "I can't imagine why you took it. If you'd listen to reason—"

"You mean take money from you?"

"Well, what's wrong with that?"

"Everything, Harry, although you're a dear to offer it." He looked helpless and furious.

"It's not so bad," Roberta said softly, "and at least it's furnished. Anyway, I can't afford anything better. And I'd much rather live here than in Lorette's penthouse watching that animal pull her down with him."

"But it's a rough neighborhood!"

"Lorette's place," said Roberta, "is loads rougher."

So she moved in with her few belongings, and Harry Burke became her private security guard. He may have made his self-appointment harder than the job actually was—there were plenty of other people living in the building who could not afford higher rents, and they seemed to survive the hazards of the neighborhood—but one night Burke collared a dish-haired youth in a shiny black jacket and jackboots as the boy crouched at Roberta's window, peeping hotly through the bars and the crack in the drapes at the undressing girl. The Scot did not call the police. He took the boy's switchblade away, kicked him in the tail, and warned him as he fled that the building was off limits to beats, kooks, deviates, perverts in all classifications, and just plain mischief-hunters, and to be sure to tell his friends. After that, Burke felt better. He even fixed the unreliable front-door lock at his own expense, saying to Roberta, "That ought to kill the myth that Scots are tight with their money." Roberta kissed him rather more warmly than his 49¢ expenditure warranted; so he bought heaven for three and six, which even in Scotland would have been held a bargain.

THIRTY-FOUR

What happened to Lorette was an old story to Ellery, who was native-born and steeped in the American juices; to alien Burke, such Anglicisms as the Profumo case notwithstanding, it was an astonishment. The heroine of the liberating courtroom, following cultural precedent, became an overnight celebrity, with all the appurtenances thereto appertaining, including a contract.

"Only ignorance accounts for your surprise, Harry," Ellery said kindly. "Over here we reward homicide as a matter of national course. We dote on our murderers. Photograph them, interview them, beg them for autographs, raise funds for their defense, fight for a glimpse of them, and burst into tears when they're acquitted. Some of us even marry them. I understand that Truman Capote has been spending his past few years—years, mind you—picking away at a particularly senseless Kansas massacre, just to get a book out of it. Just? He'll sell millions."

"But to sign her for Broadway!" Burke protested.

"Of course. You're simply not with it, Harry. These days in the U.S.A. civil rights means something. Why should a WASP of the tender sex be discriminated against because my father and the D.A. thought she'd murdered her aunt? Although I understand Lorette's case doesn't altogether conform to the democratic ideal. She's supposed to have talent."

"So has Roberta," the Scot said bitterly. "But I don't see anyone offering her a contract."

"Tell Roberta to go out and get accused of shooting somebody."

Lorette had been bombarded with so many offers—
TV appearances, nightclub work, even a motion picture
contract—that, at Uncle Carlos's tactical suggestion, she
had turned to Selma Pilter for guidance. The old veteran
of the percentage wars, whose affection for Lorette dated
from that day in William Maloney Wasser's office,
charged into the battle. It was she who captured the
Broadway contract.

"But Selma," Lorette said nervously, "Broadway . . ."

"Look, my dear," Selma Pilter said. "If you're serious
about a singing career, there's no quicker way to recogni-
tion. I don't see you kicking around the clubs for years.
If you're going to become a star you've got to command
a star's audience. And, while television is good exposure,
it's no shortcut. Look at Barbra Streisand—it wasn't until
she hit Broadway that she made it big. GeeGee climbed
to the top on radio, but that was a different era. You've
had the publicity, now you need the vehicle. And right
away, while the public still remembers you. That's why I
advised you to turn down the Hollywood offer—Hollywood takes too long. Of course, if you didn't have star
quality, it would be another story. But with your voice,
on top of what's just happened to you, you can't miss."

"Do you really think so?"

"I'm too old in this game to waste my time on medioc-
rity. So, I might add, is Orrin Steyne. If Orrin wants you
for his musical, he thinks you'll make it. He's not going
to risk nearly half a million dollars of his backers'
money, let alone his reputation, on a mere pretty face
and a few dozen yards of news clippings."

"Will I be playing the lead?"

The old woman grinned. "You're talking like a star already. Dear, this is a musical revue. Loaded with fresh
young talent—Orrin's a master at picking tomorrow's
stars. What he has in mind for you is a single—just you,
a piano, and a spotlight. He couldn't show more confidence in you. My advice is to take it."

Lorette took it and the buildup began. Between Selma
Pilter and Steyne's press agent, not to mention the likes
of Kip Kipley, she received the full treatment. Quietly,
Marta Bellina, back from her tour, gave the girl lessons
in breathing and projection. "It's the least I can do for
Glory's niece," the aging opera singer told her. "And
your voice does so remind me of hers."

Ellery, still fitfully chasing the four-letter will-o'-the-
wisp in the Guild murder, took time off to satisfy himself on that score. He cabbed over to the doddering

Roman Theater on West 47th Street, where Steyne's company was rehearsing, and with the help of a nodding acquaintance with the doorman and a five-spot, slipped into one of the last-row seats for a personal audition.

It was true. The resemblance raised goose pimples. The girl was a natural instrumentalist of the voice—the same voice, Ellery would have sworn, that came out of the ancient Glory Guild records he cherished.

Lorette sat at the grand on the naked stage, in street clothes, without makeup, a frowning preoccupation on her little face as she occasionally squinted at the lyrics on the sheets. From her throat came the same faint throb that had bewitched her aunt's radio millions. Like the intimate Guild voice, it drew its audience close, singing to the listener, not the theater; it became one man's experience, to be carried tenderly home and dreamed on. Billy Gaudens, whom Steyne had chosen to write the music for his revue, had tailor-made Lorette's numbers, fitting style and mood to the voice until they seemed of a piece. Gaudens had cleverly struck away from the prevailing beat and rock and folk sounds, going back to the impassioned ballads of Glory Guild's day—songs that grieved, demanded, yearned, sank to the roots. (Later, Ellery learned that all the other music in the show was in the modern idiom. Orrin Steyne was giving Lorette a showcase. He knew what he had.)

She's going to be a sensation, Ellery thought . . . and, as he thought it, the old lightning struck.

More sensational than the girl.

He sat for a few moments, overwhelmed, thinking it over.

There was no doubt about it.

That's what GeeGee had meant.

He crept out of the orchestra seat and went groping for a phone.

THIRTY-FIVE

"Don't ask me why it hit me at Lorette's rehearsal," Ellery said an hour later in Wasser's office, to the attorney, his father, Harry Burke, and Roberta. "Or maybe it's because she makes music—I mean makes it! —and music is the secret of this thing."

"What thing?" demanded Inspector Queen. "What are you talking about, son?"

"Face," Ellery said. "The message GeeGee left on her desk as she was dying."

"What's music got to do with that?"

"Everything." Ellery was too hopped up to talk from a chair; he was darting about Wasser's office as if trying to dodge an assault of hornets. "I don't know how I could have been such a mental dropout. It was all there in those four letters.

"You'll note," he said, "that I say four *letters*, not the word. You'll note," he said, "that I use the word *note*, which is absolutely called for."

"You'll note, Mr Queen," said Wasser, his tic ticking, "that you've already lost me."

"I'll find you again. Give me my head, Mr. Wasser. At times like these I feel as if I'd had ten drinks and then hit the fresh air. . . . Look.

"GeeGee wrote 'face.' It was evident that she meant 'face' as a reference to whoever shot her. It was also evident, and it's become increasingly so, as my headaches attest, that as a word-clue to her killer 'face' means nothing at all.

"The question naturally follows: Suppose it wasn't a word-clue?"

The Inspector frowned. "But if it wasn't a word-clue . . ."

"Exactly. If it wasn't a word-clue, what sort of clue could it be? This called for reexamination. I reexamined. I re-reexamined. I thought of everything it could be except what it is. And what it is is so obvious that none of us saw it at all.

"For if it wasn't a word-clue, it became simply a clue consisting of four letters of the English alphabet. Forming not a word, but a sequence of some sort, in some other frame of reference."

"A code?" the old man suggested.

"Don't interrupt me when I'm flying, please. Where was I? Oh, yes," Ellery said. "When you start thinking in those terms, it immediately strikes you that GeeGee wrote those four letters—wrote them physically—*as individual letters*. She separated them: *f* and a space, *a* and a space, *c* and a space, and finally *e*. True, spacing was characteristic of her handwriting generally; and to make it more misleading, the way she formed her letters made them look like hand printing rather than ordinary calligraphy. But once you think of *f-a-c*-e in some context

126

other than words, you're in the clear and on your way."

"Not I," said Mrs. Burke's comfort-and-joy. The Scot frowned. "What context?"

"Well, what do we know about Glory Guild's preoccupations? One: as a performing artist, she spent her whole life in music. Two: in retirement she was a nut on puzzles. Right? Then think of *f-a-c-e* in terms of musicology and puzzles. A musical puzzle."

There was a silence, musical and puzzled. Ellery beamed; he had achieved orbital velocity, and as always at such times he was in a state of euphoria. His father, Wasser, Burke showed no signs of intelligence. Roberta West was cerebrating as if she were on to something—the big eyes were luminous under the indrawn sorrel brows—but finally she shook her bricktop.

"I studied music as a child, so I ought to know what you're getting at, Ellery. But I don't."

"What does *f-a-c-e* stand for in music, Roberta?"

"Face?"

"There's that old devil 'word' again. Not a word, Roberta. Letters. In music."

"Oh. You mean that *f* and *a* and *c* and *e* are *notes?*"

"What else? Of course that's what I mean. Which notes?"

"Which?"

"On the staff."

"If I had a sheet of music . . ."

"Mr. Wasser, may I?" Ellery grabbed a pad of plain yellow paper from the lawyer's desk, and a pen, and sketched quickly. When he held the pad up, they saw that he had inked in the common musical staff of five parallel lines:

"Here's the staff in G clef, the treble clef. Roberta, show us where the notes *f, a, c,* and *e* go."

Roberta took the pad and pen and, after some thought, used the pen.

"Now label each note."

She did so.

127

"Have a look."

Ellery passed the pad around. What they saw was:

"So they're notes," said Inspector Queen. "And I take it Miss West's put them in the right places or you wouldn't be licking your chops. So what, Ellery?"

"The staff is composed of five lines and the four spaces between the lines. Where has Roberta placed the notes? On the lines or in the spaces?"

"In the spaces."

"In the *spaces*. Which means *between the lines*."

Ellery paused triumphantly.

"Are we supposed to put you up for mayor?" his father snapped. "I don't know what you're talking about, Ellery. You'll have to spell it out before it makes sense to my pea-brain."

"Wait." Harry Burke was gripping the arms of his chair. *"She was telling us to look between the lines."*

"Give the gentleman the cigar," Ellery said. "Yes, that was GeeGee's little musical-puzzle message. 'Look between the lines.' "

There was another silence.

"Which lines?" asked the Inspector wildly. "Where?"

"That, of course, is the question."

"Her diaries!"

"Logical, dad. But not reasonable. Remember how closely written her diaries are. Hardly any room on those jammed pages. She'd have to have had the talent of the man who wrote the Lord's Prayer on the head of a pin to have squeezed anything in between the lines of those entries."

"Then where? In one of her books?"

"Unlikely. There are hundreds of them."

"It couldn't be between the lines of anything hand-written," muttered Burke, "for the reason you gave. And yet not printing, either. Still it's got to be something mechanical, where the spacing is appreciable and regular . . ."

"You've got it, Harry."

Burke saw light.

"Something typewritten! Did she leave anything she'd typed?"

"Not necessarily that *she* typed."

"Her will," Wasser said slowly. "By God, her will!"

"That," Ellery nodded, "was my conclusion, too. That's why I asked for this meeting in your office, Mr Wasser. When you read the will to the heirs you stated that the original was already in the hands of the Surrogate; you were reading from a copy. I recognized it as the one we found in the metal box in the Guild apartment, Glory's own copy. You still have it in your files?"

"Of course!"

"I'd like to have it."

While they waited for Wasser's secretary to fetch the will, Ellery remarked, "There's another reason for suspecting that Glory's copy of the will is the hiding place of some between-the-lines message from her . . . that long list of bequests to charities. It struck me at the time as peculiar. Why had she gone to the trouble of having all those trifling donations listed individually? A lump bequest could have been more conveniently provided for, to be parceled out at the discretion of her executor. But specifying the charities one by one did accomplish one thing—it made the will a much longer document, providing plenty of space for a considerable message. Ah, thank you," Ellery said to Wasser's secretary, taking the will. "Just a moment, please. Didn't I see an electric toaster in the outer office?"

"Yes, sir. Mr. Wasser often has his breakfast in the office. That's why we keep one here."

"I'd like to borrow it."

The girl brought it in, and Ellery plugged the connection into the wall behind the lawyer's desk. He set the toaster down on the desk and turned the machine on.

"Better than the match trick, eh?" Ellery said cheerfully. "Well, let's see if the old guesser is still functioning." He held the first page of the will above the heat coming up from the toast wells, passing the page back and forth. By this time they were crowding about him, craning.

"It's coming out!" Roberta cried.

In the spacing between the typewritten lines, the unmistakable handwriting of Glory Guild had begun to appear.

"I'll be damned," Harry Burke exclaimed.

"Somebody's going to be," Inspector Queen said exultantly. "Now maybe we'll get somewhere on this case!"

THIRTY-SIX

~~~~~~~~~~~~~~~~~~~~~~~~~~~~

It was a long message, as Ellery had predicted, written for economy in minute calligraphy. It occupied the spaces between the lines on all but the bottom half of the last typewritten page.

"Dad, you read it."

Ellery sat quietly down.

I am writing this

the Inspector read aloud

for reasons that will become clear soon enough. I had wanted for some time to get away from things, and I had planned to go up to Newtown, to the cottage. I asked Carlos to drive up with me, but he begged off, saying, he was not feeling well. I fussed with his headache until he said he felt a bit better, so it was not until late afternoon that I left. (I wanted to call the trip off, but Carlos insisted that I go.)

When I got to the cottage I found that the electricity was not turned on, even though I had insructed Jeanne several days before to notify Connecticut Light & Power to restore service (I later found out that she'd simply forgotten, which was not like Jeanne at all). I would have made do with candles, except that the house was very damp and cold—the heating is electric, too. Rather than risk a virus (do singers ever get over their fear of colds?) I decided to turn right around and go back to the city.

I took the penthouse elevator up and I was about to put my key in the lock when I heard voices from the living room, Carlos's and a woman's. The woman's voice was that of a stranger. It was a shock. In my own home! He had no shame, no shame. I was furious, sick, and disgusted.

I went downstairs again and took the service elevator up, and I let myself in through the kitchen and pantry and listened from behind the dining room door. Carlos and the woman were still talking away. The door is a swinging door, and I pushed it open a crack and peeped in. I am not proud of myself about all this, but I could have strangled Carlos for having lied about not feeling well, and entertaining a woman in my home the moment I was out of the way, and I wanted to see what she looked like. She was young, and small, and fair, with red hair and tiny hands and feet (and I'm such a horse!—or rather

130

"cow," as I heard my dear husband refer to me to this girl, a cow "to be milked," he told her).

Roberta West went blue-white. "That was me," she breathed. "That must have been the night he ... And she was listening at the door! What must she have thought of me!" Harry Burke took her hand and shushed her. Inspector Queen read on, glaring at Roberta:

Carlos was doing most of the talking and the long and short of it is that *he was plotting against my life*. I am not imagining this; he spelled it out. My knees began to shake, and I remember thinking, "No, this is a joke, he can't be serious." I almost walked in on them to tell him what a bad joke I thought it was. But I didn't. Something held me back. I continued to eavesdrop, hating myself and yet unable to tear myself away.

He told this girl that if he did it himself he would be the first to be suspected. So he had to have a real alibi. (By this time I wasn't so sure he was joking.) He then proposed to the girl that *she* do the actual killing while he established his alibi, and that after he inherited all my money he would marry her and they'd live happily ever after. So it was no joke after all. He meant it. He really meant it.

I couldn't take any more. I ran out through the kitchen, leaving them in the living room, and down the service elevator, and I walked and walked, not knowing what to do, where to go, whom to turn to. I walked most of the night. Then I took my car and drove back to Newtown and had the power turned on and stayed at the cottage for two whole days, thinking things out. And not getting anywhere, I might add. If I went to the police, what good would it do? It would be my word against his, with the girl's denial to back him up; it would get into the papers and create a horrid mess. Anyway, the most I could expect from the police would be somebody to guard me, but they couldn't do that indefinitely, even if they believed me.

I could divorce him. But by this time I was over the shock and most of the fears. I was fighting mad. I knew what Carlos was, of course, and I suspected that he was chasing other women, but murder! I never dreamed he would bloody his hands. There was an unreality about the whole thing, anyway. All I could think of was that I had to get back at him some way, that would badly hurt him. Divorce wouldn't do it the way I wanted it done. He had to think everything was going his way.

Of course, I was gambling with my life. Maybe in my heart of hearts I didn't really believe it. Anyway, I've lived the best part of my life, and if it's cut short by a few years ... It will make no sense to anyone but another woman, who's grown old and ugly and fat and forgotten after having had everything, admiration and applause and fame and everything wonderful that goes with them.

131

I kept my eyes very wide open after that and soon found out that my suspicions about Carlos and other women were all too well-founded. He's even seduced Jeanne Temple, my secretary, poor thing; no wonder she's been so nervous. I don't blame the women, Carlos has something that women can't resist. Of course, I had *not* torn up our prenuptial agreement, because of my suspicions. I'd fooled him into thinking I had. Keeping it in force gives me another weapon against him, the hurtiest one of all.

I have other weapons, too—this new will, on which I'm writing in disappearing ink. I've also left a clue in invisible ink on my diary page for December first. This is all in case I am murdered. I don't know what Carlos is waiting for, maybe just the right opportunity—I haven't given him many! But something tells me the time is drawing near, something about the way he's been acting. If I'm right about his intentions, and I am convinced I am, he'll get what he deserves, and where it will hurt the most. One of the things I have done is start a search for my sister's only child, Lorette Spanier. I've left the bulk of my estate to her. That ought to wipe the charm off Carlos's face! I'd love to be able to be there when this will is read to him.

To whoever reads this: If I should die a violent death, my husband is the one who arranged it. Even though he will have some alibi, he's as guilty as if he did it with his own hands. The woman will be just his tool.

I have been trying to find out who the girl is who was in my apartment the night I overheard him plan my murder, but Carlos has been very coy about her. As far as I can tell he hasn't seen her again, unless it's been on the sly. So I do not know her name, although I have the oddest feeling I have seen her somewhere before. Here is her description: Late twenties, very fair skin, red hair, height about five feet three, cute figure, pretty eyes (I couldn't tell the color), speaks with a stagy diction (could I have seen her somewhere around Broadway, or on tour?), and she dresses sort of Greenwich Villagey. She has a prominent birthmark on her right check, high up, shaped like an almost perfect butterfly, that ought to make her easy to identify. This girl is Carlos's accomplice. She is the one who, if I am murdered, will have done the murder for him.

Signed—Glory Guild

Inspector Queen looked up from the last page. He squinted at Roberta's birthmark and shrugged. Then the old man set the will down on Wasser's desk and turned away.

"Butterfly birthmark," Harry Burke exclaimed. "That's why she thought Roberta looked familiar. Didn't you say, Bertie, you'd met her with Armando that time in summer stock? It must have stuck in her mind."

"But she got it all wrong," Roberta said in a quavery

voice. "She must have run out of the apartment that night in May before she heard me turn Carlos down cold and leave. If she'd stayed another few minutes, she'd have known that I told him I wanted no part of it or him. She'd never have written this. Not about me, anyway."

Burke cradled her hand. "Of course not, Bertie."

"And she wasn't able to track me down because I never saw Carlos again until the night of the murder, when he turned up at my apartment to use me as his alibi!" The pink butterfly on her cheek was fluttering in distress. "God, how did I ever get into this?"

Burke was glaring at Ellery, as if he expected words of wisdom or at least of comfort. But Ellery was low in his chair, nuzzling his knuckles, sucking on them and getting no sustenance.

Nobody said anything for a long time.

"So," Inspector Queen ultimately muttered, "we're all the way back to where we were. Further back. The one clue we had is a dud. Gets us not an inch closer to the woman Armando had pull the job."

"But this is evidence against him, Inspector," Wasser protested. "Now you have not only Miss West's testimony, but Glory Guild's documented corroboration of Armando's proposal to Miss West as well."

But the Inspector shook his head. "To put Armando away, Mr. Wasser, we need the woman. I notice," he added with a sour glance at his son, "that you're not saying anything."

"What's there to say?" Ellery mumbled. "You've said it all, dad. We'll have to start from scratch again."

THIRTY-SEVEN

Start again they did, and scratch they did, and what they garnered for their pains was a wealth of hindsight that told them nothing they had not known before. In addition to which Armando was being shrewdly difficult.

He was no longer seeing Mrs. Ardene (Piggyback) Vlietland, the lady of the Newport $100,000 brawl. Mrs. Gertie Hodge Huppenkleimer of Chicago and Beekman Place was no longer seeing him; apparently her taste for used toys had turned toward newer and safer amusements, and Armando was making no attempts visible to the probing eye to resume their play. Horsewoman and alcoholic Daffy Dingle was still drying out up around Boston way. Armando had also dropped Jeanne Temple, who was reported mooning about the East 49th Street apartment she shared with Virginia Whiting and going out on an occasional part-time secretarial job, her brief amour no doubt nursed to her impressive chest. Dr. Susan Merckell seemed too busy with ailing larynges at large to fiddle with Armando's, or his throat was suddenly in perfect health. Marta Bellina was off again, in Europe somewhere, on another singing tour. They did not even bother with Selma Pilter; Armando had younger fish to fry. And there was nothing, utterly nothing, on the mysterious woman in the violet veil, or any veil at all. It was as if she had been something out of a gothic romance, drifting about in limbo, the creation of someone's overheated imagination.

Armando was concentrating on Lorette Spanier, playing the role of avuncular confessor and nurseryman of a tender talent. He attended her rehearsals regularly, sitting in the empty orchestra of the Roman Theater while she tried out a new Billy Gaudens number or worked on a classic; appearing like magic backstage when she was through for the day; taking her home or to some hideaway restaurant if she was not too exhausted; soothing her when she was in a mopy mood over the way things were going. He was seen with her everywhere.

"The little fool," Harry Burke snorted. "Doesn't she have the most elementary sense of caution?"

"She's lonely, Harry," Roberta said. "You just don't understand women."

"I understand the Armandos of this world!"

"So," said Roberta grimly, "do I. But don't judge Lorette by your great big masculine standards, my love. She'll find a way to take care of herself. Most of us do; it's an instinct women are born with. Right now she needs somebody to lean on and talk to. Carlos makes that kind of thing awfully easy."

Burke snorted

"He'll take her the way he took her aunt."

"He didn't really take Glory Guild, did he? Not according to that secret message of hers."

"Then why is she lying in a copper-lined box, not breathing?"

"He isn't going to harm Lorette. He wants her money."

"And he'll get it, too!"

134

"Not for a long time, darling. Don't sell little Lorette short. She may be making a fool of herself with Carlos right now, but she'll let it go only just so far. To get the money he's got to marry her, and I have the feeling he's not going to find Lorette that gullible."

"He talked her aunt into it!"

"Her aunt was practically an old woman. Lorette's not only loaded, she's young and beautiful. This is just a phase. Anyway, why spend all this time talking about *them?* I've got to get up early tomorrow morning."

So they turned to other things, which left them both breathing hard.

Roberta had been accepted for an off-Broadway play, in which she had not a line to say; she was to appear for three interminable acts, upstage right, in a flesh-colored bikini, doing the frug. "The author tells me he wrote it while under the influence of LSD," she told Burke. "And you know what? I believe him." She crept home each night battered in every muscle and sinew.

They were consequently hard times for the Scot. While Roberta rehearsed, he spent most of his days with Ellery, hanging uselessly about police headquarters. They came to resemble a pair out of low tragedy, detesting the sight of each other, but bound together by an unseverable bond, like Siamese twins.

Their dialogue was dreary.

"Are you as sick of me as I am of you?" Ellery demanded.

"Righto," Burke snapped.

"Then why don't you cut out?"

"I can't, Ellery. Why don't you?"

"I can't, either."

"My pal."

"Put it there, pal."

Burke put his hands into his pockets.

Inspector Queen went pathetically to see the district attorney.

"How about hauling Armando before the grand jury without the woman, Herman?"

The D.A. shook his head.

"But we've got Glory's story between those lines," the Inspector argued. "We've got Roberta West's testimony." He was really arguing with himself, using the D.A. as a sounding board.

"So what, Dick? All they prove is possible intention on his part seven months before the fact. Even if I could get a grand jury to indict, which I doubt, can't you imagine what a good defense lawyer would do to my case? And you know Armando would hire the best. If you ask me, Dick, the bastard would enjoy the publicity. I'm damned if I'm going to give it to him without a fighting chance to put him away. The only chance we've got is that woman."

"What woman?" the Inspector whined. "I'm beginning to think she never existed."

Pathetic or not, the Inspector refused to give up. He summoned Carlos Armando to headquarters with cunning regularity—to keep his teeth on edge, the old warrior told Ellery and Harry Burke. But if the summonses to Centre Street were designed to fray Armando's nerves, they frayed only the Inspector's. The man seemed to thrive on the visits. He no longer howled harassment or threatened legal action. He was charming, his negative answers were oiled with courtesy, his blunt teeth grinned, and once he even offered the old man a cigar. ("I don't smoke cigars," the Inspector rasped, "and if I did I wouldn't smoke one from Havana, and if I did I wouldn't accept it from you, Armando, and if I did I'd choke on it." Armando thereupon offered the cigar to Ellery, who thoughtfully took it. "I'll pass it along to some rat I want to poison," he said to Armando with equal courtesy. Armando smiled.)

"He's got me by the short hairs," yelled the Inspector, "and he's loving every minute of it. Keeps asking me why I don't arrest him! I've never hated anyone so much in my life. I wish I'd gone in for a career in the Sanitation Department." At their puzzled looks he added, "At least I'd be equipped to handle this garbage."

The old man stopped calling Armando down to Centre Street.

Burke asked: "Then it's going into the unsolved file?"

"Not on your tintype," the Inspector snapped; he always fell back on the slang of his youth when he was upset. "I'll stick with this case till they shovel me under. But these sessions are giving me ulcers, not him. We'll lie low for a while and hope he gets too pleased with himself. Maybe he'll make a mistake. Maybe one of these days he'll contact the woman. Or she'll contact him. I've got him under twenty-four-hour surveillance."

And not only by Inspector Queen's squad. Ellery, who was losing weight he could not afford, took to trailing along with the trailers, or independently, lightening the burden on his bathroom scale still further. He saw a great deal of the Playboy Club and the Gaslight Club

136

and Danny's Hideaway and Dinty Moore's and Sardi's and Lindy's, and even more of the musty interior of the Roman Theater, and had nothing to show for it but acid stomach and an occasional hangover.

"Then why do you do it?" Harry Burke asked him.

"You know what they say about hope," Ellery shrugged. "It's a cinch I can't do any work."

"The old game," Burke sighed. "See who has more patience, the fox or the hounds. Nothing?"

"Nothing. Want to join me in this exercise in futility?"

"No, thank you. I haven't the stomach for it, Ellery. Sooner or later I'd throttle him. Anyway, there's Roberta."

There was Roberta, and Burke suddenly had better things to do than fume in Ellery's presence, being fumed back at. One night, when Roberta crawled into her hole-in-the-wall from the Village hole-in-the-wall where she had frugged onstage all day, and consequently was in no condition to resist a decent human emotion, the Scot took his courage in both brawny hands, like one of his forebears' claymores, and swung wildly.

"Bertie. Bert. Roberta. I can't stand this any longer. I mean, you can say what you like about police dogs, but they lead a damned dullish life. I'm going out of my mind, Roberta. Hanging about. I mean . . ."

"You mean you want to go *home*," Roberta said with a little cry.

"Definitely! You understand, don't you?"

"Oh, yes," Roberta said, with the thinnest layer of ice on her voice. It was her best stage voice, the one she had always yearned to employ in an interpretation of Lady Macbeth. "I certainly do."

Burke beamed. "Then it's all settled." Then he said anxiously, "Isn't it?"

"What's settled?"

"I thought—"

To his horror, Roberta began to blub. "Oh, I don't blame you, Harry . . ."

"Bertie! What on earth's the matter?"

"N-nothing."

"There *is*. Or you wouldn't be crying, for the love of God."

"I'm *not* crying! Why should I cry, for the love of God? Of course you want to go home. You're in a land of aliens. No dart games in the pubs, no Rockers or Mods, no changing of the Guard . . . Harry, please. I have a headache. Good night."

"But." Burke's transparent eyes let some honest bewilderment through. "But I thought . . ." He stopped.

"Yes. You're always thinking. You're so cerebral, Harry." Roberta suddenly turned over on the couch cover she was blubbing into. "You thought what?"

"I thought you'd realize that I didn't mean—"

"You *didn't* mean? You're so exasperating sometimes, Harry. Can't you talk simple, understandable English?"

"I'm Scots," Burke said stiffishly. "We don't speak the same language, perhaps but what I have in mind is supposed to be universal. What I didn't mean—I mean, what I meant was . . ."

"Yes, Harry?"

"Damn it all to hell!" Burke's wrestler's neck was purple with strain. "I want you to go home with me!"

Roberta was sitting up by this time, frowning a little at the mess she found her hair in. "That would be nice, Harry. I mean under different circumstances. I mean you're not very clever about propositioning girls, you don't have the *savoir-faire* of men like Carlos, or even Ellery Queen, but I suppose I ought to take it as a compliment, considering the source. You *are* a darling in your own way. Are you actually proposing to unclasp your purse to finance a trip to England for me in return for my illegal embraces? I couldn't afford it on my own, of course, though I'd love to see England; I've always dreamed of going there—Stratford-on-Avon and all that. But, darling, I'm afraid I can't take you up on it. I see I've given you the wrong impression of myself. Just because circumstances forced me to confess that I'd once had an affair with that monster Carlos doesn't give you the right to think I'm that kind of girl generally. But you are sweet, Harry; thank you at least for wanting a few nights of love with me. And now, really, I *am* tired and I'd like to go to bed—alone. Good night, Harry."

"*Will—you—be—quiet!*" the Scot roared. "you don't understand at all! I want to marry you!"

"Oh, Harry," Roberta cried. "If I'd only known!"

Whatever other mendacity she was about to utter was never uttered. The rest was smothered in powerful arms and lips.

"Well, old chap," Burke told Ellery the next day with bashful jubilation, "I finally popped the old question."

Ellery grunted. "How did Roberta get it out of you?"

"Beg your pardon?"

"The poor girl's been waiting for you to pop it for weeks. Maybe months for all I know. Anyone but a love-sick Scot would have seen it. Congratulations." Ellery shook Burke's hand limply.

They were planning to be married as soon as the avant-garde turkey Roberta was rehearsing for opened and closed, which Miss West predicted would be in nothing flat. "And we're going to bow our necks to the yoke in Merrie Olde," Burke cried. "Can't wait for that BOAC flight, chappie. To tell you the truth, I've had a bellyful of your lovely country."

"Sometimes," Ellery nodded wistfully, "I wish you'd licked us at Yorktown."

And he cursed Carlos Armando and all his gypsy ancestors, and went back to his novel.

THIRTY-EIGHT

~~~~~~~~~~~~

Orrin Steyne's revue opened to notices that read as though they had been scribbled during an orgasm rather than sedately composed in its aftermath. It had been an uninspired theatrical season, and the time was hot for critical passion.

Or perhaps it was the legendary Orrin Steyne luck. He had never had a flop; and, in the unkind little world in which theatrical producers lived and labored, success was spitefully expressed in gambling terms, not in the context of a talent for the game.

About Lorette Spanier there could be no semantics. A performer by definition performed; the only question was how well. The answer, headlined and shouted, was unequivocal. The critics acclaimed her Broadway's latest love, *Variety* said STEYNE FIND BOFFO, Walter Kerr himself pronounced her the logical successor to Glory Guild, *Life* scheduled a profile of her, the in-groups debated whether she was high camp or low, and the squares queued up at the box office and laid siege to the stage door to fight for her autograph. Selma Pilter got her Lorette Spanier on a management contract—the old woman had been working on an oral understanding—with Armando's instant blessing: "You are better off signed with Selma, *cara,* than letting yourself be exposed to every sharpie in this cutthroat business." And there was a cherished cable from West Berlin: I TOLD YOU TO KEEP PROJECTING LOVE MARTA.

The revue opened on a Thursday night. Friday afternoon Ellery telephoned Kip Kipley's unlisted number. "Can you get me two tickets for Orrin Steyne's *Revue?* I've tried everywhere with no luck."

"When do you want them for, a year from Christmas?" the columnist asked.

"Saturday night."

"This Saturday night?"

"This Saturday night."

"Who do you think I am, Jackie Kennedy?" said Kipley. Then he said, "I'll see what I can do." He called back in ten minutes. "Why I scratch your back when you still owe me God knows how much *pro quo* I'll never understand. They'll be at the box office."

"Thanks, Kip."

"You can shove your thanks, Charlie. Give me something I can print, and we're buddy-buddies."

"I wish I could," Ellery sighed, and hung up. He really did.

For, novel and deadline notwithstanding, the Guild case kept niggling him. He had no idea why he had suddenly decided to see the revue. The decision had nothing to do with the magnitude of Lorette's talent; he was willing to take Broadway's word for that. And as a rule he avoided musicals. Still, putting it down to a vague professional itch to keep his finger on the pulse of the cadaver, Ellery took his father by the resisting arm—to the girly-girly-brought-up Inspector, musicals had died with Florenz Ziegfeld and Earl Carroll; he had thought *Oklahoma!* rather dull and *My Fair Lady* a lot of fancy nonsense—and on Saturday evening they set off for the Roman Theater.

Their taxi had to fight the usual good fight with the traffic (no New Yorker in his right mind took a private car into the theater district on Saturday nights); they exchanged the usual nostalgia-spiked imprecations on the honkytonk atmosphere of the new Times Square; they did the usual elbow work on the unneighborly line at the THIS PERFORMANCE window of the old Roman; and eventually they found themselves seated in the orchestra on the aisle, sixth row center, that Valhalla of the hit-show devotee's dreams.

"Mighty nice," the Inspector said, partially mollified. "How did you do it?" He did not know about Ellery's appeal to Kipley. "These seats must have set you back half a week's salary. My salary, anyway."

Ellery said sententiously, "Money isn't everything,"

140

and settled back with the playbill. There were some things a man didn't tell, even to his father.

And there it was. *Songs. . . . Lorette Spanier,* at the end of the first act. Everyone in their vicinity, it seemed, had the program open to the same page; Ellery squinted here and there to make sure. It happened once every ten years or so, that lightning something in the air of old theaters that smelled like brimstone. It could be detected only at the birth of a new star. You could almost hear the crackle of the sparks.

Even that died away after the blackout preceding her appearance, leaving a silence so heavy it seemed about to burst from its own weight.

The darkness was as palpable as the silence.

Ellery found himself crouched on the edge of his seat. He felt his father, the least impressionable of men, doing the same thing beside him.

No one shuffled or coughed.

A tall pure white cone suddenly sprang down from the proscenium to center stage. Bathed in its brilliant light sat Lorette, at a vast rose piano, pale hands folded. A black velvet backdrop with a gigantic American Beauty rose embroidered on it was her background. She was dressed in a flashing sequined evening gown of the same color as the rose, with a high neckline and no back at all. She wore no jewelry, and her white skin and golden hair seemed stamped on the velvet. She was looking, not at the audience, but at the hands in her lap. It was as if she were all alone somewhere, listening for something not audible to ordinary ears.

She held her indrawn pose for fully thirty seconds. Then she looked up and at the conductor in the well. He raised his baton, holding it aloft deliberately. When it came down, the orchestra burst into an anguished fortissimo chord, heavily brassed, and there were gasps.

All at once the chord segued into the soft teasing introduction to Gaudens's already acclaimed "Where O Where?" The introduction died away, and Lorette raised her hands. She played a swift caressing arpeggio, threw her shining head back, and began to sing.

It was very nearly the same voice Ellery had listened to on that day of rehearsal, but not quite. A dimension had been added, an intangible something that made the difference between quality and style. Whether she had soared to the challenge of her opportunity, or Marta Bellina had taught her some unique secret of the singer's art, the fact was that Lorette now had both. The quality was Glory Guild's; the style was Lorette's own. In that sense Walter Kerr had been precisely right. In the same way that a generation sprang from its parents, carrying their genes but adding combinatons of its own to become something altogether new, the niece was indeed "the logical successor" to her aunt.

There was the old Guild vocal intimacy, inner-directed to the individual ear in its faintly throbbing passion; what made it new was a curious preoccupation with self that Guild had never had, as if Lorette were conscious of no audience at all, the inner direction being result rather than cause. It was as if she were singing to herself in the privacy of her bedroom, allowing herself an erotic freedom of expression that she would not have dreamed of expressing in public. It turned every man and woman in the audience into a sort of Listening Tom, ear squeezed to a forbidden door; it raised the blood pressure and made breathing difficult.

It was smashing.

Fighting the effect on his nervous system, Ellery tore his attention away from what was happening to him to observe what was happening to the people around him. His father was pressed forward, eyes half shut, with a grin on his old lips that had pain as well as remembered pleasure in it. The few others he could make out in the near darkness were just as embarrassing to behold. Each face was stripped of social controls, oblivious of decencies and restraints, nakedly isolated. It was not a pretty sight, and it revolted as well as fascinated him. My God, Ellery thought, she'll become a destructive social force, she'll turn neighborly communities into packs of slavering lone wolves, she'll disperse the herd yearnings of the young and replace marijuana and LSD in the college dorms. She could not possibly realize the dangerous potentialities of her power. She'll sell tens of millions of records and there ought to be a law against her.

There were five other songs: "Love, Love"; "You're Trouble to Me"; "There's No Moon Ever"; "Take Me"; and "I Want to Die" . . .

Lorette's hands returned to her lap.

The roar that shook the theater she did not acknowledge; she did not even look around. She simply sat there, as she had begun, hands folded, eyes lowered, lost in her own echoes. This was at Orrin Steyne's direction, Ellery was sure, but he did not think she would have reacted differently had Steyne never said a word.

They would not allow her to stop. The first-act curtain

142

came down, went up, came down, went up again; still she sat there, a glittering little figure at the great piano on the otherwise empty stage.

More! *More! MORE!*

It became a thunderous growl.

Lorette swung about on the bench then, all flashing rose in the spotlight; for the first time she looked her audience in the eye.

The ploy was startling. It brought instant silence.

"I should so much like to sing and sing for you," she murmured. "But there's a great deal more of Mr. Steyne's wonderful show in store, so I have time for only one encore. I don't believe Billy Gaudens will mind if I reach far back into the past. This song lyric was written by someone you probably remember in a field worlds away from music, James J. Walker; the music was by Ernest R. Ball. It was first published in 1905, and it was revived and became famous in the late Twenties, when Jimmy Walker was Mayor of New York. It was a very special favorite of Glory Guild's—my aunt."

A shrewd stroke of Steyne's—Ellery was positive Steyne had inspired it—this uttering GeeGee Guild's name aloud, hauling into the light what lurked in the darkness of everyone's thoughts.

Lorette turned back to her piano.

The same electric silence crackled.

The same breaths were withheld.

She began to sing once more.

It was perhaps an unfortunate choice musically and lyrically. Ball's music was sticky sweet; Walker's lyric, especially of the verse, evoked images of birds in gilded cages and poor sewing-machine girls:

> Now in the summer of life, sweetheart,
> You say you love but me,
> Gladly I give all my heart to you,
> Throbbing with ecstacy.
> But last night I saw while a-dreaming,
> The future old and gray,
> And I wondered if you'll love me then, dear,
> Just as you do today.

Refrain (*molto espressivo*):

> Will you love me in December as you do in May,
> Will you love me in the good old-fashioned way?

143

When my hair has all turned gray,
Will you kiss me then, and say,
That you love me in December as you do in
    May?

Lorette gave it *molto espressivo*, English music hall style. Ellery shook his head. It was a mistake, and he was willing to bet that before many performances had passed Orrin Steyne—or Billy Gaudens—would see to it that Lorette's encore number was less in the nature of a parody. From the throat of any other singer he could think of the song would have aroused smiles, if not titters. It was a tribute to Lorette's power that her audience was as passionately rapt by this song from another world and time as they had been by Gaudens's cunning music.

Listening to Beau James's youthful effusion—*Beau James* was what Gene Fowler had entitled his biography of Jimmy Walker—Ellery was reminded that the theme of Walker's sentimental lyric, especially that of the chorus, had evidently haunted him to his dying day. According to Fowler, some four decades after the original publication of "Will You Love Me in December As You Do in May?" which Lorette Spanier was now singing almost twenty years still later, as the one-time Tin Pan Alley aspirant, trial lawyer, state senator, mayor, and playboy politico sat in his darkened room during his last illness, he had suddenly turned on a light, reached for a pencil, and begun to compose the lyric to a new song. It had concluded with the lines:

There'll be no December
If you'll just remember,
Sweetheart, it's always May.

After four decades and two world wars Jimmy Walker had come full circle.

I wish, Ellery found himself thinking, I could do the same with the Guild case.

There'll be no December . . .

Ellery sat up as though touched by a live wire. As indeed, in a way, he had been. The coincidence would have been amusing in other circumstances. He had shifted his left elbow on the arm of his seat, and the movement had caused the sharp edge of the seat's arm to press into the hollow behind his elbow and the sensitive nerve beneath. The unpleasant shock almost made him cry out.

144

Inspector Queen shushed him angrily, intent on the song. To the Inspector, what Lorette was singing was a piece of his youth.

But to Ellery it was a foretaste of the immediate future. He would almost have cried out even if the nerve had not been shocked. For he was shocked in a far more vulnerable place.

"Dad."

"Shut up!" his father hissed.

"Dad, we'll have to leave."

"What?"

"At least I'll have to."

"Are you out of your mind? Now, damn it, you've made me lose the end of the song!" Lorette had finished, and the applause rose from all around them in crashing waves. She rose from the bench and stood unsmiling, white hand on the end of the rose piano, blue eyes glittering in the spot; all of her glittered. Then the curtain came down, and it stayed down. The house lights went up.

"I swear I can't imagine what comes over you," the old man complained as they shoved their way up the aisle. "You're a natural-born spoiler, Ellery. Man, what a voice!" He went on and on about Lorette; or perhaps it was about himself.

Ellery said nothing until they reached the crowded lobby. He was scowling in some sort of pain. "You don't have to go, dad. Why not stay and see the rest of the show? I'll meet you back home later."

"Wait a minute, will you? What's eating you?"

"I just remembered something."

"About the Guild case?" the old man asked instantly.

"Yes."

"What?"

"I'd rather not say yet. I have to check something first. You really don't have to leave, dad. I don't want to spoil your night out."

"You've already spoiled it. Anyway, I don't care about the rest of the show. I've had my money's worth, and then some. What a singer! About the Guild case?"

"The Guild case."

"It bugs me, too," the old man said. "Where we going?"

"Didn't you turn over that copy of Glory Guild's will to the D.A.? The one with the secret writing on it that we brought out in Wasser's office?"

"Yes?"

145

"I'll have to find him."

"Wasser?"

"The D.A."

"Herman? Now? On Saturday night?"

Ellery nodded morosely.

Inspector Queen glanced at him sidewise and said nothing more. They shouldered their way out into 47th Street, ducked into a nearby restaurant, located its public phone, and Ellery spent twenty-five minutes tracking down the district attorney. It turned out that he was attending a political banquet at the Waldorf, and he sounded nasty over the phone. The banquet was getting full press and TV coverage.

"Now?" he said to Ellery. "On Saturday night?"

"Yes, Herman," Ellery said.

"Can't it wait till Monday morning, for God's sake?"

"No, Herman," Ellery said.

"Stop sounding like the straight man in a vaudeville routine," the D.A. snapped. "All right, Mystery Man, I'll meet you and the Inspector down in my office as soon as I can get there. But this better be good!"

"Good is not the word for it," Ellery muttered, and hung up.

THIRTY-NINE

By the time he got through reading the minute chirography between the typewritten lines of Glory Guild's copy of her will, Ellery looked ten years older.

"Well?" the district attorney demanded. "Did you find what you were looking for?"

"I found it."

"Found what, son?" the Inspector wanted to know. "When I read it aloud in Wasser's office that day, I didn't leave out or change a word. What's the point?"

"That's the point. You two give me some slack on this, will you?"

"You mean to say you're not going to talk even now?" his father growled.

"Gets me away from that banquet with all the news media there," the D.A. said to his ceiling, "on a Saturday night yet, with my wife wondering if I've gone off with a chick somewhere, and he won't open up! Thank God,

146

Dick, I'm not stuck with a kook for a son. I'm going back to the Waldorf, and I won't be available for *any-thing* till Monday morning—not if I want to hold onto my wife, and I want to. When this joker is ready to let a mere servant of the people in on whatever he's trick-or-treating, let me know. Be sure you lock my door on your way out."

"Well?" Inspector Queen asked in the silence of the shadowy office after its rightful owner left.

"Not now, dad," Ellery mumbled, "not yet."

The old man shrugged. It was an old story to him, and he had learned to live with it.

They went home in a silent taxicab.

Eventually the Inspector left his pride and joy in an equally silent study, pulling on his celebrated lower lip and staring down some mysterious tunnel inhabited, to judge from his expression, by particularly revolting monsters.

FORTY

So the mystery's face rotated past its three-quarter position, and Ellery saw the whole face at last, and knew it.

4   FULL FACE

"Bury me on my face," said Diogenes;
and when he was asked why, he replied,
"Because in a little while everything
will be turned upside down."

DIOGENES LAERTIUS

FORTY-ONE

The Inspector shook him awake.

"What?" Ellery shouted, shooting up in bed.

"I haven't said anything yet," his father said. "Get up, will you? You have company."

"What time is it?"

"Eleven o'clock, and the day is Sunday, in case you forgot. What time did you get to bed?"

"I don't know, dad. Four, five, something like that. Company? Who?"

"Harry Burke and Roberta West. If you ask me," the Inspector grumbled from the doorway, "those two are plotting something. They look too damn happy to be up to anything legal."

They did indeed. The Scot was sucking on a dead pipe furiously, his sandy brows working like pistons, his wrestler's neck mottled in a flaming purple motif, and his transparent eyes doing a sort of optical hornpipe. In his blunt right hand nestled Roberta's left, being ground up and loving every bone-crushing moment of it. Ellery had never seen Roberta so vivacious. She bubbled over the instant he came shambling out in his faded old dressing gown and down-at-heel slippers.

"Guess what, Ellery?" Roberta cried. "We're getting married!"

"Am I supposed to go into a Highland fling?" Ellery grunted. "That earth-shaking event was announced to me some time ago."

"But we've changed our *plans*, Ellery."

"We're not going to wait until Bertie's show closes to go to England," said Burke excitedly. "She's chucked the bloody thing, and we're going to be married here and now."

"In my apartment?" Ellery asked sourly.

"I don't mean here and now," Burke said. "I mean in New York and today."

151

"Oh?" Ellery perked up. "And what caused this change in strategy? Sit down, please, both of you. I can't abide people who jump about first thing Sunday morning. Dad, is there any tomato juice in the fridge? I need lots of tomato juice this morning."

"It's Harry," Roberta said, slipping into one of the chairs at the dinette table in the alcove of the living room. "He's so masterful. He couldn't wait."

"Bloody well could not," Burke said, seating himself by her side and recapturing her hand. "Said to myself, 'Why wait?' Makes no bloody sense, when you think of it. And I've thought of bloody little else. All we need is a dominie, and it's done."

"You also need a little thing called a marriage license," Ellery said, "—thanks, dad!" He took a long gulp of the bloody stuff. "Wasserman, three days, and all that. How do you propose to do it all today?"

"Oh, we've got the tests over with and the license now for a week," Roberta said. "Do you suppose I might have a smidge of that, Inspector? It looks so good, and I haven't had any breakfast. Or dinner last night, come to think of it. Harry was so insistent."

"Don't put it all on Harry," Ellery said disagreeably; "he couldn't take the Wasserman for you. Well, I guess it's congratulations again. Is there anything I can do?"

"You don't sound very enthusiastic," Harry Burke growled. "Don't you approve?"

"Slip the chip, chum," Ellery said. "Why should I be enthusiastic over *your* marriage? Eggs, dad. Do we have any eggs?"

"Thank you, Inspector!" said Roberta. She sipped thirstily.

"Coming up," the Inspector said. "Anybody else?"

"I'd *love* some," Roberta said breathlessly, lowering the tomato juice. "Wouldn't you, Harry?"

"Come on, Bertie." Burke glared at Ellery. "I'll take you out to breakfast."

"*Harry.*"

"Simmer down, Harry," Ellery said. "I'm not at my best Sunday mornings. Dad makes the meanest scrambled eggs on the West Side. Have some. Come on."

"No, thank you," Burke said stiffly.

"And *lots* of toast, Inspector, please," Roberta said. "Harry, stop being a drag."

"Coming up," the Inspector said again, and disappeared in the kitchen again.

"He could show some enthusiasm," Burke complained. "What's the matter with Sunday mornings?"

"The matter is that they come after Saturday nights," Ellery explained. "This particular Saturday night I didn't get to bed until well into Sunday morning."

"Conscience, a head, or a lively bit of fluff? Or all three?"

"Dad and I saw Orrin Steyne's *Revue* last night."

Burke looked puzzled. "What of it? So did a great many other people, and from what I hear they enjoyed themselves. Sometimes you make no sense, Ellery."

"There was a song Lorette sang . . ." Ellery stopped. "Never mind. We were talking about your shotgun nuptials." He suddenly seemed to have swallowed something bitter.

Roberta looked indignant.

"Shotgun! I don't know where private detectives get their reputations. A girl is safer with Harry than with a dedicated violet. Harry and I debated whether to go see her or not," Roberta went on, failing to signal a right-hand turn, "and don't the eggs and bacon smell yummy! And is there anything more delicious than toast making? Is she as good as they're saying, Ellery?"

"What? Oh. Sensational."

"Then we won't go. I can't stand other people's success. That's something you'll find out about me, Harry. We couldn't go, anyway. We'll be in England—"

"Now that spring is here," Burke and Ellery said in unison. Whereupon Burke grinned, stuck his hand across the table, and called out, "Put some more eggs on, Inspector! I've changed my mind."

"Nuptials," Ellery reminded them glumly. "Who's committing the crime?"

"That," Roberta said, frowning, "happens to be our problem. Realize what day it is today?"

"Certainly, it's Sunday." At her reproving look Ellery said, "Isn't it?"

"What Sunday?"

"*What* Sunday?"

"It's Palm Sunday, that's what Sunday."

"So it is." Ellery looked chagrined. "I'm not following, I think. Palm Sunday?"

"Heathen! Palm Sunday is the beginning of Holy Week, remember? And it's Lent besides. Well, Harry's a renegade Presbyterian, but I'm a dues-paying Episcopalian, and I've always wanted to be married in an Episcopal church by an Episcopal minister, but you simply don't

153

get married in my church during Holy Week and/or Lent. It's against the canons, or something. So we're hung up."

"Then wait for a week or two, or whenever Lent's over."

Roberta looked dreamy.

"We can't. Harry already has our plane tickets—we're spending the night in a hotel and taking off first thing tomorrow morning."

"The solution seems to me not too snarly," Ellery said. "You could cancel the plane tickets."

"We can't," said Roberta. "Harry won't."

"Or you could fly to England tomorrow morning and put the bloody thing off until after Lent."

"It's not a bloody thing, and I wouldn't be able to hold out until after Lent," the Scot said dangerously. "You know, Queen? I don't care for your attitude."

"Ellery," Ellery lamented. "Let's keep this emotional conversation friendly. By the way, how sure are you both that you want to marry each other?"

They stared at him as if he had uttered an indecency.

Then Burke jumped up. "On your feet, Bertie! We're getting the hell out of here."

"Oh, Harry, sit down," Roberta said. He did so reluctantly, eyes spitting colorless murder across the table. "We're sure, Ellery," she said softly.

"You love this character?"

"I love this character."

Ellery shrugged. "Or you could rustle up a minister of some less canonical church to do the job. Or, easiest of all, find some civil servant who's authorized by the State to perform the tribal rites. They're just as binding and a lot less gluey."

"You don't understand," Roberta began; but Inspector Queen came in then with a hogback platter of scrambled eggs, bacon, and buttered toast, and her attention was diverted.

"And I know just the man," the Inspector said, setting the plate down. "The coffee's perking." He explored the sideboard for napkins, plates, and cutlery, and began passing them around. "J.J."

"The Judge," Ellery said damply.

"The Judge?" Burke asked in a suspicious tone. "Who's the Judge?"

"Judge J. J. McCue, an old friend of ours," the Inspector said, and went for the coffee pot.

"Would he do it?" the Scot demanded.

"If dad asks him."

"He's not a minister," Roberta said doubtfully.

"You can't have your eggs and eat them, too, Bertie," her swain said *con amore*. His good humor was on the rise again. "A judge sounds bloody fine to me. Especially the friend-of-the-family type. We can always be married over again by an Anglican priest after we get to England. I don't care how many times I marry you. Or how many blokes perform the ceremony, or where. Can you people get Judge McCue today?"

"We can try," the Inspector said, back with the pot. He poured a cupful for Roberta. "If he's in town I'll guarantee it."

Roberta frowned. Finally she nodded, sighed, and said, "Oh, well, all right," and buried her nose in the fragrant cup.

Burke beamed.

Roberta attacked the eggs.

The Inspector sat down and reached for a slice of toast.

But Ellery munched. Tastelessly.

FORTY-TWO

He was in a peculiar humor all day. He did not even perk up at his father's success in locating Judge McCue on a crowded municipal Palm Sunday golf course. So that Harry Burke's dander began to act up again.

"We'll have the ceremony here," the Inspector said, hanging up. "The Judge says he can't do it at his house— his wife comes from a long line of High Church ministers and she thinks Holy Week marriages are made in hell. Besides, he's in enough trouble with her because he's playing golf today. So he'll slip over to our place this evening. Is that all right with you two?"

"Oh, wonderful!" Roberta said, clapping her hands.

"I'm not so bowled over by it," Burke said, glaring at Ellery. "Although it's kind of *you*, Inspector."

Ellery was examining his thumb, which he had just taken out of his mouth. It looked as if a rat had been gnawing at it.

"Harry, my love," Roberta said rapidly. "Don't you have anything to do?"

"Do I?"

"You don't know *anything*."

"I've never been married before," her swain said, flushing. "What have I forgotten?"

"Oh, nothing. Just the flowers. My corsage. The champagne. Little things like that."

"My God! Excuse me."

"Don't bother about the bubbly," Inspector Queen called after him. "Ellery has a few bottles of the stuff stashed away for an occasion—haven't you, son?"

"The Sazarac '47? I suppose I have," Ellery said gloomily.

"I wouldnt take his bubbly for all the bubbles in 'em," the Scot said coldly.

"You'll have to," Ellery said, gnawing again. "Where are you going to buy champagne in New York on Palm Sunday?"

Burke stalked out.

"And cigarets, love!" Roberta called. "I'm fresh out." The door banged.

"I don't know what's come over you two," she said, "—thank you, Ellery," and puffed energetically. "It's not all Harry's fault, either. There's something on your mind. May I ask what it is? Since it's my wedding, and I don't want it spoiled."

"I have problems," Ellery conceded. The Inspector finished his second cup of coffee and glanced at him. "Well!" Ellery rose. "I'd better get the dishes out of the way."

"Here, I'll do them," Roberta said, jumping up. "I don't approve of men doing dishes, even bachelors. You haven't answered my question, Ellery. What problems?"

But Ellery shook his head.

"Why spoil your wedding day? You just said you didn't want it spoiled."

"I certainly do not! I take it all back. You can keep your old problems to yourself."

"Yes," Ellery said; and he disappeared in his study, leaving Roberta frowning a little and his father staring after him thoughtfully.

"What's the matter with that son of yours, Inspector?" Roberta demanded, collecting the plates.

The Inspector was still staring at the door.

"He's in a bind over the Guild case," the old man said. "He always acts this way when a case is bugging him." He followed her into the kitchen, carrying the coffee pot. "Don't let it upset you." He pulled out the tray of the

156

dishwasher for her. "You know, Roberta," the Inspector said suddenly, "it's given me an idea. I wonder if you'd mind."

"Mind?"

"Having a few people in for the ceremony."

Roberta stiffened. "That would depend on who they are."

"Well, Lorette Spanier, Selma Pilter, maybe Mr. Wasser, if we can get them." His tone suggested that the subjunctive mood was a mere courtesy.

"Oh, dear," Roberta said. "Why, Inspector?"

"I don't know why exactly," the old man said. "Call it a hunch. I've seen this sort of thing work with Ellery before. Gathering people who've been involved in a tough case at a critical stage seems to do something for him. Clears his head."

"But it's my wedding!" Roberta cried. "Goodness, people getting married shouldn't be asked to be guinea pigs in a—a—"

"I know it's asking a lot," he said gently.

"Besides, Inspector, Lorette wouldn't come. You know the circumstances under which we broke up. And she's in that revue—"

"Since when are performances of Broadway shows given on Sundays? Anyway, I have a feeling she would. Maybe Lorette's been looking for a chance to make up with you, now that she's hit the jackpot and can afford to let bygones be bygones. And I know you'll feel better about flying off to England without leaving any bitterness behind." Inspector Queen had an old-fashioned belief in the efficacy of "Hearts and Flowers" in situations like these. "What do you say?" he said as he followed her back to the living room.

Roberta silently began to gather up the cups and saucers.

"Be a sport, Roberta."

"Harry wouldn't . . ."

"Leave Harry to me. He's a pro. He understands these things."

"But it's his wedding, too!"

"Think about it. I'd really appreciate it."

The Inspector left her quietly and went into Ellery's study. He slipped the door to the living room shut. Ellery was sprawled behind his desk, swivel chair slued about so that he could park his feet on the windowsill and look out at the smog-smutched sky beyond the bars of the fire escape.

"Son."

Ellery kept looking out.

"How about telling me what this is all about?"

Ellery shook his head.

"Are you in the stew, or is it done and you're parked on the lid?"

Ellery did not reply.

"All right," his father said. "I've got to go down to Isaac Rubin's Delicatessen and order some smoked turkey and corned beef sandwiches and stuff for tonight. While I'm out I'd like to phone Lorette Spanier, Carlos Armando, and a couple of others—Mrs. Pilter, William Wasser. Inviting them to the wedding."

That brought Ellery's shoes to the floor in a small explosion.

"That's what you'd be doing if you saw your way clear, isn't it?"

"You know me so damned well it's illegal," Ellery said slowly. "Yes, dad, I suppose it is. But dragging a murder case into a wedding . . . Do you suppose. I'm getting sentimental in my old age? Anyway, you can't very well do it without consulting Roberta and Harry."

"I've already talked to Roberta, although I didn't happen to mention asking Armando; and I'll handle Mr. Burke. The point is, do *you* want me to do it?"

Ellery tugged at his nose, cracked a knuckle, and generally agonized.

Finally he said, "Want? Anything but. But I don't suppose I really have a choice."

"Shall I call anyone besides the ones I mentioned?"

Ellery considered. "No," he said, and turned again to the Manhattan sky, which scowled back, puzzled.

He didn't even ask me to get pastrami, the Inspector thought as he slipped out.

FORTY-THREE

Inspector Queen had remarkably little trouble with Harry Burke.

"This wedding is turning out a bugger," the Scot growled to the old man with a shake of his sandy head. "The important thing now is to marry Bertie and get the hell out of your bleeding country, Inspector. By tomorrow morning this will all be a bad dream, I keep telling myself. And Bert and I can wake up."

"That's the boy," the Inspector said warmly, and turned to Roberta, who kicked the rug and said, "Well, if it's all right with Harry."

"That's the girl!"

The old man left for the delicatessen and the outside telephone still without having mentioned Armando. With the Inspector first things came first, and the hindmost could be taken care of by the usual agency.

He had almost as much trouble working his will with Lorette as being waited on by Mr. Rubin, who was puffing about the little delicatessen trying to satiate the demands of the non-Lent-observing Gentiles of his clientele, to whom Isaac Rubin's was an oasis in the Sunday desert. But finally the Inspector succeeded in placing his order, and shut himself up in the telephone booth with some dimes, and girded his lean loins for the fray.

William Maloney Wasser was no problem; the Inspector's argument was Wasser's watchdog responsibility to the famous estate in his care, as if that had anything to do with anything; the lawyer hemmed a little and hawed a little and finally said he supposed he would have to come, even though Roberta West and Harry Burke had nothing to do with anything and he would have to give up *Bonanza* and *Open End,* and what was going on, anyway? With Selma Pilter the Inspector had even less trouble. Her medieval beak sniffed something, too. "Whither Lorette goeth I go, Inspector Queen. I warn you to handle her with kid gloves, she's the hottest property in town. I won't have her so much as bruised. Who did you say are getting married?" The old man neglected to mention that he had not yet invited Lorette, or that Carlos Armando would be there hooked or crooked.

Lorette was difficult. "I *don't* understand, Inspector. Why in the world should Roberta want me at her wedding?"

"Her best friend?" the Inspector said, registering surprise. "Why not, Miss Spanier?"

"Because she's *not* my best friend, or I hers. That's all over with. Besides, if Roberta wants me, why doesn't she invite me herself?"

"Last-minute preparations. They made their plans all of a sudden—"

"Well, thank you very much, Inspector Queen, but no thank you."

159

At this point the Inspector heard a mellifluous *"Cara"* from the background, and Armando's greased murmur.

"Just a moment, please," Lorette said.

An off-telephone discussion followed. The old man grinned in the booth, waiting. Armando was advising acceptance, as of a lark. So he was still riding high, secure in his immunity. So much the better. Ellery should be pleased. And the Inspector wondered for the umpteenth time what Ellery had in mind. And tried not to think of the dirty trick he was playing on the newlyweds-to-be.

"Inspector Queen," Lorette said.

"Yes?"

"Very well, we'll come."

"We?" the old man repeated with cunning bleakness. Two birds with one stone. He had not envisioned Armando as an ally.

"Carlos and I. I won't come without Carlos."

"Well, now, I don't know, Miss Spanier. In view of how Roberta feels about him, not to mention Harry Burke—"

"I'm sorry. If they really want me, they'll have to take Mr. Armando, too."

"All right," the Inspector said, with a not altogether contrived sigh. "I just hope he, uh, respects the solemnity of the occasion. I wouldn't have Roberta's and Harry's wedding spoiled for anything." And hung up, feeling like Judas, a feeling he chased to cover the moment it showed its accusing head.

It's going to be one hell of a wedding, the old man guiltily thought as he left the booth, and for the umpteenth-and-first time wondered what it was all about.

FORTY-FOUR

~~~~~~~~~~~~~~~~~~~

One hell of a wedding it turned out.

Judge McCue arrived at seven, a tall old party with a white thatch, a bricklayer's complexion, a nose like a prize fighter's, and blue judge-eyes. He towered over Inspector Queen like Mt. Fujiyama. The jurist was glancing at his watch even as the Inspector let him in, and he glanced at it again during the introduction of the unhappy couple, both of whom were beginning to exhibit the classic symptoms of premarital jitters.

160

"I don't like to hurry matters," Judge McCue said in his Chaliapin voice, "but the fact is I had to tell Mrs. McCue a white lie about where I was going, and she's expecting me back home practically at once. My wife doesn't hold with Lenten weddings."

"I'm beginning to agree with her," Harry Burke said with ungroomlike asperity. "It seems we have to wait, Judge McCue. Inspector Queen's invited some guests to our wedding." The Scot's stress on the pronoun was positively prosecutional.

"It'll be over soon, darling," Roberta said nervously. "Judge, I wonder . . . could you possibly perform the ceremony with the Episcopal service instead of just a civil service? I mean, I'd really feel more married if . . ."

"I don't see why not, Miss West," Judge McCue said. "Except that I don't carry a Book of Common Prayer around with me."

"Ellery's got one in his reference library," Burke said with an anything-to-get-this-over-with air.

"I'll get it," Ellery said unexpectedly. He sounded almost grateful. He emerged from his study with a battered little red-covered book, carrying it as if it put a strain on his arm muscles. "Page 300, I think."

"Don't you feel well, Ellery?" asked Judge McCue.

"I'm fine," Ellery said bravely, and handed the book to the Judge and went over to the windows, between which the enormous basket-spray of shaggy 'mums Burke had ordered had been set up by Roberta for appropriate background, and gloomed down at the street. He kept pulling at his lower lip and pinching his nose, and he looked about as festive as Walter Cronkite announcing an abort at Cape Kennedy.

Burke sniffed the cinnamony air in Ellery's direction, and muttered something.

"Here comes Wasser," Ellery said suddenly. "And Mrs. Pilter."

"Anyone else coming?" Judge McCue referred to his wristwatch again.

"And there's another cab with Lorette," Ellery announced, still looking out, and paused. "And Carlos Armando," he said.

"What?" Harry Burke shouted in 100-proof stupefaction.

"Now look, Harry boy," the Inspector said hurriedly. "Lorette Spanier wouldn't come without him. I couldn't help myself. If you wanted Lorette——"

161

"I didn't want Lorette! I didn't want any of them!" the Scot howled. "Whose wedding is this? What's coming off here? By God, for a plugged pig's bladder I'd call the bloody thing off!"

"Harry," moaned Roberta.

"I don't care a tweak, Bertie! These people have taken over the most sacred thing in our lives and they're turning it into a bloody peep show! I won't be used! I won't have you being used!"

"What is this all about?" Judge McCue asked feebly. Nobody answered him.

The door buzzed.

Roberta, half hysterical, raced to the Inspector's bathroom.

The next few minutes were avant-garde and Nouvelle Vague, with a dash of Fellini. The unwilling guests inched in together, to be met by Harry Burke's glare, Ellery's simper, the Inspector's frantic heartiness, and Judge McCue's bewilderment. The only one who seemed to enjoy the experience was Carlos Armando, whose dark face and black eyes glistened with malice. Everyone milled about in the smallish living room, passing and repassing like a deck of cards being shuffled by a clumsy dealer, to the accompaniment of confused introductions, mumbled politenesses, unresponsive grunts, hostile handshakes, enthusiastic references to the dismal spring, sudden silences, overhearty congratulations to Lorette, and —like a Wagnerian leitmotiv—queries about the whereabouts of the missing bride, chiefly by Armando, in an innocent tone of voice.

She was in the bathroom "fixing herself up" for the happy event, Inspector Queen found himself saying for the dozenth time.

Ultimately Roberta made her appearance, pale but head high, like the heroine in a Victorian play. The hush that fell over the living room did not improve the climate. Armando's charm poisoned the air; Ellery had to grab hold of Harry Burke's arm at one point to prevent that oak-muscled member from an extremity. In the end it was—suprisingly—Lorette who saved the day. She put her arms about Roberta, kissed her, and took her off to the kitchen to disinter the wedding bouquet from the refrigerator; and when they emerged Roberta announced that Lorette was to be her maid of honor; and the Inspector hastily swiped some 'mums from the basket and improvised a maid of honor's corsage, using a length of

162

white satin ribbon out of the supply he hoarded from past Christmases.

Finally everything was settled. The Judge took up a position between the windows, his back to the floral spray, with Burke facing him on the right hand and Roberta on the left, as prescribed in the liturgy, Lorette standing behind Roberta, Ellery behind Burke, and the others behind them. Judge McCue opened the Book of Common Prayer to page 300, and clamped tortoise shells on his mashed nose, and began in his *basso profundo* to read the Solemnization of Matrimony as ratified by the Protestant Episcopal Church in the United States of America in convention assembled on the sixteenth day of October in the Year of our Lord One Thousand Seven Hundred and Eighty-nine:

"*Dearly beloved,*" the Judge said, and cleared his throat.

Inspector Queen, from his premeditated vantage point to one side, kept watching Ellery. That child of his youth was a stricken man. The Inspector had never seen him so iron-stiff, so bloodless with indecision. Obviously, a worm was nibbling away at the fruit of the Inspector's loins; and, while the Judge read on, the old man kept probing for it, trying to catch and classify. But fruitlessly.

"*. . . we are gathered together here in the sight of God, and in the face of this company, to join together this Man and this Woman in holy Matrimony . . .*"

The room was filled with the odor of the unknown given off by all wedding ceremonies, an odor that is almost a threat. Roberta was unconsciously clutching to her white lace wedding frock the pink velvet muff Burke had ordered, bruising the gardenias with which it was covered; the stocky groom himself seemed inches taller, as if he had suddenly been assigned to sentry duty at Buckingham Palace—the Inspector could almost see Burke wearing a shako and shouldering a musket. Lorette Spanier looked far away and lost. Selma Pilter was secretive with the hidden envy of an old woman to whom weddings were celebrations of regret; and the Inspector was fascinated to behold William Maloney Wasser's belly doing a portly jiggle in rhythm with Judge McCue's cadences, as at some overseen fertility rite. Only Armando was his mocking, hateful self, his enjoyment of the scene evidently deepened by his own multiple experience of such obscenities.

"*. . . which is an honourable estate, instituted of God . . .*" The Judge boomed on of the mystical union and

163

the holy estate and the first miracle wrought in Cana of Galilee, and Inspector Queen returned to his only begotten son, stiff as mortality.

And the old man began to wonder with great uneasiness if he had not committed a wrong in taking matters into his own hands. Something wrong, something very wrong, was in the air.

". . . *and therefore is not by any to be entered into unadvisedly or lightly; but reverently, discreetly, advisedly, soberly, and in the fear of God."*

Why? Why?

"Into this holy estate these two persons present come now to be joined."

What's he wrestling with? the old man thought. Whatever the opponent, the struggle was fierce. A muscle in Ellery's jaw was doing a throttled dance of its own; the hands clasped before him were gray in the knuckles; he stood as rigidly at attention as the nervous groom before him. But Burke has cause, the Inspector thought. What's with my son?

"If any man can show just cause, why they may not lawfully be joined together," the bass voice continued, *"let him now speak, or else hereafter for ever hold his peace."*

Something has to give, the old man's thoughts ran. This can't go on; he'll burst . . . Ellery opened his mouth. And clamped it shut again.

"I require and charge you both, as ye will answer at the dreadful day of judgment when the secrets of all hearts shall be disclosed, that if either of you know any impediment, why ye may not be lawfully joined together in Matrimony ye do now confess—"

Ellery said, "I have a point."

The words sounded involuntary, as if a thought had found its own vehicle of expression, independent of its thinker. And, indeed, Ellery looked as shocked by what he had said as Judge McCue, Roberta West, and Harry Burke. The Judge's severe blue eyes accused him over Burke's head; the nuptial pair half turned in Ellery's direction in protest; and all the other eyes went to him, even Carlos Armando's, as if he had given vent to a natural indiscretion during silent prayer in church.

"I have a point," Ellery said again. "I have a point, and I can't keep it to myself any longer. Judge, you will simply have to stop this wedding."

"You're daft," Burke said. "Daft."

"No, Harry," Ellery said. "Sane. Only too sane."

FORTY-FIVE

～～～～～～～

"I owe you an apology, Roberta," Ellery went on. "This may not seem the time or place, but in another sense it's the only time and place. In either event, I have no choice." He said again, as if to reassure himself, "I have no choice."

He had stepped out of the tableau, while its actors remained frozen where they stood. But now he said, "You had better all sit down, this will take time," as if the concept of time obsessed him; and he moved about, pushing a chair here, settling Roberta with special care, another there, for Mrs. Pilter, and still another for Lorette Spanier. None of the men complied. Already the atmosphere was thickening up to something curiously like a lynching mood. Only, who were the posse and who was the victim?

Ellery braced himself.

"A moment ago I mentioned time and place," Ellery said. "The place may be fortuitous, but what of time? We're face to face with it. Time is of the essence in this case.

"Case . . . Because, of course, the case is what this is all about. The murder case. The murder of Glory Guild.

"I have to take you back to Glory's will, her copy of it," Ellery said, "and what she wrote in disappearing ink between those typewritten lines. What she wrote was an earwitness report of the events of that evening when she overheard her own murder being planned—by you, Armando, when you thought your wife was safely in Connecticut at her cottage, and you got Roberta West up to your wife's apartment and tried to talk this girl into killing her for you."

"You will not take me in by cheap trickery," Armando said, showing his brilliant teeth. "This has all been ably stage-managed, Mr. Queen, but I do not blurt out indiscretions under a surprise. A report in GeeGee's copy of her will? In disappearing ink? You are romancing, no doubt for my benefit. You will have to do better than that."

"The question," Ellery said, turning his back on the swarthy man, "the question is the *time* the incident of the

165

plotting took place. It's the nicest sort of question—"

But he was interrupted. "I can't imagine your doing anything more to me than you're doing at this moment," Harry Burke snarled. "Something's gone wrong with you, Queen. Your brain's begun rattling about in your bean. I don't know what you're talking about."

"The time," Ellery repeated. He took the blue-backed document from his pocket. "This is Glory's copy of her will, with her message on it. You, Harry, and Roberta and Mr. Wasser were present when my father read it aloud in Mr. Wasser's office, so you're acquainted with its contents. The Judge, Lorette, Mrs. Pilter, and Armando—especially Armando—are not. So bear with me while I read it to them."

"You probably wrote it yourself," Armando said, smiling; but there was wariness in his smile. "But read it, by all means."

Ellery ignored him. "'I am writing this for reasons that will become clear soon enough,'" he read. "'I had wanted for some time to get away from things, and I had planned to go up to Newtown, to the cottage. . . .'" He read on in a neutral, almost schoolmaster's voice, as if it were a lesson to be taught: how Armando's wife had driven up to Newtown and found that her secretary had forgotten her instructions to notify the Connecticut Light & Power Company to turn the electricity on, how the house had been "very damp and cold," and how, rather than risk a cold, she had returned to the city. How she had let herself into the apartment and overheard her husband's conversation with a girl unknown to her; her description of Roberta; Armando's reference to herself as "a cow to be milked"; his proposal to Roberta that she kill his wife while he established an alibi, after which he would inherit "all my money" and marry Roberta. And how, unable to "take any more," Glory Guild had fled from the apartment, walked the streets most of the night, and then driven back to the Connecticut cottage where she had stayed for "two whole days," thinking over her plight; and so on, to the dismal end.

The silence was puzzled, except for Armando's.

"I deny it all, of course," Armando said. "This is a forgery—"

"You be quiet." Ellery tucked the will away in his pocket. "I return to the question. And I ask you: Did you hear a single word in the account I just read you that specifies the *time* when this unlovely scene took place?" And he shook his head. "The fact remains,

166

Glory's message does not date Armando's session with Roberta."

"But Roberta told us the time!" Harry Burke growled. "The night this scum proposed the murder to her—when she ran out of the Guild apartment frightened and disgusted—was a night in May, Roberta said. So what's all this nonsense about time?"

Harry, Harry, Ellery thought.

"Humor me, Harry," Ellery said, "and let's pursue this nonsense. Glory was murdered on the night of December thirtieth last year. You, I, my father went through her diaries and memoirs, with particular attention to last year, and we found every page—in last year's diary, up to the day of her death, every page but one—jammed with day-to-day jottings. Yet not one of those entries—which means throughout May as well as in any other month last year—not one mentioned what took place in the Guild apartment the night Armando made his charming proposal to Roberta. Not one, or certainly one or all of us—trying to solve the murder—would have pounced on it and shouted it to the rooftops of Centre Street. Nowhere in last year's diary did Glory note down a word about having overheard her husband's plot. That is, directly."

"What do you mean?" Inspector Queen said, frowning. "She didn't mention it at all. You just said so."

"I said 'directly.' But didn't she mention it—as it were —somewhere in the diary indirectly?"

After a moment his father said quickly, "The blank page."

"The blank page. Which was dated what?"

"December first."

Ellery nodded.

"So, in view of its absence everywhere else in the diary, it must have been on the night of December first that Glory overheard Armando plotting her death. And there's a confirmation of this—that blank December first page contained the letters *f-a-c-e* in disappearing ink, which was Glory's read-between-the-lines clue to her copy of the will. Which, duly read, in turn revealed her firsthand account of the events of that night. December first was the date of that session, beyond a doubt.

"December first," Ellery said, addressing himself for the first time in the supercharged silence to Roberta, "not a night in May, Roberta. What's more, there can be no question of its having been a slip of the tongue. You misdated the talk as taking place in May not once but at

167

least twice that I can remember. The first time was on the morning of New Year's Day, when Harry and I had just got off the plane from England—less than thirty-six hours after the murder—and I found my father's note to call you, and I did, and you insisted on coming right over, and you told us about your affair with Armando terminating in his proposal that you kill his wife. He made that proposal to you, you told us, on a night 'a little more than seven months ago.' Since you were telling us this story on January first, 'a little more than seven months ago' placed the conversation some time back in late May.

"One misdating might have been an innocent error, although an error of over half a year takes great faith in innocence to swallow. But you misdated it a second time, the other day, when I finally interpreted Glory's clue *f-a-c-e*, brought out the hidden message in her will, and my father read her accusation aloud in your presence. You immediately placed the time of the scene in the Guild apartment as 'that night in May,' as Harry just reminded us. That was quick of you, Roberta. Before any of us, you spotted Glory's failure to date the scene in her account, and you made on-the-spot use of it to strengthen your original story to us.

"For in that original story, on New Year's morning, you told Harry and me that you had not laid eyes on Carlos Armando between 'that night in May' and the night of December thirtieth, when you said Armando showed up suddenly at your apartment and established his alibi for the murder of his wife, which was taking place presumably while he was with you.

"We know now that you did see the lover you professed to have come to loathe in May—saw him as recently as the night of December first, in his wife's apartment, the night that his proposal to you to murder her really took place, not six months earlier. Far from having dropped him in May, it's a reasonable assumption that you kept seeing him all through the summer and fall—until, in fact, that night of December first.

"And if you lied to us about that, Roberta, then your whole story becomes suspect. And if your whole story becomes suspect, we can no longer take your word for anything you told us. For example, for the alibi you gave Armando for the night of his wife's murder. And if the alibi you gave Armando for his wife's murder is suspect, then it follows that *you yourself have no alibi* for the night of the murder. Because an alibi works two ways, one of them neatly hidden. It accounts for the person

168

being alibied, and *ipso facto* accounts for the person providing the alibi. That was the really clever part of the plan. It cleared you at the same time that it cleared Armando. It enabled you to come to me soon after the murder and, by alibiing your lover, clear yourself of any suspicion that might arise in the investigation.

"Innocent people don't concoct intricate ways to clear themselves of suspicion.

"All this logical figuration, Roberta," Ellery said to the sorrel-haired girl, "leads to only one conclusion: You could have been the woman Carlos Armando used as his tool. You could have been his accomplice. You could have been the woman we've been hunting—the woman who shot Glory Guild to death."

She was standing pale as a cast; the gardenia-covered symbol of her wedding was pressed hard against her lacy frock, rupturing the flowers. The Scot at her side looked like a companion piece; Burke seemed to be retreating deeper within himself, as if the plaster were hardening; only his transparent eyes showed a tormented kind of life. As for Armando, he wet his pretty lips in the burned and pitted skin and half parted them, as if about to admonish Roberta West against speaking; but then they clamped shut, evidently preferring silence to the risk of admission implicit in a warning.

Ellery half turned from Roberta and Harry Burke, and it was clear that they had become intolerable to him. But then he turned back. "You could have been," he said to Roberta. "The question is: Were you?

"You were.

"I say this baldly because there are three confirmations of your guilt arising from the facts.

"One: In the account Glory left us between the lines of her will, she described you unmistakably, Roberta, down to the butterfly birthmark on your cheek, as the woman with whom her husband was plotting her death. Since we can no longer accept your word that you rejected Armando's proposal, the fact remains that you were the woman Glory accused. 'This girl is Carlos's accomplice,' she concluded her account. 'She is the one who, if I am murdered, will have done the murder for him.' I submit that Glory would hardly have left such an unequivocal accusation, Roberta, had she not had sufficient reason to believe, from what she overheard that night of December first, that you had given clear evidence of falling in with Armando's plan. Had you remained 'stunned' and 'horrified,' as you told us, 'unable to get a word out,'

169

Glory could not have accused you so without qualification. It follows that you must have said something that night, given some positive indication to Armando, that convinced Glory of your acquiescence in the murder plot.

"And incidentally, let's get one thing straight about the cryptic clue that culminated in the secret account on the will. When Glory sat at her desk on the night of December thirtieth, mortally shot, and managed to pick up a pen and write *f-a-c-e* on a piece of paper before she fell forward on it, it was not an inspiration that came to her from on high a mere few seconds away from death. Now we know that she had prepared that very clue almost a full month earlier, when she wrote the same four letters of the alphabet in disappearing ink on the blank December first page of her diary.

"Also incidentally, Glory's passion for puzzles was not the reason for her use of the *f-a-c-e* clue and the disappearing ink. They were only the *modus operandi* of her motivation. Had she left open instructions and an open account of what she had overheard on December first, she was afraid either Armando or Jeanne Temple, her secretary, who had access to her effects, would find and destroy them—Armando for obvious reasons, Jeanne Temple because she was having an affair with Armando and was presumably under his thumb.

"Which brings us to confirmation number two." Ellery unexpectedly turned to Carlos Armando, who took an involuntary half step backward. "When you planned the murder of your wife, Armando, you believed your premarital agreement with her—that five years' probation business—was no longer in existence; as you said heatedly at the will reading, Glory tore it up before your eyes at the expiration of the five years. Only it turned out that she hadn't done anything of the sort; she had torn up a dummy. So, when Mr. Wasser read the will to the heirs after your wife's funeral, you learned for the first time that she had duped you; that the premarital agreement was still in effect; that all the trouble you had gone to, up to and including masterminding a murder, had netted you a mere $5,000.

"To most murderers this would have been checkmate. A lesser mortal would have given up, collected his 5,000 and turned to other games. But you were made of more heroic stuff. You didn't give up—not you. You thought you saw a way to recoup your defeat in spite of Glory's defensive play. It's common knowledge that a murderer can't legally profit from his crime. If Lorette Spanier, who inherited the bulk of Glory's estate, could somehow be tagged for her aunt's murder, *the estate would have to revert to you* in spite of that premarital agreement. The reason is, of course, that with Lorette legally out of the picture you would be *the only one* left to inherit. Glory Guild had no other living heirs.

"So you extended your original plan: you framed Lorette for Glory's murder. You knew that a powerful motive could be ascribed to her—the new will naming her the principal heir; that Lorette's denying Glory had told her about the new will had no evidence to back it up. You also knew that Lorette could be charged with opportunity—the then known facts indicated only her unsupported word that she had left her aunt alive in the apartment on the murder night. With motive and opportunity there for the grasping, all you had to do, Armando, was provide Lorette with the third factor of the classical rule: means. You merely had to arrange for the gun that had shot your wife to be found in her niece's possession.

"And who could most easily have planted the gun in Lorette's bedroom closet? You were no longer living in the Guild apartment; but Lorette was, *and Roberta was,* too. So it must have been Roberta who hid the gun in Lorette's hatbox in Lorette's clothes closet. And we know it was Roberta who, when the gun fell out of the hatbox, suggested that Harry Burke and I, in the apartment at the time, be immediately informed of it.

"Third confirmation," Ellery said; and he moistened the dryness in his throat and hurried on, as if anxious to rid himself of an unwelcome burden. "A complication arose. A Bowery derelict called Spotty suddenly appeared, claiming to have information that might clear Lorette of the murder charge. You had already engineered your wife's death, Armando; you had already committed yourself to the frameup of Lorette; you wanted Glory's estate more than ever; the only thing to do, you reasoned, was to get rid of Spotty before he could testify and clear Lorette, destroying your last chance to get your hands on all that loot.

"So, Armando, you did just that. You got rid of Spotty. Since he was killed in that Bowery flophouse, you must have got in there dressed as a bum, registered under a false name, gone up to the 'dorm,' stabbed Spotty as he lay on the cot, and either walked out calmly into the winter night under Burke's nose or escaped through the rear exit.

"But the question is, how did you even know of Spotty's existence, Armando? How did you become aware of the danger he posed to your frame-up of Lorette? Most important of all, how did you learn where to find Spotty? You were not in Uri Frankell's office when Spotty showed up offering to sell his information. *Ah, but Roberta was.* And, what's more, she accompanied Harry Burke when he immediately set about trailing Spotty from Frankell's office to the Bowery. So it's evident that when Roberta left Burke on watch outside the flophouse for a few minutes and went off to that cafeteria to buy some sandwiches, she took the opportunity to phone you, Armando. It's the only way you could have found out so quickly about Spotty's unexpected appearance as a vital factor in the case, and why, when, and where to kill him.

"So there it is," Ellery said wearily, "the whole dreary *shtik*, act and scene and line. It was a magnificently clever plot, if you go into ecstasies over this sort of thing —brilliantly worked out, brilliantly executed, brilliantly improvised when improvisation was called for, and as sickening an exercise in misdirected ingenuity as I've run across in some years.

"Roberta, you were the one who got into the Guild apartment that night of December thirtieth with a duplicate key Armando provided; you were the one who insinuated yourself into the case so as to be on the inside, a reliable source of information to Armando as it arose in the course of the official investigation. By the way, you must originally have intended to shine up to me, as close to the police officer in charge; but when Harry Burke fell for you, you decided it would be safer and subtler to switch your attentions to him, knowing he would have as much access to the inquiry as I had. And you were the one, Roberta, who put us on the trail of a woman who didn't exist—the 'other' woman you led us to believe Armando must have used as his tool in the killing, when it was you all along. And you were the mysterious woman in the violet veil who, once the murder was done, was significantly never seen again. You were not only the murderer in this case, Roberta, you also acted as its prime red herring—a combination rare in the hanky-pank of murder."

There was an inexorability in the progress of Ellery's tired voice, an end-of-the-road quality, that was more frightening than a riot squad. Roberta stood immobilized by it. As for Armando, his black eyes were fixed on her

172

with extraordinary violence, straining to communicate warnings, threats, reminders. But it was as if she did not see him, or anyone.

"I'm almost finished," Ellery said, "and if I leave anything out, or get anything wrong, Roberta, you can supply the omission or correct the error." *(No!* screamed Armando's black eyes.) "I imagine that the crisis in your relationship with Armando occurred with the failure of the frame-up against Lorette—with her acquittal at the trial. From that moment your interests diverged. Glory Guild's fortune, or the share you were working toward, Roberta, was irretrievably out of your reach.

"But was it out of Armando's reach? Hardly. Armando has the instincts of a vampire bat. He got busy charming Lorette, as he had charmed so many women before her, including her aunt; and you realized, Roberta, that now he meant to marry her and so get his hands on the fortune he had failed to grasp through murder. If and when that happened, there was no place in the game for you. You were of no further use to Armando except for your mutual alibis, and that was a Mexican standoff. Being a woman, you over-reacted. You began to warn Lorette against Armando, trying to thwart his new plan . . . trying, I suppose, to salvage the only thing left to you out of the whole sorry business, Armando himself. You must have been wildly in love with him in the first place to let him talk you into committing murder for him; and now that you saw yourself losing him to Lorette . . ."

"And what about me?" Harry Burke demanded in a cawing croak, like a jungle bird.

"What about you, Harry?" Ellery said deliberately, but he did not sound as if he were enjoying himself. "Do you still dream the fairy-tale dream that Roberta is in love with you? You were a pawn in this game, Harry, a very minor piece to be sacrificed on the board."

"Then why is she marrying me? Why," the Scot wheeled on Roberta for the first time, "are you marrying me?"

Roberta moistened her lips. "Harry . . ."

"What de'il's use can I have for you as a husband?"

"Harry, I did fall in love with you. I do love you."

"With your hands stained with blood!"

Her lips quivered, and when she spoke it was in so low a voice that they all had to strain to hear her. "Yes . . ." But then it gathered strength. "Yes, Ellery's right about everything—the murder, everything—I did shoot

173

her—" *(No, no, no!* shrieked Armando's eyes.) "—but not about that. I've been trying to forget the whole nightmare. I wanted to start a new life . . ."

"Idiot!" shouted Carlos Armando. "Stupid, stupid idiot! And now you have fallen into Queen's trap. All he wanted out of you was an admission of guilt, and you have given it to him. Don't you realize even in your stupidity that if you had kept your mouth shut they could have done nothing against us? In all Queen's fancy talk, they have not a particle of evidence they could take into a courtroom! *Fool. FOOL!*"

Inspector Queen said, "Miss West, are you willing to make a sworn statement?"

Roberta looked at Harry Burke. What she saw in his face made her turn away. "Yes," she said to the Inspector. "Yes."

FORTY-SIX

~~~~~~~~~~~~~~~~~~

The jets were coming and going; the planned chaos of the airport swirled and swooped and buzzed around them unseen and unheard. They might have been in a cave on an island in a typhoon as they waited for Burke's flight to be announced.

The Scot's eyes were no longer transparent; they were the color of blood. He looked as if he had not slept or changed his clothes for a week. His mouth was zippered. He had not asked Ellery to see him off; he had made it plain, in fact, that he wanted never to see Ellery again. But Ellery had tagged along undiscouragedly.

"I know how you feel, Harry," Ellery was saying. "I used you, yes. I almost didn't. I fought with myself not to. When Lorette sang Jimmy Walker's song and that December-May business hit me between the eyes and I saw the whole thing clear, I fought the toughest fight of my life. I didn't know what to do, how to handle it. And when you and Roberta came over and announced you meant to be married right away—last night—the fight was even tougher. Because it gave me an opening, a way to get her to confess. And then my father proposed inviting the others to the wedding. He knows me through and through; he knew something final was in

174

the wind, and without knowing my destination he knew what to do to get me off the ground.

"In the end I gave in, Harry. I had to; I suppose there was never any real doubt about what I had to do. I had no choice. Armando was right: nothing in my argument about Roberta's guilt could have constituted a court case. So I had to make Roberta confess. And not only that. I also had to find a way to stop you from marrying her. I couldn't let you marry a murderess, and I knew that only an admission from her lips would convince you that she was just that. And, of course, I couldn't let a murderess go scot-free . . . no, that's a foul pun; I didn't intend it."

"British Overseas Airways flight number nineteen now loading at Gate Ten," said the annunciator.

Burke grabbed his flight bag and began to stride toward Gate Ten, almost running.

Ellery hurried after him.

"Harry."

The Scot turned on him then. He said in a murderous voice, "You go to hell," and muscled his way through the crowded gate, shouldering an old lady aside, so that she staggered and almost fell.

Ellery caught her. "He's not feeling well," he explained to the old lady.

He stood there until long after Gate Ten was empty. While the BOAC jet taxied to its runway. Until it was part of the sky, and lost.

Of course Burke was being unfair. But you couldn't expect a man to be fair when he had just had his whole life kicked out from under him.

Or the man who had done the kicking to soothe himself with the perfect music of reason.

And so Ellery stood there.

He was still standing alone on his island when a hand touched his.

He turned around and it was, of all people, Inspector Queen.

"El," his father said, squeezing his arm. "Come on, I'll buy you a cup of coffee."

A face that had a story to tell.

How different faces are in this

particular! Some of them speak not.

(Some) faces are books in which not

a line is written, save perhaps a date.

HENRY WADSWORTH LONGFELLOW

The House
of Brass

. . . for within the hollow crown
That rounds the mortal temples of
  a king
Keeps Death his court, and there
  the antic sits,
Scoffing his state and grinning at
  his pomp;
Allowing him a breath, a little
  scene,
To monarchize, be fear'd, and kill
  with looks,
Infusing him with self and vain
  conceit
As if this flesh which walls about
  our life
Were brass impregnable . . .
—SHAKESPEARE,
King Richard II, III, ii.

BRASS— / bras, bräs / *n* [ME *bras, OE braes;* c. OFris *bres* copper, MLG *bras* metal] **1:** any of various metal alloys consisting mainly of copper and zinc **2:** a utensil, ornament, or other article made of such an alloy **3:** *Mach.* a replaceable semicylindrical shell, usually of bronze, used with another such to line a bearing; a half bushing **4:** *Music.* **a.** a musical instrument of the trumpet or horn family **b.** such instruments collectively or in a band or orchestra **5:** *Brit.* **a.** a memorial tablet or plaque incised with an effigy, coat of arms, or the like **b.** *Slang.* money **c.** *Slang.* a prostitute **6:** *Furniture.* any piece of ornamental or functional hardware, as a drawer pull, made of brass **7:** metallic yellow; lemon, amber, or reddish yellow **8:** *U.S. Slang.* **a.** high-ranking military officers **b.** any very important officials **9:** *Informal.* excessive assurance; impudence; effrontery—*adj* **10:** of, made of, or pertaining to brass **11:** using musical instruments made of brass **12:** having the color brass—**brass′ish** *adj.*

Chapters

1

WHAT?

Richard was all for San Juan or St. Croix, but Jessie held out for every girl's right to one honeymoon in Niagara Falls (she said "girl" bravely, taking advantage of the technicality); so Niagara Falls it turned out to be, Richard giving in without a fight. He was so much in love he would have agreed to Hanoi.

Ellery received his father's cable in an Istanbul hotel room and collapsed on the bed. He was on a planetary junket, nibbling at police chiefs for gourmet crimes, and he had encountered no criminological recipe so outré as the Inspector's announcement. His first thought was of old fools; but when he flew to New York he found Jessie Sherwood to be, not an old man's nubile folly, but a brisk and buxom dear approaching fifty, with a young voice and young eyes, full of soft humor and authority, and without duplicity or doubts. They scouted the opposition for a moment, decided there was none, and fell into each other's arms.

The couple were married in Jessie's little church in the Village, and afterward Ellery gave them a reception at the Algonquin, out of an obscure sentiment toward the memory of Frank Case and the Round Table, in a suiteful of spring flowers. Jessie wore an Irish lace dress the color of blue violets, like her eyes, and the Inspector a summer tuxedo (peevishly vetoing Ellery's overenthusiastic suggestion of a cummerbund), and Ellery had the unique experience of giving his father away. The minister out of the quaintness of his Episcopal heart spoke of the blessings of matrimony "in the summer of our content," which Jessie thought a beautiful way of putting it, while her groom glared at the man of God, who was a good twenty years younger than he and could afford to be patronizing.

The continuation of the beginning was very, very satisfactory. The mighty Falls roared an unending welcome and offered them its shiniest sunlight, rainbow, and mist. And the fat Indian woman squatting near the railing sold them pillows

9

stuffed with pine needles that scented their double bed with sanctification.

When they got back from the honeymoon, looking well-fed, they went to the Queen apartment. Jessie had given hers up, putting her things in storage against the undiscussed future. It kept seeming as if there would always be time enough to talk about it.

"Home." Jessie crooned over the word. Then she clucked over the dust and began bustling about opening windows.

The old man dumped their bags. "Is it?"

"Why, Richard, whatever do you mean?"

"What are we going to do about Ellery?" So it came out.

"Oh, pooh," Jessie said. "I made up my mind long ago. Ellery will live with us, and that's that." She went hunting for a dustcloth.

"Maybe he will," the Inspector mumbled, "and then again maybe he'll have something to say about it. He usually does." And he began thumbing through the accumulation of mail he had found waiting for him. "We'll see."

"We won't see," Jessie said, reappearing. "You haven't lost a son, you've gained a wife."

"It's beginning to sink in," the Inspector said with a grin. "All right, let's say it's settled for the time being."

"Why does it have to be temporary? Where would we get an apartment these days we could afford? Even with me working—"

"With you what?" the retired Inspector cried.

"Working."

"You're not going back to nursing! I want a wife, not a proctologist's plumber. My police pension'll be enough, along with what I've stashed away. I didn't marry you to watch you carry bedpans for a lot of neurotic women—or *men!*—and don't you forget it, Jessie Queen."

"Yes, Richard," Jessie said meekly. But she thought: I will. We'll need the money. "What's wrong?"

He was glaring at one of the envelopes. "This is addressed to Miss Jessie Sherwood. Your first letter, and they don't pay me the courtesy of using my name!"

"Forwarded by Registry. It's probably some charity asking for money. I'm on all sorts of lists."

It was not a plea for money. Jessie looked, and frowned, and looked again. "I'll be darned."

"What is it, Jessie"

"Look at this."

This turned out to be a $100 bill.

"And that."

10

And that was half a $1000 bill.

The Inspector frowned at the pretty portraits, too. Experience had taught him that mysteries starting out with unsolicited lucre had a way of turning nasty toward the end, if not sooner. For fillip, the original of the $1000 bill had been scissored down the middle of Grover Cleveland's bust with a pinking shears in three op-art-looking jags.

"Richard, whatever can it mean?"

He was holding the bills up to the light off the end of his nose. "They're not counterfeits. How should I know? There's got to be some explanation. Look in the envelope, Jessie. There must be a note."

There was, and they touched heads bending over it. Unfolded, it became two sheets of vellum notepaper bearing a heavily engraved gold crest, all very impressive; or it would have been impressive if it had not had the foxed look of paper that has been lying around for a generation. The body of the letter was typewritten, as was the address on the envelope.

"Out of somebody's attic, looks like. Read it aloud, Jessie." The Inspector's reading glasses were over near the old leather chair. "Damn my eyes!" He regularly damned each part of his anatomy that surrendered to his years; this year it was his eyes.

Jessie's soft voice gave the contents of the note a femininity that rather got in the way of its style. " 'Dear Miss Sherwood,' " the foxed vellum said. " 'You will doubtless think it odd to receive an invitation from someone you do not know. I give you my word, however, that this is all very much to your interest.

" 'I invite you herewith to visit me at The House of Brass, my ancestral home near Phillipskill, New York.

" 'The $100 bill enclosed will serve to cover your traveling expenses. As for the missing half of the $1000 bill, it will be presented to you at the expiration of your visit. Call it a souvenir of what I think I may assure you will be an unusual experience.

" 'Taxis are available at either the Tarrytown or Phillipskill railroad stations, although Phillipskill is somewhat nearer. If you should decide to come by motor, take the second turn on your left after passing the Old River Inn on the Albany Post Road; then the first turn to the right, which is marked by a sign that says Private Road. As for water transportation, the old boat landing has been in disrepair for many years, and I cannot vouch for its safety.

" 'May I hope to expect you as soon as possible. Your arrival or absence will reply for you. In the latter case, of course, the halved $1000 bill will be of no use to you. In any case, you may retain the $100 bill.

Yours faithfully,
Hendrik Brass' "

The signature was old-man shaky, Jessie observed—an old-fashioned old man, she thought, from the language. She remarked this to Richard, who went for his glasses to see for himself.

"An old boy, all right. And of the old school. I take it you don't know a Hendrik Brass?"

"Never heard of him."

The Inspector reached for the telephone. "Velie?" he said to the Sergeant when the familiar basso blasted his ear. "Sure I'm back! Fine, she's fine. Listen, Velie—yes, I'll tell her. Remember that Fifth Avenue place called The House of Brass? What became of it. How about a man named Hendrik Brass?—Hendrik, ending in *ik*. You're a fat lot of help. Sure, first chance we get." He hung up. Jessie looked at him anxiously.

"The House of Brass used to be a high-toned jewelry store on Fifth Avenue, like Tiffany's and Cartier's. You had to have real moola to walk in there, Jessie. As I recall the place, it specialized in gold—solid gold services, that sort of stuff. They closed the shop years ago. Velie says they never reopened. Not in New York, anyway."

"But the letter talks about The House of Brass as if it's a place to live in, Richard."

"Doesn't he call it the ancestral home? I guess he just uses the old firm name for it."

Jessie's little nose twitched like a rabbit's. "I swear, Richard, I don't know what to do about this."

"I know what I'd do."

"What?"

"Send the money back and forget it."

"Would you really?" In spite of herself, Jessie felt a lick of disappointment. Her life had been a succession of stuck movie frames—night duty, whining women, unsavory bedpans, men patients who either pinched your bottom or looked as if they would like to, and the eternal triangle of nurse, intern, and supervisor. What her life had lacked was the unexpected, and here it was being offered her on a silver platter, or rather in a gold-crested letter. And Richard, dear new husband, was saying to send the bright bills back and forget the whole thing. "Oh, Richard," Jessie heard herself say in a rush, "let me!"

He was wonderful. He looked at her with his bushy-browed stare; then the whole hard face melted and ran,

12

and he took her in his arms. "How could I ever deny you anything, honey? But my advice is to get more information. How about giving this Hendrik Brass a ring and finding out first if he's got all his marbles? You can sometimes tell just from the way they sound. I'll call for you if you want."

"Would you, darling?"

"You bet," he said; and jumped for the phone.

But Westchester Information had no listing for a House of Brass or a Hendrik Brass, and he set the phone down with a scowl. "If not for the cash, I'd say it was a practical joke. Jessie, I don't *want* to deny you, but . . ."

Men had to be male, especially new husbands; Jessie was not alarmed. Instead, she kissed him. "I'm eaten up by plain nosiness, darling. Don't tell me you aren't."

"If you think I'd let you go traipsing off by yourself—"

"I wouldn't dream of it. Oh, Richard, this sounds like an adventure! What a thrilling way to start our married life."

How right she was.

"DeWitt Alistair" sounded like a made-up name in a third-rate play played by a fourth-rate company. But it happened to be Alistair's legal monicker, which he used only when the mark needed a particular kind of softening up. As it had turned out, he would have been better advised to use something that sounded as if it came out of *Pilgrim's Progress*, like John Repentance or Reuben Disappointment.

To make matters grittier, Mrs. Alistair, who had had her doubts from the beginning, kept throwing the biter-bit bit in his teeth. She managed this feat without opening her mouth, an accomplishment that few appreciated but her husband, who had long since given up admiring it.

So the Alistairs were not in connubial harmony when they entered the lobby of the shabby-genteel hotel in the West 60s that Alistair had insisted reflected their working image and that, it now appeared with bitter clarity, their true image could not afford. The fish had taken their bait, slipped the hook, and vanished downstream, leaving them hungry and furious. The immediate problem was to find a less knowledgeable trout, and the wherewithal to land him. They paid only perfunctory attention to the impressive-looking envelope in their box. Impressive-looking envelopes did not impress them. They had mailed too many of them.

Both were thinking deeply.

Upstairs, in their shabby-genteel room, Alistair tossed the envelope on the bed, sat down near the dusty window, and turned to the racing news in the paper he had picked up from a lobby chair. Mrs. Alistair unlocked one of their two suitcases. From it she took an electric plate, a whistling teakettle minus the whistle, a spoon, two plastic cups, and a nearly empty jar of instant coffee. She filled the kettle at the tap in the bathroom, placed it on the hot plate, plugged the plate in at the outlet behind her husband's chair, and returned to the bathroom to repair her face, which was aristo-cratic-plain, well-preserved, noncommittal, and served her purposes. When she came out she planted herself before her spouse and looked at him. After a moment he lowered the paper.

"Well, what are you looking at?" DeWitt Alistair had a thunky voice, with a British edge to it that gave off a faint thud of counterfeit. It was. He had been born in Weehawken, New Jersey.

"Well," Elizabeth Alistair replied, "not very much." Her speech was entirely unaffected. What there was of it.

"There you go again!"

"Haven't said a word."

"Haven't you!"

"Quote me."

"I'll clip you!"

His wife seemed undaunted. "What do we do now, Machiavelli?"

"I've got to think about it," he said shortly.

"You won't find the answer in the harness entries."

"Let me alone, will you!"

"Any money left?"

He returned to his newspaper, shrugging.

Mrs. Alistair spooned out the coffee, added the water, stirred, and set one of the cups down at his elbow. Then she did the same for herself. All in an exhausted way. It was one of their longest dialogues in months.

She sat down on the bed and sipped her brew, giving herself completely over to thought. The process was evidently not agreeable; it foretold disaster for someone.

Suddenly she picked up the letter and opened it.

Alistair grunted something unpleasant to himself and turned the page. He looked like Walter Pidgeon, but with mean little eyes like a *corrida* bull. He was not a good man to meet in an alley. Or to play cards with.

"DeWitt."

"What now, for God's sake?" He glanced over. She was holding up a mint $100 bill and what looked remarkably like half a mint $1000 bill. He extended his hand quickly. She gave him two sheets of rusty-looking vellum notepaper. The bills she retained.

14

"I'll take the whole one," he said. "You can keep the half."

Mrs. Alistair smiled at his transparency. She handed over the $100 bill and tucked the mutilated bill away in her cleavage. Alistair held the $100 bill up to the light. Then, without comment, he placed it in his wafer wallet and turned to the letter. When he had finished reading the letter he stored it carefully in his breast pocket.

"What do you think, Liz?"

"Come-on."

"I'm not so sure."

"That's an improvement," she said, and rose.

"Nothing to lose. And there's the other half of the grand."

"Pigeon bait," she said reflectively.

"What can he get out of us? So we bite. Agreed?"

She shrugged.

Alistair picked up the telephone, said, "Time, please," listened, and hung up. "Twelve minutes to checkout," he said to his wife, and rose, too.

Elizabeth Alistair washed the cups and spoon and dried them on a hand towel, deposited them in the smaller suitcase along with the jar of coffee and the hot plate, and locked the case. Her husband put on his Tyrolean hat and charcoal-gray Wales of Boston weatherproof, and picked up the larger of the two cases. His wife went to the closet and got out her Russian lynx coat, a memento of a bygone bonanza which she kept in rack-new condition. She tucked the beige velvet toque carefully on her dyed hair, looked around, picked up the smaller case and, as an afterthought, her husband's stolen newspaper, and preceded him from the room.

Neither looked back.

It was indicative of Dr. Hubert Thornton's quality that the patients of the South Cornwall Medical Group called him "Doc," while they addressed his three medical partners as "Doctor." To the partners this was symptomatic of his weakness, and they were forever chiding him about it. "All right, so you're a kindly old g.p.," the heart and lungs man of the Group jeered. "But do you have to lay it on so thick, Hube? It makes the rest of us look like medical sharks."

"I don't try to," Hube Thornton protested. "It just comes out that way."

"Take the Andersons' bill. It's been deliquent for seven months. What's so great about the Andersons? You sleeping with Mrs. Anderson or something?"

Thornton flushed. "Mrs. Anderson has a prolapsed uterus and a peptic ulcer," he said stiffly.

15

"Neither stopped her from buying two cases of bourbon and Scotch for that wingding they threw last Saturday night. If the dame can buy booze in case lots she can damn well pay her medical bill. The trouble with you, Hube, is you're trying to be South Cornwall's Albert Schweitzer. Who's going to pay our bills?"

"You're right, of course." And Thornton took out his fat old Waterman pen and wrote the Medical Group his personal check for the amount of the Andersons' bill.

It made for an embarrassed silence.

"That ties it," said the pediatrician of the Group with a snap of his jaws on the cigar in his mouth. "You have a genius for making me feel like a son of a bitch, Hube. You can take your check and shove it." He tore it up. "All right, men, we wait some more. Hube Thornton Rides Again."

The tall surgeon of the Group shook his Ivy-League-barbered head. "Hube, you should have gone into the Public Health Service. You spend more time in that clinic and make more night calls than the rest of us put together."

"Somebody has to," Dr. Thornton said feebly.

"You were born in the wrong century. You know you've got bags under your eyes an inch thick? Ozzie here insists you're an incipient TB. And why the hell don't you get your glasses fixed? You look like a Skid Row bum. And buy another suit?"

They ran through a long list of chronic grievances.

Thornton remained silent. He had tried more than once to withdraw from the Group for the sake of the common weal; to his bewilderment they always jumped on him as if he had proposed that they start performing illegal abortions.

He was forty-seven years old, scalpel-thin, with hair turning to cancer gray and a high-temperature mustache that was too much trouble to keep trimmed—hell, he thought with a chuckle, if it doesn't make me look like Dr. Schweitzer at that! Food meant nothing to him, although a brandy once a night, before bedtime, usually did. The eyeglasses charge was also justified: a shaft had snapped months before and he had mended it with adhesive; he had simply never found the time to have a new shaft fitted. As for the sartorial lapse, you always had to have a suit pressed or a Merthiolate spot removed, or waste good time buying a new one.

After a while Hube Thornton stuffed his hairy ears to the three-man recitation of his vices and virtues—virtues that always seemed, in their view, to be vices in themselves—and thought of other things. He was brought back to time and place by a sharp pronunciation of his name.

"What?" Thornton said.

"I said," the pediatrician said, "that girl out there with the hairdo is one continuous pain in the gluteus. Put a letter addressed to you in my mail. Third time this week." He tossed a heavy envelope over. "Maybe it's someone paying a bill, God forbid."

His partners suddenly began to talk golf, lying their heads off. Dr. Thornton opened the envelope. He took out what was in it and gargled.

"Good God!" the heart-and-lungs man exclaimed. "It's money! Hube's caught himself an honest patient."

"Honest my foot," the pediatrician cried. "He's loaded. Say, isn't that thousand dollar bill cut in half?"

"At least the hundred's whole," the surgeon said. "But who pays in cash these days?"

"Where?" Thornton paused in his reading. "I mean, where is Phillipskill?"

"Near Tarrytown," said the h.-and-l. man. "House call? With that kind of fee, I'd make it myself."

"I'll be jiggered." Thornton wagged his big head. "Will you for heaven's sake read this?"

The two sheets of vellum were passed around. There were appropriate comments from his colleagues.

"But you can't get away from this money," Thornton said. "They certainly look genuine. Do you suppose he's psycho?"

The three modern doctors exchanged glances. The surgeon nominated himself spokesman.

"Hube," he said earnestly, "here's your chance."

"Chance for what?"

"To get off the treadmill. Why not take the guy up on this? He's probably an oddball millionaire who was on the right side in the Medicare fight. How about it, Hube? Hell, it'll be a ball."

"Besides," said the pediatrician, "you can use a vacation."

"And how," said the heart-lungs man. "Or one of these days, by God, I'll find your sputum full of mycobacterium bugs, and then you'll get a vacation that'll cost you."

"But I can't just go off! What about my practice?"

"We'll get Joe Adelson to fill in—he's full of the milk, too," said the surgeon. "And if there's still some slack, Hube, we'll take it up. Go on, for once in your life act human. What have you got to lose but your bags?"

"My clinic patients—"

"We'll handle them, too."

It took them thirty-five minutes by the office clock to talk Hube Thornton into responding affirmatively to the mysterious Mr. Brass's summons. By that time the outer office was jammed with the usual early-morning prothrombins, low-

17

grade upper respiratory infections, and emergency hangovers, and Hube said all right, but only if they let him clear his appointments calendar for the day, even if it took him, Schweitzer-wise, far into the night.

Miss Openshaw found the squarish envelope in her letter box in the vestibule, mixed in with the usual pleading letters from the Institute for the Indigent Blind, the Ocapoosa Indian Mission School, the Leper Hostel, and other desperate institutions of good works, and set about climbing the two flights of the brownstone to her maidenly apartment.

En route she had to brave the morning ordeal, which consisted in passing Mr. Bailey's apartment door. The man was appalling, with all too obvious designs on every female spoor whose path he crossed. It made her blood run cold to see that mysterious door open a crack and the evil brown eye leer out at her.

Sometimes he opened his door to the fullest, so that she could see him in all his male vulgarity. He had a coarse way of not buttoning his shirt, exposing the ugly hair on his chest. Once he had actually dared to accost her. Oh, he had been clever. An innocent-sounding "Good morning, neighbor." It was the only time she had ever heard his voice, which was deep and gruff and—oh, what word was there but *male*!— and she had heard herself with absolute stupefaction asking him up to her apartment for tea. To her apartment! What under Heaven had come over her? By a miracle she had gone unscathed. Actually, the man had refused. She could picture, only too graphically what would have happened had he accepted her inane invitation. It had been a narrow escape.

Miss Openshaw's step slowed as she approached the Bailey door on the landing this morning and, inevitably, passed it. That was strange, because her heart was bumping and her mind was telling her that she must hurry before that door opened and he revealed himself in all his disgusting hairiness; but somehow her limbs would not obey her.

Fortunately, nothing happened. His door remained closed, and Miss Openshaw went on up the other flight to her door, clutching the mail and her fears to her bosom.

Cornelia Openshaw was thirty-nine and, as the saying went, "never kissed"—at least since childhood, and even then only sparingly by her mother, who had favored boys, and never by a father who was as remote as Jehovah. She gave the impression of being not so much plain as unused. Ordinarily she was mouse-mannered, but there were times when she seemed touched by a live wire; at such times she appeared about to leap. She was always heavily made up; she

18

spent hours at her vanity, which was crowded with choice items from Helena Rubinstein's cosmetic counters. She invariably made her toilette before her morning descent to the mailbox and the dangerous crossing of the first-floor landing.

She hurried into her apartment, locked her three locks, slipped the guard-chain into its slot, and ran over to pull down a windowshade that showed four inches of daylight. She had a horror of Peeping Toms, although of late she had noticed with some perturbation that she was becoming forgetful about the shades.

She sat down on her Regency sofa to go through the mail. The tea she had poured before going downstairs was cold, and she rose to heat it; there was no urgency about the mail; she never received any of importance except the modest estate checks on which she lived. When the tea was hot, she reseated herself and, sipping daintily, reached for the first envelope.

It was heavy and squarish.

The elegance of the vellum warmed her. One rarely saw notepaper of such quality in these days of mass cheapness. Whom could it be from?

When the money fell out she gasped.

She read the letter avidly.

Its contents immediately suffused her. Who was Hendrik Brass? It sounded like a foreign name, and Cornelia Openshaw did not like foreign names. Beware the Greeks bearing gifts. . . . Gifts. Of course! It was the beckoning candy to the innocent child, with who knew what at the giving end. His courtly style might be a lure. After all, he was inviting her to come to a place that was very likely, from the sound of it, miles from a police station—probably in a wooded area, where her body might not be found for years, after his will had been done on her. Miss Openshaw was an indefatigable reader of true crimes, books like *The Boston Strangler* and *In Cold Blood*, shuddering at every detail and trying to imagine the unimaginable others.

The sensible thing to do was to take the letter and money straight to the police.

She reached for the telephone.

But something drew her back—curiosity, or a dollop of common sense in the confusion that made up her diet. There was the aged notepaper. Surely a rapist would not go to such lengths?—and the severed $1000 bill. Why so much? They could only come from wealth, she decided, hereditary wealth, and that way lay Victorian drawing rooms and a tall dark handsome gentleman who invariably dressed for dinner.

The more Miss Openshaw contemplated Hendrik Brass's invitation, the less perilous became the prospect.

In the end, with excitement in her sharp blue eyes, she decided to take the plunge.

Still, there was no point in being foolhardy. Cornelia Openshaw rose from the sofa and went to her Queen Anne desk. Here, seating herself, she wrote out a check for three months' rent, inserted it in an envelope, addressed, sealed, and stamped the envelope, and deposited it in her purse for immediate mailing. Then she took up a sheet of her Tiffany stationery and poised her pen.

Twenty minutes later, with the wastebasket rich with false starts, she read over the irreducible minimum of her final draft. It said:

> *If I am not back by the time*
> *my rent next comes due, please*
> *notify the F.B.I. at once.*
> Cornelia Openshaw

She Scotch-taped the note to the frame of her gilded mirror, attached Hendrik Brass's letter to the mirror, where it would be noticed, packed her alligator suitcase with her frilliest things, notably the lingerie, tucked the whole bill and the bisected bill in her purse, and departed on the dreadful quest.

Like discharged veterans since wars began, Keith Palmer was in a hangup when the letter came. He had had his tour in Vietnam, and the fact that he had come out of it with a whole head was almost beside the point. He could still remember his sweats in the helicopters.

At first they had had him on K.P. at the base five miles from Danang, which was a ball, except for occasional night mortar attacks by Charlie, when you couldn't see a thing except the explosions. Then, with entrenched military logic, they had made him a machine gunner in the birds without a single flight in training. Thereafter it was one crash landing after another. There had been a sort of logic in that, because Keith had come into the service from the junk and scrap iron business. But it was too beautifully logical to have been anything but a coincidence.

One thing, though, they hadn't got him scrubbed. He had won a sprained ankle in one crash, and once he had come down the sole survivor of the crew and been picked up by a rescue craft in exactly sixteen minutes; but that was all. Four of the men with whom he had gone through boot in Tennessee had been shipped back to the States in flag-draped boxes, one had returned an amputee, and one had contracted V.D. during R. and R. in Hong Kong. All Keith had come back with was his life. Of course, there was Joanne waiting, and little Schmulie, as Bill Perlberg called him; but they were another story.

The hangup was that, after Vietnam and the crashing birds, the scrap iron business lost its charm and nothing appeared to take its place. There was a kaleidoscopic succession of stupid jobs, and even one interlude when he hid himself in a freight car headed for nowhere, wife and child notwithstanding (after that one Joanne said, making with the chin, that the next time it happened *she* would take off, with little Sam, and not in any freight car, either); so it had not been all beer and pretzels. What to do? That was Keith's preoccupation when the letter came from Phillipskill, New York.

He fingered the crackling C-note and the scissored $1000 bill unbelievingly as he sat in the dinky office over whose front door the *Palmer & Perlberg* sign still waved (Bill, his ex-partner, had come back from Vietnam to the firm still hoping). Keith had dropped in on Bill expressly to show him Hendrik Brass's letter, and also because it was a dismal Saturday morning and Joanne was home and he had changed Schmulie's diaper six times and Joanne was in one of her I-dare-you-to-start-something moods.

"What do you think, Bill?"

Bill was digesting the letter in his slow way. "Reads to me like a kook."

"Not to me," Keith said. Outwardly they were both twenty-five, good clean American boys, the second-squad football team type. "To me it's something out of an English novel."

Bill shook his head. "The Englanders don't throw their dough around. It has to be an American kook. What are you going to do about this?"

"What would you do, Bill?"

"I'm damned if I know. It sounds real cool, but I have our junk business to run."

"I told you it's not mine any more! Anyway—"

"There's two anyways. Joanne and Schmulie. Have you talked this over with the frau?"

"I chickened out. She doesn't know a thing about it."

"Sounds like one hell of a marriage. Why?"

"Because she's a working wife. What do you think we're living on? We can't get by on the few bucks I'm making working for the town on the roads."

"I'd talk to her."

"You're not married to her."

21

"To anybody," Bill said with fervor, "and don't you forget it."

"I can't just walk out and go chasing after the missing half of a thousand bucks that may be phoney for all I know. Not after that freight train. Or can I?"

"You're beginning to sound like that schmo Hamlet."

"Joanne wouldn't go for another walkout. She thinks I'm an all-around strikeout as it is."

"Then there's your answer."

"On the other hand, how can I ignore it?" Keith said, nursing on his knuckle. "It's such a gorgeous-sounding setup."

"For what? That's the question."

"Sure it's the question. That's what makes it so gorgeous."

"Look, man, you'd better make up your mind."

"That's why I'm talking to you, isn't it?" Keith Palmer asked his best buddy bitterly.

There was a Great Outdoorsy something about Lynn O'Neill, especially when she laughed, which she was doing now. She evoked motion pictures of long chestnut hair blowing in the prairie wind, Conestoga wagons, rifles across long-skirted knees, and horses. She gave off scent clouds of newmown timothy during morning breezes. It was all done with mirrors, because Lynn was a strictly seventh-decade-of-the-century girl. The last time she had been on a horse he had thrown her, cracking three ribs. That's the kind of decade it was.

She was laughing at the time she opened the squarish envelope—not, certainly, at what fell out of it, because that produced a squeal, but at the whole ridiculous notion of buying life insurance. She had nothing against life insurance per se, but she was confidently going to live to be a hundred, or at least fifty, and whom would she leave insurance to, anyway? And if she had been inclined toward that sort of deal, she surely would not dream of buying a policy from Tom, or Dick, or—no—his name was Harry. Harry was a calculating drip. Lynn wouldn't have given him a sale, let alone a date, if he had been the only whole man in Wagon Springs. He had red hairs creeping out of his nose, and a domed head from which protruded the eyes of a cuttlefish, of a nauseatingly poisonous green.

"Hey!" Harry said. "That's U.S. money you're throwing around, Miss O'Neill."

"It just fell out," Lynn said. "Would you excuse me? I don't ordinarily open my mail while listening to people, but this seems so queer I'm dying of curiosity."

22

"Take your time," Harry said, performing marvels with his skinny neck.

Lynn read Hendrik Brass's letter. She read it a second time. Then she opened her mouth in a perfect O and said, "Oh!" and "Oh, my!" and read it a third time.

"Somebody leave you a bundle?" Harry asked, panting.

"Not exactly," Lynn said. "Not ever exactly. Oh, I don't know what to do about this."

"Allow me," Harry said, and to her astonishment he plucked the two sheets of vellum paper from her hand and began to read the letter.

"Hey," Lynn said, topaz eyes sparkling. "That's my letter."

"My advice is to keep the dough and throw the letter away. Now about this policy—"

"Some other time," Lynn said, and rose.

"Then we'll sleep on this for a while?"

"You sleep on it, Harry" said Lynn, still burned about the letter; and she marched to the door. When she came back, sans Harry, she picked up the $100 bill and the pinked $1000 bill and read the letter for the fourth time. Out West, where men were men, Lynn had acquired plenty of experience fighting off temptation; could this Brass character be on the make? He sounded old, which did not take him off the hook; the old ones were often the stickiest. On the other hand, there was a kind of humorous sweetness about his style that did not seem to fit with advanced lechery. All in all, it might turn out a gas.

What decided Lynn finally was economics. Worry did not form a significant part of her nature, but the need to eat did, and the fact was she had been one of a number of low-seniority employees who had just received their severance pay, along with the usual printed form of regret.

Her geographical distance from Phillipskill, New York— wherever that was—made flying, and even the moribund railroad, a luxury that would deplete her meager savings; she did not know whether $100 would cover the transportation, but she did know that a bus was the cheapest way to travel; so she telephoned the terminal and got facts and figures, and then she set about tying off knots.

Go East, young woman, Lynn O'Neill said to herself as she packed, and see what gives with this Hendrik Brass.

23

2

WHERE?

Richard and Jessie Queen spanked sedately along in the Mustang.

Jessie had allowed herself one luxury upon changing names: she had traded in her droopy Dodge and bought the new car, which was fire-bucket red, red-bucket-seated, and sported every gadget in Mr. Ford's repertoire. Richard, whose automotive needs until his retirement had been taken care of by the City of New York, greeted the Mustang like an eight-year-old on Christmas morning.

Being an old-fashioned man, he was taking an old-fashioned route, the Saw Mill River Parkway. There was probably a shinier way to go, but the old Saw Mill had served him lo these many years, and by God it would serve him now.

It was a day as crisp as peanut brittle, and the Inspector had to admit that his blood was crackling. The crackle was only a little damped by the small encyclopedia of facts he had collected at the 42nd Street Library and a newspaper morgue of his acquaintance.

"You're thinking," Jessie said accusingly. "What about?"

"These Brass monkeys."

"Then isn't it time to let me in on what you've found out, Richard? Seeing that it's my letter."

"They came from Holland originally, name of van der Bras or van den Bras. Eventually it turned into a double *s*, without the fancy stuff."

Jessie settled herself, snuggling. The queerness of the mystery had long since made simple nosiness turn to alarm. For the hundredth time she counted the blessings of her union with this admirable man. How had she ever lived without him?

"Go on," Jessie said.

The original migration, the admirable man went on, had come two centuries ago. The Brasses had been metalworkers even then. Having arrived in patroon country well-off, it was not long before they were rich; and with their affluence came

24

the purchase of the present estate, which lay between the then small villages of Tarrytown and Phillipskill. They soon outgrew the house. In a few decades it swelled to baronial proportions, with one wing given over entirely to workshops. Inevitably their creations included the use of precious stones. But they became best known for their gold and sterling pieces, and later platinum.

Jim Fiske was reputed to have spent at least five hundred thousand of his legally stolen dollars at The House of Brass on his statuesque companion, Josie Mansfield. Boss Tweed, the story went, lavished almost as much on his daughter for wedding gifts. But on the whole the clientele of The House were respectable monoliths of finance like rufous-nosed old J.P. Morgan the Elder.

"Then these Brasses must be multimillionaires," Jessie said, looking relieved, as if the possession of multimillions gave automatic absolution from wickedness.

The Mustang was galloping now, and the Inspector took time out to admire the Hudson at its loveliest. "Could be," he said. "It's hard to get rid of that kind of money. Although I got the feeling the family went to pot. I do know there's only one Brass left kicking, this Hendrik, at least up in Phillipskill. He's lived there with one servant for more than ten years now. Sort of a hermit existence."

"Just one servant in a place like that?"

"That's what the news story I dug up said. Seems he takes care of the old man and the house, too."

"How old is he?"

"Who, Brass? Must be seventy-six by this time."

"And the two of them rattle around in a *castle*?"

"It's screwier than that, Jessie. Some local people interviewed by the last reporter to nose around claimed the chimneys in most of the layout show no smoke, sometimes in the dead of winter. But they say there's always smoke from the chimney over the workshop wing."

"Sounds like somebody out of the Middle Ages," Jessie said with an uncertain smile. "I'll bet he walks around in a fur gown with little stars all over it, and a skullcap on his head."

"I don't like how any of it sounds," said Richard Queen in his old inspector's voice. "You sure you want to go through with this, Jessie?"

"I feel the same way, Richard." Jessie even managed to shudder, which under the circumstances was not difficult. "But now that we've come so far, it won't hurt to take a peek, will it? We can always say, 'No, thank you,' and leave."

25

He snorted and began hunting for the Albany Post Road. Eventually he found it, and they bowled along in a thickening silence.

"There it is!" Jessie said suddenly. "That tavern, Richard."

The Old River Inn had come upon them almost by stealth. It was a sprawling structure of weathered stone and brick, with a wooden gallery that sagged like an old woman's abdomen.

"Didn't he say the second turn to the left after passing the Old River Inn?"

"Damned if I know. Better look at the letter."

Jessie looked, and nodded. "Second to the left."

They parted company with the Post Road to plunge into a rapidly aging past. The paving vanished, the road grew unpredictable, clutching trees tried to get at them from both sides; in one place, a sudden wooden bridge took them precariously over black water. It was Sleepy Hollow country, all right. Jessie had not the least trouble imagining the Headless Horseman "in the very witching time of night" in pursuit of a terrified Ichabod Crane on laboring Old Gunpowder.

"Richard, you almost went past! The *first* turnoff, he said. To the right. There, where it says Private Road on the sign."

The Inspector swore and steered into the byroad. There were more carnivorous trees, an ever-narrowing lane, and everything gone to seed; finally, a colicky bend in the road ... and there it was, a branch of old Europe grafted onto the American landscape.

The House of Brass was made up of a series of nested buildings snuggling into one another like whelps at their dam's teats. The original building was low and long, with fieldstone walls and a shingled upper story capped by a gambrel roof which swooped down in two stages from a high ridgepole; the major slope was pierced by a soldierly line of dormer windows. The gable ends were clapboard; each slope-edge of the roof was staggered in a series of setbacks, looking for all the world like flights of foreshortened steps, as on Washington Irving's Sunnyside.

From this mother house ran a family of ells, each a house in itself, it seemed, each with its own gambrel roof, each part-fieldstone, part-shingle, part-clapboard, even part-brick. Two of the roofs descended into "kickups," either to avoid darkening the windows below or to shed rainwater from the house; they made Jessie think of the turned-up caps on the Old Dutch Cleanser labels. And all over the roofs, like a bumper crop of mushrooms, rose whitewashed chimneys of different heights and shapes, tall, thin, short, squat, all making erect silhouettes against the sky. Each room of this vast dwelling, it appeared, must have its own fireplace. There were at least thirty chimneys.

The front door of the maternal building was strangest of all. It was of solid, blinding brass. Even before they pulled up in the Mustang they could see that the brass was elaborately decorated in a design that made Jessie think of a medieval tapestry. Brass! Of course. Someone—if not Hendrik Brass, then one of his forebears—had exercised a sense of humor in a sort of architectural pun.

Jessie remarked rather happily about this to her husband as they parked, but all she elicited was a grunt. The Inspector's lifelong chase of wickedness had made him suspicious of all deviations from the conventional; the great brass door was only the climax of a whole chapter of deviations, as far as he was concerned; and Jessie sighed, already knowing him well, and wondered if the scowl was going to become a permanent feature of his dear face.

There was no sign of life.

"You know, darling," Jessie said as she got out and stretched the legs her husband admired so, "this must once upon a time have been a charming place."

"Once," her husband said, "upon one hell of a long time!" Everything looked neglected except the brass door, which glittered as if it had been polished to its highest luster only that morning. Even the vines that crawled over the walls were rachitic-looking. And where there must once have been neat Dutch gardens ran a wasteland of weeds.

The Inspector stumped across the blackened red bricks unevenly paving the driveway, seized the king-sized knocker, and let fly. As he waited, he saw that the tapestry-like design on the brass door was really an arrangement of representations of scales, crucibles, the kind of hammers used in goldbeating, graving tools, and the like. Even the knocker was decorated with them.

Jessie, who at that moment was not interested in doors or knockers, hung back, expecting anything and hoping for nothing at all, an excuse to turn round and go away.

But there was something.

It really did jump, that door, springing like a bird into flight. And there—Jessie almost thought of him as It—there he stood ... whoever he was ... filling the doorway with little to spare, an outsized figure of a man that would have been majestic if it had not given off an effluvium of not quite human stupidity.

For one awful moment Jessie heard herself giggle. The apparition was too, too much; she could not decide whether he looked like Mary Shelley's monster or Lurch, the butler on the old Addams Family TV show.

In her nursing career Jessie had seen her quota of patients suffering from dysfunction of the pituitary gland, but usually the condition was restricted to enlargement of the bones of the head and the soft parts of the hands and feet, with the rest of the body relatively normal. This man's acromegaly seemed to have invaded all of him. It was not his fault, naturally, but it did not render him peaceable to the eye. Jessie shut hers for a moment to regain her professional poise. When she opened them the man was looking at her over her husband's head.

Oh, dear, Jessie thought, he saw that. And firmly stepped to the Inspector's side, to reassure the man as well as herself.

He had very little forehead, and small, dull, flawed-looking eyes of a scuffed green, like cheap marbles that had scraped about in a boy's pocket. It was his eyes, Jessie decided charitably, that were responsible for his stupid look. He was wearing the traditional striped apron over a dusty black suit, and a little black tie whose knot was almost buried under his prognathous chin. Undoubtedly Hendrik Brass's factotum.

What Richard Queen thought of Hendrik Brass's factotum could not be detected except by an expert. But Jessie, who was rapidly becoming one, thought she heard an I-told-you-so in his voice.

"We're the Queens."

"Queens?" His voice was froggy, with a booming vibrato, rather like the bass note of a piano that had not been tuned in years. A stained paw went into the striped apron and emerged with a stiffish paper—the same kind of paper, Jessie noted, which Brass had used for his invitation.

There is no Queens on here."

He stepped back, clearly intending to shut the door in their faces. "Hold on there," the Inspector said. "I forgot. I mean you ought to have a Sherwood."

"Sherwood?" The green marbles ran over the paper again. "Yes. Jessie Sherwood."

He backed off. Jessie and Richard stepped over the threshold. The giant immediately presented his bulk to Richard.

"Not you," he said. "Her."

"Now just a minute, please," Jessie said. "No, dear, I'll handle this. Mr. Brass evidently didn't know I'd got married. I don't go anywhere my husband can't go. If Mr. Brass wants me, he'll have to take Mr. Queen too. You march right in there and tell Mr. Brass that."

The oversized lips writhed. "I will go and see," he said, and slammed the door. They had to jump back.

"And you still want to go through with this, Jessie?" Richard asked in a dangerously mild voice.

"Oh, Richard, the poor man can't help it. He was born that way. Let's wait and see what Hendrik Brass is like."

"Anybody who'd hire a guy like that to answer doors has to be a chandelier swinger. Take my word for it, you're stepping into something you'll wish you hadn't."

"Now, darling, you promised—"

"This might even turn out risky. That hulk has a hundred and fifty pounds on me."

"He's probably the most harmless man, darling. I've known loads of acromegalics. They're very gentle people."

"And bright?"

"Yes."

"Well, this one isn't. Whatever's in that head of his, it's not brains. I tell you you can't predict what one like that'll do."

"You sound positively bigoted, Richard Queen! Can't we just wait and see?"

The brass door swooshed inward again, startling them.

"Come."

"The two of us?" The Inspector sounded disappointed.

The man nodded and stepped aside.

"You see, Richard?" Jessie said. "Really, I should have let Mr. Brass know you were coming, too. It would only have been good manners."

The Inspector grunted his opinion of good manners, and they stepped into Nieuw Amsterdam. Or what might have been Nieuw Amsterdam if not for the brass.

Brass winked and flashed everywhere. Articles that might have been true specimens of early and Revolutionary Dutch were transformed by it into things neither authentic nor beautiful, only brassified. Brass handles had even been fitted to old hearth hairbrushes and brooms, and they saw a basket whose original wicker was now a mere lining to a brass container.

They were standing in a wide hall that ran the depth of the house. The front parlor was almost wholly visible through the broad doorway at their left. Its dominant feature was a man-tall fireplace with a brass mantelpiece and brass side-pieces; only practical considerations, they felt, had kept their brass-mad host from plating the old Dutch firebrick and the black iron door to the Dutch oven. But the fire tools were of brass, and so was the wood box.

Brass's man, who had suddenly named himself Hugo, had gone out to the Mustang for their luggage; now, with a bag under each gorilla arm, he nodded at them and led the way to the staircase. It was of the Dutch boxed-in type, dating from the time when the upper floors were used for the storage of provisions, hay, and spinning and weaving materials and consequently did not, in the burgher's view, require heating; the boxing was, of course, laminated with sheets of brass. What had probably been a mahogany handrail had been replaced with a brass one; the original delicate spindles were now brass as well. On the steps, screwed down, were brass foot-plates showing the scratching of many years of use. And what were evidently ancestral portraits, primitives by justifiably forgotten artists, showing patroon and *goede vrouw* faces overlaid with hairnets of fine paint-cracks, marched up the stairwell in step with the risers, each portrait massively reframed in ornamented brass.

The hall upstairs was a cramped place with shadowy crooks where it angled off into the ells; the whole thing boded Tom Thumb bedrooms. Nor were they disappointed. As they followed Hugo past open doorways—some doors were shut—they saw into empty, dim, tiny bedrooms remarkable only for their brassy interiors—doorknobs, beds, lamps, fireplace tools, candlesticks, sconces, snuffers, clock pendulums, cornices, and chandeliers (some of which had been converted to electricity; others were still fitted with gas mantles)—all, all of brass.

Hugo kicked open a door and stumped through, jerking his great head in a follow-me signal, and they found themselves in a miniature sitting room paneled from floor to ceiling in brass, the metal covered with the same designs they had seen on the front door. The little room was furnished with falling-apart Dutch settle-like pieces. The chairs looked as uncompromising as pews.

The giant edged through another doorway which made him stoop, and dropped their bags, the Queens following dumbly into a bedroom. The room looked crowded, as much because it was overfurnished as undersized. The same worn-down furniture was everywhere.

The brass double bed was swollen with featherbedding that looked soft but not quite clean. Nothing looked quite clean. Jessie's heart sank. A few courageous rays of sun managed to get through the dormer-window shutters, which were of the Dutch batten type, with saw-cut openings in the shape of half moons, hearts, and pots of flowers.

To Jessie's relief, the brass chandelier was electrified. At least they would not go blind if they wanted to read something at bedtime. But when she looked around, there wasn't a book to be seen, nor even a magazine. And they hadn't thought to bring any reading matter. Oh, well, Jessie thought, I'll cross that bridge when Richard gets to it.

In one corner lay a huge can of brass polish and a pile of dirty rags. Hugo had apparently been interrupted by their arrival.

"You must buy polish by the case lots, Hugo," Richard Queen remarked with menacing softness. "What is this brass thing with Mr. Brass?"

"I," Hugo said proudly, "made the brass."

"You? Made all of it?"

"Most. Mr. Hendrik taught me. Down there," the long arm descended like an ax, "in the workshop."

"Well, I'll be," the Inspector said. "Okay. When do we get to see your Mr. Hendrik?"

Hugo shook his improbable head. "I am to answer no questions. Mr. Hendrik said to say he would see you all later this afternoon. Meantime you are to unpack and rest."

"See us *all?* All who?"

"All Mr. Hendrik's guests. You are the last."

"How many of us are there? I didn't see any cars outside."

"I have put them in the coach house. I will put yours away, too. Key?" The impossible hand reached.

The Inspector looked stubborn. But then, catching a wifely glance, he handed over the ignition key. Hugo scooped up the rags and polish and left.

Husband and wife engaged in a duel of stares. Jessie decided on a strategic diversion. "Goodness, a girl needs a bathroom. I'd hate to have to use an outhouse," and she investigated another door, which she knew perfectly well must lead to a bathroom, as it indeed did—a surprisingly large one, with a ceiling that made her feel like whoever had been down in the Pit while the Pendulum swung, and with an old room-sized tub replated in brass down to its claw feet, and brass fittings everywhere. She shut the door, wishing she had been married long enough to get over the traditional embarrassments.

Richard hung about outside. "Blast it all, Jessie, the more I see of this setup the less I like it. What do you say? Be a good girl and let's get the hell out of here."

"Without even meeting Mr. Brass?" Jessie said through the door. "Richard." What Richard responded was drowned by the plumbing.

When she came out he was stooped over the nearest leg of the bedstead. "Look at this," he muttered. "The damn bed legs are *screwed* to the floor. I told you this Brass is off his rocker."

"Oh, hush. You know, considering how old this house must be, it's in wonderful condition. The floors don't sag at all. And the ceiling looks so sturdy. . . ." She wanted to mollify

31

him, so she dropped that line and said instead, "But it *is* on the gloomy side."

"You're damn tootin' it is!"

"Do you have to swear about everything, dear?" Jessie sat down on the bed. She sank deep into the ancient counterpane and simultaneously raised a splash of dust. "Whoo! We can't sleep in this, Richard. You throw open those shutters and windows, and I'll dust and air the bed things, and ... What are you doing *now*?"

He was wrestling with a walleyed female van den Bras framed in the ubiquitous brass. He wrestled in vain. "The painting is screwed down, too!"

"I know, dear, I know," Jessie said in the tone she had employed with young women in labor, although she hadn't noticed the screws in the wall at all; and she got him busy with the windows to take his mind off Hendrik Brass.

But the first thing Richard saw when he opened a shutter was their Mustang disappearing with a weird finality, as if driving itself, behind the farthest ell.

It struck another portentous note.

What sort of place had they got themselves into?

3

WHY?

Jessie was stretched out on the aired and cleaned bed when the brazen thunderclap came. She had removed her dress and slipped into one of her trousseau negligees, but the filmy stuff had parted when she turned over in the doze, and Richard was standing over her admiring her C-cups, the length of her lashes, and her other remarkable attributes. The crash made her eyes fly open in telltale terror, and brought him around to the door with an agility that would have done credit to a man half his age.

"What in the world was *that*?" Jessie whispered.

The Inspector uncoiled. "A Chinese gong. Brass, what else? I have a hunch we're about to meet Chief Hazelnut himself."

"Everyone in the parlor!" Hugo was roaring.

When they got downstairs they found six people assembled. Hugo had vanished.

32

The Inspector took inventory. None of the three men present was old enough to be Hendrik Brass. One—large and formidable-looking, with a country squire's complexion and unblinking little eyes—might have been taken for sixty by the innocent; but to the Inspector, who had sized men up for a living, the red-faced man was considerably younger; a hard and shabby life had left its premature mark on his flesh. The second male of the sextet, a stooped and skinny six-footer with a red mustache, wearing horn rims one shaft of which was taped with adhesive, was no more than middle-aged. The third, with the physique of an inactive football player, was in his late or mid-twenties.

Jessie paid more attention to the three women. The one seated in the chair behind which the country squire was standing made her feel uncomfortable on sight. She was in her forties, slim and elegant, the elegance ever so slightly tarnished, with an imperious tilt to her too perfectly coifed, dyed brown-blonde hair and a deadly quiet something in her face. Jessie knew intuitively that they made a pair, legal or otherwise. She did not like them at all.

The second woman, in her late thirties, was so heavily made up that she looked grotesque. Her swift appraisal of Richard as they came in, and her equally swift dismissal of him, made Jessie want to slap her face. The creature immediately went back to what she had evidently been doing before their entrance, devouring the footballish young man with her dental eyes. Jessie put her down as Inhibited Female, probably Spinster, and unquestionably Man-crazy.

The third woman was no more than a girl. Jessie decided to like her. She was pretty, with a fresh look, topaz eyes of spirit, and a pile of natural chestnut hair that begged to be shaken out and brushed. The young man of the group was showing signs of interest; and from the way the girl ignored him Jessie knew that she was pleasantly aware of his interest.

"Welcome to the club," the young man said, advancing with outstretched hand. "I saw you people drive up from my window. My name is Keith Palmer."

"Richard Queen," the Inspector said, shaking Palmer's hand with a vigor that told Jessie the young man had passed muster. "My wife Jessie."

"Mrs. Queen. May I present Mr. and Mrs. Alistair?" He indicated the deadly woman in the far chair and the florid man behind her. "Miss Cornelia Openshaw"—that was Miss Hot-Pants, Jessie nodded to herself, and unmarried as deduced. "Miss Lynn O'Neill"—the fresh-faced girl. "And Dr. Hubert Thornton." And that was the tall stooped man with

33

the broken shaft. "You folks wouldn't know what this is all about, would you?"

The Inspector shook his head. "My wife got a letter from this Brass with money and instructions in it, and that's all we know."

"We all did," young Lynn O'Neill said. "We've compared letters, and they're identical except for the addresses."

"Did anybody here *know* anybody else before today?" Jessie asked.

There was a general disclaimer.

"I don't know why I came." Dr. Thornton lit a cigaret from the end of a butt and tossed the butt into the cave of the fireplace, where a monumental log was blazing away. "The whole thing sounds like the product of hardened arteries to me. I ought to turn around and drive back to South Cornwall."

"Not so smart," Alistair said from behind his wife's chair. He was all smiles, all but his eyes. "There's money in this, and who can't use money?"

Mrs. Alistair said nothing. She's the one to watch, the Inspector decided. She's not so sure there's money in it, but if there is it will be a tossup as to who grabs first, she or her husband.

"Anybody else coming, do you know?" he asked.

"Hugo says we're the lot," Palmer said. "Where is this Brass, anyway? Letting us stew this way."

"Old trick," Mrs. Alistair said suddenly. Then her linear lips clamped shut, as if she had caught herself in an indiscretion.

"Here's Hugo," Lynn O'Neill said, cocking her head. "Who else would sound like the Giant in Jack and the Beanstalk?"

"I wonder what Mr. Brass looks like," Miss Openshaw wondered thoughtfully.

All heads swiveled.

Hugo appeared, a gigantic illusion.

Clinging to his arm was a miniaturized ancient with twiggy arms and legs and a little gray face whose nose seemed bent on making contact with his pointy chin. The face was connected to the shoulders by a long neck that did not look as if it had the strength to support the head. He carried a brass cane that quivered; and he was wearing a faded red velvet jacket with brocaded lapels, a woolen scarf about his shoulders shot with moth holes, and old carpet slippers on his feet. The few white hairs on his bone of a skull were at attention, like the gallant remnants of a defeated regiment.

But the most remarkable thing about Hendrik Brass's appearance was his eyes, or rather the absence of them. They were invisible behind dark glasses of coy, extreme design, more fitting for a bikini-clad beach girl. They concealed half his little face.

"Well, well," Hendrik Brass chirped. And indeed his voice, like the rest of him, made them think of an aged bird. "Are they all here, Hugo?" He seemed to peer.

"Yes, Mister Hendrik."

"Good. I am going to call your names, my friends. Please answer to them." Calling a *roll*? "Mr. Alistair."

"Here," Alistair said at once.

"No, Mr. Alistair, say something more. Repeat your name."

"My name is DeWitt Alistair. Is that all right?"

Brass nodded, and the brass cane twitched. "I believe your wife is with you, sir?"

"My name is Elizabeth Alistair," said Mrs. Alistair. She was staring at him as if she were puzzled.

"Dr. Thornton."

The red-mustached doctor said, "I'm Hubert Thornton, Mr. Brass." He was looking puzzled, too, but it was the puzzlement of a clinician with a problem.

"Miss Cornelia Openshaw? Mr. Keith Palmer? Miss Lynn O'Neill? Miss Jessie Sherwood?—I beg your pardon, Mrs. Richard Queen, I understand. And Mr. Queen?" One by one they humored him. "Good, good, you've all come. Couldn't resist, eh? Well, you'll find out what this is all about right now. I didn't mean it to sound mysterious." He cheeped, and it was as if a sparrow had burst into laughter—a rather wicked sparrow, Jessie thought emotionally "Hugo, you oaf, are you going to let me stand here forever? My chair."

Hugo rushed over to the fireplace, plucked an overstuffed paterfamilias chair of elaborate design (some of the stuffing, Jessie noticed, was coming out) with one hand, and rushed it back to the doorway.

He set it precisely behind the old man, and Hendrik Brass sat himself on the edge of it, gripping his cane between his bony knees. In this position he was facing all of them, but he seemed to be staring into the fire rather than at them, because his head did not move at all during what followed, even when someone spoke.

"It is really a simple matter," he began. "I am the only survivor of the Brass family. I have no heirs. I'm old, I'm sick, and I'm rich. Six million dollars rich. You hear me? Six million. I'd be worth a great deal more," he said with a vicious little tweet, "if the government didn't take big chunks of it and give it away to a lot of greedy foreigners. I'll be damned if I'll let 'em have all of it when I die."

Hugo stood guard behind the armchair, one hand on it as if to be ready should it fall apart suddenly, as indeed it looked as though it might. No one said anything at this point. The $6,000,000 confidence took savoring. Keith Palmer looked incredulous, Dr. Thornton thoughtful, Miss Openshaw delighted, Lynn O'Neill astounded; only the Alistairs retained their sniffy expressions, as if testing the wind and unwilling to believe the evidence of their noses.

"So," continued Hendrik Brass with a smack of his little blue lips. "Of you eight, I have sought out six—you, Mrs. Alistair, and you, Mr. Queen, are here only because of your spouses. Actually, my friends, I set out to locate nine people. My information now is that two of them are dead, and no trace could be found of the ninth, a certain Harding Boyle. Do you follow me?"

He tilted his head at this. There was a general mumble, none of it projectile. What could anyone sensibly say? The old man was either in a high flight of paranoia, or he was pulling their collective legs in a senile joke. The property must once have been impressive, but everything they had seen so far was racked and riddled with age and neglect. To think of this seedy little septuagenarian in his motheaten scarf and worn-down carpet slippers as the possessor of $6,000,000 called for absolute faith.

"Now why did I pick you six out of two hundred million people to stand in line for my money?" their host went on. "Good question? The one you're asking yourselves? I'll tell you why. The reason, my friends, is that each of you is either the son or daughter of someone who gave me a helping hand during a crisis in my life. And yet none of you has ever heard of me. Right? Speak up."

No one spoke up. They were so many children with bubble-gum balloons at their mouths, afraid to breathe and so burst them. There was a fantastic something about Hendrik Brass and his chirping, no doubt helped out by the enormous flicker of the fire and the glitter of the overpowering brass, that made the old Dutch parlor seem like a stage set and everyone in it a character in a play, with Brass its author-producer-director.

Old Hendrik apparently took their silence for applause. "Am I right, too, that your parents are all dead? I'm told they are, or I promise you I'd have had them here instead of you. The virtues of the fathers shall be visited upon the children, eh?" He smacked his lips at his wit.

And DeWitt Alistair said suddenly, as if he had made up his mind to leap a dangerous gap, "Mr. Brass."

"That would be Mr. Alistair," the old man said, staring

36

into his fire; and the Inspector solved one of the mysteries and was irritated with himself. Hendrik Brass was blind. He should have realized it at once from the cane, the dark glasses, the fixity of the old man's head, and his having made each of them say something. "Yes, Mr. Alistair?"

The big man said smoothly, in his thunky voice, "You refer to the six of us as 'standing in line' for your money. What d'ye mean by that?"

"You stand in line, Mr. Alistair, you're waiting. And you don't know if you're going to get to the teller's window before it closes. I may decide to leave my fortune to one of you, or two of you, or all of you, or maybe none of you. Depends."

"On what, Mr. Brass?" Cornelia Openshaw asked suspiciously.

"Just be yourselves is my advice, Miss Openshaw. I warn you, I'm a hard man to diddle."

He flourished his cane, and the firelight caught its brass like a sword.

"Since none of you knows me, or what my connection was with one or both of your parents, I'll tell you." He stabbed with the cane in Jessie's direction. "You, Jessie Sherwood— excuse me, Mrs. Queen—your father was a medical doctor. Dr. Sherwood's skill saved my life when I was very sick. I've never forgotten."

Jessie looked startled. She was about to say something when Richard's pressure on her shoulder stopped her.

"In your case, Dr. Thornton, it was—bless her—your mother. At the lowest time of my life she hauled me to my feet again, restored my confidence in myself. If you're half the man your mother was a woman, Doctor, you're going to be a lucky fellow.

"Mr. Alistair," the old man continued, "it's my pleasure to inform you that one time when I was deep in financial difficulties and had exhausted every possible source of help, your father lent me money I needed. Of course I repaid the debt, but I can never forget that he came to my rescue when everyone else turned me down."

The con man looked profoundly astonished; and the Inspector only a little less so.

"Miss O'Neill," Brass said to the pretty girl, "I spent some years in the West at one time in my life, and it turned out I was accused of stealing a horse. The sheriff saved me from lynching. What's more, he saw to it I got a fair trial—in fact, proved I was not guilty and had to go against public opinion to do it. That sheriff, Miss O'Neill, was your father. I could hardly do less than remember him with gratitude."

37

Lynn O'Neill frowned. But she was silent.

"Keith Palmer." The old man hesitated. "No, I'd best not go into details in your mother's case. Our—well, friendship—meant a great deal to me, a great deal. Let's let it go at that."

"Whatever you say, Mr. Brass," Keith said. The Inspector grinned to himself. Palmer was trying to visualize the old gnome as a young blade seducing a fair maiden, and he was clearly having trouble doing it.

"And that leaves you, Miss Openshaw."

"Yes? Yes?" Cornelia Openshaw said, open-mouthed.

"When I was a young man, I went through a period of extreme depression. I was determined to commit suicide. I actually tried to. Your parents saved my life. A man doesn't forget people like that, even after half a century."

Miss Openshaw turned misty-eyed. "I had a very wonderful father," she said.

Hendrik's old head nodded. They waited. Finally he stirred. "So that's why I've had you all come. . . ."

"For how long, Mr. Brass?" Alistair demanded.

"For as long as I need to make up my mind about you. Testing period, you might say. I'll be watching you all, and I don't need years for that. You're free to leave at any time, of course, and when you do—whether it's before I'm ready or not—you'll at least get the missing half of the thousand dollar bill. You understand that if any of you should leave before I've made a decision, you can forget about sharing in my estate. A gamble worth at least a sixth of six million dollars ought to be worth the investment of a few weeks' time."

"And when you've decided?" Elizabeth Alistair said.

"Then, Mrs. Alistair, I'll make my will. Meanwhile, my friends, we'll try to make you as comfortable as this old place will allow. I'm having some extra day help come in, and Hugo will be doing the cooking. You ask him for whatever you want. Well, well," Hendrik Brass said irritably, "get me up, Hugo! All this talk has tuckered me. Hugo, do you hear, idiot?"

He turned in the paterfamilias chair and lashed out with the cane. Hugo paid no more attention to the blows than if they had been delivered with jackstraws. He hauled the old man gently to his feet; and then, huge jaw hanging, he led his master away like a gigantic hound, out of the parlor and up the staircase, until the sideshow pair disappeared from view.

The Scotch broth was almost cold, the pork was underdone, and the vegetables were cooked to a fare-thee-well.

"If tonight was typical of Hugo's cooking," the Inspector grumbled when he and Jessie finally escaped to their rooms, "we'll die of dyspepsia before that old curlicue makes up his mind. I'm going to have to stock up on milk of magnesia."

"Richard," Jessie said. She sounded so unhappy that he turned in alarm. "There's something I have to tell you."

"I knew it," he exclaimed. "I knew it the minute he talked to you!"

"To tell the truth, I don't know what to make of this. There's been some mistake."

"What mistake, Jessie?"

"Richard, my father never was a doctor. He was a civil service employee all his life—worked in the post office till the day he retired. I was just going to tell that to Mr. Brass when you stopped me."

"A mixup," he muttered. "Whoever did old Brass's tracking for him located the wrong Jessie Sherwood—it's not that uncommon a name. It makes me wonder . . ."

"What, Richard?"

"If you're the only one."

Jessie stared. "You mean others of these people may be the wrong ones, too?"

"Why not? If your case is a sample, no one ever bothered to interview the people Brass wanted found. Sounds to me like a hurry-up job by somebody who didn't give a damn. How would the old man know the difference? Another thing. How come the Harding Boyle that the old boy mentioned wasn't located at all? This is starting to get interesting."

"Oh, you and your—your coppiness," Jessie moaned. "The question is, what do I *do*? I don't see any way out of it. I'll have to tell Mr. Brass I'm not the Jessie Sherwood he's looking for."

"Well, sure," the Inspector said; he was tugging at his ear. "But does it have to be right now?"

"You mean we're to stay on in spite of—?"

"There's something rotten about this setup, Jessie. I'd like to know what it is."

"I simply don't understand you! First you didn't want me to come. Then when I did, you pestered me to leave. And now that you know I have no right to be here at all, you want me to stay!"

"Can't a man change his mind? Honey, you look beat. Why don't you go to bed?"

"And what are you going to do?"

The Inspector managed to look and sound remarkably like his remote son. "Think."

Jessie flounced into the bathroom.

39

Richard Queen seized the opportunity, stealthily, while she was out of sight and hearing, to lock and bolt their doors.

The featherbed was so deeply demoralizing that sleep came late and wakefulness early. The Inspector, who had the habits of a monk, was used to a hard mattress; and Jessie had had to massage too many aching backs to approve of a soft one. With dawn prying at their eyes, Jessie thinking Richard asleep and Richard thinking Jessie asleep, each had turned noiselessly over so as not to disturb the other, when disturbance would have been a relief.

So they were both fully awake and on their feet at opposite sides of the bed, even though it was two hours later, before the echo of the first shriek died away. The shriek, a woman's, was followed quickly by a muffled shouting that they realized had been going on for some time; that was followed by a ponderous running and stumbling about that they now recalled had anticipated the shriek as well. Then there was the second shriek in the same female timbre, and a thud, sex indeterminable.

"I knew it!" Richard snarled, although what it was he had known he did not explain, even to himself. He grabbed his robe. "Jessie, lock the door after me—"

"Not on your life," Jessie panted, grabbing, too. "You're not leaving me in here alone, Richard Queen!"

He went first, shoving her behind him and holding her there. He had an impression of disheveled heads protruding from doorways and peering around the ells at the ends of the hall; but it was no more than a camera flash, because it was immediately shut out by the sight and sound of Hugo thundering up and down the hall like a bull elephant in musth, trumpeting, "He is dead! Dead! Ah, help, help!" while his extraordinary features worked in all directions, totally disorganized. The source of the thud they quickly identified. Miss Openshaw was lying across the threshold of her room in a sheer black nightgown that half revealed her virgin udders; her eyes were shut and the hairnet she had slept in had slipped down over one of them; her lips and what could be seen of her chunky legs were on the blue side. Young Palmer, in pajamas, fortunately opaque, knelt by her, slapping her cheek with one hand and trying to stop Hugo with the other as the giant crashed past. (They learned later that Miss Openshaw had opened her door at Hugo's bellow, caught the word "dead," shrieked, asked who was dead, was answered, shrieked again, and fainted.)

It was Hendrik Brass, it seemed, who was dead. The Inspector, who had jumped out into Hugo's path and stopped him by sheer force of character, was able to elicit that much and no more.

"Where's that doctor?" the Inspector roared.

Dr. Thornton appeared from one of the ell corridors. He had thrown a topcoat over his nightshirt, and he had a wild look in his eye.

"What now, for heaven's sake?"

"Hugo says old Brass is dead. You'd better come with me." The Inspector stopped. "Come where?" he demanded of the Almighty. "I don't even know where he beds down! Hugo, where's Mr. Brass's room?"

Hugo gaped at him.

"I know where it is." DeWitt Alistair began to run. He stopped very short opposite the landing. "It's in there." He made no move to follow the stab of his meaty forefinger.

Mrs. Alistair hovered somewhere in the background, intent as a cat on a tree; she wore a threadbare, slickly ironed black flannel robe and gold bedroom slippers with some of the gold threads missing. Lynn O'Neill and Jessie were helping Cornelia Openshaw to her feet; the spinster shrank against them at the sight of poor Hugo, who seemed in shock. Keith Palmer ran down the hall toward the Inspector and Dr. Thornton to see what had to be seen.

They were blinded by brass; and then they wheeled on the old man in the bed. He was lying askew on a bloody pillow; his sunken eyes were shut; his face was grayer than gray where it was not scarlet. Dr. Thornton plucked the twiggy hand from the coverlet, feeling for the artery.

Hugo croaked from the doorway, "He is dead, dead," a froggy requiem, deep and dolorous, conveying fundamental distress.

The doctor looked up. "No such thing," he said sharply. "There's a good pulse." His glance swept professionally over the still bleeding head. "Somebody fetch my medical bag from the garage. It's on the back seat of my car." Young Palmer said quickly, "I'll do it, Doctor," and vaulted down the stairs. "And one of you women get some hot water."

Jessie said from the doorway, "You do it, Miss O'Neill. I can be more useful here," and she came in and said, "I'm a registered nurse, Doctor," as calm as a barge on a windless day; and Richard felt a fine warmth. Then he got busy using his eyes.

The bedroom was very like the room they had been assigned, full of decrepit furniture, only brassier if that was possible. There was a fireplace with a profusion of brass fire tools; it was faced with Dutch tiles that were cracked and faded-looking. But he was not concerned with the condition of Hendrik Brass's heirlooms. He was trying to make a different assessment.

When Palmer returned with the black bag, the doctor was carefully going over the old man's head. Jessie seized the bag and began pulling things out, anticipating Dr. Thornton's needs; they worked in silence.

Lynn O'Neill came in with a steaming kettle. Jessie took it from her and shooed the girl out. At that moment she caught sight of her husband. "What are you *doing,* Richard?"

He was on his knees, lean rump uppermost, near the foot of Brass's bed, delicately raising the corner of the pulled-over coverlet, which showed smears of blood.

"Here's what did it." There was a long brass poker on the floor, half under the bed. The tip looked as if it had been dipped in strawberry jam. He glanced over at the fireplace; the poker was missing from the rack of fire tools. "He was hit over the head, probably in his sleep. How many wounds are there, Doctor?"

"Three. The only reason he's alive is that the pillow must have taken most of the force of the blows. He looks in a lot worse shape than he actually is. These scalp wounds can be messy."

"Any skull fracture?"

"Not that I can see. By God, the old fellow is all ready to come around. He's either got the constitution of a horse or he was born under a lucky star."

The sightless eyes were beginning to flutter under the pain of Dr. Thornton's stitching.

"Don't anybody touch that poker. Hugo, what happened?" The Inspector had to repeat himself. Hugo shook like a dog.

"I bring Mr. Hendrik breakfast in bed every morning. I found him all full of blood. I thought—he looked—"

The Inspector nodded. "Where's the telephone?"

"No phone. Mr. Hendrik does not like them."

"He wouldn't." The Inspector started for the door.

"What do you want a telephone for, Richard?" Jessie was swabbing the blood from the old man's face as Dr. Thornton bandaged the bald head.

"I have to make a call." He shook his head at her, and she nodded in wifely understanding. What a team we'd have made twenty-five years ago! he thought. "Better make sure nobody touches anything."

He went out, shutting the door, and began to push through. To their questions he merely said, "He's not dead. Had an accident," and went to his and Jessie's bedroom, where he rapidly dressed. Then he hurried around to the old converted coach house, retrieved the Mustang, and drove out

42

of the grounds and back the way they had come the day before, to pull up at the Old River Inn. It was still not open for the day, but he located a public booth at one side of the building.

"Get me the Phillipskill police," he said to the operator. When he was connected he said, "I'm reporting an assault on Mr. Hendrik Brass," gave his name, made a suggestion, hung up, went out, got into the Mustang, and drove back looking grim.

Incredibly, he found the old man sitting up in bed, demanding his breakfast. Brass had put his dark glasses on, and with his bandaged head he looked like some ancient delinquent who had just taken part in a rumble. Dr. Thornton and Jessie were trying to reason with him, and the argument about his breakfast, which they lost, was succeeded by his absolute refusal to hear another word about Thornton's recommendation that he check into the nearest hospital for head X-rays and observation for possible concussion.

Richard left them arguing, to slip out of the house and look around. He was still checking doors and windows when a police car drove up and two uniformed men got out. One was carrying a fingerprinting kit, and the other wore a chief's badge on his blue coat.

"Are you the man who phoned headquarters?" the chief's badge demanded. He was a burly, farmerish sort with a red face and a big belly. "I'm Chief Victor Fleck."

The Inspector nodded. "I'm Richard Queen. Retired police inspector from New York City."

Chief Fleck did not seem overjoyed by the news. "What are you doing here?"

The Inspector told him, and ran down Hendrik Brass's guest list and the story of the morning's events. "My guess is that whoever clobbered him thought he'd killed the old man. He hit him three times, and there was blood all over him and the bed; he looked dead enough. In my book it was attempted murder."

Fleck grunted. "Doesn't surprise me. Everything the old screwball does, from the stories, is way out."

"Ever been in the house, Chief?"

"No."

"It's a doozy," the Inspector said.

"Before I go in, Queen. You understand that, even if you weren't retired, you'd have no jurisdiction here? Far as I'm concerned, this case is my case and you're just another character named Joe, up to and including being a suspect. Right?"

"Right."

"But as long as we're talking—was anything taken? Could this have been a burglary?"

"I don't know. Dr. Thornton just brought the old man to, and I haven't had a chance to question him." The inspector kept a straight face.

"What were you doing when I drove up? I mean out here."

"Looking for signs of forcible entry. There aren't any."

"Inside job?"

"Looks like it to me."

"Any idea who?"

Richard shook his head. "Not a notion." Something told him that the likeliest candidate for the assault was DeWitt Alistair, but it was only a hunch. Let Fleck find out, if he were capable of it. He had met Flecks before. These small town chiefs were usually over their heads in anything more complicated than a hit-and-run.

"Oh, one other thing," Chief Fleck said, turning at the door. "Why your suggestion about bringing fingerprint equipment?"

"The poker," Richard Queen said gently.

"Oh," Fleck said; and they all went into the house.

They found Hugo fork-feeding the old man from a loaded tray. The Inspector recalled Brass's statement that he was a sick man. Sick with what? It could have nothing to do with his digestion. There was a half-inch slab of ham cut into small pieces, three fried eggs, a mound of buttered toast, and a pot of coffee; and the recipient of all this waited greedily between forkfuls, making sucking sounds.

Jessie and Dr. Thornton hovered, unbelieving.

At the tramp of the three men Brass stopped in midchomp.

"Who is that?" he mumbled. "There are three of you."

"It's Queen, Mr. Brass," the Inspector said. "I've got Chief Fleck of the Phillipskill police and one of his officers with me."

"You've got *who*?" Hendrik Brass wheezed, spitting egg. "Who authorized you to call the police? Get them out of my house!"

"Mr. Brass," the Inspector said, startled, "somebody tried to kill you."

"And whose business is that? If I want police I'll call 'em. My family's lived on this property for two hundred years and never once asked anybody for help—anybody from the *government*!—not even during the Rent Wars. Get 'em out!"

"Now just a minute, Mr. Brass," said Chief Fleck, man-to-man. "If you've been assaulted, it's my job to come in on it—"

"Who said I was assaulted?"

"Why, this man here. Queen."

"And what's he know about it? Did he see it happen?"

"That poker didn't hit you over the head by itself, Mr. Brass," the Inspector said. "Unless you did it yourself?"

To their amazement the old man heehawed. "Yes, sir, that's what happened, all righty, I hit myself over the head. And you prove I didn't." He screamed suddenly, "Get out, I said! Off my property!"

Hugo hastily put some ham into his mouth.

Chief Fleck had turned beef-colored. Dr. Thornton hurried over and whispered, "My advice is to drop this for now, gentlemen. At least leave the room. There might be a concussion, and he shouldn't be excited."

"You the doctor Queen told me about?"

"I'm Dr. Thornton."

"They why don't you sign a commitment paper for the old birdseed? Anybody can see his brain's gone to jelly. You through with that poker, Bobby?"

The officer set the poker down and put his equipment away. "No prints, Vic. Must have been wiped."

"The hell with this." Fleck raised his voice. "Look, Mr. Brass, I was called here and I've got to put something down for the record. You're not going to press a charge against anybody, or make a complaint?"

"That's it."

"It's all right with me." The chief nodded curtly at the Inspector, who followed him and his man into the hall. "This isn't the end of it by a long shot, Queen. You know it and I know it."

"I'm afraid I do."

"If he denies an assault and won't lodge a complaint, I can't do anything. But if something else happens to him I want to be notified. Understood?"

"For two cents plain," muttered the Inspector, "I'd chuck the whole thing."

"Then you're not staying? Can't stop you."

The Inspector shrugged. "You know I am. I haven't any idea what my wife and I are mixed up in here, but I'm still enough of a cop to want to find out."

"What I thought," Chief Fleck said with a heavy grin. "And that's why I'm warning you, Queen. Something happens here, I'm not standing by and watch some ex-New York cop grab off all the publicity. Like I said, this is my neck of the woods."

45

"Whatever happens, Chief," Richard said solemnly, "I promise you: you can talk to the reporters."

The burly policeman seemed to detect a whiff of irony. "Okay, Queen," he said gruffly, "as long as we understand each other." The officers clumped downstairs, and a moment later he heard the police car peel off.

The Inspector went back into the bedroom. Dr. Thornton was filling a hypodermic, and Jessie was dabbing the old man's spindly arm. Hugo was preparing to leave with the tray, and the Inspector took it from him. "I'll take this downstairs. I have a job for you."

Hugo looked stupid.

"You know somebody tried to hurt Mr. Hendrik?"

The massive head wagged.

"Well, the job I want you to do, Hugo, is to keep watch over him. So nobody can get near him to hurt him again. Know what I mean? Don't leave this room, not for a second. If there's anything funny, yell."

"The cooking—" began Hugo.

"The women can take care of that."

Hugo looked torn. But then he nodded.

Jessie took the tray from Richard, and he followed her and Dr. Thornton out. The last thing he saw before he shut the door was Hugo settling down at the foot of the brass bed, little eyes fixed on his master's face.

While Jessie dressed, the Inspector slipped downstairs for a cup of coffee and a few minutes alone with his thoughts.

He was enormously puzzled. The assault on Hendrik Brass made no sense. According to Brass he had not yet drawn a will. He had certainly not chosen his heir or heirs; the whole point of his invitations was to enable him to weigh the chosen six in the balance and cull the unworthy from among them, a procedure that had barely got under way. Old Brass had mentioned "weeks."

Why had someone—presumably someone in the house— attempted to kill off the goose before it could lay the egg? The only beneficiary, had the murder attempt succeeded, would have been the treasury of the State of New York.

Yet it must make sense of some sort. Unless the assailant was as off-balance as Hendrik himself, there was a motive hidden somewhere that related to at least one of the guests. A motive that was stronger than $1,000,000.

He tried to imagine such a motive. Maybe one of them was loaded—so loaded that $1,000,000 meant little to him; one man's million was another man's spending money. But, thinking over the five people besides Jessie who were involved, he could not see any of them so fortunately situated.

Barring that, the Inspector thought wryly, whoever did it is a nut, like old Hendrik himself. Nuts made no sense except to other nuts. It was the only explanation, unsatisfactory as it was, that he could think of for someone's trying to commit the wrong crime at the wrong time.

It was also the kind of baffler that would have drawn Ellery to the point like a setter in the field at the first flutter of a wing. But Ellery had gone back to Turkey.

I'm my son's father, Richard decided with a grimace.

He finished his coffee and prepared a breakfast tray for Jessie, a service she always protested and secretly cherished.

An act of Congress could not have made him return to New York.

"First things first, Jessie," he said.

Jessie looked up from her sausages and eggs. He had bolted the doors, and he was speaking in a voice that would have defied any but the latest electronic bug.

"What things?" Jessie asked.

"We have to start somewhere. And the only fact we have to go on is that you're not the Jessie Sherwood Brass was looking for. So the question has to be answered: How many of the others aren't the genuine article, either? I can't leave you here alone to find out, and even if I could it would take me too long. We need help."

"But who, Richard?"

"My West 87th Street Irregulars," the Inspector said with a grin. "So hold down the fort, will you, honey? I've got to get to that inn again and make some calls."

The great stone fireplace of the Old River Inn had gagged to death long ago, to be replaced by a malodorous oil heater whose fumes pervaded the food, such as it was, and gave the drinks a bouquet of creosote. Otherwise the spready, low-ceilinged dining room was little changed from the days of the Hudson River steamboat trade, when the captains and crews of the *Ben Franklin* and the *Mary Powell* took their pleasure there during layovers. But none of the six men at the scarred and bleached round table in the middle of the dining room was in a mood for nostalgia. The Inspector had insisted on treating his five guests to the grandest feed the Inn afforded, with a bottle of Irish to make it palatable, before getting down to the business for which he had summoned them; and they were plainly chafing for enlightenment.

The old men listened in professional silence as the Inspector outlined the situation at "the bughouse," his least colorful characterization.

They were ex-police officers, retired by the New York City

47

police department at the mandatory age of sixty-three. Wes Polonsky, a massive man with a mashed nose, had been a detective first grade on the Automobile, Forgery, and Pickpocket Squad. Pete Angelo, Polonsky's old working partner, was even more massive; he had been a terror to hoodlums, and Polonsky, who had been pretty good himself, swore that Angelo could still stack them in a brawl like cordwood. Al Murphy, whose red hair refused to fade, had been a sergeant on radio car patrol in the 16th Precinct at the time of his retirement. Hugh Giffin had come out of the Main Office Squad with a set of broken knuckles and a knife slash across his face; he had a gentle disposition that had never interfered with the heroics sometimes called for by his job. The fifth ex-cop, Johnny Kripps, had been a lieutenant in Homicide. With his black-rimmed glasses and soft white hair he looked like a teacher or librarian.

"What I had in mind," the Inspector said, "is going to call for legwork, maybe a lot of it. None of us is getting any younger—"

"Cut the baloney, Dick," said Pete Angelo. "You wouldn't have thrown us this life preserver if you didn't think we had the muscle to grab it."

"I take real good care of my feet, Inspector," Polonsky said quickly. Of the quintet he seemed the most devastated by time; the hand holding the cigaret shook, and there were red streaks on his eyeballs. "You don't have to worry about us."

The Inspector hesitated. They were all put out to pasture through the cruel chronology of age, when most of them could still run a respectable race; it was about Polonsky that he had his doubts. But to have left out old Wes would have been unthinkable. He made up his mind to give the big Pole the easiest job without making a point of it.

"Wes, you tackle the Alistairs. I'm betting they have more yellow sheets here and yonder than Carter has pills. There's just got to be something on them. Root around the B.C.I., talk to some of the boys, get as much dope as you can dig up. My hunch is they've used aliases all over creation. I figure Alistair for pure con, with that Beast of Belsen wife of his badgering for him. If she is his wife."

"Will do." Old Polonsky's bloodshot eyes were giving off sparks.

"Murph, you tackle this Dr. Thornton. Hubert Thornton, South Cornwall, seems involved in a medical co-op and clinic. Find out especially about his mother, if she ever had a connection with Brass."

Al Murphy reached for the bottle with a red-furred hand.

"I'm great on mother cases," he said with a grin. "I remember one time—"

They hooted him down.

"You, Hughie, draw Cornelia Openshaw," the Inspector said to Giffin. "She's a sex-crazy old maid whose parents are supposed to have saved Brass from committing suicide." He slid over a slip with her address, and the scarred ex-M.O.S. man tucked it away. "I want to know if that story is true."

Angelo was looking expectant. "Okay, Pete, your baby is this young fellow Palmer, Keith Palmer." He handed the big man another slip. "Brass claims Palmer's mother was once a good 'friend' of his. From the way he said it, she shacked up with him when he was something to look at without turning your stomach. It will probably take delicate handling. I don't want word of this to get back to Palmer, so just concentrate on the mother background."

"Leave it to me, Dick."

"Lynn O'Neill is yours, Johnny," the Inspector said to Kripps. "This one may take some doing. The girl is from Wyoming, and her father, the man Brass says saved him from a necktie party, was a sheriff there somewhere. You may even have to fly out."

"Let me give it a long-distance try first," the ex-Homicide lieutenant said. "Just before they put me out to grass I had to pick up an extradited murder suspect at the sheriff's office in Cheyenne, and I got pretty friendly with the chief deputy. I could maybe dig this all up by phone."

"Well, if you can't and you find you have to fly out, Johnny, I'll pick up the tab."

"I wouldn't think of it, Dick." Kripps had turned a brick shade. "Only these days I have to play it close to the vest. . . ."

"It's my case, and I pay the expenses. That goes for the whole crew. Just let me know what you lay out. Or if any of you needs an advance—?"

"What'd you do, Inspector, come into a million?" Polonsky growled. "Look, I'm so damn glad to have something to *do*. . . ."

The rest was friendly argument and what was left of the bottle of Irish. They broke up at last after setting a meeting date at the Inn for progress reports; then Richard Queen went back to The House of Brass feeling far better than when he had left.

4

WHAT!

Lynn O'Neill and Keith Palmer were the only two young people within reaching distance, so they naturally reached.

The atmosphere of the place was no hindrance. There was something about the house and even its tenants that made people uneasy about being left alone. If not for the ever-winking brass, The House of Brass would have had all the hominess of a castle in Transylvania. Lynn especially hated the bedtimes, when she had to lock her door and face the long night in solitary. She could hardly wait for the mornings and the sight of Keith Palmer's rugged and—she was sure of it (or was she?)—decent young face.

"I really don't know what I'm doing here," Lynn confided to Keith on the second morning after the assault on Hendrik Brass. They were strolling through the piny woods behind the outbuildings, Keith kicking fallen branches aside and Lynn picking her way across the ankle-trap terrain; Brass's grounds were as dilapidated as his house. "I ought to go home."

"Oh, I hope you won't do that," Keith said quickly.

"Why not?"

"Because, well, there's all that loot."

"Is that," asked Lynn, sending a sidelong glance his way that sparkled with topaz, "the only reason?"

"Well, no."

"What's another reason?"

"Well, you."

"Oh," Lynn said, and lapsed into encouraging silence.

"I mean, you're a damn attractive wench."

"Oh, dear," Lynn sighed. "I was afraid you were going to say something like that."

"Why afraid?"

"Should I be flattered? Any girl my age would look yummy in this zoo. Who's my competition? Cornelia Openshaw? Not that she wouldn't like to be. The way she looks at you is absolutely pornographic. Or Mrs. Alistair? I imagine it would be like trying to make love to a cougar. Of course, there's that darling Mrs. Queen—"

"Look, it's *you*."

"I don't grasp your meaning, Mr. Palmer."

"I mean," Keith exploded, "you'd stand out in Atlantic City during Miss America week!"

"Why, thank you," murmured Lynn.

"Anyway, what would you do back in Wyoming?"

"Look for another job. They automated me out of my last one."

"You see?"

They zigged along for some time, breathing deeply. In Lynn's case, Keith thought, it was a rousing sight. And a fine day it was. Sun shining, and all that. The farther they got from old Brass's mausoleum the finer the day came, the shinier the sun, and the more energetically Lynn's sweater bounced.

"And another thing," Lynn said suddenly. "It doesn't fit."

"What doesn't fit?"

"Any of this. I'm beginning to feel . . ." Lynn stopped. "Never mind."

"Now you can't do that! What were you going to say?"

"It'll sound square."

"Try me."

"It's . . . evil." Lynn searched his face. But he failed to smile, and she was cheered. "It's not just that eerie old man or his Frankenstein monster. It's nearly all of them—the Alistairs, that Openshaw freak, Mr. Queen always disappearing somewhere. . . . The only ones who give me any feeling of security are Dr. Thornton and Mrs. Queen, and sometimes I'm not sure about them."

"How about me?" Keith asked carelessly.

Lynn squatted on a smooth boulder beside the path. She was wearing blush-pink slacks, and the way they tightened over her flanks when she sat down tickled him.

"How about you, Keith?"

"That was my question."

"Let me ask you a question. I don't have any right to ask it, so you don't have to answer. Are you married?"

Keith was stricken. He stood there.

"I thought so," Lynn said. The sun's rays squeezing through the pines unaccountably dimmed. Lucky Lynn, she thought.

"Now hold on there," Keith stammered. "Just hold your horses. You asked me a question, give me a chance to think how to answer you—"

"Oh, come off it, Keith. How many kinds of answers are there to a question like that? Yes or no, and that's it. Not that it's any of my business, of course."

51

"I'd *like* it to be your business. I mean—"

"Yes?"

"You asked whether I'm married, and you said there are only two possible answers to it, yes or no. Well, they're not the only possible answers, Lynn. That's what's hanging me up."

"They're not?" Lynn said derisively. "All right, Mr. Palmer, you give me another possible answer."

"Yes *and* no."

Lynn's mouth opened, and she jumped to her feet. "That's the most insulting doubletalk, do you know that? I'm beginning not to like you at all, Keith Palmer!"

"But it's the truth," he protested. He was in the grip of some obscure agony. "In one way I'm married, in another I'm not. I—well, I can't explain it any more definitely than that. Not right now I can't. I mean—"

"You're putting me on. And you needn't bother to see me back to Horror House, thank you. What kind of fool do you take me for?"

Lynn galloped off. He stood there glaring, half hoping she would turn an ankle so that he would have a face-saving excuse to go after her. But she was as agile as a filly. All too soon her nubile young figure was lost among the pines.

Keith Palmer kicked at the boulder. Unfortunately his aim was impeccable. So he sat down cursing his foot, and cursing Keith Palmer and all his works, which included a wife named Joanne and a small boy named Sam, alias Schmulie.

On the fifth night after Hendrik Brass's head's adventure with the fireplace poker, at dinner, Richard Queen rapped on his wineglass, which was still full of Hugo's vile Chablis.

"If you don't mind, Mr. Brass," Richard said, "I'd like everybody to meet in the parlor. Especially including you, sir."

"Oh?" said old Brass. "And if I do mind, Mr. Queen? Aren't you making rather free with my house?"

"Somebody made rather free with your head a few nights ago," the Inspector retorted, "and you didn't seem to mind that, which strikes me as pretty broadminded of you, if you'll pardon the pun. But that's not what's sticking in my craw, Mr. Brass. It's another of your peculiarities, if that's the word."

"And what is that?" asked the old man amiably, as if they were bosom friends. "We can talk here. What's bothering you?"

"What's bothering me, Mr. Brass, and what's going to

bother everybody at this table before I get through, is that you're one of the world's biggest liars."

The Alistairs drew in their heads in tandem, like a brace of trained turtles. They then glanced at each other, whereupon as one they turned their attention to Hendrik Brass. Lynn O'Neill's eyes widened. Keith Palmer's narrowed. Dr. Thornton's reflected the watchfulness with which he seemed increasingly infected. Only Cornelia Openshaw remained unmoved. She was digesting young Palmer from across the table, what could be seen of him, piece by piece.

"I'm a liar?" old Brass said calmly. "Indeed. And wherein have I lied?"

"You said that Jessie Sherwood's father, Dr. Sherwood, once saved your life when you were very sick. Isn't that what you said?"

"It's exactly what I said."

"Well, far from saving your life, Dr. Sherwood nearly killed you. He made a wrong diagnosis and prescribed a treatment from which you almost died. If a specialist hadn't been called and corrected both the diagnosis and the treatment, you *would* have died. When you recovered, you went to a lawyer and actually started to sue Dr. Sherwood for malpractice. Only the fact that the specialist wouldn't testify against a fellow-physician made you drop the suit. And that's how grateful you had reason to be to Dr. Sherwood!"

"I see," said Hendrik Brass, and he hawked. "I see," he said again, and he smiled. "Is that all, Mr. Queen?"

"I'm just starting. Take DeWitt Alistair's father." Alistair's floridity lost some of its bloom; but Elizabeth Alistair contrived to gather herself in an almost visible ripple of muscle. "One time, you said, when you were hard-pressed financially and couldn't find a soul to help you out, Alistair's father lent you what you needed to save you from bankruptcy. Didn't you get it hindside to, Mr. Brass? Alistair's father didn't come to your rescue. He didn't lend you a cent. What really happened was that you owed him a big gambling debt, and he made your life miserable trying to get you to pay up. It was his demands for payment, in fact, that almost drove you *into* bankruptcy. That's what Alistair's father did for you that, according to you, Mr. Brass, brings a lump to your throat at his memory."

It was an index of DeWitt Alistair's need for some providential black-ink bookkeeping that he directed the full volume of his malevolence, not at Hendrik Brass, but at the Inspector. But Richard Queen had been audited by such glances before, and he ignored it. As for Elizabeth Alistair, she lidded her stony eyes like an Internal Revenue inspector.

53

"Go on," said Brass. "Because I take it you're not through?"

The Inspector looked around as if for refreshment and settled on Lynn's lovely face. "Miss O'Neill is another victim of your lying. Her father didn't save you from a lynching. And he didn't come to your defense at your trial. He caught you redhanded with the stolen horse and was the prosecution's most important witness against you. The only reason you didn't wind up in jail is that he committed a technical error—search and seizure without a warrant—and the presiding judge happened to be a stickler for the fine points. If you've got any reason to remember somebody with gratitude, it's the judge, not Sheriff O'Neill. He felt so bad about your getting off that he ran you out of his county, threatening to string you up himself if ever he caught you horse-thieving again."

Hendrik Brass's long neck stretched; he ran out his gray tongue and made a hissing noise. Then it all turned to cackles.

"You've been doing a lot of homework, Mr. Queen. There's more?"

"Oh, yes," the Inspector said, turning from Lynn, who was trying not to make a spectacle of herself. Her expression said: There goes my million. "Let's go to Keith Palmer here. You said that you and Palmer's mother were very close. You know how close your mother was to this man?" he said to Keith. "She couldn't stand the sight of him. She queered his act with her best friend, whom he was trying to marry, by proving to the girl that Brass was a skunk who'd left a trail of broken hearts, and that the only reason he was after her was to get his hands on her father's money. And he has the gall to imply that he and your mother had an affair!"

"Is that true, Mr. Brass?" Keith asked the old man. "For God's sake, why would you make up a story like that?"

"Mr. Queen has the floor," Hendrik Brass said, unveiling his dentures. "Let him answer your questions."

"Next case," the Inspector said, unveiling *his* dentures. "That's you, Dr. Thornton. Whose mother is supposed to have hauled him to his feet at a low point in his life, and restored his confidence in himself, I believe he put it. Doctor, your mother had about as much use for this man as Palmer's did. He tried to get her to marry him, and put on a campaign of harassment that lasted six months—one time she had to call the police to get him out of her hair. She finally shook him when she married your father, and even then your father had to threaten to break his neck if he didn't leave your mother alone."

54

Dr. Thornton seemed unsurprised. He examined Brass through his heavy glasses as if the old man were a specimen under his microscope.

Brass was silent this time. He merely waved his gray hand at the Inspector. The crooked smile was still in evidence.

"Which brings me," the Inspector said, "to Miss Openshaw—"

"Stop! I don't want to hear it!" cried Cornelia Openshaw; she was completely engaged by now, Keith Palmer forgotten. She actually stopped up her ears.

"Sorry, you're part of this, Miss Openshaw, and in fairness to the others I can't leave you out. In your case the finding is negative. Brass claims your parents saved his life when he tried to commit suicide. There's not a record or a recollection on the part of anyone in a position to know that it was true. In view of what we've learned about the parents of the others, it makes more sense to assume that, whatever relationship your father and mother had with this man, it left him not with gratitude toward them but with some gripe he's nursed for a generation."

"You can't prove that," snapped the spinster. "I for one am ready to believe anything Mr. Brass says."

"That's your problem. Well, Brass? That's the record. Want to correct it?"

"So that's why you've been making all those trips to the Old River Inn," the old man tittered. "Hugo wondered about that, and so did I."

"Look, Brass, you've been caught dead to rights in at least five whoppers, and the time's come for you to start leveling. All these people's parents are dead, so you can't take anything out on them. But they left children. If you're the sort of man who carries over his hates, you hate them. Then why have you invited them here? To make them your heirs, as you claim? After what I've dug up about you, nobody in his right mind would believe it. And there's at least one of these people who didn't from the start—the one who tried to wallop your brains out. If you ask me, he thought he was beating you to the punch! So what's this all about, Brass? Did you get them here so you could have Hugo dose the lousy food he serves with arsenic? From the samples of his cooking, we wouldn't be able to taste the difference. Come clean!"

Old Brass, who had been nestled in the recesses of his big chair at the head of the table, inched forward and up until he was perched on the edge, the whole process recalling a horror movie in which the 3000-year-old mummy suddenly sits up in his sarcophagus.

"Hugo," he said briskly, "more coffee."

Hugo jerked, shambled forward with the coffeepot, and refilled the old man's cup. He remained behind the chair, pot aloft, electric cord trailing, so that he looked like a plugged-in robot.

"Ah." Brass set the cup deftly down on the saucer. "You were asking me a question, Mr. Queen, and you've earned an answer. All that running about between here and the inn, meeting with your hirelings—if that's what they are—getting their reports and so on—a bunch of incompetents, if you ask me, because they got everything right but the only thing that counts."

"What are you talking about?" The Inspector looked startled. "What didn't they get right?"

"Why, they dug up the facts," sniggered Hendrik Brass, "about the wrong Hendrik Brass."

The snigger became a laugh that became a spasm that left the old man choking. He was slapping his skeletal shank with the marvelous humor of it all and trying to get his breath at the same time. There was rack-brained silence around the board until he achieved it, and after.

"What d'ye mean the wrong Hendrik Brass?" Richard Queen roared. "Make sense, man. There's more than one Hendrik Brass—that's your story? You'll have to do better than that!"

"It's easy enough to check," Brass gasped; and to the Inspector's disgust one of the birchbark lids came down over its sightless eye in a wink. "But you'll find out I'm not lying. There's been more Hendrik Brasses than you can count. It's a family tradition?"

"*What's* a family tradition?"

"Two traditions. One: The family business has always been inherited by the eldest son. Any other sons take potluck. Two: The eldest son is always named Hendrik, after the founder of the Brass fortune. My father had two sons. I was the younger. My elder brother was baptized Hendrik Willem—sometimes the eldest was given a middle name; optional, you might say. But always Hendrik. When I came along I was named Simon."

"Then why are you calling yourself Hendrik?"

"Because Henk is dead—I used to call Hendrik Henk. That left only me, you see. So I had a lawyer apply to the court to change my name legally to Hendrik Simon Brass. It's been Hendrik Simon ever since."

"Hold on! Are you saying that the Hendrik I've been talking about, the one who bedeviled the parents of these people, was your older brother?"

"I am." The old man grinned his grisly grin. "And a wild one he was, too, in his young days, when Father was still alive and running the business. Almost as wild as I was. Got around the country quite a bit, Hendrik Willem did. But when Father died, Henk came home and settled down. Turned out a regular jackass for work, like Father. Work, work, work, that was Henk. Didn't even take time enough off to get married, though he'd doodled around with women a-plenty in his early days. And one fine day Henk dropped dead from plain overwork, and the business and the money and this property fell into my lap. And here we are. Does that satisfy you, Mr. Queen?"

The Inspector glared at him. There had been no reason for Polonsky, Angelo, Murphy, Giffin, and Kripps to suspect a different Hendrik Brass; it was the last thing anyone would have thought of. Still . . .

"You haven't straightened this out at all, Mr. Brass. It's crooked as my Aunt Minnie's arthritis—crookeder! Your brother did all those things? But you led us to believe *you* did. The identical involvements couldn't apply to both of you, even if you both raised hell as young men. *Two* near fatal mistakes by the same doctor, one involving you and one your brother? *Two* arrests for horse-stealing by the same Wyoming sheriff of the same brothers at different times? And so on? That would be a fairy tale, Brass. Or are you trying to make us believe that the stories you told us about the nice things those folks did were things done to you, but the stuff my friends dug out about the nasty things they did were things done to your brother? The same people? That would be an even taller story!

"The way I see it, Brass, you personally had no contact at all with the parents of these people here. That being the case, you personally can't possibly owe them a thing—not gratitude, not even hate. Or are you carrying on a feud in your brother's name?"

"That," old Brass chuckled, "is for you to find out."

"Well, I don't buy such a fairy tale, either. Feuds went out with the Hatfields and the Whatchamacallems. You've got some other reason, Brass. Why did you ask these folks to come here? It still gets down to the same thing: What's this all about?"

"Yes, that seems to be the six-million-dollar question, doesn't it. Inspector?" said the old man with gummy enjoyment. "Oh, dear, I let the cat out of the bag, didn't I? I don't suppose anybody here but your wife knows. You didn't know I knew you were a retired police inspector from New York, did you?"

"No," said the Inspector with something like respect, "I did not."

Which made them all stare at him, emphatically the Alistairs, who looked as if they had just turned over a rock with the usual unpleasant results.

"I may be blind," chortled old Brass, "but there's nothing wrong with my head, hey? Or with my sources of information? All right, Inspector Queen, you've had considerable experience solving mysteries, suppose you solve this one. *You* find out what this is all about, eh? What say?" And all of a sudden his merriment drained out. He grimaced, and stamped his foot, and yelped, "I've had enough fun for one night. Hugo, you barrel of fish guts, my cane!"

5

WHICH?

Hendrik Brass's "sources of information" turned up the next morning, in the singular.

It happened while Dr. Thornton was attempting to dress the old man's head in the brassy bedroom. Jessie was there to assist, Richard Queen was there because Jessie was there, and Hugo was there because of Richard's standing order— humped in a corner not being used for the moment, flawed eyes trained on the bandages swathing the aged skull across the room as if they were about to reveal something rare and wonderful.

Dr. Thornton said, "Peroxide, please," and Nurse Queen obliged, and the doctor poured, soaking the old bandage above the wound. He waited while the peroxide bubbled and the caked blood underneath softened, and then gently unwound the bandage, Hendrik Brass lying there after his fit of temper with a mummified expression, sunken eyes shut; at the last deft pull the dressing came away like a charm, the eyes opened, and the old man said suddenly to his ceiling, "You have healing hands, Doctor."

"Thank you," Dr. Thornton said. " 'I dressed his wounds; God healed them.' "

The ancient imp looked puzzled.

"What?"

"Something I read somewhere."

"God! I don't believe in God."

The wound was ugly. There was a marked swelling along the puckered line of laceration, tightening the stitches so that the bald skull looked like a football with its laces showing.

"I don't think we'll rebandage," the doctor said. "Let the air get at it. I'll remove the stitches in a day or two. Right now we'll clean away the mess. Have you been having any headaches or head pains? Dizziness? Faintness?"

"No."

"The God you don't believe in has been good to you, Mr. Brass."

He and Jessie got busy with the clotted blood around the wound, Richard admiring his wife's smooth movements; so that he was startled at the sound of Hugo's voice.

"The man is here, the man is here!"

To the Inspector's ears as he whirled it might as well have been "I smell the blood of an Englishman!", in so ferocious a bass had Hugo uttered it. And then he saw the man.

He stood lounging in the doorway, hands in pockets, with a smile that was half jeer, half sneer, and all of it nasty. It was hard to tell exactly what amused him, whether it was Hugo's mastiff growl, the Inspector's choreography, or the wound on Brass's skull.

Hugo took a step.

"Watch it, Shorty," the man in the doorway said. "I may not be as big as you, but I'm betting I'm a lot quicker on my pins. Not to mention hands."

Hugo took another step. The newcomer did not move, either forward or backward. But the Inspector saw him set himself.

"He doesn't like me," the man said. "I don't think we'll ever make the scene."

"Who are you?" Richard demanded.

"The name, dad, is Vaughn." He kept his eyes on Hugo.

"Who, who?" shrilled old Hendrik from the bed. "Vaughn?"

"That's right, Mr. Brass."

"Hugo," the old man said peevishly. "I told you the last time. Stop."

Hugo stopped. The man uncoiled and advanced at a saunter into the bedroom.

The Inspector was a peaceable citizen, but there was something about the newcomer that made him itch to push the fellow's face in. For one thing, his very walk was an affront—a cross between a slither and a strut, engineered either to pounce or to strike an attitude, depending on

59

circumstances. For another, his survey of Jessie was a laser performance, penetrating deep; it stripped her quite naked and, worse, discarded her in a sort of regretful contempt; he might just as well have said aloud: Twenty years ago, baby ... maybe.

You and I, the Inspector told him silently, were born enemies.

He took a survey of his own.

Either Vaughn's custom pinstripe was made too small for him, or he had grown too broad and thick for it; it revealed rather than covered his body, which looked overmuscled. His hair was stiff and sandy and cropped short. His light gray eyes had diamond-chip glints in them. His nose was flattened in an otherwise angular face; perhaps it was the jaw that made the Inspector think of a cartoon, for it jutted out of his face like a 1925 cowcatcher. His skin was pitted and unlovely and shrieked of sunlamps. The Inspector would not have been surprised to see him produce a racing form and a slice of Lindy's cheesecake. There was a Bersagliere-type hat on his head (he's a sharpshooter, all right, the Inspector thought); he had not bothered to remove it. His shirt was navy blue and his tie was daffodil yellow. The hands were big and scarred. Yet there was intelligence in the spying eyes; or perhaps a primitive wisdom that had been picked up in back rooms and alleys. It was impossbile to imagine a decent man liking him or a woman of any sort turning her head away.

Anyway you looked at him, he was bad news.

"What happened to your noggin?" Vaughn asked with the passion of a coroner.

The old man said petulantly, "I will discuss that with you later, Mr. Vaughn."

"You should have contacted me. That overgrown slob is no security. Even a blind man ought to be able to see he's got nothing between his cauliflowers but air."

"You," Jessie said, "are a boor!"

"Sure, doll," Vaughn said, and dismissed her.

"Please, please," the old man said. "The rest of you get out."

"Hold it." The Inspector's mustache was bristling. "My wife, not to mention the others, has a vested interest in what goes on in this house. I want to know who this man is and why you've had him come here."

"You make like a cop," Vaughn said before Brass could answer. "Say, I catch. Your name is Queen and you just got tied to Jessie Sherwood—I take it this broad here. Right, dad?"

"You're right, sonny, and nobody calls my wife a broad. *Nobody!*"

"Pops, you turn me on." The way the muscular back presented itself to him made the Inspector angry indeed. But Jessie put her hand on his arm. "You. With the lip rug. Which one would you be?"

The doctor's red mustache bristled, too. "I'm Dr. Thornton."

"Oh, yeah. Okay, you heard Mr. Brass. Out, the lot of you."

"I'm not leaving this room till I've had my answer," the Inspector said. "Who is this hood, Mr. Brass?"

"It's all right, Vaughn," Hendrik Brass said. "On second thought I want them to know. Why, Inspector, Mr. Vaughn is the private detective I engaged to find your wife and the others. He is also an attorney. He will draw up my will when I've made up my mind who gets my money."

"Attorney! Which school did you graduate from, Vaughn? Ossining?"

"Harvard, Yale, Barbers' College, what's the big deal? You want to see my degree, dad?"

"I'd like to see the permit for that gun you're packing in the shoulder holster."

"And I thought this three-hundred-buck custom-built hid the heater. I better change tailors. Don't fret your old gray head, Inspector. I've got a permit. Also, if you're interested, a New York detective agency license."

"They're letting anything operate in New York these days. All right, Mr. Brass, he's your one-man Gestapo, and I can't do anything about that, but I want it understood now that he'd better not try any rough stuff. Especially with the women. I know the breed."

Vaughn shrugged. "What's the matter, granddad, aren't the wedding bells swinging anymore? Look, if it's like war you want, okay, only I choose my own turf. And just so we understand each other, watch that fat lip. An ex-cop is nothing by me." He gave the Inspector no time to reply. "How long's this job going to take, Mr. Brass?"

"As long as it takes." The old man looked sly. "How long can you be away from your place of business?"

"That's up to you, you're picking up the tab. While we're holding hands—and since I have to hang around here anyway—you're not serious about letting Man Mountain there keep muscling for you, are you? If that hit on your skull says anything about his work, you better get yourself a new boy."

"That's what I had in mind, Mr. Vaughn. You're also to take over as my bodyguard."

Hugo stirred. "Not me?" He looked appalled.

"Beat it, Godzilly," Vaughn said. "You heard your lord and master."

"Not me?" Hugo said again; this time it sounded like a whimper.

"No," the old man yapped. "You go back to your polishing, Hugo. And be sure and do whatever Mr. Vaughn tells you. Hear?"

Hugo's shoulders sloped. "Yes, Mr. Hendrik." He slunk from the room. Jessie could have wept for him.

"All right, folks, Outsville time." Vaughn jerked a hammerhead thumb toward the door. "Mr. Brass and I have some yakking to do."

Richard held the door open for Jessie and a fuming Dr. Thornton. He was about to follow them out when, to his stupefaction, he saw Vaughn reach, produce a battered silver flask from his hip pocket, and unscrew the cap. The last time had had seen anyone carrying a hip flask was during Prohibition. Maybe they were coming back. Or Vaughn had been reading Dashiell Hammett. If he could read.

The last thing the Inspector saw as he closed the door was Vaughn taking a long pull from the flask.

"Great spot you've got here, Mr. Brass," he heard the private eye laugh. "But like I say, it'll never take the place of Acapulco."

Before Vaughn's coming, life in the old house had settled into a restless routine: breakfast between eight and nine; drives into Phillipskill or Tarrytown for newspapers, magazines, books (the Brass library, such as it was, had apparently stopped growing in the time of William Dean Howells and F. Marion Crawford), cigarets or toiletries; then lunch at noon, after which some strolled about the grounds or down to the half-submerged boat landing, or occupied themselves in other ways—Jessie knitting a pullover for Richard with needles and yarn she bought in the Phillipskill Emporium; the Alistairs playing poker for toothpicks, or Mrs. Alistair engaging herself in a carnivorous solitaire while her husband pored over his racing news, purchased in Tarrytown; Dr. Thornton reading the latest issue of *Playboy,* ignoring the copies of the AMA journal and *MD* which had been forwarded to him from South Cornwall; the two young people reading paperbacks, ostentatiously avoiding each other in all but spirit, Lynn giving Keith the nose-in-the-air bit signifying outrage, Keith taking it like a superfluous puppy and looking so miserable that Lynn wanted to put her arms around him and assure him that everything was all right, which was ridiculous, since everything was all wrong; Cornelia Openshaw roasting Keith with her superheated glances while her posture and behavior spoke of absolute propriety; and over all old fox Queen, here and everywhere, but never far from their host who mingled with his guests, present but aloof, pale ears cocked for nuances, like an old conductor listening to a new orchestra, with a smile on his lips that positively smoked, it was so infernal. It made peace of mind and dreams of millions difficult. But even this became routine, and after a while most of them ignored Hendrik Brass except when directly addressed, at which times they leaped to his question or bidding, smiling anxious smiles in return, as if he could see.

Vaughn's appearance on the premises changed the quality of their discomfort. It was like being enclosed suddenly in a huge spherical sneer from which there was no escape.

Like the Inspector, Vaughn had apparently taken the measure of the Alistairs; he kept delivering little seminars on confidence games he had run into, and pretending forgetfulness of the fine points and appealing to them for help. It unsettled the pair wonderfully, since Vaughn deferred to their expertise within hearing of old Brass, who listened in enigmatic silence.

On Dr. Thornton he spewed the venom of an evident animus against the medical profession. All doctors, he would remark, were butchers, money grubbers, or out-and-out quacks. The doctor suffered with dignity. But equanimity grew harder for him by the hour, especially when Vaughn took to making gentle duck sounds at his approach. Thornton began to tug at his mustache, show his tobacco-stained teeth, and make fists. Yet Vaughn always stopped short of lighting Thornton's fuse. Apparently it was a way of amusing himself.

His technique with Cornelia Openshaw was basic: he told her dirty stories. In the beginning this sent her stalking out of the room, or drove her into incoherent splutters. But the Inspector noticed that Miss Openshaw's indignation threshold became higher as time passed, until finally she stopped stalking and spluttering, and listened in a simulation of total deafness.

Toward Palmer Vaughn adopted the man-to-man ploy. It consisted of little unexpected jabs to the ribs, like punctuation marks: "Y'know what I mean, man"—*jab* exclamation point; or a powerful slap between the shoulder blades that rocked Keith, big as he was: "What d'ye say, pal—*slap* question mark; or a hard forefinger stabbing at Keith's chest like a row of hemstitching: "You can bet your sweet asafetida, fella"—*stab-stab-stab* period ... always uttered and delivered in the friendliest fashion, so that it would have seemed churlish to take umbrage. The procedure consistently reduced Keith to speechlessness. After a while it was embarrassing to see Keith backpedal or sidestep at the approach of Vaughn, like an outclassed fighter suddenly thrust into the ring. It was a question how long he would take Vaughn's badgering.

But it was Lynn O'Neill who became Vaughn's serious target. His technique was to pretend not to see her until she came close; then to start with pleased surprise; then to begin at the crown of her chestnut hair and go over her slowly from north to south like a photoelectric eye searching for hidden treasures, lingering on those he found, until he reached her feet, when he reversed his field and repeated the process from south to north. He said hardly a word to her; his eyes spoke for him. Since his only passes were ocular, Lynn could find no graceful way to slap him down. She developed a chronic blush, which infuriated her, and fled as soon as she could.

"The poor girl," Jessie said indignantly. Said Richard, "He's softening her up." "What do you *mean*?" "It takes a powerful gal to resist such flattery." "Flattery!" "To her sex appeal. Do you see Keith Palmer getting anywhere with his droopy looks? A woman likes a man who wants her, doesn't she?" "Not a man like *that*!" "You couldn't be wronger," Richard said; and there developed between the newlyweds a certain coolness that lasted the better part of a morning.

Richard had to admit that, as far as Vaughn's day-to-day assignment was concerned, his work could not be faulted. During the day he was rarely beyond arm's length of Hendrik; and when the old man went to his room for the night, Vaughn set up a cot in the hall straddling the doorway. If a door was opened anywhere, or a footfall or a voice got to his ears, he was out of the cot like a shot, hand darting to his holster, either to investigate or to wait where he was until he was satisfied that the sound augured no threat to his charge. He bathed and changed his clothes in the afternoons in Brass's bedroom, when the blind man took his daily nap, and then only after latching and locking the bedroom door.

There were no incidents, only a clotting of relationships. The Alistairs remained a duo, rarely separating—once Alistair drove down to the Old River Inn to make a telephone call, he said, and his wife paced the parlor until he returned; after dinner they usually played cards, ignoring the others. Hendrik Brass and Vaughn formed another set, with Hugo lumbering dumbly along on their periphery. The others, with the indecisive exception of Cornelia Openshaw, constituted the largest clique; Miss Openshaw could not seem to make up her mind between the Brass-Vaughn-Hugo group or the one that included young Palmer. She flitted from one to the other like a disoriented bee.

One night after dinner the spinster wandered over to the ancient cabinet Zenith and began to play with the dials. Nothing happened, which was not surprising, since the Inspector had seen her go through the same routine at least twice before. "Goodness, not even the radio works," Miss Openshaw said. "Mr. Palmer, would you mind driving me over to the Inn? They have a TV there."

She was obviously on the prowl. Keith flushed.

"I'd like to, Miss Openshaw, but Miss O'Neill and I have a date to go walking. Don't we, Lynn?"

He fully expected to be thrown to the wolverine. Instead, Lynn said, "Of course, Keith. I'm sorry, Miss Openshaw. I'm sure Mr. Palmer will be happy to oblige some other night. Coming, Keith?"

Outside, Keith, hustling Lynn along, blurted, "Thanks a million. It was the only thing I could think of."

Lynn giggled. "She really has a thing for you."

"That's the way it's been all my life. The ones I go for won't give me the time of night. The ones that go for me are dogs."

"Oh, I'm sure that's not true. Didn't you say something about being married—in a way? Whatever that meant. Or did you marry a dog?—what a nasty word!"

"No! I mean ... Look, Lynn," Keith said, "about this marriage business ... Oh, damn it, I simply can't explain! I mean, all I can say is I'm not a two-timer. It's not my nature. Lynn, trust me. I want to get to know you—"

"Why?" Lynn said remotely ... not quite as remotely as during their last walk, but remotely enough to let him know she wasn't to be taken in by a lot of sweet talk from a married man on the make.

"Because—Hell! Why does a man usually want to get to know a girl?"

"Do you really want me to answer that?"

"Well, of course that becomes part of it—"

"Of *course*."

"But not the whole part, or even the most important part—"

"Oh, I don't know," Lynn said. "It's pretty important. Anyway, let's drop the subject and enjoy the woods. Lovely country, isn't it? So different from Wyoming."

They exchanged biographies, feeling better. Lynn's original family home had been in a coal-mining town which went ghost after the veins ran out. "Easterners have an idea everybody from the West is a cowhand. Wyoming has more sheep than cattle, and darn few of either where I grew up. Daddy died when I was thirteen and my mother went a few years ago. I could certainly use that million dollars. I don't even have a job."

"You," Keith said warmly, "could get a job in Hollywood, and not processing food, either."

"*Mister* Palmer. That's one of the oldest lines there is," Lynn said in a weary-wise tone. Secretly she was pleased; he had said it almost as if he meant it—well, really as if he *had* meant it. "And what's your tale of woe?"

He seemed to brace himself, and spun an abbreviated account of his partnership in a junk and scrap iron business "with a marvelous guy named Bill Perlberg"; then of Vietnam and the Saigon bars and the wily Cong, and so on; and in none of it appeared the names Joanne and little Sam, or even the words wife and son, which might have explained the abbreviation, but of course Lynn didn't know that, although she suspected all sorts of things. As for Keith, he tried to change the subject.

Lynn listened critically, walking in judgment, and decided to let him have it. "You're leaving things out," she said, as Zola might have said, "*J'accuse!*" "Why, Keith?"

He was saved by a fluty soprano tootling, "Oh, Mr. Pallllll-mer! Mr. Palmer?" Or was he? For it was Miss Openshaw, skittering. "Oh, there you are! It's really Miss O'Neill I'm looking for."

"Me?" Lynn said.

"Mrs. Queen wants you. Right away."

"I'll take you back, Lynn," Keith said in a rush.

"No, Mr. Palmer, Mrs. Queen doesn't want *you*. Why don't I keep you company until Miss O'Neill gets back? Miss O'Neill, Mrs. Queen is *waiting*"—and she gave Lynn a friendly shove, and at once latched onto Keith's arm—"oh, I'm so glad to get out of that *house*, Mr. Palmer. That old man gives me the jeebies. Do you know I sometimes get the feeling that he's *looking* at me? I know that awful creature Vaughn definitely is. . . ."

Lynn had to suffer Vaughn's examination as she passed him taking Hendrik up to bed from the parlor. This time something was added. He brushed against her, and his big hand somehow made contact with her bottom. She was about to whirl on him when he said politely, "Pardon *me*, Miss O'Neill," and went on up the stairs. His back laughed at her.

Lynn strode indignantly into the parlor. "Miss Openshaw says you want to see me, Mrs. Queen."

Jessie was knitting; the Inspector was reading yesterday's New York *Daily News*. They both looked up.

"Well, I'm always glad to see you, dear," Jessie said in a puzzled way. "But—"

"What my wife means, Miss O'Neill," the Inspector said with a grin, "is that she was wondering out loud if everybody wouldn't like some tea, and she happened to mention that she didn't see you here. That was all the excuse Miss Openshaw needed. Before anybody could say 'Keith Palmer!' she lit out."

Lynn said rather carefully, "She's pathetic."

"But persistent," Dr. Thornton snapped. He was reading a learned piece by Hugh Hefner angrily. "My advice, Miss O'Neill, is not to waste your sympathy on her. Women of her sort can become dangerous. If I were you, I'd tell Palmer to stay out of her way."

Lynn shrugged. "He's a big boy, Doctor, and I hardly know him. Oh, dear, I'm getting a headache. I think I'll go to bed."

"Four aces," DeWitt Alistair said to his wife, and reached for a mountain of toothpicks.

That was the night the Inspector decided to check with his Irregulars on their last assignment. It was taking too much time, and his nose told him that time was growing short.

"You should have been chairman of the board, Inspector Queen," old Brass said with his gummy grin. "What's the purpose of this conference?"

He was perched on the edge of his paterfamilias chair like some Lilliputian monarch, sucking on the handle of his cane, the lights bouncing off the brass onto his bald head with its football lacing. Vaughn and Hugo flanked him. There was a full audience. For once they were more interested in the Inspector than in their benefactor; there had been something in the Queen voice when he sounded the tocsin that rang through the musty house like the last trump.

"I'll make it short, Mr. Brass," the Inspector said. "You got all these people here on the yarn that you're worth six million dollars—"

"Yarn?" the old man interrupted. He was sucking, twitching, cocking his ears with every appearance of anticipation.

"Yarn," the Inspector repeated. "Because I've had my investigators checking for ten days. In Phillipskill. In Tarrytown. All over Westchester County. In New York. In Boston and Philadelphia, where there's a lot of Back Bay and Main Line money deposited and invested. In New York, Boston, and Philly I set a reliable agency to work on it. What I wanted was quick but thorough coverage, and my crew couldn't do it all themselves. And what they've come up with is this."

Something like horror had leaped into every eye.

"My people haven't been able to find a single checking or savings account or safe deposit box anywhere in the name of Hendrik Brass. Or any record of stocks or bonds, or of financial holdings of any kind. They've found no trace of real estate except this house and the grounds. The house is rated a white elephant by the local real estate people, and the land is worth just about the amount of the outstanding mortgages, of which there are two. In other words, there's practically no equity in your House of Brass."

"Indeed," the old man said with enjoyment. "Your wife isn't the only one who's been doing her knitting, I see."

"I'm not through knitting yet," the Inspector retorted. "My people also turned up the fact that you're over your head in debt to tradespeople in Phillipskill and Tarrytown. The butchers and grocers are carrying you with at least six months' bills. You haven't settled your last winter's fuel bills and come next winter, as I understand it, you'll either pay up or you'll have to go back to heating this antique the way your ancestors did. You're in your third month of arrears to the power company, and one of these days, unless you clear the account, they're going to shut off your service. And the reason you don't like telephones is that the phone company did cut off your service eight months ago for nonpayment. So how many millions can you have, Mr. Brass? And where are they? The way it looks now, the only estate anybody can inherit is a bunch of IOUs."

His audience looked as if he had just announced that they had been enjoying the hospitality of Typhoid Mary.

"Well, Mr. Brass?"

"About the unpaid bills," the old man replied calmly. "Why should I hurry? Yes, some of them are becoming impatient, but let 'em. They'll get over it. Didn't you know they'd rather have a rich man owe them than a poor man pay?—because they can keep adding interest to the bills. As for the telephone company, who needs a telephone? I paid their damned fixed charges for years, and for what? Ninety percent of the calls people make are a waste of time, anyway—jaw-jaw-jaw. Does that answer your question, Inspector?"

"It wouldn't satisfy a two-year-old. But the money you owe is the least of it. How about the money you're supposed to have? You haven't answered that."

The withered mouth parted, and the old man had to make a grab for his false teeth. He seemed delighted with himself;

worse, with Richard Queen, as if the Inspector, like a small boy, had run to him with some treasure of the field to admire. The falsetto of his amusement filled the flickering parlor and its dusty furniture and ricocheted off the time-cracked portraits of the he-Brasses in their stocks and the she-Brasses in their crinolines. They could only gape at him as if he were about to announce that he was the Wizard of Oz.

Hendrik Brass wiped his sightless eyes with a frayed handkerchief.

"You've made me very happy, Inspector Queen." But his voice was now shrewd and cruel. "I'm glad you've snooped. It gives our little game a zing—you know? Think you've caught the old scamp, hey? Well, that's as it may be. I leave it to these good people to decide. Whom will you believe, ladies and gentlemen? This man, who claims I'm a lying pauper, or me? Think it over, my friends. Make up your minds whether I'm penniless, in which case you can leave my house tomorrow morning—with the missing halves of the thousand dollar bills, as I promised—or whether I'm a millionaire and stay. It's up to you." He rose and said peremptorily, "Dummy, your arm! Vaughn, come."

"Daddyo," Vaughn said with admiration, "you blow my cool!"

Silence followed the trio out of the parlor and up the stairs and beyond. It was a long time before it was broken.

Then the Inspector said, "As the old filbert says, it's up to you."

Dr. Thornton had been shaking his head. "I don't know," he said. "I just don't know whether to stay or go."

"What do you think we ought to do, Inspector?" Cornelia Openshaw asked anxiously. "What are you going to advise your wife?"

"Me? I wouldn't leave for ten times the millions he's dangling in front of your noses."

"But I thought you said—"

"Something's going on that isn't right, Miss Openshaw, and I'm staying till I find out what it is."

"Well." Miss Openshaw seemed in agony.

Lynn O'Neill was tossing her chestnut locks. "I simply don't know what we're panicking for. Inspector Queen and his friends can't possibly have covered every place. Mr. Brass could still have his millions on deposit or invested somewhere. I've read that lots of rich people have their money banked in Switzerland, or somewhere else abroad. I'd stay if I were you, Doctor. Think how you'd feel if you found you'd walked out on a million dollars."

"That's his bait," Thornton muttered. "But I do admit that if there is a fortune . . . With a million I could enlarge our clinic, buy the latest equipment, expand our services. . . . I suppose I'll stay. How about you, Keith?"

Young Palmer grinned. "A fire and flood couldn't drive me away. I don't care what you found or didn't find, Inspector. The way I look at it, he's playing poker with us. You don't get up and walk away from a pot like this."

"Even" asked the Inspector dryly, "if you suspect you're playing with a stacked deck?"

"All my chips consist of is time. And I've got plenty of that."

The Inspector was heard to mumble something about P. T. Barnum and the birthrate of suckers, but only by his wife.

"He could have hidden assets," Jessie said suddenly. "All this brass, for instance."

"Why, that's *true*," Cornelia squealed. "And none of us saw it but Mrs. Queen. The brass must be worth a fortune!"

"You said you'd been in the scrap metal business, Keith," Lynn cried. "Do you know anything about brass?"

"Some." Keith picked up the wicker basket with its brass casing and went over it carefully. Then he examined one of the brass lamps, hefting it repeatedly. Then he examined a late Dutch trundle bed in the same fashion—it had been plated with the omnipresent brass and converted into a magazine rack. He shook his head. "In my opinion all this stuff is ordinary brass of average composition, weight, and workmanship. Maybe below average."

"Even so," Dr. Thornton protested, "there must be tons of it lying around here."

Keith shook his head. "I don't think you could figure the total value in more than thousands. What could you do with sub-par brass in all sizes and shapes but strip it and have it melted down to scrap?"

"Well, I still think we oughtn't to give up hope," Cornelia declared. "Mr. Brass did send us those bills, and if he's a pauper where did he get them? Didn't you say they're genuine, Inspector Queen?"

"The ones my wife got are."

"There, you see?"

The Inspector shrugged.

"Just—one—minute." Lynn was looking around. "This house if full of antiques. Some of them are probably rare."

"Whatever he's got that was worth anything, Miss O'Neill, he's spoiled by plating it with this brass. Anyway, it's all falling apart."

Silence.

"Say!" Keith exclaimed. "The House of Brass used to deal in precious stones, too, didn't it? Why can't his millions be in jewels? Diamonds and stuff wouldn't take up much space if you wanted to hide them. They could be under our noses!"

"It's possible." The Inspector did not sound excited. "The only ones," he went on slowly, "who haven't expressed an opinion are you people." He was staring at the Alistairs. "What are you intending to do? You staying or leaving?"

DeWitt Alistair opened his mouth.

"Staying," his wife said, and took a fortune in toothpicks with a straight flush.

A day passed, and another. Keith and Lynn, spelunking in the cavernous cellar, which was full of fat spiders, broken furniture, and shelving loaded with old kerosene lamps, corroded pipe fittings, empty wine bottles, boxes of rusted nails and screws, and other junk—apparently Hendrik Brass never threw out anything—found no treasure but a mildewed phonograph cabinet and a boxful of ancient records, some of them in undamaged condition. The phonograph was one of the early massive Victrolas, wound by hand, and many of the records were thick platters with Red Seal labels and blank backs—Carusos, Melbas, Schumann-Heinks, Louise Homers, Geraldine Farrars, Titta Ruffos, Mary Gardens, Alma Glucks—some departed Brass had evidently been fond of opera—and a selection of popular recordings of a simpler day.

They lugged and tugged the old machine halfway up the cellar stairs, where Hugo, investigating, discovered them; he completed the portage by himself as easily as if it had been Hiawatha's canoe.

Hugo deposited the Victrola in the parlor and tracked down a pot of usable grease; he came back with the pot and the records, and Keith set about cleaning and regreasing the machine, while Lynn went through the box, sorting the records and dusting them. There was even a packet of steel needles in the box, miraculously never opened. Keith began to crank.

" 'On the Tamiami Trail,' " Lynn read one label. "I never heard of it."

"I have," Richard Queen said. And, as the Victrola burst into scratchy, faraway song, he said formally, "Mrs. Queen, may I have the pleasure?"

Before Jessie could jump to her feet the music stopped with a dying screech, and Richard turned in protest to find Vaughn straightening up from the machine, leering over his

71

rape like a Vandal, while old Hendrik stood in the doorway, smiling. He had a thin portfolio tucked under one arm.

"You'll have to postpone your dance for some other occasion, Inspector. This time I'm calling the meeting."

He felt his way to his favorite chair and settled himself. Hugo moved a low table to a position before the chair. The old man patted the table, nodded, and placed the portfolio on it. Vaughn and Hugo took up a rather ominous stand flanking the chair.

"It's two weeks or thereabouts since the attempt on my life was made by—as Inspector Queen would put it—person or persons unknown," the old man began in his lip-smacking way, "but here I am still alive and kicking, as they say, and here you all still are, waiting on the old lunatic's decision. Well, I've decided."

DeWitt Alistair inclined his head as if listening for distant drums. Elizabeth Alistair sat steady as an Indian chief, but the Inspector noticed that she was holding her breath. So she belonged to the human race after all.

"I don't hear anything," the old man said. "You're wondering now what the old fool's going to say. How many of us? Eh? Which of us? Who gets? And who doesn't? Well, ladies and gentlemen, my conclusion is that there's not much to choose among you."

And this smells high to heaven, Richard Queen told him in the voiceless colloquy he was conducting. Alistair was an all-round no-goodnik, and Mrs. Alistair was about as attractive as Sinjanthropus's wife. And to claim that there was little to choose as between, say, Lynn O'Neill and Cornelia Openshaw was the clearest example of blindness he had yet seen in the blind man.

Brass rapped on the floor. "I've instructed Mr. Vaughn, in his capacity as Attorney Vaughn, to draw up my will, and he has done so."

"Yes?" burst out Miss Openshaw, and put her purple-tipped claws to her mouth.

"Ah, my dear, can't wait? I understand. You see how much good your meddling's done, Inspector? Why, ladies and gentlemen, I have left my estate—all six million dollars' worth, as advertised—to the six of you, share and share alike. How's that?"

There were sighs, signifying thankfulness. The Inspector felt let down. He had had some wild thought that the old man meant to set his prisoners to springing at one another's throats by leaving some of them out; but who, with the possible exception of DeWitt Alistair, would resent sharing a gratuitous fortune with five other people when each share was worth $1,000,000?

"However," said the old man, and paused.

Ah, the Inspector thought.

"There's a proviso. I told you that Mr. Vaughn was not able to locate another of my candidates, the person named Harding Boyle. Well, if Boyle should turn up no later than one month after my death, he will be included as an equal legatee, so that the estate would then be split seven ways instead of six. Oh, yes, and I have left a special bequest in my will to Mr. Zarbus."

"To *who*?" asked the Inspector, his grammar showing.

"Zarbus, Hugo Zarbus, O good and faithful servant, et cetera. This dumbhead here. It won't much affect anyone's share, however; you can afford to be generous."

Why can't I believe a word the old rascal says? the Inspector demanded of himself in despair. Maybe it was the result of a total misreading of superficial signs—of the mendacious way old Brass chomped, sucked, leered; the derisive chuckle and titter. Could it be that this appearance of insincerity had nothing to do with his character? After all, he was rewarding the man who had cooked his meals, polished his tons of brass, taken care of his creature needs, suffered his abuse, day in and out for years. The Inspector shook his head. He simply could not see Hendrik Brass being grateful to anyone for anything. No, there was a gimmick in all this. Only what was it?

As for Hugo Zarbus, the announcement of his windfall left him looking exactly as stupid as he always looked.

The old man was opening the portfolio. From it he took a blue-backed document and spread it flat.

"Mr. Vaughn, will you ask Sarah and Emma Hotaling to step in here?"

Vaughn said nothing nastily and went away. He returned herding the two women Brass had hired for the duration of his visitors' stay. The Hotaling sisters were Phillipskill spinsters who seemed to have been born frightened. They crept about the premises making beds and pretending to dust, and all but ran after the dinner dishes were put away; they never left without giving the impression that they were not coming back. But they did. So Brass must be paying them. But where was he getting the money? He must have some hidden away, probably in the same cache from which he had taken the $100 and $1000 bills.

"A pen, Mr. Vaughn."

Vaughn produced a ballpoint pen and placed it in the old man's hand.

"Guide me to the signature line."

The private detective-lawyer set the hand in place.

"Sarah and Emma," Hendrik Brass said, "I am now going to sign my will. I ask you to witness. Do you understand what I'm talking about?"

The two women nodded in terror.

He wrote laboriously. There was no sound but the swish of the pen.

"Now, Mr. Vaughn, have the Misses Hotaling sign as witnesses."

The sisters frantically wrote their names where Vaughn's stabbing finger indicated.

"By God," Vaughn drawled, "they can write."

"Are they finished, Mr. Vaughn?"

"Yup."

"Then thank you, ladies. That's all."

Under cover of the sisters' flight, the Inspector drifted across the room to glance down at the will. Vaughn was watching him with a grin. But there was no question that the "Hendrik Brass" the old man had shakily written was in the same hand as the signature in Jessie's letter of invitation.

"That's enough, dad," Vaughn said, and picked up the will. "You'll wear the ink out. Anything else, Mr. Brass?"

"One thing. You people need be in no hurry to leave. In fact, I should like you all to stay on. Eat! Drink! Be merry! For who knows? Tomorrow the old man may die, and then you'd only have to come back. But with what a difference, eh? Rich! Does my heart good to think of it. Ah, what a wonderful thing it is to give. The question is, will I receive?"

The cackle this time was prolonged. He sounded exactly like Basil Rathbone's Witch in the "Hansel and Gretel" recording the Inspector had once given Wes Polonsky's daughter's firstborn.

"Of course, if you want to go . . ."

It seemed to the Inspector that Brass allowed his voice to dribble out deliberately. *If you want to go . . .* Then what happens?

"Look, Mr. Brass," the Inspector said. "Wouldn't this be a good time to let these folks know just where your money is? If you've got it tucked away somewhere, it might put everybody to a lot of trouble trying to find it. Not to anticipate your death, but you brought the subject up yourself."

He could have sworn that the sunken eyes in their liverish pits saw him.

"Giving you a bad time, Inspector? Well, sir, I don't choose to tell you. No sir. What do you think of that?"

He chuckled and held out his arm to Hugo.

They heard the old man complaining all the way upstairs, Vaughn stalking behind; whining that Hugo was going too fast, too slowly, too clumsily, until the querulous voice was cut off by the snip of a door.

"Well?" Richard demanded. "You people going or staying?"

Young Palmer was rubbing his hands. "He seems to want us to stay. Far as I'm concerned old Hendrik can do no wrong—not after today! How about you, Lynn?"

"I've nowhere to go, and I'm in no hurry to get there." Lynn wriggled. "Golly! A whole million dollars!"

"I wonder," wondered Cornelia with Chinese eyes, "where he's hiding it."

"That's his hook," the Inspector said wearily. "He's playing you people like fish. He's got some cockeyed reason for wanting you here. In my book that's good enough reason to get out."

"Then you're leaving?" Dr. Thornton asked.

"Somebody has to watch over you babes in the woods. Who knows what's in that head of his?"

"I noticed he didn't say anything this time about giving us the other half of the $1000 bill if we left," the doctor muttered. "Well, I've invested this much time, I'll stick a few days longer."

"You, Alistair?"

The beefy man did not hesitate. "If I had dough, I'd say this was some crazy con. But Liz and I are kind of on the short side. I'm playing the hand out."

To which Mrs. Alistair nodded.

"In that case," Richard said to his tender half, who had been sitting there having the creeping shivers over the mess she had got them into, "we may as well take up where we left off. Miss O'Neill, would you put the phonograph back on?"

And to the scratchy strains of "On the Tamiami Trail" he grabbed Jessie around the waist, swept her out into the middle of the parlor, and launched into a Warren G. Harding-type foxtrot.

"We'd better be getting back, Mr. Palmer," Lynn said. "That moon is doing things to you."

Keith mumbled something. He turned off the portable radio he had bought in Tarrytown and scrambled to his feet. The moon was sending a message across the Hudson that ended gloriously at the half-sunken dock. But then it had touched Lynn, too. Maybe she was immune.

Lynn took his arm cosily as they strolled back.

He wished she wouldn't. It brought them into contact. Of course, contact was what he wanted more than anything, but what good was contact without cooperation?

So he walked stiffly. Lynn did not seem to notice. She kept chattering away about an insurance guy named Harry, the wonders of food processing, and other memorabilia of Wagon Springs. That last kiss had been something all right. But from the way Lynn was acting, it might never have happened. Maybe the music had been wrong. The jockey had put on Zero Mostel. Keith cursed himself. He had tried to find some schmaltzy love songs on the transistor, but no dice.

"What?" Keith said. She had broken contact. He felt a sense of inconsolable loss.

"I left my purse down at the dock, darn it. We'll have to go back."

"Oh. I'll go. You wait." He plunged off, taking the flashlight with him. Why, the poor guy, Lynn thought. Leaving me without a light in the woods. I did get him flustered.

She rapped her shin against a big rock and sat down, rubbing her leg.

In the dark.

In the very dark.

It was so dark suddenly that Lynn began to be furious. Getting him hot and bothered was lovely, but this smacked of petty male revenge, which wasn't in the rule book. I'll make him pay, Lynn thought, and immediately felt better.

Light blinded her.

"Hi, babe," said the voice behind it.

Vaughn's voice.

Lynn leaped. But he was too quick for her. She felt herself smothered, surrounded, immobilized, befouled. His hands were everywhere. She squirmed and tried to kick and bite. He laughed. He was not even breathing hard.

"Yup," Vaughn said. "You feel even better than I thought you would."

Lynn tried to scream. But he had his forearm against her throat.

"Now you don't mean that, baby," Vaughn said. He began gently to bend her backward. "Yell your head off. I like it that way."

"Wait, wait!"

"Why fight it, baby? If you can put out for a square like Palmer, think what a real man'll feel like."

He must be vulnerable somewhere, Lynn thought desperately. "I thought . . . you had . . . a job guarding Mr. Brass."

"Beddy-bye behind a locked door. Quit stalling, chick, and awayyyyyyy we go."

The next thing Lynn knew she was flat on her back and he was straddling her. He looked twenty feet tall. Lynn gathered all the breath in her body and shrieked, *"Keith!"*

Keith was coming on the run. She could hear his big feet crashing through the brush. A crazy light began bobbing in her direction. Lynn rolled over and away. Vaughn swore, and laughed, and turned off his flash. Lynn shut her eyes. Poor Keith. Now, on top of everything else, he was going to take a beating. For her. Vaughn would break him in two. How he would hate her. Oh, Lynn. She found herself crouching behind a tree, afraid to look.

She heard sounds. Feet sounds, nose sounds, lung sounds, fist sounds, and finally whole body sounds. Then no sounds.

I'd better start running, Lynn thought dully.

But then a man came around the tree and took her arm roughly and said, "Tough boy won't bother you anymore. I found out something."

Thank you, God.

"Oh, Keith, he gave you a bloody nose!"

"Hell, no. I ran into a tree coming up the path."

"Found out?" Lynn found herself hugging him. "Found out what?"

But Keith seemed remote in a manly, majestic sort of way. "The guy has a glass jaw."

As soon as Richard locked and bolted their door that night, Jessie said, "Richard, I want to get out of this. I mean it."

"Palmer took him," her husband said, shaking his head. "I'll be damned."

"First thing tomorrow morning I'm going to that old man and tell him his monster Vaughn made a mistake in my case. Then, darling, we're *leaving*."

"What? Oh, no, not yet, hon." He was frowning. "We can't. At least I can't. But I wish you would."

"Richard Queen, I'm your excuse for being here. You know I won't go one foot without you."

"You're a stubborn woman."

"You're a—you're a policeman!"

"Honey, I think we're in for a rough time. That will Brass had Vaughn draw up was a bad mistake. He's practically asking for it."

"Asking for what?"

"A box and six feet of Westchester County. You mark my words, Jessie. With this setup, the will that old idiot signed today is going to be his death warrant."

Two days later he was proved a prophet.

6

WHO?

The evening before had been remarkable in only one respect. The Queens encountered Hugo on their before-dinner walk back from the woods. He was an extraordinary sight. He was dressed in a blue serge suit that fitted him like a coat of mail and trailed whiffs of mothballs; enormous oxblood-colored shoes; and what in the Inspector's youth had been called an "iron hat"—a derby. And he was chugging out of the driveway on an aged Honda.

Hugo braked, and the Inspector asked gravely, "Where you going all dressed up? Got a date?" He tried to visualize the female who would date Hugo, and could not.

"It is my night off, Mr. Queen," Hugo said proudly. "Mr. Hendrik gives me four whole nights off a year."

"Can he spare 'em?"

"Have a nice time," Jessie said; and Hugo tipped his derby and chugged on his way. "Poor man. Why, Richard, it's practically *slavery*."

"He must get paid something if he can afford to go to town. Wonder where he goes. And what he does."

"And how little," Jessie said grimly, "Mr. Brass pays him."

Mr. Brass seemed out of sorts at the dinner table. The Inspector put it down to Hugo's absence. The old man was neither japish nor tittery tonight; for the most part he munched in silence, feeling around for his food. Occasionally Vaughn, who was still showing a purpled souvenir on the southeast corner of his jaw, speared a slippery piece of meat for him. Once Brass called testily for wine, and Vaughn went down to the cellar and came up with a tall dark slender bottle, stagily dusty and cobwebbed. The old man fingered it and sniffed at the cork.

"This claret is older than I am," he squeaked. "Always meant to keep it for an occasion. Ah, well, who knows? Fill my glass, Mr. Vaughn. And the others'."

They sipped to Hendrik Brass's health. He seemed to derive a derisive pleasure out of that, and cocked his head evilly at them in turn, looking more like himself. The claret had turned to vinegar, and none of them finished it. Shortly afterward Vaughn took the old man up to bed. In the flicker of the candles the wine left in their glasses sparkled like fresh blood.

The Inspector found himself sitting up in bed, every nerve alert. Beside him Jessie slept. He listened, wondering why. No wind rattled branches outdoors or made the old house groan; no one had cried out—he was sure of that. Yet he had been awakened by something.

He slipped into his robe and slippers and noiselessly unlocked and unlatched the bedroom door and stepped out into the chill hall. The red night light was a misty wound in the shadows. He strained his eyes in the grayness, and his ears. He could just make out the big blob down the hall before Hendrik Brass's door that was Vaughn, lying on his guardian cot.

Then he heard it clearly. It was Vaughn snoring. Of course. The man had to sleep, and the Inspector had made no sound. Still, he thought, I could tiptoe up to him and put him out of commission before he could reach for his gun. Maybe Keith's haymaker to his jaw had taken the starch out of him; he certainly had been acting sheepish since the battle in the woods.

Suddenly the short hairs on the Inspector's neck rose and a cold finger ran down his spine. Those were no snores he heard, but the rough and broken sounds of a struggle for breath.

He began to run.

Once more Dr. Thornton and Jessie Sherwood Queen tended a patient, sponged blood, administered hypos, and sutured and dressed a wound.

"He's lucky," Thornton said. "In spite of all his boozing he's in good shape. He'll be all right."

Lynn O'Neill, who had been staring fascinated at her sedated attacker of two days before, said, "And Mr. Brass?" She moistened her young lips.

"Mr. Brass," Dr. Thornton muttered, "is dead."

Keith Palmer said, "Lynn, I'd better get you out of here."

He took her away. The others were in the hall, where Chief Fleck had sent them.

Fleck licked his lips, too. There was triumph in his small eyes, and anticipation, and the hope of many, many reporters. He asked jovially, "Could this Vaughn have stabbed himself?"

Thornton shook his head.

"Impossible," the Inspector said. "The angle of the wound shows that he was stabbed from behind as he lay on his side facing the door. The knife slid in under his shoulder blade at an upward angle. He couldn't have done it himself if he were a contortionist."

Jessie fastened the last strip of adhesive tape across the man's naked, hairy back. They had put him on the couch in old Brass's sitting room. In the adjoining bedroom the last of the Brasses lay dead in his tall brass bed. There was no doubt that he had died in it. There was also no doubt that he had been murdered in it.

The Phillipskill police chief stalked back into the bedroom for another look. Richard and Dr. Thornton followed, leaving Jessie with the sedated Vaughn.

Hendrik Brass's eyes glared up at his wrinkled ceiling, as blind in death as they had been in life. The mouth gaped toothless—his dentures were in a glass beside the bed—gray-blue as the gray-blue face. It seemed to the Inspector that he was smiling, enjoying his joke to the end, and beyond. The blade that pinned his bloody nightshirt to his flesh was buried to the haft.

"County Medical Examiner's M.D. ought to been here long ago," Chief Fleck grumbled. "What's your opinion, Dr. Thornton?"

"I could tell more if I removed the knife."

"Then do it. I authorize you. But be careful about prints."

Thornton was still wearing surgical gloves. He grasped the ends of the crosspiece, avoiding the haft, and lifted gently. The knife came out of Hendrik Brass's heart as if it had impaled a piece of cheese. A trickle of blood oozed out, and stopped.

"Brass," Richard said. "What else?"

It was all of brass, and it was rather short—although it had been long enough—and the blade as well as the handle was intricately chased with the tiny crucibles and other symbols with which its owner had seemed obsessed. Thornton scrutinized the blade, its length, its shape.

"My guess is it's the same blade that wounded Vaughn. And of course it's what killed Brass, though the autopsy will make sure of that. Unless there's one just like it around somewhere."

"I saw this one—or its double—on Brass's desk downstairs as late as last night," the Inspector said.

Fleck's man, who had been dusting the room for prints, was sent below. He came back shaking his head. "It's not there now, Vic."

"Then this is the one, all right. I wonder what kind of knife it is. Never saw one like it." Fleck's little eyes sought Richard Queen's, and looked away.

"It's a fancy letter opener," Richard said. "And it was on his desk in plain sight. Anyone could have taken it."

"Then it's probably another inside job, like that hit over the head a couple weeks back." The police chief glanced about. "Oh, Doc," he said, relieved. "Looks like I've drawn a big one at last."

And the Inspector knew that Chief Victor Fleck had no intention of turning the case over to a higher authority. He had probably not even notified the State Police; no troopers had shown up. He wondered if Fleck would even call on their crime laboratory facilities. He would fight tooth and nail to keep on top of the case; he must have visions of himself running for Sheriff out of the publicity.

Richard turned to the newcomer.

The Medical Examiner's physician was a brisk, balding young man with tired eyes who seemed to know Chief Fleck of old. He nodded curtly, said nothing, and set about his examination. He paid no attention to the others.

The chief's man looked up from the letter knife. "No prints I can raise, Vic. Either they won't take on all this engraving, or whoever used it wore gloves."

"Tag it for the files, Bob, after Dr. Ash gets through with it. I guess we've pulled a cute one. Well, Doc?"

The country doctor straightened up. "Is that the knife?"

"It's the one we took out of his chest."

Dr. Ash looked it over. "I'll take it along for comparison purposes during the P.M., but it certainly looks as if it did the job. I'll arrange for removal of the body."

"Do you have to take him to the county seat?"

"Where do you suggest I do the autopsy, Chief, on this bed? Sure I have to."

"Well, all right."

"Dr. Ash," said the Inspector.

"Yes?"

"How long would you say he's been dead?"

"Yeah," said Fleck, fast. "How long, Doc?"

"I may know more exactly after the post, but my preliminary opinion is that he died between four and six this morning." He jerked the topsheet over the dead man's head and brusquely left.

"How's it sound to you, Thornton?" the chief demanded.

"Between four and six A.M., yes."

"Then it looks pretty clear to me. Middle of the night, and Vaughn was sleeping on the cot across the old man's doorway. Whoever committed this crime sneaked up on Vaughn in the dark, stuck the knife in his back, pulled it out, and got

81

into Brass's bedroom and let the old man have it with the same knife. That stack up to you, Queen?"

"Sounds likely."

They found the private detective sitting up on the couch, and Jessie breathing indignation.

"He won't do a thing I tell him to, Doctor," she said. "He actually wants to get up!"

Vaughn took the flask from his lips and cursed. "She tells me the old man got it in the heart. Who the hell got past me?"

"That's what you'd better answer, mister," Fleck said.

Vaughn gave him the fish eye. "Who are you? The local fuzz, I suppose. How do I know who it was? I was catching some shuteye." His arms flexed, and he winced. "When I catch the joker who stuck that shiv in me—"

"Any notion who might have done it?"

"Fanny Farmer. How do I know? I was sleeping, I tell you—"

"Sleeping off a drunk, if you ask me," the Inspector said. "How many belts did you have last night?"

Vaughn chose to ignore him. "Look, fuzz," he said to Fleck. "Old man Brass was my job. You haul your fallen arches back to Phillipskill and give some Joe Tourist a speeding ticket. Leave this caper to me. When I've got him I'll dump him in your lap. If he'll fit under your front porch, that is."

Fleck's face had turned from red to purple.

"You want to see the inside of my pokey? Watch that big mouth when you talk to me!"

"Look," Vaughn sneered, "I happen to be a lawyer, and I specialize in suits for false arrest. So cool it, man. Damn it, Thornton, this dressing stinks. I can feel myself bleeding again."

"If you'd remained quiet, as Mrs. Queen told you to," Thornton snapped, "it wouldn't be. We'll have to redress it. It's all right, Chief, I can handle him. If he gets tough, I'll just yank on a suture."

They left Vaughn with Thornton and Jessie, Fleck raging. He bellowed for his other assistant, a crosseyed man he called Lew, and ordered him to watch Vaughn. "If he gives you any trouble, slap him in cuffs!"

"What are you going to do now, Chief?" the Inspector asked. He was genuinely curious.

"Find out where everybody was," the chief said, glaring. "Starting with you."

It was a wary group that Fleck assembled downstairs.

Everyone but Palmer was in a robe. Everyone was watchful. Everyone spoke with loving care. Over the parlor and its lively brass hovered the spirit of $6,000,000. Someone there had hastened the great day, and he—or she, or they—meant to survive undetected to enjoy its reward. The Inspector, sensitive to such atmospheres, felt it in every cell. Poor Jessie could only sit and shiver in the chill of morning.

"Between four and six?" Ellery's father said. "That's a bad time to have to prove an alibi. I was in bed with my wife. It had already happened when I got up to see what had wakened me. Mrs. Queen was sleeping."

"Not when you got out of bed," Jessie said. "After all those years as a nurse I sleep with one eye open. I saw my husband get up and go out, Chief."

"What time was that?" Fleck wanted to know. And added hopefully, "I suppose you didn't notice?"

"Yes, I did. I always wear my watch to bed, and as you can see it has a radium dial. Part of my training, too. It was seven minutes past six."

Fleck grunted. "How about you, Miss O'Neill?"

Lynn looked angry. "I wish I could prove I was sleeping. But I was, even if I can't. Sleeping like mad. I always do. I didn't even know anything was wrong till all the noise this morning woke me up."

"You, Palmer?"

"Sleeping," Keith said. "The noise woke me, too. Inspector Queen asked me to get to a phone and notify you, so I dressed and did. That's all I know."

"Miss Openshaw? Can you prove where you were between four and six A.M.?"

"What do you think I am?" Cornelia asked in shrill outrage. "I was alone in my bed. Where else would I be? I'm a decent woman, I'll have you know!"

"No alibi, either. You, Mr. Alistair?" He looks like a Met fan after the last out, the Inspector thought. Fleck had come to the game expecting a home run first man up.

Just a shade too quickly Alistair said, "My wife and I were like the Queens, Chief, in bed together."

"That," said Hube Thornton, "is a damn lie."

From Mrs. Alistair's look at Thornton, Richard expected him to slide to the floor at their feet. But the doctor merely said to Fleck, "I'm a restless sleeper, and I woke up about three o'clock. So I read a medical journal I'd been meaning to get caught up on. At half-past three or so I heard noise from the Alistairs' room, which is next to mine. A few minutes later I heard their door open and close. I wondered what was going on and got out of bed and opened my door. I saw Alistair pussyfooting it down the hall. He disappeared around the corner and I went back to bed."

Chief Fleck said, "Aha!" The Inspector could not believe his ears. "Why didn't you yell?"

"For what? I hadn't seen him do anything, and I knew Vaughn was stretched out across the door to Brass's room. He's been doing it every night. But I definitely saw Alistair leave his room."

"So you lied," Fleck shouted at Alistair. "That's going to cost you, mister!"

The country squire was not florid now. But his voice was persuasive. "I didn't want to get involved, Chief. You can understand that, after what's happened. It was a mistake, I see that now. I'm sorry."

"Where did you go?"

"I've suffered from insomnia all my life. Last night it was particularly bad. So I got up and put on my robe and slippers and slipped out of the house for some air. This damn place is like a tomb."

"What did you do out there?"

"Just walked. In the woods. At one point I went down to the boat landing. Sat smoking there till dawn. I got back a few minutes to six and fell right asleep. I didn't wake up till my wife shook me and told me the news."

Smooth as snake oil, Elizabeth Alistair said, "I heard my husband get up, and I heard him come back. I'm a light sleeper, too. It's just as DeWitt says."

"Except you can't prove he spent all that time at the landing," Fleck said. "Or where you were, Mrs. Alistair!"

"In *bed*."

"Alone. Between four and six. Nobody has an alibi, not even you, Queen—you know yourself the police don't give house room to a husband and wife alibiing each other. The only one caught lying outright is Alistair, and I'm tucking that away, mister, in my little black book." Alistair looked displeased; his wife looked deadly. "Oh, Hugo. How are you? Feeling any better?"

Fleck could only have said it out of some crude fellow-countryman kindness. Hugo looked as if he had had a memorable night. His derby was missing, but he was still in his blue serge suit and oxblood shoes. The suit was rumpled and dirty and gave off a strong malty odor; the shoes were scuffed; one lace trailed. The little eyes were red-veined and puffed, the huge jaw shaking.

He was suffering from hangover as well as grief; they had found him sprawled on his bed, fully dressed, snoring like a whale and smelling like a brewery after his night in town.

Fleck had questioned him, but he remembered nothing. He had gone to a tavern outside Phillipskill and performed prodigies of beer consumption. He did not recall leaving the tavern, or getting home, or where his Honda was (they found it near the entrance to the Brass property, where he had evidently fallen off). And as far as time was concerned, it had not existed for him.

Hugo did not answer Chief Fleck's question at once. He rubbed his bushy massif of a jaw as if he had a toothache, and he said in his *basso vibrato*, "Mr. Hendrik is dead. Oh, he is dead." Then he answered it. "And my head hurts."

"I'm leaving my two men here till I finish my investigation," Fleck announced before he drove off, "and nobody better try to cop out, because I'll take it hard. Don't leave the grounds, except if you need anything from town one of the ladies can do it. Oh, and if anybody decides he's got something to say to me, tell one of my officers. Okay?" Then he left, almost skipping.

There was nothing else. No fingerprints had been found in Brass's sitting room or bedroom—or on the door Vaughn had been straddling—that should not have been there. No evidence of any description had turned up. They were immured with a murderer, and the Inspector felt challenged.

"But Richard dear," Jessie protested, "all we have to do is tell Chief Fleck I'm not the real Jessie Sherwood and he'll let us go. He'll know *we* can't be mixed up with that six million dollars. I see no reason to stay on. We're not even able to help that poor old man anymore."

That was when her spouse took her hands in his and said, "Honey, I've got to hear the other shoe drop. One of these people murdered old Hendrik. Who? I can't leave till I find out."

So all Jessie could do was stand at her bedroom window and watch the county meat wagon cart away the remains of their baffling host, dissection-table-bound. There were other faces at other windows, all glum, watching, too. Even if the late Hendrik had died fortified by the prayers of the Dutch Reformed Church (which he had told them in his wicked way he had not attended for sixty years), they would not have felt comforted. Not, at least, until the pall of murder was lifted from The House of Brass; or for relief, the six million untraced dollars were dealt among the lucky innocents.

And that seemed a long way off, for Vaughn in his legal entity assured them that the law debarred any distribution of the estate for at least six months. He seemed to take joy in the assurance.

It occurred to more than one of them that, suddenly, in some magical reversal of reality, they had exchanged one tormentor for another.

7

AND WHERE AGAIN?

Burial was to be in the family plot on the grounds at Hendrik Brass's express request, Vaughn said. "He told me F.D.R. got planted in his Hyde Park turf, and he had as much right to dig his own dirt as any Democrat that ever died."

"May I inquire," inquired Mr. Pealing of Pealing & Pealing, the Phillipskill morticians, "if the deceased left any provision—?"

"If you mean you're buggered about your bread, Mac," Vaughn said, "I wouldn't advise making with the super-deluxe bronze. There's some question about the scratch. The best I can promise you right now is that your bill will give you a creditor's claim on the estate."

"No insurance policies, Mr. Vaughn?"

"No policies."

Mr. Pealing sighed. "Well, my father buried his father, and my grandfather buried his grandfather, so I suppose I can't do less than bury him. And if the estate can't settle the bill, we'll write it off to goodwill." Mr. Pealing allowed himself to smile at this.

"I never met a body snatcher yet who'd give you the scraps out of his embalming pail. You'll deduct it from your income tax."

Mr. Pealing retreated.

"Why do you have to be so unpleasant to everybody, Mr. Vaughn?" asked Jessie. "Mr. Pealing said that out of the goodness of his heart."

"That noblesse oblige crud?" Vaughn laughed and went about his business, which at the moment was to make Hugo's life even more miserable than it was.

The old Sleepy Hollow Church had been shut down for years except for an annual service, to Jessie's disappointment;

but the police chief vetoed any church rites, and the funeral was held from the house. The modest casket was not opened. The only outsiders present were a Tarrytown minister, Mr. Pealing and an assistant, and Chief Fleck's crosseyed Lew. The small Brass graveyard in its hollow near the road was a thicket of triumphant weeds and leaning stones, some with gasping cherubim on them; a sumac had planted itself before the doorway of the single half-ruined mausoleum. The minister read a simple service, watched Hugo and the undertaker's assistant fill in the grave, shook hands, and fled. The others followed suit, all but Richard and Jessie, who lingered among the stones, stepping over those that had fallen, reading all but obliterated epitaphs, and after a while clasping hands for communication.

The stone that sent them hurrying back to the house was a thin slab, sandy brown, on which were incised the words POMPEY—*Faithful Unto Death*. As Jessie remarked, Pompey might as well have been a horse.

They found Fleck waiting in the parlor with the others. The Inspector grinned. The chief had been playing it with coziness. Not a newsman had shown up; there had been no mention in the local papers of old Brass's murder, only of his death. Fleck was sitting on the homicide, saving the news for the great day when he could announce not only that it had taken place, but that he had solved it.

The chief sat very still before the fireplace, as if in hope that its dimensions would diminish him. He took no part in what followed.

Vaughn said, "Settle down, boys and girls. *Vino* on the house. We've guzzled the last of that lousy claret, today we polish off the port, and what's left downstairs wouldn't make a vinegar dressing. Anybody want to hear decedent's last legal words?"

He had slipped a soiled T-shirt over his bandages; only a slight brown tear under his right shoulder blade and a certain caution of gesture reminded of his stab wound. His shoulder holster with its nuzzling .38 was very much in evidence. He opened the blue-backed will.

It began, "I, Hendrik Simon Brass, a single man, of the Town of Phillipskill, County of Westchester, State of New York, being in full possession of my faculties, but sensible of the uncertainties of this mortal life . . ."

So he dictated the wording, the Inspector decided. It was the Brass style, all right. He noticed that no one was reaching for the port.

Vaughn read through the appetizers. After a while he got

to the meat, and paused for their slavering benefit. Then he laughed and read on.

"I give and devise to my manservant, Hugo Zarbus, my house and lands situate in the Town of Phillipskill.

"The remainder and residue of my estate I give and bequeath to DeWitt Alistair, Lynn O'Neill, Cornelia Openshaw, Keith Palmer, Jessie Sherwood, and Hubert Thornton, share and share alike, if living at my decease.

"If by the expiration of one month after my death one Harding Boyle, whereabouts unknown to me, shall appear in his person and make claim to participation in my estate, he shall receive an equal share with the six legatees named in the paragraph preceding. The executor of my estate shall have full authority to identify the said Harding Boyle and to certify his claim or reject it.

"At the expiration of the one month above-mentioned, the contents of my house and outbuildings shall be sold at public auction for the benefit of the residuary heirs.

"I nominate herewith, and appoint as executor of my estate free of bond, my attorney Vaughn J. Vaughn . . ."

When Vaughn J. Vaughn had concluded, there was a fascinated hush. Then Richard Queen said, "That's one daisy of a will, Vaughn. What kind of lawyer are you? Nothing is said about payment of debts. Nothing is said about the value of the residuary estate or, more important, what it consists of—"

"Or where it is!" screeched Cornelia Openshaw. "You drew up this will. Where is it?"

Vaughn poured himself a slug of port, shrugged, winced, and tossed the wine down. "Don't ask me, baby."

"And don't you 'baby' me! I want to know what I've just inherited. I have a *right* to know. He named you his executor. You've *got* to know!"

"All I know is what I just read in the paper."

Alistair was trembling. He said in a very flat voice, "Look, Vaughn, you know what's at stake here—"

"You certainly do," Lynn said. "Do you mean to tell us that Mr. Brass didn't tell you where his fortune is?"

"Brass was an old mule. He insisted on dictating the will word for word. When I suggested ordinary legal additions he wouldn't listen. When I asked him to specify what his estate consists of and where the six million dollars' worth is, he cackled and clammed up. Anything else you want to know, friends, consult a crystal ball. Tennis, anyone?"

At that moment Lew came in and whispered to his chief. Fleck got up heavily and went out and a moment later came back with two men. One was fat, the other was thin. Both had eyes like pack rats.

"Mr. Fluegle and Mr. Channing," Fleck said. "Lawyers from Phillipskill. You can take it from there." And he squeezed himself before the fireplace again.

Mr. Fluegle said in a fat voice, "I represent the creditors of the late Hendrik Brass in Phillipskill."

Mr. Channing said in a thin voice. "*I* represent the creditors of the late Hendrik Brass in Phillipskill."

Mr. Fluegle glared at Mr. Channing. "You didn't lose any time getting here."

Mr. Channing spat at Mr. Fluegle, "And ditto!"

"Now, girls," Vaughn said. "I'm the late etcetera's executor and I dig you've split the wolf pack between you. Where are the tabs and how much do they come to?"

Each lawyer produced a briefcaseful of bills. They thrust them at Vaughn in a dead heat.

Vaughn riffled through them. "Gas, electric, hardware, butcher, baker—I suppose there'd be a candlestick-maker if Brass hadn't made his own. And so on far into the night. How much does your clients' share of the loot come to, Fatty?"

Mr. Fluegle said, "$3,025.11."

"Skinny?"

Mr. Channing snapped, "$4,443.13."

Vaughn pushed the wine aside, produced his flask, unscrewed the cap, and threw his head back. When it had sought its level again he said, "This here lightning calculator makes that $7,468.24, right, pardners? Well, all valid claims will be settled in full when that fathead police chief over there lets me out of here long enough to file the will. Assuming, of course, there are assets sufficient to cover them, on which point said executor has no scuttle yet. Any other remarks? Don't bother. Hugo, heave these bloodsuckers out."

Hugo blinked. Then he advanced on the two lawyers, rather like a glacier. They departed with all deliberate speed.

Vaughn took another pull on the inexhaustible flask. (He must have brought a case with him, the Inspector thought.) "Come on, cats, you're sitting around here looking like you're in the same bag. Get with it. Who's going to start the action?"

"I'll do it," Richard said. "For openers, I point out that the will makes no provision for maintenance of the house or us during the month waiting period. The stores certainly aren't going to extend any more credit, nor after what those lawyers just heard. If we stay on here we've got to have power and we've got to have food. Looks to me as if we're going to have to pool our resources."

"*If* we stay on, Cornelia said bitterly, "and *if* Hugo doesn't mind. It's his house now."

"At least he knows what *he* inherited," Keith said.

"What Hugo inherited," the Inspector said, "is the doubtful equity in a twice-mortgaged piece of property nobody would take as a gift. Do you mind, Hugo?"

Hugo looked frightened. "Mind, Mr. Queen?" he said nervously. "Mind what?"

"Don't waste your time talking to dickybird," Vaughn said. "Anyway, nothing is anybody's till the will goes through probate and all claims on the estate are settled, which is going to take at least six months, as I told you, more likely a year. If you squares want to toss your bread around supporting this pad, it's okay by me, but my advice is to go home and wait for what the Surrogate and Allah provide."

"That would be good advice," the Inspector said, "except for two little details."

"What's one, dad?"

"Brass was murdered. Fleck won't let us go."

Chief Fleck stirred and nodded cautiously.

"And the other one?"

"I can't believe that Brass didn't say *something* about the whereabouts of that alleged six million."

"I agree," Dr. Thornton said. "He was having too much fun mystifying us not to have left some clue, even if it was cryptic."

"You holding out on us, Vaughn?" Alistair said, his voice even flatter than before.

Rather slyly, the Inspector thought without charity, Vaughn began to act as if he were in pain. "Sheest!" he said, grimacing. "This air hole in my back hurts like hell. You sure you didn't get your degree in dentistry, Doc?"

"You're lucky to be walking around," Thornton growled. "And don't try to change the subject. Just what did the old man say?"

"Nothing, I tell you. Nothing that means anything."

It was Elizabeth Alistair who got the first exclamation in. "Then he did tell you something! What?"

Vaughn shrugged and winced again. "He said it was somewhere in the building."

"This building?" Lynn cried.

"This building."

"But where?" Cornelia Openshaw demanded.

"I asked him. He wouldn't say." He got to his feet. "Doc,

my back's crucifying me. How about some pain killer? I don't even smoke grass."

"Damn Hippocrates," Dr. Thornton muttered. "Hugo, help me get this hood upstairs."

When Thornton returned, the Inspector said, "We've been waiting for you, Doctor. We've agreed some kind of action has to be taken. Chief Fleck has the right to say yes or no to whatever we decide on, of course. He's said he'd at least listen. That right, Chief?"

Fleck's barnyard eyes were muddy with suspicion. He said, "Yes?" Then he said, "Yes." Then he said, "Depends on what action."

"I know what I'd do," Cornelia said viciously. "You men ought to take that *thing* upstairs down to the cellar and thrash him. He knows more than he's letting on. Beat it out of him!"

"What action?" Fleck repeated.

"One step ought to be taken right away," Richard said. "According to Vaughn, Brass said the six million—in whatever form it is—is somewhere in this house. We have to search the house." He held up his hand at their cries of enthusiasm. "It's no job for amateurs. Not if it's to be done right. Chief, I have five old cronies, retired from the force like me, who've been helping me out in this merry-go-round. With your permission I'd like to make up a search party of myself, you, your own officers, and my five friends. They're pros, and they won't want a thing out of it but to get off their duffs. What do you say?"

The chief looked at him, pondering ponderously.

"And if there's any trouble with Vaughn about it," the Inspector added in a helpless way that made Jessie want to pinch his perfidious hide, "why, Chief, you can handle him."

Fleck at once said, "Okay."

No structure of such complexity was ever so thoroughly searched. They examined every nook and cranny, closet and cabinet; went over every piece of furniture; probed every artifact and household article; dissected each mattress and counterpane. They took up the rugs and the carpets, they tapped the floors and ceilings and brass paneling, they thumped the walls inch by inch, and they gave the cellar the going over of its cluttered life, including the furnace. They investigated the toilet tanks, the stovepipes, and all the fireplace flues. They mounted ladders to look into the chandeliers. They unscrewed gas mantles. They removed the lining of the refrigerator door. They explored the attics and their moldering contents. They found two safes for which no combination was noted down anywhere, and opened them as if they were boxes of soda crackers; one of them contained a cashbox concealing $187 in small bills and sixty-five cents in coins ("My God!" DeWitt Alistair shouted. "Is this what's left out of what he's been running the house on?"), among other items less negotiable. They measured each room to the last cubic inch, and then they measured the halls for arithmetic discrepancies, of which there were none.

Not that their search was without fruit. Among their more exotic discoveries were some tattered IOUs, well-foxed; a small tole box of baroque pearls, hopelessly flawed; a dented pewter porringer inscribed in dainty flourishes *Beloved Baby, 1827*; bootleg 19th Century editions (British) of *My Secret Life* and the nude drawings of Aubrey Beardsley, both of which looked as if they had gone through the Florentine flood; and three U.S. two-cent pieces in worthless condition and a doughnutlike hunk of stone that Johnny Kripps claimed was a sample of Yap Island money. They found (in the safe containing the cashbox; the other had guarded the aged IOUs and the box of fourth-rate pearls) several booklets of Masonic ritual in code, which produced excitement that died a horrible death when the Inspector decoded them and stated that they were Masonic rituals in code. They also found a moldy velvet bustle, plum-colored; a letter of marque; a chromo photograph of A. Lincoln's letter to Mrs. Bixby; $10,000 worth of Confederate money; and a bottle of bathtub gin with drowned ants in it. But for sheer volume their most rewarding finds were wornout molds for making brass; there were hundreds and hundreds of them. . . . Things like that. Things like that were all they found.

"Well," the Inspector said, "we certainly gave it the old college try. Thanks, men," he said to Giffin, Polonsky, Kripps, Angelo, and Murphy. "Don't be surprised if you hear from me again." And the five old men shook hands all around, even with Chief Fleck, who had got underfoot at every turn, and left looking happy.

"Now what?" said Jessie. With Hendrik Brass's death she had stopped bedeviling Richard about pulling out. Instead, she had followed him around the house during the search as if she were an heir in fact. "What next?"

"The house has to be torn apart." This from DeWitt Alistair. He was stripped quite down to the spiritual buff, mean-eyed, starveling, and ready to bite.

"You mean literally, Alistair?" Dr. Thornton said.

"The old man told Vaughn that the money or whatever it is

92

is *in* the house. My hunch is it's bricked over or cemented into one of the walls."

"That might be why the tapping didn't produce anything," Keith said in his slow way. "Alistair could have something."

The Inspector scowled. "It's a possibility I've been hoping we wouldn't have to face. But I admit I can't think of anything else. Can anybody?"

But there were complications, all of them entangled in law. The structure itself had been willed to Hugo. More urgently, there were two mortgages on the property, the first held by the Phillipskill Savings and Loan Association, the second by the Hudson Valley Trust Company of Tarrytown. In law, Vaughn pointed out, the mortgagees held priority.

The president of the Phillipskill bank, a jolly-eyed man named Jacobus, and a vice-president of the Tarrytown bank, a sad-eyed one named Claffey, were invited to visit and listen. Their joint conclusion was that the buildings had no marketable value. No one in his right mind could be expected to buy such a sprawling ruin (it was also half eaten away by termites, as the Inspector found a strategic place to point out) for purposes of residence. Various zoning regulations debarred a sale to an institution. As Jacobus put it, the place was a brass elephant.

"When we originally granted the loan," the Phillipskill bank president said, "the house was still worth something, and of course there was the land. The house probably wouldn't pay the cost of tearing it down, which would have to be done eventually anyway because of the value of the acreage, which has gone up considerably."

Mr. Claffey of the Tarrytown bank frowned at what he evidently considered an unbankerish admission on the part of Jacobus. "The question is if the land has a value in excess of the property's indebtedness."

"Let's talk turkey, gentlemen," Richard retorted. "You not only have no objection to the house being wrecked, you'd actually welcome it, isn't that so? Because eventually you'd have to have it done yourselves, and by our doing it now we save you money. Number two, there's been a jump in land values around here in recent years, especially river frontage. Even if the present value of the land mightn't be in excess of the mortgages, which I don't concede, it's bound to become a bonanza, with the demand for housing, the superhighways, and Phillipskill's increasing access to New York for commuters. It strikes me it's worth your while not only to agree to the house being torn down, but also to compensate Mr. Zarbus for it, because it's a cinch the cost of wrecking is going to go up in time, too. What do you say?"

"Mr. Zarbus's consent would certainly be required," Claffey said carefully. "And I think we might see our way clear to paying him a little something for it, eh, Jacobus?"

Jacobus nodded carefully, too. "Would that be agreeable to you, Mr. Zarbus?"

Mr. Zarbus was absent in all but body. He gaped at them. Vaughn said curtly, "I'll handle it for the pinhead," and the bankers looked crestfallen. In the end they closeted themselves with Vaughn and Hugo, and from the sour looks on their faces when they departed the Inspector knew that Vaughn had made a good deal, not so much positively for Hugo as negatively against Claffey and Jacobus. Banking was a pursuit Vaughn seemed to hold in even greater contempt than medicine. In fact, he said so. To the bankers, as they left.

The next problem on the agenda was the wrecking.

"It isn't necessary to raze the house to the ground," the Inspector said. "The whole purpose is to find a hiding place. All inside walls should be stripped to the studs; all flooring should be ripped up, but it can be laid back down afterward for our use till we leave. The old bricks in the fireplaces can be taken out without tearing down the chimneys; and so on. It will leave the house a shell, but at least it'll still be usable on a temporary basis—we can rig up blankets between bedrooms, for instance, for some sort of privacy. Any objections?"

"As long as they don't miss anything," Alistair said.

"We'll see to it they don't."

Several companies were asked to submit estimates; the lowest came from a small one in White Plains in the large person of a gentleman named Trafuzzi. "We got to work on time plus labor," Mr. Trafuzzi told them. "Considering what you folks want, it ain't no ordinary wrecking job. You got to put up $3,000. Might not come to that, but that's what you got to post."

He wandered off while they talked it over.

"Anybody got three grand?" asked Vaughn, ever cooperative. "Come on, you millionaires. Ante up."

The spontaneous silence was eloquent.

"Couldn't we float a bank loan?" Keith asked at last.

"On whose credit?" Vaughn jeered. "Alistair's?"

Alistair murdered him with a glance. Mrs. Alistair's followup cut his corpse into little pieces.

It was agreed that a bank loan was out. The Alistairs had no credit, Lynn said she had no credit, Keith said he had no credit, Cornelia Openshaw said she had but wouldn't lift a finger—the responsibility should be shared, like the legacy it was aimed at; a point so self-evidently fair that Jessie was relieved of the difficulty of having to reply at all, which was also the case with Dr. Thornton.

Vaughn was not a man to let an opportunity for bad works pass. "Why's your lip buttoned, Doc? You leeches have all the dough there is, with what you steal from Uncle, not to mention what you suck from your victims."

Dr. Thornton laughed. It was a short laugh, not expressing merriment; but since it was the only laugh of any kind he had released in weeks, it startled them.

"How much have I charged you, Vaughn?" And he made a secret of his mouth.

The Albert Schweitzer of South Cornwall had been bothering Richard for some time. He seemed troubled, as if he were wrestling with a disagreeable problem. Indeed, the Inspector was surprised that Thornton had remained away from his practice for as long as he had. He had made several calls to his colleagues, each time coming back looking unhappier. It was another piece of the puzzle.

"We have those halves of the thousand dollar bills," Lynn said suddenly.

Vaughn, who since the night of his K.O. had been relatively respectful toward her, winked. "Half a bill is as good as no bill, doll. To the U.S. Treasury it isn't money. Next suggestion?"

"Wait a minute," the Inspector muttered. "Miss O'Neill may have a point. I forgot about the bills."

"But I just told you, dad—"

"I told you to stop dadding me!" the Inspector said, not muttering. "I'd like to see those six halves all together."

"Why?" The Beast of Belsen, instantly.

"Call it a hunch, Mrs. Alistair."

Predictably, the heirs were able to produce their bisected Grover Clevelands on the spot from assorted locations on their anatomies. The Inspector glanced at Jessie, and she handed over the one she had received, looking overjoyed to be rid of it. Her husband dragged over a table and they surrounded it, each clutching his ragged piece of bill. "I'm not going to take them away from you. I just want to make a test. Mind putting 'em on the table?"

Vaughn hung about, craning. "Hey, man," he said to Alistair. "Old Sleuth here knows a con or two his own self. Five gets you ten he palms one."

And indeed Old Sleuth was engaged in a sort of shell game, switching half bills around in this spot and that, but always setting two halves in juxtaposition. In the end there was an awful silence. He had managed to arrange the six halves in such a way that the variously jagged edges of each fitted into a companion half, forming three perfect bills.

"The thought crossed my mind when we didn't find the six halves Brass was supposed to be keeping for you—I mean during the house search," the Inspector said, "but in the turmoil I forgot about it. We don't have—we've never had—the six halves of six different bills. What that old shtunk did was halve three bills and send one to each of six people as *if* they came from six bills. So it cost him not six grand but three. Smart."

"*Dishonest,*" yelped Cornelia.

"He was a dishonest old man," Dr. Thornton said heavily. "Among other things even worse." And he added, with astonishing savagery, "The world is better off without him."

"Anyway, we do have $3,000 among us," Lynn said, "and that's exactly what Mr. Trafuzzi is asking. You know, it's eerie? Almost as though Mr. Brass had foreseen all this."

"I wouldn't put it past him," Keith grunted. "But the question is, do we pool 'em or don't we? I'm for it."

Alistair glanced at Mrs. Alistair; she inclined her head a fraction of an inch, and he promptly said, "So am I." Lynn voted yes. Cornelia, agonized, voted yes, too. And Dr. Thornton looked weary and went along. Jessie, of course, had to play her part.

So they called Mr. Trafuzzi back in.

There was an ancillary consideration. Demolition would leave them facing the great outdoors while it was in progress. None of them seemed to feel that sleeping on the ground wrapped in shredded counterpanes would contribute to a good-neighbor policy. The solution was offered by Richard. According to Vaughn, Brass had specified the house itself as the hiding place of his treasure. That eliminated the coach house, which had five tiny rooms in its upper story unused, from its accumulation of cobwebs, dead insects, and strata of dust, for generations. The Inspector suggested that they clean the rooms, rent some cots, and move in while Mr. Trafuzzi's crew worked on the main building. Lynn and Cornelia, Keith and Dr. Thornton, Vaughn and Hugo, could double up; the other two rooms would serve for the Alistairs and himself and Jessie. The women would have to cook outdoors, but only until they could move back into the shell. The utilities and appliances in the kitchen would still be usable.

A vote was taken in mounting excitement, the resolution was passed without dissent, and they set to work, even the Alistairs. Vaughn kept his private eye on things, nipping regularly at his flask; Hugo hung about with a bewildered look, useless as a child, until out of pity Jessie asked him to help. After that he tagged after her looking happy.

That night there was trouble in the fusty old dining room. The Inspector had been half expecting it; nerves had shown multiplying symptoms of frazzle. Vaughn was regaling the company with accounts of his extracurricular activities with the wives of husbands he had been hired to get the goods on, until Cornelia Openshaw could bear it no longer. "Is it absolutely necessary for you to talk with your mouth full, Mr. Vaughn? You're disgusting!"—to which Vaughn replied through a mouthful, "It isn't what's going into my mouth that's bugging you, Corny, it's what's coming out, right? I bet you take Henry Miller to bed with you. Never met an old babe yet who could keep her mind off her ovaries"—setting off a scene that ended with Jessie's taking a hysterical Miss Openshaw upstairs, while Lynn gave him a generous piece of her mind. After dinner Keith invited Vaughn to come outside and be taught all over again how to treat decent women, Vaughn replying with a hasty grin, "Don't let that fluke punch go to your head, buster. If I didn't have this hole in my back . . ." and the Alistairs got into a wrangle over a pile of toothpicks, exchanging charges of cheating.

So it was a relief when, the next morning, Mr. Trafuzzi and his wreckers arrived and with happy cries set to work tearing the innards out of The House of Brass under a thin red line of quivering eyes, not excluding Chief Fleck's, who had begun to look desperate. As far as Richard could tell, the Phillipskill policeman had done nothing whatever toward solving the murder of Hendrik Brass but hang about, as if waiting for providence to drop a confession into his lap. Brother, he told Fleck silently, with this crew and setup you're going to have a long wait.

That afternoon, on a summons from the Inspector, the West 87th Street Irregulars were back on the job, equipped with an electric drill, a metal detector, picks and shovels, and other equipment he had had them rent in the city. While Trafuzzi's men worked inside, the Irregulars pried out the brickwork of the driveway immediately surrounding the house to examine the foundations. Then they invaded the cellar, broke up the cement of the floor, and dug down for several feet. They used the metal detectors in the cellar and around the foundations. The five men bedded down that night in their cars; early the next morning they were back at it. Wes Polonsky began to show signs of wear and tear; Pete Angelo performed prodigies; the others labored in anger at their infirmities.

But they did the job, and what they found for their pains

97

were: five Indian arrowheads and a crumbled calumet; an automobile license plate for the year 1915; a whale-blubber try-pot eaten away by rust; the skeleton of a small dog; the boiler of a Stanley Steamer; a metal box full of handmade iron nails fused into an irregular mass; and a whole collection of unrecognizable objects that would not have brought five cents from a pop artist.

And what Mr. Trafuzzi and his men found was nothing but sand plaster and several historic rats' nests, in one of which lay a scrap of time-browned paper that had come, according to its legend, from a copy of *Godey's Lady's Book* of November 1844.

That night, around the cooking fire on what remained of the brick driveway, the only sounds audible came from nature's lesser creations. Her noblest were speechless.

Until Lynn cried in despair, "It's an out-and-out fraud, that's what it is. That old man was pulling our legs. There's no six million dollars. There's no six *hundred* dollars."

"I don't believe it," whimpered Cornelia. "I *don't*."

"Somehow," Keith mumbled, "neither do I. Maybe it's because I don't want to not believe it."

"It's here," DeWitt Alistair said between his large teeth. "It's got to be!"

"I hope," began Dr. Thornton; and stopped there.

Mrs. Alistair glared into the fire as if she meant to challenge it with her bare hands.

As his wife looked anxiously at him, Richard Queen muttered, "Somehow I get the feeling it's here, too. But, damn it all to hell, where?"

They moved back into what was left of the house. There were two days left of Hendrik Brass's time limit of one month.

8

AND WHY AGAIN?

They waited without knowing what they were waiting for. Of course, approaching was the auction, but what could be expected from that? There was almost $7,500 worth of known outstanding indebtedness; time and the publication of the notice required by law would undoubtedly produce more. Still, the place was a magnet, holding them fast. (There was a general tendency to forget about the murder; it seemed irrelevant. Only Chief Fleck's sulky shadow reminded them of it from time to time.)

It certainly held Lynn and Keith fast. But they were held by a magnet far older than Hendrik Brass or his elusive millions. It was this attraction that led to the newest *bizarrerie*.

Dr. Thornton had become progressively more interesting as a study in indecipherable behavior. He had taken to long solitary walks, hands behind back, head bowed, brow furrowed, like a philosopher pondering the perplexities of the universe or a prisoner chafing from confinement. In the one posture he was certainly getting nowhere; in the other he could formulate no plan of escape. In either or both he was unerringly unhappy. Could it be their failure to unearth the secret of Brass's hiding place—his Schweitzerian wish, indeed his need, for the riches that would do so much for so many? The Inspector did not think so. That might be part of it, but it was not the greater part. No, it was something else.

What it was emerged on the evening before the scheduled auction. Richard and Jessie, out for a constitutional, found Dr. Thornton sitting in the woods on a rock, alone as usual, chin on his fist. He had been neglecting himself beyond even his capacity for self-neglect: his sandy-gray hair was creeping down his neck like jungle brush; his red mustache had raggedly overgrown his lips; he needed a shave; and his suit, ever shabby, was disreputable. Also, the adhesive around his eyeglass shaft had come loose; it was barely holding the broken ends together, and he had not bothered to retape it.

"Oh," he said, spying the Queens; and rose, uncertainly.

"Hi," Richard said, and would have passed on; but Jessie said, "Why don't you join us, Doctor? It's such a lovely night for walking, with this moon and all. Unless you'd rather be alone?"

"My God, no," Thornton said; and he fell in step with them. But mutely; Jessie could not even get him to talk about his youthful experiences in Papua, where he had made a pioneer study of yaws—one of his fondest reminiscences. So after a while the Queens abandoned their efforts, and the three trudged in silence toward the Hudson.

They came on Lynn and Keith as the best things—and the worst—are so often come upon, with shocking unexpectedness. The two young people were lying on the ruins of the dock, in the moonlight, passionately embracing. From the stormy music of their breathing and the wild dance of their hands it was all too clear where the pas de deux was tending; and Richard and Jessie jumped back in embarrassment, expecting Dr. Thornton to follow. But to their amazement the amazing doctor uttered a strangled *"No!"* and sprang forward, shouting, "Stop! Please, please! Stop!"

Jessie could have died. Lynn and Keith scrambled to their feet, looking madly around, Lynn smoothing her skirt, Keith making absurd brushing gestures, and both crimson in the moonlight.

"We-were-you-are," stammered Keith.

"We-were-admiring," and that was as far as Lynn could get too. They just stood there on the dock, and in it, condemned.

"I beg your pardon," Dr. Thornton said; he was gasping as if he had asthma. "I beg your pardon must humbly. But you don't know. You can't know. Nothing in the world but one thing would have made me . . ." and he was struck dumb again, as if this venture into words only proved how wise he had been in his taciturity. Then, with a great effort, he said, "This has gone too far. I have gone too far, I mean, to back out now. You'll forgive me when you hear what I have to say. We had better go back to the house. This—believe it or not—involves everybody."

How they got back to the eviscerated cadaver that was now The House of Brass Jessie never clearly remembered. All she could recall afterward was the crunching of five pairs of feet, that of two pairs receding rapidly before them— Lynn running, Keith running after her. Then Jessie found herself in the wreckage of the parlor surrounded by eyes, with Richard gripping her shoulder from behind; and the guilty pair at bay, Lynn still smoothing her skirt, Keith still brushing himself, both unconsciously, and both as angry white as they had been crimson.

"What's the hangup this time?" Vaughn asked, lowering his flask to stare. "The hippies been swinging?"

"You shut your foul mouth," Thornton said to him; and, oddly, Vaughn did. The voyager from South Cornwall turned to the young couple with resolution; he had set his course, and he was not about to trim his sails. "Miss O'Neill—Lynn, if you don't mind my calling you that—and Palmer, Keith, you won't understand at first why I'm going to talk about your most personal feelings publicly this way. But believe me, please, you'll forgive me before I'm through.

"It's given me a hard time," he said, "a very hard time. Watching your relationship grow. Reluctant to interfere. Hoping it wouldn't come to this—"

"What business is it of yours, Doctor?" Keith demanded, tight-lipped. "Or anybody's? Lynn and I haven't made any secret of our interest in each other. You'd think we were committing a crime!"

"You were about to."

"What year are you living in, Doctor?"

"No, no, you don't understand—"

"I still can't believe that a person as decent as you, Doctor, could do what you've done tonight," Lynn said in a very controlled voice. But Jessie saw her hands trembling. "I suppose you're referring to the fact that there's a Mrs. Keith Palmer and a little Palmer named Sam. Well, it so happens I know all about them. He told me."

"I don't know what you're talking about, Lynn," Dr. Thornton said. "If Keith is married and has a child it's news to me."

"It's none of your business!" Keith growled.

"Please, Keith, let me get on with this thing. The fact that you're married and may be contemplating divorce in order to marry Lynn, if that's your intention—"

"That's his intention," Lynn said with a snap. "Yes, Doctor, that's exactly his intention. Isn't it, Keith?"

"Well," Keith said, "yes. Yes, sure. Of course. What else?"

"—doesn't alter what I have to say one bit. Except to make my speech even more necessary. May I go on?"

The Queens saw the young couple exchange glances. They were no longer marooned in anger: now they were at sea.

"All right, Doctor," Keith said; oddly, he seemed to brace himself. Lynn saw it, and it brought the slightest cloud to her sunny face. "Speak your piece."

Thornton began to pace, marshaling his thoughts. The Alistairs looked alarmed, Vaughn alert, Cornelia Openshaw sniffishly eager, as if she had stumbled on a dirty book and was in the act of reading it before complaining to the police.

"I hardly know where to start," Thornton began; but he did know, or he found the answer as he spoke, for he went on abruptly. "We've all been tangled up in a mystery since we got here—three mysteries.

"The first: Why did Brass make six people he didn't know—and had never seen before—his heirs?

"The second: Does the six million dollar fortune exist? And if it does, in what form and where is it?

"And third: Which of us killed him for it?"

The Inspector in his intentness nodded. Thornton was exactly right. Those were the problems. On second thought, it was natural that the doctor should see them so clearly and express them so succinctly. He was a man trained in the observation and analysis of facts.

"I'm not a detective. I can't answer the second and third questions. But unfortunately I can throw light on the first."

Hugo had laid a fire—the spring nights near the river were chilly—and the firelight as usual was playing with the brass. Its twinkling illuminated Thornton's shagginess and made him look larger than life, and somehow menacing.

"For some time I've been trying to decide whether to tell you what I know—what I've known since the night Brass told us his baptismal name was Simon, not Hendrik. Tonight," he said, glancing at Lynn and Keith and away, in despair, "my hand was forced. I simply couldn't allow you two young people to go any further in your romance. Just before my mother died she told me something that had been on her conscience for half a lifetime and that she had kept a secret from everyone, including my father . . . the man I had been brought up to believe was my father. Well, it seemed he was not. And Mother told me the name of the man who was."

Dr. Thornton paused, and they paused with him, groping for the truth.

"And who was that, Doctor?" the Inspector asked, as though he had not already guessed.

"Simon Brass, the man you know as Hendrik Simon Brass." And the doctor went on in a great hurry, as if he were eager for his destination that he might rest, "You see what that means. . . . the only thing that makes sense, that explains why Hendrik Simon Brass gathered six people he had never seen and willed them his estate in equal shares, is that—like me—you five are also the illegitimate children of Simon Brass. And that, I'm terribly, terribly sorry to have to say, must include you, Lynn, and you, Keith. You're closely related by blood. Far too closely. You're half-brother and sister."

His blunt workman's hands, which had been raised in a sort of exorcism, fell exhausted to his sides; and he dropped into the chair in which Chief Fleck was accustomed to diminishing himself.

So the pathology lesson was over. The nature of the disease was known.

Lynn O'Neill did not seem to understand. Jessie read the girl's face as though it were a hospital chart. First she whitened—shock, a total incomprehension. Then her eyes took on the gloss that came over the eyes of all the newly dead Jessie had ever pulled a sheet over. And finally understanding, in a flood; and with it horror, shame, sickness of spirit—the debris of a cataclysm of nature.

The most inhuman cry she had ever heard from a human mouth came to Jessie's stupefied ears. And Lynn ran out, almost toppling Dr. Thornton in her flight.

Keith, like some alarmed house dog, raced after her.

And, to Jessie's astonishment, Richard ran after Keith.

What pigs people are, Jessie thought. Even me.

All through the ensuing babble—Cornelia Openshaw's strident protestations against the very notion that her heavenly father might have been a cuckold; DeWitt Alistair's spitting routine (into the fire just past Dr. Thornton's head), his profane refusal to consider any possibility of his mother's fall from grace (Alistair, who Jessie would have taken her oath possessed the filial allegiance of a Dungeness crab)—throughout the confusion Jessie sat with closed eyes, torn between her suffering for Lynn and her prayers of thankfulness that she was not the Jessie Sherwood fate and Hendrik Brass had decreed. Jessie had strong memories of her parents. Her mother had held Victorian convictions in the sole ownership of wives by their husbands; and her father, if he had ever looked on another woman with lust, would have dropped to his knees before the Baptist God he worshiped throughout the week, up to as well as including Sundays, and risen cleansed.

The protests had run their course and dropped off to mutterings when, unexpectedly, Richard Queen returned with Lynn O'Neill and Keith Palmer in tow. He was herding them like a shepherd; and—it was beyond belief—they seemed exactly as untroubled as sheep. Lynn was alive again. Bewildered, but alive. And more. And Keith looked like the proverbial condemned prisoner immediately following his reprieve. The couple stood to one side, hands entwined, quietly.

And the Inspector strode to the middle of the parlor and said briskly, "Dr. Thornton."

"Sir?" Thornton raised his head.

"That the younger brother, Simon, the one we knew as Hendrik, could have had an affair with every woman his older brother had run afoul of in this case would be just too much of a coincidence to swallow. I don't believe it for a second."

"That's what I've been telling him!" cried Alistair.

"Take your parents, Alistair. Wes Polonsky, who investigated your family for me and found out that the original Hendrik—Hendrik Willem—had been pushed to the wall by your father over a gambling debt, has found out subsequently that the younger one, Simon—our Hendrik—belonged to the old Lawn Tennis Club around the same time that your mother was a member. But there's no evidence they even knew each other. Or, if they did, had more than a nodding acquaintance."

"One man's nod," said Dr. Thornton; and bit his lip, avoiding the two young people whose lives he had sickened and who, miraculously, seemed to have regained their health.

"Granted, Doctor. But I have conclusive evidence in at least one case, thank the Lord. Johnny Kripps did some followup work for me on Simon, and he discovered that throughout that whole time when Hendrik Willem was raising hell out West and getting into that trouble with Sheriff O'Neill—and out of it by a technicality—Simon was here back East. As a matter of fact, there's reason to believe that Simon never in his life even set foot in Wyoming. Miss O'Neill, what did I ask you when I ran after you?"

"Whether my mother ever lived anywhere but in Wyoming," Lynn said dreamily.

"And what was your answer?"

"That she was born there and died there—lived there her entire life."

"So there goes your theory, Doctor, about all of you being Brass's illegitimate children. In your case we have to accept it as true, since your mother told you the story on her deathbed. But I see no basis for believing it about any of the others."

"Then I ask you again," said Dr. Thornton. "If we aren't all Brass's bastards, why did he ask us here? Why did he make us his heirs?"

"Because he *thought* he was the father of all six. In my book, Doctor, the old man was senile. You saw his behavior. He might have been on the borderline—clear about some things, hallucinating about others. And I don't have to tell you about sex delusions in senility. His mind must have been a hodgepodge of memories about his older brother's wild-oats days, and he simply took them over—applied them to himself, and twisted nearly all of them in the process; my men proved that what Hendrik Simon claimed about his older brother was just the opposite in every case. Incidentally, I'm no psychologist, but I'm betting there's a connection between Simon's identifying with his brother's life at the same time that he followed the family tradition and took over the name Hendrik when the real Hendrik died."

"Could be," Thornton said, but he did not sound convinced. "At any rate, Inspector, all you've settled for sure is that, of the six people involved, Lynn is in the clear."

"And me," Alistair snarled.

"Not you, Alistair. As far as I'm concerned, your case has to be listed as doubtful. And by the way, Lynn, I'm overjoyed about what the Inspector's friend found out. It removes any impediment between you and Keith."

"Yes," Lynn said. "Oh, yes."

"Oh, yes?" hissed Cornelia. "And what about his wife and child? No impediment! I've never in all my life heard of people acting so shamelessly. Mr. Palmer, you can be very sure I'm going to tell your wife what's been going on here!"

Mr. Palmer said nothing.

"I'm with you, baby," Vaughn said. He rose, stretched, yawned, made a face, and said, "How about our vittles, chicks? Or is Hugo back in the kitchen? I'm hungry as a wolf."

"It appears that you're not the only wolf around here, Mr. Vaughn," Cornelia snapped, distributing her largesse.

Mercifully, Hugo appeared. From some antique trunk, and for some incredible reason, he had resurrected a butler's outfit, green with age.

"Dinner," said the heir to The House of Brass, *molto vibrato*, "is ready."

Dinner was ready, but it was also inedible and dismal, unbrightened by the dining-room fire and the fat candles sputtering in the great brass sconces on the table. Nobody had an appetite but Vaughn, who ate wolfishly, as predicted. After the coffee (there was no dessert, to Vaughn's uninhibited disgust) they all took refuge in their blanket-hung shells of bedrooms. Plaster dust coated everything. The pinned-together bedding and linen they had contrived for the walls had gaps in them, and Jessie undressed in the dark. Her husband blundered about, kicking things.

"Oh, Richard," Jessie whispered (whispering, too, had become a necessity with the demolition of the walls), "I'm so proud of you."

"Huh?"

"I mean for clearing up that awful situation between Lynn and Keith. That poor baby. To be hit between the eyes by something like that . . . and you coming along to make everything all right again . . . I could hug you. In fact, I'm going to." And Jessie did, after some groping.

He was not displeased. But being Richard Queen, he grumbled, "There's more important things to worry about. . . . Okay," he argued to the darkness, "at least one of 'em's Hendrik Simon's bastard, maybe more. But it's a cinch not all of them. Anyway, he thought they were, which explains why Brass called them here and left them six million dollars we can't find. But those other whys! Not to mention the whats and the wheres. How do we answer *them*?"

"Richard, where are you going?"

"To search the coach house. Should have done it before. Maybe the old pagan was lying to Vaughn when he said his fortune was hidden in the main building."

The Inspector was up half the night searching the coach house, upstairs and down.

He found nothing.

9

AND WHAT AGAIN?

"Name is Keller folks how do," the long-nosed man said, playing with the lodge emblems a-dangle from the chain across his corporation. The Tarrytown auctioneer had been recommended to Vaughn by Chief Fleck. Keller had a look of sleepiness which the Inspector knew was an illusion; he had tangled with auctioneers before. "We'd better wait a while longer not enough hot ones here yet to warm up a hen coop." He chuckled.

No one shared his good humor. Most of the smaller contents of The House of Brass were scattered about the driveway area; for all their flashing in the sun it was a dreary scene cast with dreary people. Their only bright moment had come that morning when the Inspector pointed out that "a certain Harding Boyle" had failed to show up within the thirty days called for by the will, and that therefore a possible seventh heir was automatically eliminated from sharing in Brass's fortune. "What fortune?" Cornelia Openshaw whinnied. So that moment dimmed, too.

There were antique hunters from out of state, chiefly Connecticut, but they were only a handful; and the few local people present seemed drawn more by curiosity than a desire to possess one of the late Hendrik Brass's household treasures. No city newsmen had shown up, and the two reporters from the local gazettes were part-time correspondents, so-much-per-liners. A yawning state trooper had parked on the road. The entire police force of Phillipskill was on hand to see, apparently, that he stayed there.

For the rest, Brass's heirs, the Queens, Mrs. Alistair, Hugo and Vaughn made up one group; Messrs. Fluegle and Channing, representing the creditors, and bankers Jacobus and Claffey, representing the mortgagees, made up another; and conspicuously by himself a weasel-eyed little man with a tipstaff look about him—a process server, the Inspector guessed—whom no one seemed to know. He was studying a carbon copy of the list of auction items Keller had distributed.

"Well, looks like nobody else is coming," Keller said. "We better get going." He stepped briskly up on an improvised podium, was handed a tagged item by his assistant, and held up a piece that had come from the parlor. "Here's item number one on your list folks an old Dutch bench can be used as an elegant end table real antique dating from about 1780 it's covered with brass but you could strip that off and you'll find it's prob'ly painted black underneath and decorated in lots of colors like the authentic ones come who'll start the bidding with fifty dollars fifty do I have fifty—"

A woman's voice said distinctly, "Two dollars."

"The lady is making a funny hahaha who'll bid forty-five anybody forty-five forty-five. . . ."

The auctioneer stopped, pained. All heads had swiveled. A bright red pickup, horn blasting, was charging around the driveway scattering people. It was driven by a big man with a purple face. The man killed his engine, leaped out, and dashed at Keller as if he meant to tear him apart with his formidable hands.

"Hold it, hold it!" he shouted.

There was confusion. Chief Fleck quickly stepped in to diffuse it. After a colloquy the chief introduced the invader to Vaughn as one Mr. Sidney Carton Sloan, a building contractor from Phillipskill.

"Vaughn's the man to talk to, Sid," the chief said. "He's executor of the old loony's estate."

"What's the beef, Mac," Vaughn said.

"Now you just look here, Mr. Vorn," the contractor said. "I just got back from a Caribbean cruise, first thing I hear is Brass's kicked the bucket and they're holding an auction, well, nuts to that! You cancel and terminate this here sale and order all moneys to be turned back so my company can get our fair share of what's owed us—"

"Quit flapping those papers in my puss," Vaughn said. "What are they?"

It turned out that, several years before, Hendrik Brass had called Sloan in for an estimate of the cost of putting in "extra steel beams and columns," Sloan said, "to forestall a

107

possible collapse" of the floors and ceilings of the main building. The contractor had given Brass an estimate of $8,000 "more or less," the old man had approved, and the work had been done.

"The exact figure come to $8,327. He'd gave me an advance of $500—"

"By check?" Richard Queen asked swiftly.

The big man stared at him. "Who are you? No, cash. Ask anybody around here, he always paid cash. When he paid." To this there was a general head-wagging, led by lawyers Fluegle and Channing. "Come the job's done, he hands me another two thousand. So I wait. After a while he gives me another five hundred. After another while he gives me three hundred twenty-seven. 'Leaves a nice round five thousand owing you,' he says to me. 'I like round numbers, don't you?' I tell you he was bats. But I says fine, who's worried, not me, and goes my way. You know that old man never paid me another nickel? He keeps putting me off, complaining the work ain't right, some flooring's still sagging, and et cetera. What could I do? Take him to court? How would it look, me suing a Brass? I figure I'll give him more time, him being a millionaire and all. But now he's dead I want my five thousand. Here's the contract he signed, and his signature on this one showing the work was done. And don't try to tell me you got receipts showing he paid me more than three thousand three twenty-seven, because you can't have, and you do have they're forgeries—"

"Don't start yapping about forged receipts, Mac, till you see one. Let me look through the estate papers."

"I'm going with you," Sloan said doggedly.

Vaughn went into the house, the contractor at his heels. The Inspector followed the contractor. Chief Fleck followed the Inspector. Two people walked over to the road, got into different cars, and drove angrily away.

Brass's cupboard-type desk was still in the parlor, one of the heavier pieces Keller had left where it was for later auction. Vaughn opened a drawer, took out a fat portfolio, and began going through papers.

"Here they are," he said. "Yump. The estimates, the contract, and your receipts for the moo you say he paid. I'd assumed he paid the balance, because this dates back years ago, and his records are a godawful mess."

"Then I want my money," Sloan said.

"It's not that simple, friend."

"Just a minute," the Inspector said. He was rubbernecking over Vaughn's shoulder. "What's that about repairing some chimneys in your original estimate? You didn't mention anything about chimneys, Mr. Sloan."

"Because I never repaired 'em. You'll notice that was a separate estimate. The old man'd had some chimneys blown down during a hurricane, and he'd gone all over creation getting bids to repair 'em. He asked me to bid, too. I gave him a figure, and even though he admitted mine was the lowest bid he'd got, he said I wanted too much. Well it was the cheapest I could do it for, and in the end he decided to have me just put in those extra beams and columns. That should have been my tipoff," the contractor said bitterly. "But that Brass name fooled me. Well, Mr. Vorn, do I get my five grand?"

"There's a long line in front of you," Vaughn said. "You have a valid claim, from these papers, but there are whole squads of other creditors."

"I want my five thousand!" screamed Mr. Sloan, looking like a fried eggplant.

Vaughn shrugged. "Get yourself a lawyer, Mac. Now go cool off with a couple of beers or something, you're holding up the auction."

But Mr. Sloan had held up nothing. When they got back outside they found Auctioneer Keller busily declaiming over the rare qualities of a threadbare early American red rug for which he was suggesting an initial bid of $200. "Dandy example of the period and if you can't use a rug this size why cut it up for scatter rugs haha do I hear one fifty?"

"One dollar fifty cents," said a local.

"One *hundred* fifty——"

"How much did that church bench bring?" the Inspector asked Jessie, sotto.

"Three and a half dollars. Oh, Richard, this junk isn't going to bring *anything*."

"Anybody special doing the buying?"

"That little man there." Jessie indicated the weasel-eyed stranger Richard had mislabeled a process server. "For *peanuts*. It's a shame."

The rug went to the little man. "Sold to Mr. Phil G. Garrett for $23," said Keller, banged his gavel with eyes raised to heaven, and turned to the next item.

The Inspector studied the odd Mr. Phil G. Garrett. He became very thoughtful. Then he began walking restlessly up and down.

More rugs were offered and sold; then a lot consisting of milk glass, from a once extensive servant's table, in wretched condition; then an assortment of old chinaware, mostly chipped—all to the same Mr. Garrett for bids that, according to Mr. Keller, were a disgrace to his honorable calling. Keller was just warming up to the next lot—household ironmongery, from cookie cutters and trivets to rust-eaten flat-irons and skillets—when Richard Queen stopped his prowling and, in stopping, contrarily made his move. His hand shot up and caught the autioneer in midharangue.

"Not finished describing the lot," Keller barked, as if the Inspector had committed an antisocial act. "What's it this time for gawsakes?"

"Stop," cried the Inspector. "Stop the auction."

He gathered the heirs in the stripped house, while two more people left and Keller sat down on Hendrik Brass's paterfamilias chair in the driveway and began to wipe his neck with a red handkerchief. Chief Fleck accompanied them, treading on heels and looking dangerous. Vaughn listened for a few minutes, shrugged, and wandered off to replenish his flask which, notwithstanding the early hour, he had already emptied. Hugo hovered in the background, blinking.

"I may have this licked," the Inspector snapped. "One of our three problems, as you put it, Doctor, was: Is there really a fortune and, if so, what and where is it? I think there is a fortune, and I think I know at least what form it's in."

The outcry was as rousing as the Anvil Chorus.

"Wait, wait." He held up his hand as a fascinated Jessie laved him with love. "A few years back old Hendrik called in this contractor Sloan and made a deal for the installation of extra steel beams and columns. The reason Brass gave Sloan was that the floors and walls might collapse."

"So what, Inspector?" Keith Palmer interrupted. "This house must be over two hundred years old. It's a wonder it didn't fall in long ago."

"I don't doubt the work was necessary. In fact, that's why it didn't strike me as queer before, when Trafuzzi wrecked the house and I saw those relatively new beams and columns in the walls and floors. I just assumed the old house had needed strengthening. But Sloan's estimate used the term 'extra beams and columns.' Why *extra*?"

Lynn said, "But Inspector. They're 'extra' to differentiate them from the original beams. What else could it mean?"

"More than necessary," the Inspector said, and paused.

"Don't get you," DeWitt Alistair said, frowning.

"At all!" said his wife.

"Look. Suppose old Brass had installed something in this house that weighed a lot more than the original supports were built to carry?—so much more that it had to have extra shoring to keep the unusual weight from collapsing the building?"

110

The Inspector paused again, looking like Ellery.

"I don't follow a word of this," Cornelia Openshaw said, fretting her purple-red nails.

"None of us does, I think," Dr. Thornton said.

"We're trying to find a fortune, aren't we? A big one? Maybe so big we haven't been able to see the forest for the trees we've been rooting around in. Like that yarn of Poe's where the letter he was looking for was right under the detective's nose all the time."

"What are you getting at, Inspector?" Mrs. Alistair demanded.

"You assume a fortune of six million dollars, you think in terms of paper money, stock certificates, bonds, jewels—all light stuff. But if the fortune is in something heavy enough to warrant putting in 'extra' steel beams to support it, how about—?"

"*Gold!*" Keith shouted. "My God, you know he could be right?"

Hugo gaped. But Lynn clapped her hands. "Six million dollars in gold!"

"In gold?" Alistair and his wife said together, hoarsely.

"Gold!" Cornelia screamed.

"Gold," Dr. Thornton muttered.

"Gold?" And that was Chief Fleck, gaping like Hugo.

"Gold," the Inspector nodded. "And what do we know this place is filled with? That even looks like gold?"

And they cried together, Jessie among them, in a great breathy outburst, like the wind that blew Dorothy to Oz, "The br*aaaaaass*!"

They whirled on poor Hugo. The old man had taught him how, and he had made a great deal of the brasswork in the house. Was it brass? Or was it gold?

"You come clean, halfwit," Alistair snarled, making fists. Big as he was, dancing before the Goliath, he looked like David. "It's all gold, this stuff! Isn't it? *Isn't it?*"

Hugo looked indignant. "Brass," he said.

"He's lying!" shrieked Cornelia. "Lying!"

"Brass," Hugo insisted. "Mr. Hendrik said brass."

"Then Mr. Hendrik was the liar! Oh, what's the use of talking to this—this—"

"Keith," Dr. Thornton said. "Do you know anything about precious metals?"

"I took some metallurgy courses once," Keith said, and sprang out of the house, followed by the pale and chattering group. The auctioneer was still sitting in Hendrik Brass's chair; the little man named Garrett and the would-be bidders

111

and onlookers were standing or sitting about on the uncut grass. Keith mowed through them and seized the first brass object he could lay his hands on, which happened to be a serving tray with the familiar symbology of The House of Brass all over its face. Keith hefted it, looked thoughtful, hefted it again, frowned, pulled out the blade of his pocketknife, scratched a trench in the tray, and turned the scratch this way and that to the sun.

Then he said, "Solid brass."

He tossed the tray aside and grabbed an object they had been using as an ashtray, which might have been a communal rice bowl of some slant-eyed family twelve thousand miles away except that it was covered with the same Brassian symbols, and balanced it and scored it and peered at it and balanced it again. . . .

"Solid brass," Keith said.

He picked up an old 19th Century fire bucket and ripped off the plating and gave it the same treatment, while Cornelia whimpered like a dog, the Alistairs bared their teeth, Dr. Thornton and Lynn drooped, Hugo looked vindicated, and the Inspector's lips compressed further, Jessie's heart bleeding for him.

"Solid brass," Keith said; and he attacked object after object over Keller's protests, darting about the area like Jack the Ripper, slashing and hacking and discarding, until the driveway and the grass were strewn with the flayed corpses of Hendrik Brass's possessions, and there were no victims inviolate.

"Brass," Keith said, "all brass, through and through."

"No cigar, Queen," DeWitt Alistair said. "Why the hell don't you retire to some old folks' home?"

At which palpable injustice Jessie tore into him, until Richard stopped her with a mumbled, "Maybe he's right, honey," and there was a silence far heavier than the brass would have been had it been gold, which was not lightened when they heard Vaughn's hated voice jeer, "Well, kiddies, you all through playing?" and he bellowed, "You—the auctioneer cat. Get on with it! We've had our laughs for the day," and he laughed and laughed until Jessie wanted to claw him to death.

They could only stand about as Keller resumed his litany. Mr. Phil G. Garrett continued to outbid the other bidders, although now that so many lots were denuded of their brass skins the bids were even lower. People continued to leave. Some new ones came. Among the departed were the two local reporters.

So the second of Dr. Thornton's three questions remained a mystery, too.

What constituted the fortune?

What form was it in?

If any.

10

WHAT and WHERE?

But Richard Queen said suddenly to the heirs, "I'd like to talk to you people for a minute in private."

"Again?" said Mrs. Alistair, not politely.

"Do you want to find that six million or don't you?"

This was a self-answering argument. They joined him in the parlor. There was trouble with Chief Fleck, but the Inspector said something to him aside that Jessie was sure, from the look on her beloved's face, was mendacious; whatever it was it worked, for Fleck nodded and remained where he was. Vaughn watched them leave with a grin. He seemed to be enjoying himself.

Richard held forth for some time. "It's a trick I feel ought to be tried," he concluded. "Call it a hunch. But even if it fails, I'm not committing you people to anything. Any hitch and I'll take the rap. It won't cost you a cent."

"But darling—" Jessie began; she was looking alarmed.

"Trust me, honey."

They followed him back outside. Five automobiles of honorable lineage had pulled up during their absence; the five Irregulars were standing about.

"What are you doing back here?" the Inspector demanded.

"We caucused," said Al Murphy, "and we decided the old man needed some old-man reinforcements."

"We're here," said Johnny Kripps, "for the duration."

"And we won't take no for an answer," said Hugh Giffin.

"Bless you," said Richard Queen and he went over to the auctioneer, who was chanting, ". . . and if you don't want these trifle molds and the mesh egg boiler for yourself think what a beautiful gift they'd make for the lodge or church of your choice—" and said loudly, "Hold it, Keller."

A male voice called, "Throw him out. What kind of an auction is this, anyways?"

"What is it now?" Keller snapped.

"Hendrik Brass's heirs have just held a meeting and have authorized me to speak in their behalf. In their name I'm prepared to put in a blanket bid for the entire contents of the house—"

"Wait wait some lots have already been sold I can't legally—"

"All right, we'll except those items. Let's apply my bid to everything still unsold, including the pieces that are still in the house."

"I won't agree to any such deal!" shouted Mr. Fluegle. "My clients have a claim—"

"So have mine," shouted Mr. Channing. "I won't be party to any deal that might jeopardize the full amount of their claims."

"Neither will I!" Fluegle shouted.

"I understand that, gentlemen," the Inspector said. "We intend to protect your claims, also the claim of the contractor, Sloan. Among you people the bills still owing—including Sloan's for five thousand—come to a grand total of around twelve thousand five hundred dollars, a little under, actually. Speaking for the heirs, I bid twelve thousand five hundred dollars for the entire contents of the house less those lots already sold."

"Nothing doing," said the auctioneer with great fluency. "That wouldn't take care of my legal fee."

"We will guarantee your fee, Keller, over and above the twelve five."

"Oh, in that case," said Keller in an altogether *gemütlich* tone. "Would that meet with you gents' approval?" he asked the two lawyers.

Fluegle and Channing conferred hastily. Fluegle said, not shouting, "Our only concern is in getting our clients' bills paid. It has our approval." You bet it has, the Inspector thought; at the rate the auction was going there would not be nearly enough realized to cover the outstanding indebtedness, and this was a guarantee of payment in full.

"Slow down," said Vaughn, strolling over. "As executor of the estate, I have a say in this."

"The hell you have," Richard said. "All that Brass's will specifies is a public auction of his household goods. It doesn't bar the heirs; they're members of the public. If they want to bid in on the whole kit and caboodle, Vaughn, you don't have a damn thing to say about it."

To Jessie's surprise Vaughn immediately said, "Well, now,

popsy, you've got a point," and retired into the background for another visit with his flask. The Inspector shook his head and returned to the wars.

"Okey-doke folks I guess we can wind this up in short order Mr. —what's your name sir?" asked Keller.

"Queen."

"Mr. Queen bids twelve thousand five hundred dollars for the entire contents of this here auction less the items already sold do I hear a higher bid Mr. Garrett I got a feeling you ain't going to let this gorgeous collection of Dutch and early American lots go for a measly—"

Mr. Garrett had been pumping up and down on his neat little toes during Keller's spiel. His eyes were darting about like goldfish.

"Thirteen thousand," he said nervously.

The Inspector was watching him. "Thirteen one," he said.

"Thirteen two!" cried the little stranger.

"Thirteen five," said the Inspector.

"Fourteen!"

"I bid," said Richard Queen, "fifteen thousand dollars."

Jessie was whiter than her husband's mustache. "Richard!" she whispered. "Where on earth would we get—?"

He pressed her hand and kept looking at the little man, who by now was blotting his brows with a handkerchief that was rapidly saturated.

"Fifteen thousand bid do I hear sixteen you're not licked are you Mr. Garrett just have yourself another look-see at that list take your time sir but not too much haha fifteen bid"—Mr. Keller was obviously seeing a commission far in excess of his expectations—"fifteen bid once—"

Garrett was looking about frantically. All of a sudden his panic flushed away. He said in a calm, clear voice, "Sixteen thousand."

"Sixteen bid," Keller cried enthusiastically, "I'll entertain your bid for seventeen Mr. Queen do I hear seventeen—"

"Eighteen thousand dollars," said Mr. Queen.

"Twenty!" barked the little man.

"Twenty-one."

"Twenty-two!"

"Twenty-three," said Mr. Queen.

Garrett hesitated. His eyes sought heaven and earth, and finally came to rest on the Elk's tooth trembling on Keller's watchchain. "Twenty-four thousand dollars," he said.

"Twenty-five thousand dollars," said Richard Queen. The little man's mouth opened. "One minute, Mr. Garrett. Are you intending to make a further bid?"

"Why do you ask?" There was a squeak in his voice, as if some part of his speaking mechanism had run out of oil.

"Because in that case I'd like to ask for a recess so I can consult with my principals."

"No, no, no!" said Mr. Garrett. "I object, Mr. Keller. I have a right—"

"Who's running this auction Mr. Garrett," said the man on the podium, "I am and I'm expected under my license to get the maximum bid I can't favor nobody you got your recess Mr. Queen how long do you want?"

"As long as it takes," said the Inspector; and he nodded to his dazed "principals" and strode ahead toward the house. This time he was followed by not only the heirs and Jessie but Chief Fleck and Vaughn J. Vaughn and, bringing up the rear, the five old bruisers from the five bruised cars. "Oh, I forgot," the Inspector said, halting in the door. "Mr. Garrett, would you come, too?"

Mr. Garrett's little jaw loosened. "Me?"

"Yes, you."

Mr. Garrett came, at a pace that suggested he had just been invited into a Gestapo headquarters. Perhaps the fact that the Irregulars formed a hollow square around him had something to do with it.

Inside the despoiled house, feet echoing on the derugged floors, the echoes died and the Inspector said, "Mr. Garrett, the time has come for the payola question. Are you bidding for yourself, or for somebody else?"

Various faces looked startled; some did not. But the Inspector was not studying physiognomies at the moment. All his attention was on the little man, who stepped on his own shoe and squirmed and bit his lip and finally said, "I don't have to answer that."

"You don't have to," Chief Fleck said unexpectedly, "but I'm the law around her, and the law around here would take it friendly-like if you did."

"Well. All right. I suppose ... You're acting as an agent, sir," he said to the Inspector. "So am I. Yes."

"That's what I thought," the Inspector said. "But you have an advantage over me, Garrett. You know the people I'm acting for, but I don't know whom *you're* acting for. Who?"

"That," said the little man with instant dignity, "is a question I positively will not answer. It constitutes a confidential relationship. No, sir, I'm not telling you who my client is."

Vaughn lowered his flask: "Now how about getting on with the auction?"

The Inspector said, "I'm not finished."

"With what, with what?" asked Fleck. "What you getting at here, Queen?"

"Come on with me." He did not seem perturbed over Garrett's refusal.

He led the way up to the landing and into what had been Hendrik Brass's bedroom. Nothing remained but the bedstead, which Trafuzzi's crew had screwed back into the flooring when they restored it before their departure, and one empty picture frame which they had screwed back into the wall studs to which it had originally been attached. The family portrait that had occupied the frame had long since joined its brothers and its sisters and its uncles and its aunts in the portable miscellany strewn about Keller's podium outside.

"Well?" demanded the chief, looking around.

"You're looking at two samples of the clue to old Brass's fortune," the Inspector said, "that I'm afraid everybody's overlooked, including me."

"What? Where? The only things I see are the bed and that brass frame on the wall. Don't tell me they're valuable antiques—"

"There's not a valuable antique in the joint," the Inspector said. "If Brass had any decent ones he must have sold them off years ago. The others he spoiled with his brass plating. What's left is junk. Lift that bed up, Chief, and see for yourself."

"What do you mean lift it up?" Fleck scowled. "It's screwed to the floor."

"Then move that frame on the wall."

"It's screwed down, too. What are you giving me?"

"A look at the clue I mentioned. They're both screwed down. Exactly. As all the picture frames were. As all the beds were. Not to mention the brass plating that was permanently nailed to most of the walls. Why would the old man screw down brass beds and brass picture frames and paper his walls with brass?"

"Because he was dipsy-doodle," Vaughn said promptly.

"Sure. But even lunatics have reasons for what they do. What's another reason? What did Brass accomplish by it?"

Nobody answered, not even Jessie, who was cerebrating furiously in the unchallenged competition for her husband's esteem.

"It's another case of the too obvious. What the old man accomplished by it was to make the stuff *immovable*. And why would he do that?"

They chewed the problem as if their teeth had been extracted. Only Keith Palmer digested it. Without removing his

117

arm from about Lynn's waist he said slowly, "So no one could accidentally move them . . . lift them. And the only reason he could have had for that was to conceal their weight."

In the dawn of reason Richard Queen nodded. "Nutty he may have been, but it was a mighty shrewd nuttiness. He figured that if people ever got the notion that his brass wasn't brass, the first thing they'd do is what Keith did—heft it to judge its weight. What did Keith heft? The *loose* stuff. And what did he find? That the loose stuff *was* brass. That was the old man's red herring. Then what was he covering up when he fixed it so other objects of brass were immovable? He was covering up the fact that they weren't brass at all. All the picture frames, all the bedsteads, all those heavy old Victorian bathtubs, all the metal Trafuzzi's men stripped from the walls and tossed into the cellar when they made a shell out of this place—*it's all brassplated gold*. There's your fortune, ladies and gentlemen. Strip the plating off and you'll have Hendrik Brass's six million dollars."

What. And where.

11

WHEREFORE?

They were all for running down to the cellar and retrieving the beautiful hidden weight of the gold-filled wall sheeting that had been dumped there unsuspected; but the Inspector said, "That can wait. This can't," and turned to the little stranger. "And now, Mr. Garrett, will you change your mind about telling us who your client is?"

"First of all you have to understand one thing absolutely and positively," Mr. Garrett said rapidly. "I don't know a thing about any brass-plated gold. I was just hired to bid up on the contents of—"

"You going to tell us or aren't you?"

"But I can't! It's confidential. It's like I'm a priest—"

The Inspector made a disgusted sound.

Big Wes Polonsky said, "See you a minute, Inspector?"

He retired to the hall with his aged quintet of cronies.

"We've been talking this over, Dick," Johnny Kripps said. "I'm pretty sure I remember this guy."

"Me, too," said Hugh Giffin. "And if he's who I think he is, he steers for backroom abortionists and chases ambulances for extra-busy shysters. A real dirty operator who'll do anything for a buck."

"So," Wes Polonsky said, "how about we use a little muscle on this character?"

"Leave me alone with him for three minutes," said Pete Angelo, "and I guarantee he'll sing high C while he goes crawling after another ambulance."

And Al Murphy put in, "I'm putting in for a piece of him, too."

"Wouldn't that be ex-police brutality?" the Inspector said with a grin. "No, boys, I think I'm going to have to make like Ellery. Thanks all the same. Damn it, I wish he were here! Well, he isn't, so here goes."

"But just how you going to do it, Dick?" asked Kripps.

"I told you. Like son, like father. Play God Almighty. Maybe I can make it sound kosher enough to give this Garrett a serious case of religion."

They looked doubtful as they followed him back into the bedroom.

"Well," demanded Chief Fleck, "is it back to the auction, or what?"

"It's or what," the Inspector said. "The fact is, Chief, there just might not be any more auction."

"You on a trip, dad?" Vaughn laughed. "There's got to be an auction. It's in the will."

"Maybe as the executor of said will you'll change your mind when you hear what I have to say to Mr. Phil G. Garrett. Because I'm about to tell this pimple who it was hired him to bid in on the contents of Brass's house, which would include the brass-plated gold nobody suspected."

"How are you going to do that? With mirrors?"

"With deduction."

"With *what?*"

"Listen and learn, Vaughn. In fact, I'm going to do more than deduce who hired Garrett. I'm going to prove who murdered Hendrik Brass, too."

Mr. Garrett was beginning to turn greenish around the earlobes. The others seemed too numbed by this time to look surprised. All but Chief Fleck, each of whose two hundred and forty-five pounds quivered to life.

"You do that, Queen," he said. "By God, you do that!" And he lumbered over to block the doorway, straightening his uniform for his appearance before the world's press.

Richard Queen spoke slowly, sternly, remotely, like the Voice from the Burning Bush. Jessie, who had not taken her eyes off him, heard her stomach gurgle, one of her chronic telltale vexations. It always signaled trouble. Please, dear Lord, she implored, let him be right this time!

He began with the first violence, reminding them that the blow which killed Hendrik Brass had not been the only attack on the old man; there had been a prior one, with the bedroom fireplace poker, which had proved unsuccessful.

"What was the motive behind that first attempt to kill Brass?" the Inspector said. "It couldn't have been for the fortune—at that time the old boy hadn't even made out his will. Remember, he told us then that he had no heirs at law. So if that attack with the poker had been successful, he would have died intestate and his estate would have gone in toto to the State of New York.

"Therefore the attacker's motive couldn't have been gain.

"If the motive for that first try couldn't have been gain, what could it have been? Well, what did we subsequently find out? That at least one of the people Brass was to designate his heirs was his illegitimate child. A bastard who's been abandoned by his father in infancy can't have any tender feelings for him. But he can have feelings of hate—and he can want revenge. So logically hate-revenge was the reason for that poker attempt on the old man's life. The hate, the desire for revenge, were so powerful that the attacker couldn't wait for his father to make out a will and possibly leave him part of the six million. He was out for blood. Nothing else would satisfy him."

"But that would make it Dr. Thornton," cried Cornelia Openshaw. "The doctor knew after he got here that Mr. Brass was his father—he told us so himself! And none of the rest of us knew—"

"That last is an assumption, Miss Openshaw," said the Inspector, "not a fact. Any of you but Lynn O'Neill could also have been Brass's bastard and just pretended not to know it. The very point that Dr. Thornton disclosed his own bastardy to us when all he had to do was keep his mouth shut about it takes him off the hook psychologically. If he hadn't talked we'd never even have suspected a bastardy pattern to the puzzle. Now it doesn't necessarily make it Dr. Thornton. You're *all* possibilities but Lynn."

The doctor applied a handkerchief to his mouth. The cheeks under his stubble had grown pale. But with absolution he regained a little of his color; and he tucked the handkerchief away with a cautious movement.

"Now watch what happens," the Inspector went on, "after

that try that pooped out. Days go by, nights. A week. More. Does the poker lad make a second try at killing Brass? He does not. Why not?"

"I'll answer that one, pops," said Vaughn. "Because Vaughn J. Vaughn 'd showed up packing a .38, hired to protect the old squirrel, that's why."

"And did such a bangup job of it," retorted Richard Queen, "that one night somebody crept up on you, put you out of commission in your sleep, and stepped over you and into the old man's bedroom and buried a knife in his heart. It won't wash, Vaughn. Your coming here made it harder, that's all. And not very much harder at that, because when the killer got good and ready he managed to knock off old Brass as if you weren't here."

Vaughn's sneer wavered and died. His glance at the Inspector was purely malevolent. But beyond a venomous "You're real groovy today, dad, aren't you?" he said no more.

"The point is," the Inspector went on, "that at any time between the first attack and the one that succeeded the killer could have made a second try. But he didn't. There's only one possible answer to why not. After the unsuccessful attempt *he decided to wait.*"

"Why?"

"Well, what actually happened? When *did* he act? He killed the old man *after* Brass made out the will. Then that must have been what the killer was waiting for.

"He had changed his mind about killing just for hate-revenge. By holding off until he became an heir under the will, he got not only his revenge but also his cut of the fortune. If it had turned out that he wasn't named in the will, he could always go back to his original plan to kill just for revenge. He'd had second thoughts, you see. Why not kill two birds with one stone? That's how he must have figured. It's the only explanation for his holding off."

And the tempo of the Inspector's baton quickened. "Now a killer who's willing to wait for one reason ought to be willing to wait for another. Whoever pulled this homicide is no underworld enforcer, used to taking life as a business. He's an ordinary citizen churned up by unusual events and critical situations. Ordinary citizens have more fears of punishment than professional killers. Unless they commit a murder in the heat of passion they'll control themselves and look for a less dangerous way out of their problems. Especially where gain is involved. What use is a million dollars if you're caught and sent up for life? In this case the killer had a very good excuse for not taking a chance on committing murder. Hendrik

121

Brass was seventy-six years old. By his own admission he was a sick man. How much longer could he live? All our man had to do was wait and let nature take its course. Then he'd inherit his million legitimately, with no danger to his freedom to enjoy it.

"But in spite of every normal reason to wait after he was named in the will, this man didn't. He went ahead and murdered a sick old man anyway. Was his hate for his blood-father and/or his need for money so strong that they destroyed every dictate of common sense? Could be. But in my book, which has a lot of pages, there's a likelier explanation."

The Inspector paused deliberately; Ellery had not inherited his sense of timing from his mother. There was nothing to be heard in that room, nothing. Until Richard Queen said suddenly, "Between the time the first murder attempt failed and the time old Hendrik signed his will, the killer did one thing the rest of us weren't able to do: *he solved the mystery of what Hendrik's fortune consisted of and where it was stashed away.*"

He had them hardly daring to draw a breath—hanging on every syllable. The man named Garrett in particular, the Inspector's chief object, was in thrall. Chief Fleck had his fat lips parted; only his breathing was noisy.

"You see where this takes us?" the Inspector said. "The killer's normal inhibition against killing and possibly being punished for it and not getting to enjoy the fruits of his killing was weakened by a new factor: his discovery of the fortune. He must have felt sure, from our actions, that none of the rest of us had solved the secret. But now he was under a lot of internal pressure. The longer he allowed Hendrik to go on living the greater the chance that one or more of us would solve the secret, too. But with Hendrik dead as soon as possible, the killer would be the only one to know where the gold was, and he could then gamble for stakes so high they overbalanced every other consideration: *he could grab off the whole fortune for himself instead of inheriting a mere one-sixth.* All he had to do was to get legal possession of the contents of the house—and the gold in it—without the rest of us knowing why he was doing it—or even, as it's turned out, that he was doing it at all.

"There was only one person," the Inspector went on, conducting his verbal orchestra *accelerando furioso*, "who was willing to pay a ridiculously high price for the contents of a household that to the rest of us was worthless junk. *That was the person who hired Garrett to bid in for him on everything*—up to and past the nonsensical $25,000 mark

122

that I deliberately made Garrett go to. When I pulled my trick you all saw Garrett sneak a look around, then all of a sudden start bidding me up like mad. He might as well have said out loud that he was looking for the nod from the man he was working for—his permission to keep bidding me up till I quit. And he got it, because that's just what he proceeded to do. Do you want better proof than that?

"I've shown that the killer knew the secret of the fortune. And we know now that the man who hired Garrett to bid for broke had to know the secret of the fortune. So the killer and the man behind Garrett have to be one and the same. The man who employed Garrett is the man who murdered Hendrik Brass.

"Now you'll talk," the Inspector said, whirling on Garrett, and every word came out like a clash of cymbals, "unless you want to go up as accessory to murder one. Who hired you, Garrett? Talk, or Chief Fleck books you here and now."

Mr. Phil G. Garrett, ambulance-chaser, procurer for abortionists, and bird of very little brain retreated as far as he could go, which was Hendrik Brass's dusty window, cracking his pale little knuckles as he backed up.

He prepared his lips for speech. When they were in working order he said, "I don't know anything about any murder, I didn't take this job on for a bum rap like that—"

"Who?" thundered the Inspector in tympani tones.

A shaking finger pointed.

"That man there. Mr. Vaughn."

12

WHO'S WHO?

Richard Queen did not expect Vaughn J. Vaughn to cave in like his errand boy Garrett. Notwithstanding his glass jaw, the legal beagle was a tough and cynical customer, knowledgeable in the ways of evidence. With Ellery, the brilliant analytical haymaker in the last round never failed to make his adversary toss in the towel; but Ellery did not usually square off with characters like Vaughn. So Queen *pére* waited for his opponent to get off the floor.

Vaughn's knees barely touched the canvas; he was on his psychological feet in a bound.

"Poop," Vaughn said comfortably. "All poop, pop. That's a wild scene you make out. But where it counts is in a D.A.'s office and the courts. You can scare the pants off this schmo here—all he's good for is to shmear a bellhop to open a bedroom door and then head for the woodwork—but I'm a pro, popsy. You haven't got a wooden leg to stand on."

The Inspector said nothing. He was watching for another opening.

"Try spieling that yarn in White Plains, dad. The D.A.'ll toss you out on your tokus. D.A.s want evidence, not fancy speeches."

He thought he saw one. "Garrett's fingering you is no fancy speech, Vaughn. Do you deny you hired him to bid in on the contents of this house for you?"

"Deny it? Who's denying it? Sure I hired the punk. I never get involved personally if I can help it. But now that you know, so what? There's nothing illegal about it."

"Oh, no?" shrieked Cornelia Openshaw. "What do you call trying to steal six million dollars?"

"I wasn't trying to heist anything, doll. That's what grandpa here said. Let him prove it in court."

In the impasse the puffing figure of Auctioneer Keller appeared. This time he spoke with punctuation. "Lookit *here*. When's this going to break up? I can't keep these folks hanging around forever. Are Mr. Garrett and Mr. Queen going to keep on bidding, or what? I have an auction to finish."

"There's going to be no finishing of this auction," Chief Fleck growled. "Pack up, Keller. I'm calling it off."

"On whose authority?" cried the auctioneer.

"On my authority. There's something come up that in my judgment—and I'm the law around here—calls for further investigation. The auction'll have to wait."

Vaughn sloshed his flask about. "The Surrogate's going to have a little something to say about that."

"You threatening me?" the police chief bellowed.

"Me? Heavens to Betsy. But one of these days, Chief, this mishmash is going to zap you. But good."

"What about my fee?" Keller asked shrilly.

"This whole thing is a mess right now," Fleck grunted. "Put in a nominal bill or something, Keller. Now clear out, will you?"

The auctioneer cleared out, invoking the laws of God and man. Mr. Phil G. Garrett cautiously edged after him. When he saw that no one was paying attention to him the little man darted over the threshold and scuttled downstairs, out of the house, off the Brass grounds, and presumably back to the world of sanity, where a man could chase an ambulance and be reasonably sure of the result.

"Which brings us back to the question," the Inspector said. "Vaughn, you say your action in hiring that little shill to bid in for you is legal. Your law smells. An executor has legal responsibilities to the estate under his trust, one being to see that nobody steals it. That includes himself. You're in big trouble, Vaughn. Miss Openshaw is right—you tried for the six million yourself. Where I was brought up that's called attempted grand larceny."

The private eye became thoughtful. He seemed to be weighing the plating of the Inspector's argument to see if it contained gold.

"Conceding nothing," he said at last, "and just for ducks, you might say, I'll follow along with that as a theoretical proposition. The only thing is, dad, I don't know anything about any gold under the brass. Never did. All I was doing was pulling a Garrett."

"Talk English."

"I hired Garrett at the instructions of somebody who hired me to hire him."

"Come again?"

"Middleman. I was between the little guy and the big guy. Your beef is with the top banana."

The Inspector took hold of himself. "And who is that?"

Vaughn put the flask to his lips.

"Who hired you to hire Garrett?" thundered Chief Fleck.

"Well, I'll tell you," Vaughn said, wiping his lips with the back of his hand, "seeing that charges of larceny are being tossed around. It was old buddy-boy here. Alistair."

So the audience of eyes turned on DeWitt Alistair, whose own mean specimens were turned on Vaughn J. Vaughn with all the amicability of *el toro* facing *la espada* at the moment of truth. His wife's face was simply terrible.

"You dirty name," Alistair shouted. "You lousy rat fink. I should have known better than to believe your promise you'd keep this confidential!"

"Sauve qui put, Mac," Vaughn shrugged. "I take the rap for no cat, especially the likes of you."

"Well." The Inspector was beaming. "We finally seem to be getting somewhere. So you were the one who figured out where the gold is, Alistair, and tried to latch onto it through two intermediaries. Or was it your wife? On second thought, you don't have the mental equipment. It has to be Mrs. Alistair who figured it out. Wasn't it you, Mrs. Alistair?"

Mrs. Alistair's specimens spat at him.

"My advice," said the Inspector kindly, "is for one or both of you to talk, fast. Wouldn't you say, Chief?"

Fleck said, not kindly, "I'd say!"

The four Alistair eyes held a silent conversation during which an issue was resolved. Alistair spoke, not bitterly, not belligerently, but with stuttery feeling, as if he were being held for softening up in the back room of a pre-Miranda station house.

"Liz—my wife—figured it out. Yes. The answer came to her in the middle of one night. She woke me up. I saw right off she'd got hold of something. So we got up and unscrewed one of the picture frames. We agreed it felt heavier than brass ought to be. Gold. It had to be gold."

"So you made a deal with Vaughn who made a deal with Garrett to bid in on the contents of the house for you," said Richard, "and freeze the suckers out. Nice going."

The Alistairs again held their ocular conversation. This time it was Mrs. Alistair who testified, as if she no longer trusted her spouse to cope with the prosecution.

"Suppose we did."

"Then one or both of you knocked off Hendrik Brass."

"You're not sticking us with *that*."

"I proved it, Mrs. Alistair."

"I repeat what Vaughn said. Not in a court of law."

"Maybe. But you're in this up to your four ears."

"We're in nothing! Anyway, it isn't four, it's six."

"I beg your pardon?" said Richard Queen.

"We had a partner. So if you're going to throw accusations of murder around, you'll have to include him in." It was too long a colloquy for Elizebeth Alistair. She stopped, panting.

The Inspector rolled with the punch and came up fighting. "Let me get this straight. You and your hubby wanted to grab off the whole six million, but you took in a partner? Why was that?"

"Because we didn't have the scratch to swing it by ourselves," DeWitt said quickly.

"No? You've led us to believe you hadn't any scratch at all."

"Well, we've got a little something tucked away that we never touch. In case a big one comes along. This looked like the bonanza. We decided to risk it. But it wasn't enough. So we had to take him in to make sure we could outbid everybody else, in case it was a hot auction."

"Take who in?" demanded the Inspector.

"Dr. Thornton."

The exercise in mass optics swung dizzily in the direction of the Albert Schweitzer of South Cornwall. That laborer in the humane vineyards sank onto the late Hendrik Brass's bed with a clash of lamenting springs, like a threnody, averting his face from his mourners.

"*You*, Doctor?" Lynn O'Neill gasped. "*You* tried to do the rest of us out of our shares? I'll never trust anybody again in my whole life!"

And poor Jessie had to cough and cough to drown out the sludge pump in her stomach.

As for her groom, this time he was down for the count. Dr. Thornton a crooked conniver? It was more than flesh could bear. It shattered the Inspector's trust in his own judgment of men, based on a lifetime of toiling in the laboratory of human copouts.

"Is that true, Doctor?" He still could not believe it.

Dr. Thornton was chewing his mustache like a starving man. When he raised his eyes it made Richard wish he would look elsewhere. "Yes, Inspector," he said in a strangled voice. "I've wanted to do something big for so very long. I mean with the clinic. For $3,000,000 ... It wasn't for myself, God knows. I mean not for my financial benefit.... I know that's no excuse. ..."

"You figured you being Brass's son you had a right to the whole thing, maybe?" The Inspector was still seeking a saving grace for Thornton, or for himself.

"No. Really it wasn't that. They might all be his children and have as much right ... for all I knew. ... I can understand now how a trusted bank teller can work honestly for twenty years and one day walk off with a suitcaseful of other people's money. I'm so sorry. Lynn ... Keith ... Miss Openshaw. ..."

Because he was disappointed in Thornton—or in how he must look in Jessie's eyes—the Inspector grew very angry. "I never came across a bunch like this in all my days on the force! Damn it, half of you doing your damnedest to double-cross the other half—"

"Let's not talk about double-crossing, shall we?" said Elizabeth Alistair with a lightning swipe of her paw. "Who are you to act holier-than-thou?"

Jessie shut her eyes. Here it comes, she thought.

"What? What do you mean?" huffed Richard, rocked back on his heels.

"I mean your nose isn't so clean, either, *Inspector* Queen!"

"It sure as hell isn't," her husband jeered. "You didn't know we knew, did you?"

127

"Knew *what*?"

"We heard you and your wife talk it over. Twice. Through the bedroom wall."

"Talk over what?" He was growing red; Jessie had already grown white.

"How your wife isn't the real Jessie Sherwood, that's what." Alistair turned to the others. "Didn't know that, did you? She's a phoney. For all I know he is, too. Inspector! This woman has no claim on the estate, Vaughn. You made a mistake when you traced the Jessie Sherwood old Brass meant. I heard her say so. Her father wasn't a doctor, he was a mail carrier."

"He was *not*. He—he worked *in* the post office!" It was the only riposte Jessie could come up with.

"In the words of the immortal Fiorello, when I pull a boner it's a beaut." Vaughn looked revitalized. "Well, well, so you Queens are crooks, too. Why you standing there with your mush open, Chief? Cuff 'em."

It took Richard Queen and the five Irregulars fifteen minutes to convince Chief Fleck that he was indeed a legitimate ex-inspector of the New York police department; and another ten to explain, at least to Fleck's satisfaction, why he had not disclosed Vaughn's error.

"We'd have had to leave, Fleck," the Inspector pleaded. "Try to understand the spot I was in. I was so fascinated by this setup—"

"All *right*," the chief said hotly. "But *nobody's* talked straight. Not to me!" He about-faced. "We through with the true confessions? Or is somebody else holding out on me? This is your last chance, damn it. I find out you're still hiding something, by jing and by jee you'll wish I hadn't! Well?"

Lynn O'Neill and Keith Palmer glanced at each other. And Lynn gave the slightest, fondest nod. Keith turned to the chief. He was pallid around the gills, but otherwise he held himself straight and tall and fully packed, like a he-man should.

And Keith Palmer said bravely, "I'm not Keith Palmer."

And Chief Fleck howled, "You're *not*? Then who in the holy blazes are you?"

"My name is Bill Perlberg," the false Keith Palmer confessed. "Keith is my best friend—we're in business together, the scrap metal business, well, junk, really. Grew up together, served in Vietnam together—"

"I don't care if you were shacking up together! How come you're here pretending to be him?"

"It's kind of complicated," Bill Perlberg said apologetically. "He got this letter from old Brass, see, and he wanted to come, only he couldn't—"

"Why not?"

"Because he has a wife named Joanne and a kid named Schmulie—I mean Sam—and he got back from the war all bollixed up, couldn't work, couldn't find himself, tried to run away, made a mess of his marriage, and Joanne said if he ever left her again she'd leave *him*, taking little Sam with her—"

"He loves her, you see," Lynn said with the confidence of one who has just become privy to top secrets, "and he didn't want to lose her."

"Who asked you to put your two cents in?" the chief snapped. "Okay, Perlberg, so what?"

"So Keith talked me into being his proxy," Bill said out of a rosy face. "Said he'd take care of the business if I'd come here in his place. Made me promise I wouldn't give the ball game away, because he didn't know but that it might cut him out of whatever was being passed out. The letter sounded as if there was a pot of money in the thing, whatever it turned out to be, and Keith could sure use money. He couldn't tell his wife about it, because Joanne's very practical and to her it would have been like him going off on another of his wild-goose chases. Why I let him talk me into this I'll never know. He's probably running the business into the ground."

"I'm not sorry," Lynn said softly, clinging to Bill's hand, "though for a time there I was sort of confused. Keith is married, you see, but Bill isn't."

"Here's my driver's license," said Bill, "and my social security card, and my Diner's Club—"

"Oh, stuff 'em," Chief Fleck said; and he smacked himself in the chin with the heel of his hand and went over to where the wall used to be and leaned heavily against a stud. "What's gonna happen next?"

What happened next began with Miss Openshaw, who had a few well-chosen opening words for men who took females in by pretending to be what they weren't—she was furious with Bill-Keith, and even more so with Lynn, who kept hanging on to his hand—and then got down to gold tacks.

"I for one," proclaimed Miss Openshaw, "want to be shown. I'm through taking anyone's word for *anything* in this dreadful place. You make out a fine-sounding case for the immovable brass being gold, Inspector Queen, and I certainly want to believe it, but why don't we make sure?"

"Sure," said Inspector Queen unsurely. At this point he was not sure of his own name.

"Why don't we tackle those panels stripped off the walls?" Bill suggested. "That's where most of the weight would be. I'll see how much of my metals course I can remember. Besides, I've always wanted a look at that home foundry. Somehow never got around to it." Miss Openshaw was heard to mutter something about "I wonder *why*," as she glared at Lynn. "Where's Hugo?"

Hugo said, "I am here," from the landing. He had been standing there throughout in an invisibility of total quiet.

"How about bringing up a couple of those brass sheets from the cellar, Hugo? To the workshop, where I can test them."

Hugo clumped down the stairs and disappeared. Alistair led the way to the workshop wing with the surefootedness of one who had indeed got around to it.

It was an astonishing place of annealing furnaces, cast-iron molds, dozzles, thermal couples, scales, bins, casting rooms; supplies of copper, zinc, charcoal, rosin, graphite, black lead; a cabinet of acids, chiefly sulfuric (used, Bill said as he roamed about in wonder, in the "pickling" process); sodium and potassium bichromates (for what he called "bright dipping")—it was rather like a Walt Disney conception of Vulcan's forge, dim and blackened and peopled with the ghosts of busy little men.

"I'm surprised the old man was able to teach Hugo how to make brass," Bill said. "It's a process that calls for a lot of precision. Oh, Hugo. Dump 'em right here."

"Be *careful*!" wailed Cornelia.

Bill found a hacksaw and sliced off a piece of brass sheeting and went to work with scales and a file and some nitric acid . . . ringed by eyes, to no sound but breathing.

After a while he cut a piece off the other panel and repeated his tests.

"Bring up the rest of those panels, Hugo."

"But *is* it, Bill?" cried Lynn.

Bill said nothing, eloquently. It became a long hot afternoon of lugging, sawing, testing, the air in the workshop growing heavier with each discarded sample. When the wall panels were all tested, Bill had Hugo bring in the picture frames. Then the brass railing of the staircase. Then pieces cut off the brass beds. And more, and more.

And when he was finished, and there was no brass left to test, Bill wiped his hands thoughtfully on his slacks and said, "There's some alpha-beta stuff here, but it's mostly alpha—about sixty-three percent copper, the rest zinc."

"But how much gold?" asked Elizabeth Alistair voraciously.

"None," said Bill. "Every piece here is solid brass."

"I've got some gold fillings in my teeth," Vaughn laughed. "How much am I offered?"

13

WHEN, WHERE, WHO, WHY

That was a hard time. In view of the brass that turned out to be brass, it was a wonder that the group did not break up and dissolve in various directions, never to meet again, except for Lynn and Bill, who others than Cornelia Openshaw suspected were already in indissoluble union.

What held them fast to the wreckage of Hendrik Brass's domain (aside from Chief Fleck, whose grip was weakening from sheer attrition, and who was seen very little now—how could he hold them much longer?) was the very hopelessness of their quest. They were like the Hebrews to whom Paul wrote, "Faith is the substance of things hoped for, the evidence of things not seen." The gold was hoped for, and it was not seen. Only faith could find it. So they stayed.

The case of the Queens was rather different. Jessie would have gone to hell provided her beloved were by her side, and she would have remained there for as long as he chose to roast, roasting with him. And Richard chose. And it was hell. Vaughn saw to that. And the virulent Openshaw. And the Alistairs. And even Dr. Thornton. Richard chose because he was Richard, *el ingenioso hidalgo*, as stubborn as the man from la Mancha.

"I've got to hear the other shoe drop, Jessie. I've got to."

"Yes, darling."

Since faith was the heirs' buckler, they attacked the house again, or what was left of it. The Irregulars were in the forefront. The cellar was dug up another two feet. The furnace was dismantled into its components, and the components torn to peices. The workshop underwent a particularly drastic reexamination: the annealing ovens were taken apart; everything of metal was subjected to tests to see if it might not be gold plated with copper, or zinc, or iron, or whatever. Nothing was.

There was a moment of exaltation when, after a session of

brooding, Richard brought forth, *"The new steel beams!"*
Everyone made for the nearest reinforced wall, and Bill
resurrected an ancient acetylene torch from somewhere and
fired away at the handiest beam. But it was steel through and
through. A prophet is not without honor and so forth and, in
The House of Brass, Richard was excoriated for his prophecy. He suffered the injustice, unlike a prophet, without philos-
ophy.

Then they tackled the grounds. The Irregulars labored
mightily here, too, although Bill and Dr. Thornton pitched in
with shovels, and even DeWitt Alistair deigned to soil his
hands. They tore up what remained of the brickwork of the
driveway and dug down several feet. They excavated behind
the house, and to its sides, and all around the coach house.
At the end, they razed the coach house, notwithstanding
Richard's solo nighttime search long (it seemed) before. And
finally they had to face the unexhilarating fact that Hendrik
Brass's gold was simply not in or around his building.

"The only other place it can be," Bill said, "is buried
somewhere in the woods back there. He may have given
Vaughn a bum steer just for the hell of it."

"But Bill dear," Lynn objected, "you can't dig up the
whole woods. There's acres and acres of it."

"A metal detector," Bill said; and made certain inquiries,
and drove twenty-eight miles for a gizmo rented at his own
expense ("I've got to protect Keith's investment," he explained); thereafter he could be seen creeping about the
woods with the detector, being crept along with by the heirs,
through the daylight hours and twice into the evening. On the
second day his detector detected something. Alistair and Dr.
Thornton dug fiercely, and they unearthed a rocker plane
inscribed "Patented 1864," and even this dubious find (it was
all but pulverized, and indeed when Bill tried to grasp it it
crumbled into rusty dust under his fingers) caused outcries
and an energetic renewal of the search.

Meanwhile, relationships deteriorated, too (in one case, as
Richard was to find out, they were corrupted). A typical
firelight exchange:

Alistair: What happened to my racing news, damn it?

Cornelia: Don't look at me if your nasty little paper is
missing!

Vaughn (*to Alistair*): What happened to your British
accent, DeHalfwit?

Alistair (*to Vaughn*): Bumbler! Shut your mouth!
(*Vaughn laughs and takes a swig.*)

Cornelia: Oh, you all make me tired. Especially you Alistairs and old Dr. Kildare over there.

132

Dr. Thornton (*harassed*): People who throw stones. I think we all know what *your* trouble is, Miss Openshaw.

Cornelia: Oh, you do! The AMA would just love to hear what an ethical member *you* are.

Liz Alistair (*acid*): Old maid.

Cornelia (*alkaline*): Shall we match birth certificates, dear?

And so on, far into the night when the Inspector discovered the corruption. He was finding the brass bed intolerable, and in his insomnia he had taken to getting out of it quietly and prowling. On this night, as he happened to turn the corner of the east ell into the main hall, he heard a door somewhere ahead being opened with thrilling caution. So he froze. The night light was on and he could see well enough. The door that opened was from the bedroom Vaughn J. Vaughn had preempted after Hendrik Brass's death.

Vaughn appeared. All he had on was a pair of jockey shorts.

He tiptoed down the hall. Richard followed, his felt carpet slippers making no more noise than Vaughn's bare feet. Where was the man bound? For a moment the Inspector almost leaped; but Vaughn without a glance passed the door behind which Jessie was sleeping and rounded the corner.

To Richard's stupefaction Vaughn stopped at Cornelia Openshaw's door. Vaughn looked about—Richard snatched his head back—and Old Sleuth heard Young Sleuth rap lightly but definitely on the spinster's door—raprap, rapraprap, rap raprap; it sounded unbelievably prearranged. Then the sound of the door quietly opening and closing. Then no sound at all.

Richard waited for the scream of rape. What else could Vaughn's goal be? He had already tried it once, and had been balked; his libido was not made to go unexercised for very long.

But there was no scream. There were certain other noises—furtive whispers, an excited chuckle, a gasp or two, and then a cautious settling on the irrepressible bedsprings. After that Richard went away, back to his own room.

But not to bed. He paced to the rhythm of Jessie's breathing.

He should have foreseen it, he told himself. The Miss Prims were easy if you knew how, and if the particular Miss Prim was a biscuit shell over a boiling interior. The approach must have been made out of earshot of the others—Miss Prim would insist on that—and the assignation settled.

At dawn he heard Vaughn coming back. The Inspector watched him from between two of the hung blankets as he passed. The private eye was yawning and scratching his glistening chest.

Sic transit virtus.

But Richard Queen's vigil produced more than a refresher course in human foibles. His pacing had been accompanied by thought, and his thoughts had given birth to a remarkable child.

He was still looking it over like a newly made father when nature offered a fortuitous suggestion.

Jessie came hunting for him in the woods, where he was absently wandering after the metal detector and its prospectors. "Guess what I just heard on Bill's radio!"

Huh?" Richard said.

"There's a storm on the way. A big one. It's supposed to be practically a hurricane. *Richard.*"

"Yes, hon?"

"You didn't hear a word." She repeated the radio warning and he came back to her headlong.

"What do you know about that! Did they say what time it's due to hit?"

"Around midnight."

"That's *fine.*"

"What's fine about it? The house is a shell. If the winds get strong enough—"

"Sure," her husband said in a hand-rubbing tone. "That's it."

"What's it?"

But he did not tell her. It could be another bust, he thought; he had suffered enough in her eyes.

This time he did not rush in. He held back, waiting.

The search party gave up and straggled back to the house before sunset. The sky was glum; the woods were like night; a whining wind was rising; gusts of rain were already slashing the windows; there were faroff rumblings; fireworks began to explode across the black heavens.

They scurried about making shutters fast, locking windows. The women were nervous. Even Vaughn looked uneasy.

"I wouldn't worry too much," Richard said to the assembled company. "The outside walls are still sound, and if worst comes to worst we'll be safe in the cellar. The only thing could happen is the chimneys might come tumbling down, but they won't hurt us in the cellar, and anyway the house is slated for complete demolition one of these days, so what's the difference?

After their makeshift dinner the power failed. As if it had been a signal, the wind died, and an eerie quiet fell.

"It's fixing to be a hurricane, all right," Richard said as Hugo began to distribute candles. "If it gets really bad make for the cellar. Personally, I don't feel like sitting around all evening by candlelight. I'm going to bed. Coming, Jessie?"

A procession of candles made its way to the upper floor. Hugo remained downstairs cleaning up. When he was finished he blew out the lamps and left, too.

"Jessie," Richard said, shaking her.

Jessie awoke with a start. He was holding a lighted candle aloft; shadows were leaping all over the bedroom; the house, Jessie could have sworn, was rocking. There was a steady roaring outside. "What's the matter, Richard? Is the—are we—?"

"Get dressed quick, hon. Put your coat and galoshes on, and something around your head. I've got to wake up the others. I'll meet you in the hall."

"But . . . what time is it?"

"Near midnight. I just got the signal from Johnny."

"Signal—?"

But he was gone.

When Jessie stepped out into the hall she found a rather belligerent gathering, some with candles. They all had coats or slickers on. There was no sign of Richard.

"Where's my husband?" demanded Jessie.

"He's gone to wake up Bill Perlberg," Dr. Thornton said. "What's it about this time, Mrs. Queen?"

"I have no idea. There they are."

Richard and Bill appeared from around the corner. The group immediately surrounded the Inspector.

"Hold it, hold it," he said to their questions. "No time to explain anything. We're going outside."

"In the *storm*?" squealed Cornelia Openshaw.

"In the storm. Put the candles out, please. I don't want any light to show."

Bill and Lynn began to grope their way down the stairs. The doctor hesitated, then followed; the Alistairs' nostrils trembled, but they followed, too.

"This another one of your windups, dad?" Vaughn said.

"The last one, I hope. Get going, will you? Or you'll miss all the fun."

Cornelia slipped her hand under the private eye's arm and said coyly, "I'll go with you, Vaughn—Mr. Vaughn."

"The trouble with you, dad," Vaughn said, "is you've got no follow-through." Nevertheless, he blew out his candle and

135

led Cornelia downstairs. Richard nodded to Jessie. He did not snuff his flame until they were at the front door, where the rest were waiting.

"Everybody hold onto the one in front of him," the Inspector said. "Bend into the wind. I'll go first."

He opened the door; the roar roared in. Making sure that Jessie was hanging securely on to his coattails, he lowered his head and lunged into the storm. They were drenched before they moved three feet.

The whole world seemed to be howling. Through it they could hear the trees groaning in protest. For a moment they ran into a wall of wind that stopped them in their tracks; they had to fight their way forward by main strength. No one had the breath to protest, even if a protest could have been heard. At the head of the stooped-over Conga line Richard clawed his way around the swamp of the dug-up driveway, leading them toward the belt of trees between the house and the road. Faintly, as they reached the partial shelter of the trees, he heard Cornelia somewhere behind him scream in terror.

But it was only the five cars of the Irregulars, drawn up side by side in battle array, facing the house. Because of the slope of terrain here, the hoods of the cars were higher than their rear ends. The winds were prying at them, trying to flip them over backward.

The Irregulars sat in their cars; only Johnny Kripps got out of his. He struggled to the Inspector's ear and shouted something, pointing toward the house; and the Inspector nodded and, bracing himself, went from one to another of his streaming audience, yelling, "Hold onto the cars and face the house! Face the house and watch!" And when they were crouched among the cars, dripping, furious, bewildered, he waved to Kripps, and Kripps crawled back into his car and signaled; and then, like one man, the Irregulars turned their brights on, and the roof of The House of Brass sprang into being as in a magic illusion, wavering through the curtain of rain.

And what they saw in those ten blinding beams was the figure of a man scrambling about on the roof among the mushroom chimneys casting Wagnerian shadows against the heavens in the illumination from below; now leaping, now sliding and slipping on the rain-slick shingles; now maneuvering inch by inch with legs braced; now down on all fours, crawling along the ridgepole like a monstrous spider spinning its web.

For he had rigged up a lifeline running between the bases of two of the chimneys, and he was scuttling along this line exactly like the spider he resembled, in a whipping tangle of rope; flinging a coil around a chimney here, anchoring it there, skittering from chimney to chimney, teetering until the women shrieked, recovering, and pulling and nipping and tightening his web of ropes while the night split apart and the sky fell and the wind tore at his clothes and he triumphed over all of them.

He did not seem aware of the lights that held him impaled. Perhaps he thought they were made by the storm, or he had lost his sense of time and place. He seemed bent to a frantic, insane, almost holy mission: to secure the chimneys so that they might not fall and be strewn in all their parts by the winds of chance to God knew where.

And then they screamed together for his life. He was clinging to a corner of the roof, knotting a rope. The whole corner rose in the wind and broke into a flock of shingles carried instantly away. It almost carried the man with it, as if he too were a shingle. They saw him for one moment standing on nothing at all, his mouth open like Aeolus, hands scratching at the air for purchase; and then he fell.

He fell out of the light into the abyss below. And the rope to which he had been attached came bouncing back into view with a frayed end and danced over the shattered roof and out of sight, as if gleeful at being relieved of its burden.

The five lowered their beams. Along this path of light they all made their way, clawing at the wind, for the place where the man had fallen.

And they came upon him at last around the corner of the building, half buried by the piece of roof that had given way under him, so that only his torso and his head were visible, the head lying at an impossible angle, rain pelting the blood out of his sodden hair and down his grotesque face and into the earth.

"Broke his neck," Dr. Thornton shouted, looking up. "He's dead."

At that moment, by some freak of the storm, or as if it had been waiting for a cue, the wind died, the howling stopped, the rain fell off to a whisper, and Richard Queen said distinctly, "It's just as well. He murdered Hendrik Brass."

It was the butler, Hugo.

Mr. Pealing came out from town and very kindly buried Hugo Zarbus beside his master, giving the lie to the detractors of the mortuary profession, and departed not to be seen at The House of Brass again. Only then did Richard Queen, in spite of the universal demand, led by Chief Fleck, voice the elegy.

"We figured out long ago," the Inspector said, "that old Hendrik had the walls and floors strengthened because he expected to put a strain on them—extra weight they hadn't been built to support. And that the extra weight had to be his fortune—in gold. The question is, Why didn't we find it? Why was the immovable stuff—the wall paneling, the picture frames, the beds, the bathtubs—not brass-plated gold after all, but brass through and through? Why can't we locate gold in any form in the house, where Brass told Vaughn the fortune would be found? Was Brass lying? Or had he been telling the truth—*the truth as he believed it to be?*"

"You mean," cried Bill, "the old man thought the gold was in the house when all the time it wasn't?"

"I mean," replied Richard Queen grimly, "that the old man was fooled, yes. And when I realized that, everything gelled. It's easy enough to fool a blind man about a thing like that if you set out to. Once the permanent work was done and the frames, for instance, were screwed to the walls, how could Hendrik tell they weren't gold? He couldn't make chemical tests. They were immovable, so he couldn't make weight tests. All he could do was touch the things, and touch wouldn't tell him he'd been double-crossed.

"And who could have double-crossed him? Only Hugo Zarbus. Hugo was his only companion in the house. Hugo did all the lifting and carrying. Hugo did all the metals work in the workshop! So it had to be Hugo who disobeyed Hendrik's orders and made everything out of plain brass. And Hendrik never knew the difference."

DeWitt Alistair said something irreverent about the recent dead; but he subsided quickly, following the Inspector's lips as if he were deaf.

"When I saw that," the Inspector said, "I saw that now I had to look, not for Hendrik's hiding place, but for Hugo's.

"Where could Hugo have hidden the gold? Of course, it could have been hidden anywhere—in the woods, in the family burial ground, at the bottom of the Hudson offshore, or for that matter twenty miles away. But then I re-evaluated what our searches had consisted of. Had we really exhausted every possible hiding place of the gold as far as the house was concerned? We definitely had not. We'd searched in the house, under the house, around the house—everywhere but on top of the house, *on the roof*!

"The minute I saw that," the Inspector went on, "I saw the confirmation of it. Remember that estimate of the contractor's for repairing some chimneys that had been blown down during a hurricane? Hendrik told Sloan it was too much and didn't give him the job, even though Sloan had made the lowest possible bid. So it figured that Hendrik hadn't contracted for the job with anybody. But Mrs. Queen and I, when we arrived, saw no evidence of blown-down chimneys. So somebody must have repaired them for free. Hendrik couldn't have done it. Who's left but Hugo? And if Hugo repaired those chimneys, there I was right back to the roof—which we hadn't searched.

"Well, I searched it," the Inspector said, "the same night I figured it out—the night before the hurricane—climbed up there by an extension ladder, and examined those chimneys. Not even my wife knew about it. And here's a sample of what I found."

It was a whitewashed chimney brick. The Inspector pulled on it, and it came apart in his hands; he had obviously split it beforehand. And they saw that the brick had been hollowed out. In the hollow—they crowded round, too thunderstruck to do more than devour it with their eyes—lay an ingot of dull yellowish stuff.

After an eternity someone—it was Lynn O'Neill—whispered, "The gold."

And someone else—it was Mrs. Alistair—whispered, "Say two hundred bricks to a chimney—thirty chimneys—that would make six thousand bricks ... if each brick contained only two pounds of gold it would work out to twelve thousand pounds. Six *tons*. A million a ton? For God's sake, doesn't anybody *know*?"

"Wait," the Inspector said; like a skein of wild geese, they had wheeled as one toward the door. "The bricks up there won't go away. I'm not finished. I said last night that it was Hugo who killed the old man—"

"Yeah," Chief Fleck said heavily; he was staring at the contents of the broken brick as if he could not see enough of it. The Inspector's violent verb brought him back to his old vision of the press conference and his day in the sun. "If he stole the gold out from under the old man's nose, why did he wait all this time? He could have knocked off Brass years ago—"

"Even Hugo's limited intelligence—although it wasn't half as limited as he led us to believe—realized that if he did that, Chief, he'd be collared for it. With the two of them living alone, who else would be the logical suspect?

"But when Brass gathered these people here Hugo saw the whole thing fall into his lap. They were heirs to the fortune. With the gold safely stashed in the chimneys, and a bunch of made-to-order patsies as suspects, Hugo made his play. He sneaked into Brass's room, attacked him with the brass poker, and left him for dead. He was really shook up after-

139

ward—not because one of us had tried to kill the old man, as we assumed, but because *his* try had failed.

"His second try he took no chances. That was the night, you'll recall, when he took one of his few nights off and went to that beer joint. He must have guzzled just enough to make his drunk alibi look good the next morning, sneaked back to the house in the middle of the night, crept up on Vaughn and stabbed him in the back with the brass knife, then yanked the knife out and gone into the old man's bedroom and this time made sure. He deliberately left his Honda in the bushes off the road and got into bed with his clothes on to support his drunk alibi."

"That hunk of lard?" Vaughn said incredulously. "He did all that?"

"You'd better believe it, Vaughn. He pulled the wool over everybody's eyes, including old Brass's blind ones."

"But proof," Fleck said fretfully. "I got to have proof."

"Who else could it have been, Chief? Take that first try of his—the poker attempt that failed. At the time it didn't seem to make sense. We naturally figured one of the heirs had done it. But the try was made before the old man wrote his will. I built up a fancy case about hate-revenge, but I was wrong about the heirs to the six million dollars. The fact remained that at that particular time no potential heir would have attacked the source of at least a million dollars—not with the payoff just around the corner. So that let the heirs out. That meant it was done by somebody who was *not* an heir. And how many of us were not heirs? Me, my wife, Mrs. Alistair, and Bill Perlberg—Vaughn wasn't even here. My wife and I certainly didn't have any reason to try to kill old Brass. Mrs. Alistair would have cut her arm off before she did anything to hurt her husband's chances of inheriting a bonanza. Bill Perlberg? He wasn't personally involved at all, except in protection of Keith Palmer's interests.

"There was nobody left it could have been but Hugo."

"I don't understand something," DeWitt Alistair muttered. "Why did Hugo have to kill the old man? He already had the gold, and Brass had no way of knowing he had it. All Hugo had to do was wait for the old boy to kick off naturally—"

"Hate," the Inspector said. "It has to get back to that, with the heirs eliminated. For years Hugo'd been practically a slave to Hendrik Brass—abused, insulted, worked like a dray horse . . . held in such contempt that what the old man in his malicious way left Hugo in his will was a worthless house and a hopelessly mortgaged piece of land the banks would take away from him the first thing. Our coming here triggered Hugo's hate. He saw his opportunity, and he took it."

140

"But when you solved the mystery of where Hugo had hidden the gold, Inspector," said Cornelia—even in her joy resentful—"why didn't you tell us right away?"

"Because I was looking for a handle to force Hugo's hand. In my own mind I was satisfied that it was Hugo who'd bricked up the gold in the chimneys. But all I had was a mental process. Crimes are people, not mental gymnastics. With the near-hurricane coming, I saw a way to make Hugo betray himself. I made a special point of saying to everybody—which included Hugo—that the chimneys might be blown down in the storm. The last thing Hugo wanted was to have his gold scattered to hell and gone, not only because he wanted it intact but because he wanted the secret of its location to stay that way. I knew, if he made a try, it would be after we all were in bed asleep and he thought the coast was clear. I alerted my five friends, and when they spotted him climbing up to the roof with his ropes they flashed me a signal we'd agreed on, and you know the rest."

A long breath was expelled en masse.

"Well," Dr. Thornton said; there was life in his eyes again, even humanity. "Shall we go up to the roof and get our gold, ladies and gentlemen?"

This time there was no silence, but a stampede.

"Wait," the Inspector said again. "Don't you think—as long as we have a sample here—that Bill ought to test it for quality? See what grade it is, and so forth?"

"That's a smart idea," Alistair said hoarsely, running back. "I'll get your testing stuff from the workshop, Bill!" And he ran off.

They waited. Bill was turning the yellowish brick over in the light of the lamps with a peculiar expression. When Alistair came rushing back Bill went to work with the acid and the scales.

And finally he looked up.

"This isn't gold," he said. "It's brass."

"I know it," the Inspector said in the total hush. "I tested it the night I found it. Plus a number of other bricks from other chimneys, picked at random. They're all brass.

"There never was any six million dollars, in gold or any other form," Richard Queen said. "It was all a pipe dream, neighbors. A lunatic's fantasy and a halfwit's dream. Old Hendrik was probably down to a few thousand dollars in currency, and in his dotage he built up this big deal about gold. I'm sure he thought his brass *was* gold. And he sold poor Hugo on it, too—what did Hugo know about gold, or brass, or anything else? So the lunatic fooled the halfwit, and the halfwit double-crossed the lunatic, and they both made monkeys out of you. Hendrik led you down his particular garden path, dangling the brass he thought was gold under your noses and having himself one whale of a time. What that fool's gold did to you individually you can live over in your nightmares."

So it was all answered—the when, the where, the who, and the why.

14

WHO and WHY?

It was the Alistairs who led the diaspora, fleeing before who knew what threats of the Gentiles. By the time Richard and Jessie were packed and stowing their bags in the Mustang, the Alistairs were gone without an echo.

"And good riddance," Cornelia Openshaw said; but not with her usual venom, rather in a sort of reflex, or to keep her oar in. She was standing outside with her alligator suitcase at her feet, powdered and rouged and lipsticked and eye-shadowed and looking altogether like something out of a psychedelic poster. Still, Miss Openshaw had blossomed since the night of her Introduction to Life. She would never be a fullblown rose, but at least she had budded in a pinched way; Jessie had hopes for her, although she couldn't help wondering how long it would last, considering that the man was the kind of man he was.

"Can we give you a lift, Miss Openshaw?" Jessie asked, to the Inspector's consternation.

"Or we could send a taxi for you from Phillipskill," he said, avoiding his beloved's eye, knowing he would hear about this incivility.

"Oh, no, thank you," Cornelia said tenderly. "Mr. Vaughn has very kindly offered to drive me back to Manhattan. Here he comes now."

Vaughn's battered Austin-Healy crept into view. Its chauffeur did not look very kindly. In fact, he was scowling. He jumped out and flung Miss Openshaw's elegant suitcase into his car and vaulted back behind the wheel without even opening the door for her. Through her cosmetic mask Miss

Openshaw clearly colored. She took her seat beside him, however, head high. Jessie had to look away.

"I thought you'd be staying on, Vaughn," Richard said, "to clean things up."

"What's there to clean?" Vaughn snarled. "Whatever has to be settled with the estate—some estate!—I can manage from my pad in town. If I ever get the estate papers back, that is. That square Fleck lifted my whole portfolio—said it was part of his case record, and I'd get it back when he was good and ready. I sure bought a pig in a poke when I took this job on. I won't get a Siberian zloty out of it. You ready, Corny?"

"Yes, dea—Mr. Vaughn."

"Hang on to your falsies." He peeled off in a vicious shower of mud that made the Queens jump back.

"The honeymoon," Richard remarked, "seems to be over."

Dr. Thornton came around and braked to a stop. He had shaved and trimmed his red mustache; there was a busy sparkle in his eye; he looked quite his old self.

"I'll be glad to be getting back," he said, "to the sane world of brawling brats and women who call me in the middle of the night because they've got a few menstrual cramps. That old nightmare."

"Why, Dr. Thornton," Jessie said reprovingly. "He was your father."

"I'd have been better off never knowing it. What the smell of money does to a man! I'm well out of it."

"But Mr. Brass was a sick man."

"Mrs. Queen," said Dr. Thornton, "my life consists of sick men. For real satisfaction give me a healthy one any day. Starting with myself. Well, you're not interested in my psychological problems. Goodbye. And if there's been any ray of sunshine in this business, you two were it. Thanks for everything." And he drove away.

Richard and Jessie were just getting into the Mustang when Lynn O'Neill and Bill Perlberg appeared. Bill was lugging two suitcases, and Lynn was clinging to his arm like a limpet. "And you two?" Richard asked, leaning out. "What are you going to do?"

"First," Bill said, dumping the bags, "I'm going back home and beat hell out of Keith for putting me through this meat grinder. Then I'm carrying this chick off to the nearest padre and making it permanent."

"Bill wanted us to be married by a rabbi," Lynn said, "and I wanted a Mormon, so we've compromised on a Congregational minister."

"She's going to be the first lady Secretary of State," Bill said with a grin.

"And we're going to have four children."

Bill looked startled. "Two and a half is the American average."

"Four," Lynn said firmly. "Two boys and two girls."

"Four boys."

"Darling! I didn't know you had anything against girls."

"Just little ones, not big ones."

They both laughed, and Lynn came around to kiss Jessie, and then back to kiss Richard; and they left the pair in a continuation of the long argument that constitutes marriage in a democratic society. Hendrik Brass and his fictitious $6,000,000 seemed light-years away.

Their last glimpse of The House of Brass was the thicket of brass-bricked chimneys on top of the gambrel roofs.

By prearrangement the Queens and the Irregulars rejoined at the Old River Inn for a snack before heading back to the city.

"May as well clean up the leftovers," the Inspector said over the coffee. "There's no point, boys, in continuing the hunt for the real Jessie Sherwood, whoever she is. There's nothing for her to inherit—whatever's realized out of that pile of trash will go to the creditors. As for the estate itself—the house and grounds—it's just a mess now; they may never straighten it out. Well, that's Vaughn's and the Surrogate's headache, not ours. Only thing I'm sorry about is that I dragged you boys into this."

"Sorry!" Al Murphy exclaimed. "It's been more fun than two barrels of monkeys."

Each grizzled head nodded vigorously.

"I think it's marvelous how you men have pitched in to help Richard," Jessie declared. "It's a shame you can't work together all the time."

"It sure is," Wes Polonsky said wistfully. "I wish there was a way...."

Johnny Kripps said, "Maybe there is. Or there would be if the six million had turned out to be for real. One of the heirs might have slipped Dick and us ten or fifteen grand for our trouble, and then we'd have been able to open an agency."

"Say!" Pete Angelo said. "That's an idea. The Richard Queen Detective Agency, with a staff of five. What do you say, Dick?"

"I say great," Richard said with a grin. "We could set up an office on Madison Avenue—"

"And show these young twerps on Centre Street," chortled Hughie Giffin, "that life begins at sixty-three."

"We've got among the six of us about two hundred years of know-how," Al Murphy nodded. "The more I think of it, the better it sounds."

"Could be, could be," Richard murmured in the general euphoria.

"Two hundred years of experience," Polonsky pointed out with a sigh, "and no dough."

It brought them back to reality. They sat staring into their coffee cups. Jessie could have shed tears. She wanted to gather the six to her bosom and tell them something reassuring, but what could she say? Old Wes was right: business took capital, and all they had was the subsistence pensions on which they lived. They were society's discards, rejected for the jobs they could still do, and without the means to strike out on their own.

"Well," Jessie said briskly, "I don't see why we're sitting here as if we've just come back from a funeral—"

"We have," her husband said grimly; and at that instant the nemesis that had been dogging him throughout the Brass fantasy struck again.

It came in the person of Chief Victor Fleck—puffing, red-in-the-face Fleck who swooped down on them in all his disgruntled flesh as if he meant to arrest them for indecent exposure.

"I got a radio call from my man Lew," he wheezed, dragging a chair over. "He saw you stop at the Inn here. And a good thing, too! I got news for you."

"Yes?" Richard Queen said. His heart was down around his lap somewhere, trying to tell him something. "What's happened, Chief?"

"What's happened," said the chief, "is that I'm all through listening to you, Queen. How you ever got to the rank of inspector in the police department I'll never figure out. You ain't qualified to stand at a school crossing!"

"What have I done now?" The Inspector was pale.

"You're given me another bum steer, that's what! All that hop about how old Brass was bumped off—"

"I proved it to you."

"I ain't going to tell you what you proved to me, Queen!—there's a lady present, even if she is your wife."

"What," Richard repeated, "have I done?"

"I was getting my records on the Brass case together back at my headquarters, trying to work out in my head how I was going to handle this thing with the newspapers, I mean my killer being dead and all and not even any proof except that flapdoodle you pulled on me, which ain't no proof whatsoever, anybody with half a brain could see that. Anyways, I got this file in my hand, there's a lot of it and it's bulky, and a paper falls out of it, and I pick it up and take a gander at it like you do, and by God it's one I never laid eyes on before. Damn it to hell, nobody told me about it. Bob just slipped it in the file. And, brother Queen, you didn't know about it, either, or you'd never have spilled that hogwash."

"What hogwash?" His heart was in the neighborhood of his knees now. Jessie shut her eyes. Then she opened them and felt for his hand under the table. He held onto her like a drowning man.

The Irregulars were deathly quiet.

"Remember when Hugo had his night on the town and got tanked up in the tavern? Well, it so happens my wife's mother got took sick that night, they thought it was a heart attack, and I had to drive the missus out to Long Island, all the way to hell and gone, Patchogue—that's where the old bat lives—and it turns out the damn fool'd et some fried clams for supper that she ain't supposed to ever eat any fried stuff, and it was only a case of acute indigestion, and anyways it was well into the morning before I got back to Phillipskill and found the call-in about old Brass's being murdered. I was too busy to look over the night sheet, and after that I got so snarled up in the case I never got back to it. I wish I had! If I hadn't happened to drop that memo Bob'd slipped into the Brass file I wouldn't know about it yet."

"What memo, Chief? About what?"

But Fleck chose, in his pique, to tell the story by way of Canarsie. "Hugo'd gone to this ginmill, Brookie's Place, and he got beered up quick, which you never know with these big guys, you'd think with all that beef they could drink gallons without showing it, but it goes right to Hugo's pinhead, and anyways Brookie sends him on his way around midnight. Okay. Now comes the beauty part. Around two in the morning back he comes into Brookie's, and he wants more beer. Well, he looks like he's sobered up, so Brookie figures what the hell, a buck's a buck, and starts serving him all over again. It don't take half an hour and he's stinking again. And getting out of hand—pounding on the table with that hamhock of his, cussing at the top of his voice, wanting to fight everybody in the joint—"

"*Hugo*?" said Jessie.

"You wouldn't figure him for that type, would you, ma'am, and I guess your hubby here," and Chief Fleck favored Richard with a remarkably hostile glance, "he

146

wouldn't *ever*. Well, nobody wants to tackle a gorilla like that, and he's starting in on the furniture, so Brookie puts in a hurry call to headquarters, and my night man radios Bob, who was out on car patrol, and Bob drives over and picks Hugo up and it took Bob and the night man, both of 'em, to get him locked in a cell."

The Inspector moistened his lips. "What time was it when your man booked him?"

Chief Fleck said with the bitter satisfaction of one who has been long put upon, "Two forty-six A.M."

Silence.

"But they let him go after an hour or so, didn't they?" Johnny Kripps asked sharply. "They must have."

"Oh, they let him go, all right," said Chief Fleck, even more sharply. "At seven A.M. o'clock in the morning is when they let him go, friend. And he was still in a fog, Bob tells me. Bob wanted to drive him home, but Hugo insists he's got to get his Honda, which was parked over at Brookie's, so Bob gets him over there, Hugo picks up his machine, and off he wobbles for home. And there's your killer, Inspector Queen—by God, he ain't mine!—locked in my pokey all that night, between two forty-six and seven A.M. And what time did the docs say old Brass'd got it in the heart? Between four and six, wasn't it? So how could Hugo have done it? I ask you!"

They sat there numbly until long after Fleck stamped out of the Inn.

"Darling," Jessie said, squeezing and squeezing his hand. "Darling, it's not the end of the world—"

"It's mighty like it, Jessie," her husband said, "mighty like it." He withdrew his hand gently and pushed back from the table. "I don't know about you chickens," he said to the Irregulars, "but me, I'm heading back to my pipe and my slippers, where I belong. To hell with The House of Brass. I've had it."

And so Richard Queen—as he thought—dropped the case of Hendrik Brass and his ghostly millions and the still unsolved mystery of his demise. Leaving unanswered the two paramount questions he thought he had answered:

Who?

And why?

WHO, HOW, and WHY FINALLY

A wise man, Sam Johnson said, is never surprised. But the Inspector had come to question his wisdom, so it was not surprising that he was surprised, and joyfully, at what he found when he unlocked the door of the Queen apartment and followed Jessie through the foyer into the living room. What he found there, and Jessie, too—spread all over the sofa with a glass of sherry in his hand, leafing through a notebook covered with squiggles—was the best surprise of all.

"Hi!" said Ellery.

The Inspector was so surprised he was speechless. Ellery set his glass and notebook down and embraced them both with the ardor of the prodigal son who has no doubts about his reception. Then he held them at arm's length and went over them critically.

"Dad, you look awful. Jessie, you're a vision of bridesmanship. Where in God's name have you two been? I've written, I've cabled, I've phoned twice, without an answering peep. I had to fight not to call the Missing Persons Bureau. What did you do, go on a second honeymoon?"

"Son," Richard said, hanging onto Ellery's hand. "Son. When did you get home?"

"Three days ago. What's wrong?"

"Nothing," Jessie said softly, "now."

"Then something is wrong. Let me take your things, and then you two freshen up and tell me about it. I'll make some coffee."

"Not in my kitchen you won't," Jessie said. "I've already had that out with your father, Ellery. Bachelors never seem to want to give a woman her due."

"I'm a quick study." And Ellery kissed her and with a grin watched her march off, flustered, to the kitchen. "I don't know why you didn't marry that woman years ago, Dad."

"I didn't know her years ago," the Inspector said. "I wish I had."

"Then it's working out?"

"I've never been happier in my life."

"You don't look it."

"That has nothing to do with Jessie. Fact is, I don't know what I'd have done without her. Son, you're just what the doctor ordered. I'm sure glad you're home."

"You sound as if you've had a rough time."

His father made a face. "I wish I'd known you were back, Ellery. "I'd have called you in on it before I made a complete fool of myself."

"In on what, Dad? Let's have it."

But the Inspector waited until Jessie came back with the coffeepot. Only when she sat down beside Ellery on the sofa did he begin to patrol his most sacred precinct and let his son have it in every incredible and harrowing detail.

They were well into the small hours before he concluded. Jessie had supplied details he had forgotten, and between them they had excavated the case for Ellery in depth.

"And that's it?" Ellery said. He was pulling his nose, his invariable aid to cerebration.

"That's it, son. I was positive I had the answer. But with that alibi Fleck dredged up on Hugo, my whole case—gaflooey. Can you see where I went off? Where did I go wrong?"

Ellery answered with a question. He nodded at the answer, asked another question, rejected that answer, probed again, frowned, discarded again, reexamined in a different context, and frowned once more.

"Would you be a love and refuel the pot, Jessie?" he said at last. "I think this is going to take the rest of the night."

It was dawn before Ellery came to the end of his analysis. The Inspector kept shaking his head at his blindness. But he seemed at peace, even eager and that was what mattered to Jessie.

"It adds up, all right," the Inspector muttered. "But what I still don't get is *why*. What in the blue blazes was the motive behind it?"

Ellery smiled lopsidedly. "In Whozis's immortal words, I'm glad you asked that question. Dad, didn't you say the file on the Brass estate—all the estate papers—were commandeered by Chief Fleck?" His father nodded. "Then they must still be in Fleck's possession."

"What's the point, Ellery?"

"I want to look them over. As soon as possible."

"That's too soon," Jessie decided, rising. "Your father hasn't had a decent night's sleep, Ellery, in I don't know how long. And now he hasn't had any at all. Richard, you're going to bed this minute."

"No, hon, no! I couldn't sleep. I feel full of beans. Son." The Inspector was looking years younger. "How about we drive up to Phillipskill right away? Now?"

"Richard," Jessie wailed.

"Honey, I want to! I've got to get this thing off my back. Unless ... " He took her in his arms. "I'm sorry, Jessie. I forgot all about you. I guess I've still got a lot to learn about married life. You must be out on your feet. We'll put it off till you've had some rest."

"Me? I'm not a bit tired," Jessie said quickly. God in His mercy gave us the gift of lying, she thought, when He gave us the gift of love.

"Why don't you go to bed, while Ellery and I—?"

"Richard Queen, are you trying to get rid of me?"

"That'll be the day!"

"Then we'll all go. Together, like a family should. Oh, dear! I forgot I've inherited a writer for a son. *As* a family should. It's those darn TV commercials."

"Jessie," Ellery said solemnly, "I love you. Go get your face on."

So they piled into Jessie's Mustang, and Ellery drove them back up into Washington Irving country. They crossed the Sleepy Hollow bridge; passed a crooked and crumbling mile-post whose inscription, *Phillipsk ... 2 mi,* was just legible; passed the Old River Inn and the by-road that led off to The House of Brass; and so on into the village of Phillipskill, which after a hundred-year effort to obliterate three hundred years of American history, seemed on the brink of succeeding ... stone houses built by the patroons, which had sheltered the patriot warriors of the Revolution, now ravished by pizza parlors, hamburger heavens, Real Kentucky Frankforts stands, Bar-B-Q bars, loan-shark cubbies, real estate offices, saloons-turned-grills—all in a forestry of neon signs; or casually erased by parking lots and stucco false fronts from which was hawked the garbage of the glorious present.

The police station and lockup were housed in a still inviolate early 18th Century building of Dutch brick and field-stone. As Ellery pulled the Mustang up at a POSITIVELY NO PARKING AT ANY TIME sign, the Inspector said, "There he is now," and Ellery saw a red-faced, overfed man in a blue uniform, wearing a gold-braided cap, just getting out of a police car drawn up before the building. "That's Fleck."

"You give it to him good, Ellery," Jessie said with undeniable vindictiveness. "I'll *never* forgive him for the way he talked to your father!"

150

Ellery got out of the Mustang. Chief Fleck had stopped to glare at him.

"Didn't you see that No Parking sign, mister? Let me have your driver's license!"

Ellery said, "Yes, sir," and produced it.

"Ellery Queen ... Ellery *Queen*?" The cigar sagged in the chief's mouth; he had spotted the Inspector and Jessie in the red car. "What the devil you two doing back here?" You just left!"

Richard helped his wife to the sidewalk, grinning. "You know how it is with bad pennies, Chief. This is my son. Just back from Europe, and I've told him all about the Brass case. First thing he said to me was, 'Dad, let's go up to Phillipskill and straighten Chief Fleck out.' "

"Again?" Fleck growled.

"For positively the last time," Ellery smiled. "Chief, I have to talk to you. But first I'd like to see the executor's portfolio with the Brass estate papers in it that I understand you confiscated. Do you mind?"

"Are you the Ellery Queen who ... ?"

"Well," Ellery said. "I don't know of another."

"Well," Chief Fleck said, taking a grip on his cigar. "Pleased to meet you."

"Thank you."

"Don't see why I can't stretch a point and let you have a look, Mr. Queen. Come on in. Oh, excuse me, Mrs. Queen." And he held the door open for her with the gallantry of a Raleigh. Jessie went past him like a lady, not scratching his eyes out. The Inspector strangled a chuckle. Fleck had not forgiven *him*. He was the last one in.

The chief dug the Brass estate file out of his office safe, which looked as if it had come out of New Haven under the personal eye of Elihu Yale, and Ellery seized the bulging portfolio and sat down at Fleck's desk and with maddening deliberation began to go through it. He went through it one item at a time, rubbing each paper between thumb and forefinger as if to make sure he was not bypassing any. This went on for a good ten minutes, while the portly chief looked increasingly less hopeful and cordial.

"I don't see what you expect to find in those," he grumbled as Ellery tackled a sheaf of papers clipped together. "They're all tax bills."

"Not all," Ellery murmured, yanking a paper deftly out of the sheaf without unclipping it, "not all, Chief. Though I don't doubt that's what you were supposed to think. Did you go through these? I mean really go through them?"

"Sure. Well, I flipped through—"

151

"As anyone would who wasn't looking for something specific. Here you are, Dad. The motive."

The Inspector and Jessie and Chief Fleck craned over Ellery's shoulders.

The Inspector said with awe, "I'll be damned."

That should have been the end of it; Ellery being Ellery, it was not.

Several days passed, during which Richard's beloved stayed home putting the Jessie Sherwood Queen stamp on the Queen stamping grounds—"I'm one of those rare nurses," she confided to her stepson, "who can't abide living in a disorderly house" (a remark that made him kiss her again for her lovely innocence)—while the Inspector and Ellery were off on mysterious business. Then one morning the Inspector consulted the yellow pages, tracked down a number, and dialed.

"Vaughn Detective Agency," said a too, too familiar voice.

Even though he had initiated the call, the Inspector stiffened. The man sneered even when he answered what might have been a client. "This is Richard Queen."

"Heigh-ho, pops," Vaughn said. "I thought you'd crept back into your hole with that old broad of yours. What's on your so-called mind?"

"Listen, Vaughn," the Inspector snapped, "I don't like you for hash, and I wish to hell I didn't have to call you. But you're still the legal executor of the Brass estate, and I have no choice. Do you want to get in on this, or don't you?"

"In on what?"

"There's something new in the Brass case."

"You're a born loser, pops, you know it?" Vaughn chuckled. "What is it this time? Some more brass in the sky?"

"We found a note Hugo Zarbus left that tells where he hid the fortune. Or rather my son Ellery found it—he just got back from abroad and when I told him the story he headed straight for that paper as if he'd stashed it away himself."

"You're turned on!"

"Okay, Vaughn. Nice talking to you."

"Hold it! I've got to wrap up that estate. Where did you say this genius of yours found the note?"

"I didn't say," the Inspector said dryly. "We're on our way up to Phillipskill to check out Hugo's information. You want to find out you can meet us there—personally, if I never laid eyes on you again I'd live ten years longer."

"Is it in gold?"

152

"No, it's not in gold. That's what fooled us. Look, I want to get this over with."

"You're still batting zero zero zero," Vaughn laughed. "Okay, pops, I'll be seeing you."

The Austin-Healy was parked in the dried-up mud of the debricked driveway when they pulled in. Vaughn was leaning against the hood smoking a deformed black stogie. He narrow-eyed Ellery as the Queens got out of the Mustang.

"So you're Elmer," he said.

"Ellery," Ellery said.

They looked each other over like two dogs.

"You don't look like such-a-much," Vaughn said at last.

"You do," Ellery said pleasantly. "You positively glister."

"I what?" Vaughn stared. "Say, are you for real?"

"Try me," Ellery said, waited, was not challenged, and stepped into Hendrik Brass's house. The Inspector, grinning, followed on his heels. Vaughn frowned, tossed his stogie away, and hurried after them.

Ellery was standing in the foyer, looking around at the ruins.

"I want to see that note of Hugo's," Vaughn said.

"Why?" Ellery said.

"Why? Because it's probably a phoney."

"If it is, we'll soon find out. Either there's a brass box where the note says it is, or there isn't. Right now it's the box that counts, not the note."

"It's in a box?" Vaughn muttered. "That must mean treasury notes, securities, maybe jewelry!" He rubbed his hands. "That's more like it. Let's go, Elmer. Where is it?"

The Queens started upstairs, crowded by Vaughn.

"In Hugo's room," the Inspector said.

"What kind of crud you handing me? Why, Hugo's room was searched a skillion times, along with the rest of this crummy pad!"

The Inspector shrugged without turning around. "That's where the note says it is."

"Then it is a phoney," Vaughn said as they reached the landing and the Inspector turned left, leading the way. "It can't be in the ape's room."

"Yes, it can," Ellery said.

"How? Where does the note say it is?"

"In his mattress," the Inspector said.

"Oh, come on, pops. You searched that mattress yourself."

"I know I did," the Inspector said unhappily. "So did a lot of others, Vaughn, including you." He had paused in the doorway to Hugo's bedroom, a tiny box of a place, high in the house, under the eaves. It was hot and full of bugs

153

streaming in through the open window and denuded of everything but the screwed down brass bed with its lumpy old
torn-up mattress, and a huge built-in wardrobe closet of
fumed oak that covered half a wall, its doors slightly ajar and
groaning a little in the breeze coming fitfully through the
window. Beyond they could see the Hudson and smell its
swampy tang. "But my son here has an explanation."

"The search went from room to room, as I understand it,"
Ellery said. "It was broken up by meals, sleeping periods, and
other interruptions. All Hugo had to do was keep one step
ahead of you, Vaughn. When he knew you were all heading
for his room, he took the box out of the mattress and hid it
somewhere else, probably in a room you had just searched.
When you were through searching his room he took the first
opportunity to retrieve the box and put it back in his mattress. During a second search, or a third, or a tenth, he
simply repeated the dodge. I'm amazed none of you thought
of it."

Vaughn's mouth was open. The Inspector was shaking his
head.

"Well, what are we waiting for?" Vaughn cried.

But Ellery gripped his arm. Vaughn looked down, surprised. "I think," Ellery said, "we'd best let my father do it."

The Inspector's footsteps crunched across the plaster dust
on the chestnut floor. The old random boards, which had
been loosely replaced by Trafuzzi's house wreckers, gave
under his weight here and there, making the journey haz-
ardous. But he paid no attention; he was intent on the bed
and its ripped mattress; and so were the two onlookers in the
doorway.

Richard Queen stooped and felt all over the mattress.

Suddenly his hands stopped.

"By God," he said; and plunged them into the mattress's
vitals and, with effort, brought them out, dragging a sizable
flat brass box. He set it down on the bed and stared at it as if
he could not believe his eyes. Ellery ran over and examined it
quickly. It was chased all over with the familiar scrollwork of
the House of Brass, and it was locked with a brass lock.

"This lock shouldn't give us any trouble," Ellery said. "Is
there a tool somewhere we can use as a pry?"

"Don't bother, Elmer," said Vaughn; and the Queens
swung about to find Vaughn with a .38 revolver in his hand
which was pointed at the Inspector's belly. The man's face
was a cartoon in voracity and brute triumph. "Get over near
the window. *Move.*"

Father and son communicated with each other in silence
and, as one, obeyed. Vaughn went over to the bed, treading

carefully, not taking his eyes from them. He had some trouble picking up the box with one hand. But he managed it, and tucked it under his arm, and laughed.

"With all this weight it's got to be mostly jewelry," he said. "Maybe I'll be lucky and find some cash, too. With ice you always take a beating from the fence. Six million bucks' worth! Don't you wish you could live long enough to see it?"

Ellery said, "You're going to kill us?"

"Sorry, pal."

"Hold the execution," Ellery said. "As long as we won't be around to testify against you, Vaughn, you haven't anything to lose. You murdered Hendrik Brass, didn't you?"

Vaughn laughed again. "I knocked the old bastard off, sure. Why not? Fourteen-plus percent of six million is still a lot of bread. Only now, Elmer, thanks to you, I get to keep the whole *shtik*. My big problem is how to get rid of the corpuses. Probably sink you both in the Hudson."

"You have a bigger problem than that," Ellery said in a conversational tone. "I think, Chief, you and your man can come out now."

Vaughn spun. The doors of the wardrobe closet had been flung wide, and from the closet stepped Chief Fleck and his man Lew with Police Positives leveled.

"Drop the gun, Vaughn," Fleck said; and as he said it Vaughn's forefinger jerked on the trigger of his .38 and three shots deafened the Queens. Vaughn's bullet clipped a chunk of oak out of the top panel of the closet; Fleck's and Lew's tore two holes in Vaughn's heart. He flipped over backward like a trained dog, struck the far wall, and thudded to the floor to lie there in crumpled isolation, half on his back, wounds spurting. After a while they stopped spurting and began to ooze. And some time after that the oozing stopped, too.

Lew came over in the ear-splitting silence, pursed his lips, widened his cross eyes, and dropped Hugo's mattress over the body.

Ellery picked up the brass box. It had been flung clear of the blood.

"You heard his confession, Chief?" the Inspector said.

"Every word." Fleck wiped his streaming face. "You know, I never fired this gun at anybody before? It's a funny feeling. . . . Lew took it down word for word. . . . Vaughn." The chief stared down at the mattress and shook his head; he seemed shaken to the giblets. He's not thinking of the reporters now, the Inspector thought, but give him time, give him time.

"I agreed with Dad's reasoning up to a point," Ellery said. "He was right in deducing that the first attempt on Brass's life—the unsuccessful one, with the poker—since it occurred before Brass made out his will, must have been made by a non-heir, which could only mean Hugo; and for the reason Dad gave—sheer hate. Where you went off, Dad, was in assuming that, because Hugo attacked Brass the first time, he must also have attacked him the second time. Hugo didn't kill Brass, as you found out when Chief Fleck came up with Hugo's alibi. Since Hugo couldn't have made that second, successful attempt, who could have?"

They were gathered in a private dining room at the Old River Inn—the three Queens, the five Irregulars, and Chief Fleck and his man Lew, who was taking notes and whose surname they never learned. They were guests of Fleck, who had of course recovered from the shock of the shooting and was preparing for the press conference he had already scheduled for the following morning.

"But how did you know it was Vaughn, Mr. Queen?" the chief asked anxiously. "Lew, be sure and get this down."

"With Hugo eliminated as the stabber of Brass," Ellery said, "the whole picture changes. Here's how it must have gone: Hugo takes a night off, goes to the tavern, pretends to get loaded on beer, and is kicked out around midnight. He immediately goes home on his Honda to try to kill Brass—his second try. This time he has to contend with Vaughn, who's sleeping on a cot before the old man's door. Vaughn proves no problem. Hugo used the brass letterknife from the desk downstairs to stab the sleeping beauty in the back. But he *didn't* go into the old man's bedroom and stab him, too—we know he didn't, because Brass was murdered between four and six A.M., and during those two hours, and for a considerable period before and after, Hugo was locked up in one of Chief Fleck's cells. So obviously, after stabbing Vaughn, Hugo must have got cold feet, lost his nerve; and he went back to the tavern and this time got really loaded, to land in jail.

"That leaves Vaughn alone outside Brass's bedroom with the knife in his back.

"Now a knife in the back," Ellery said, "sounds like a serious, quite incapacitating wound, and ninety-nine times out of a hundred it is. But was it in Vaughn's case? No. When Dad found him in the morning he was a very lively casualty. He was conscious. He was able to sit up in short order. In fact, he was on his feet and was his old self in a wonderfully short time. In other words, his wound was superficial.

"Which makes it possible for Vaughn to have come to

around, say, four A.M. and crawl off his cot. What would he do? Realizing he had been attacked, which could only have been to get Brass's bodyguard out of the way, he would naturally go into the bedroom to see if the old man had been attacked, too. But no, old Brass was asleep, untouched, quite alive. And in a flash Vaughn saw that, through sheer luck, he had been handed a perfect setup for murder. From the position of the stab wound in his own back, it could not possibly have been self-inflicted. If he killed old Brass with the same knife and then went back to his cot and pretended to pass out, who would connect him with the old man's murder? Dad and Fleck would have to think that Vaughn and Brass had been attacked by a third person.

"So that's just what Vaughn did, and that's just what you thought, Dad, when you found him out in the hall in the morning, and Brass in the bedroom with the knife in his heart."

"But why?" Johnny Kripps demanded. "Why kill the old man at all, Ellery? That's what I can't dope. What did Vaughn hope to get out of it?"

"Obviously, Johnny, he must have hoped to get a great deal out of it," Ellery said. "And the only thing of value connected with Hendrik Brass was the six million dollars he kept dangling in front of his heirs' noses. So *Vaughn must have had a legitimate claim on that fortune.* That's what sent me looking for documentary evidence in the estate records. And when I found the evidence—a notarized statement by one Harding Boyle that he was the Harding Boyle named in Brass's will as one of the heirs, with the claim certified by Vaughn J. Vaughn as executor of the estate—I had the indisputable confirmation of Vaughn's stake in the crime and his guilt."

"Boyle," Chief Fleck mumbled. "The heir that never showed up. ... You mean, Mr. Queen, Vaughn had some kind of a hold on this Boyle?"

"It seemed likelier to me, Chief," Ellery said gently, "that Vaughn *was* Boyle, as Dad's confirmed in the last few days by digging into Vaughn's past."

"Hugh Giffin here did the actual digging," the Inspector said. "Tell 'em, Hughie."

"Harding Boyle—they used to call him 'Hard' Boyle—was Vaughn's real handle," Giffin said. "He was a Chicago slum kid who got into all kinds of trouble—did time on A.D.W. raps, mugging, stuff like that; the law degree he claimed to have, by the way, was a lot of hooey, because the only law he knew was what he picked up in the Joliet library during a stretch there—and took the name Vaughn to shake his past. He'd never got a detective agency license otherwise."

"Let me get this straight now," Phillipskill's police chief said. "He was one of Brass's bastards, too, right? Hated the old man's guts, right?"

"I'm sure he did," Ellery said, "although in Vaughn's kind of rat race revenge would run a poor second to six million dollars as a payoff."

"Put that down, Lew!"

"If Vaughn was Boyle," Al Murphy objected, "how come he didn't identify himself as Boyle? Hell, he was actually named in the will. Why didn't he do it all open and above-board?"

"As Boyle, there was a warrant out for his arrest in Illinois," the Inspector said. "He played it safe, Al. He hid under the Vaughn alias while the six million was being hunted for. If it was never found, he hadn't broken his cover. If it was, he could take it from there. Remember, he protected himself by stashing that sworn statement among the estate papers, certifying—as Vaughn the executor—that he, Boyle, had presented himself and been duly identified as a legal heir."

"And that's another thing," Pete Angelo said. "Why be dumb and leave that paper in the portfolio? Granted he hid it among some bills, where he figured it wouldn't be found easy. But why do it at all? You say protection. That was damn dangerous protection."

"As it turned out," Ellery said, "it most certainly was. But he had to cover himself, Pete, if the fortune was ever found. It was a risk he simply had to take. Remember, he couldn't know that Chief Fleck would take the portfolio away from him. That was a smart move, Chief."

Fleck beamed. "I figured it might be." His man Lew looked at him, then bent back to his notes. Fleck coughed and downed the rest of the New York State champagne in his glass.

"There's still one thing I don't understand." Jessie said apologetically. "All right, Vaughn was Harding Boyle, one of the heirs. How on earth did he also turn out to be the 'lawyer'-bodyguard-executor that Mr. Brass hired? Wasn't that a whopping coincidence, Ellery?"

"It wasn't a coincidence at all, dear heart," Ellery said. "Brass didn't seek Vaughn out—it was the other way round. Vaughn either knew or learned that Brass was his hit-and-run father, did some research on him—the newspaper morgues are full of yarns about the Brasses—and made a deliberate play for the job. It wasn't hard for him to weasel his way

158

into the old man's confidence, with his private detective agency credentials, his fake legal background, his fast talk, and his willingness to work for Brass at a low fee.

"He could be sure of at least a seventh of the six million—he really believed there was six million dollars in the pot; that old dingleberry took Vaughn in as well as the rest of you—but I don't doubt he kept his eye peeled for a chance to find the whole bundle and somehow manage to keep it all for himself. In fact, that's what I counted on when I set up the trap. There was no note from Hugo, of course, and no fortune, but I figured that Vaughn, who'd killed for it, would snap at any bait that might land him the prize he'd given up for lost; and that's how it worked out, with Chief Fleck's cooperation. Well, Chief, I think you've got all you need. Thanks for the dinner. We'll be heading back to town."

But it was Chief Fleck and Lew who left first, Fleck's belly jiggling as he hurried out, blue sleeve unconsciously wiping the visor of his cap as if getting it spit-and-polished for his consummate appointment with the gentlemen of the press.

"Oh, Dad, one thing before we go." Ellery reached under the table and with considerable difficulty brought forth the brass box he and the Inspector had planted in Hugo Zarbus's mattress to tempt the heart and force the hand of Vaughn J. Vaughn. "To be placed," Ellery said with a grin, "among your souvenirs."

The Inspector looked down at it without happiness.

"What did you and Ellery put in it, Richard?" Jessie asked hastily.

The lock had been removed, and Richard smiled suddenly and raised the lid.

Glowing up at Jessie was a treasure of recently polished metal—bolts; nuts; pipe fittings; ashtrays; some bullet molds; a time-pitted pestle; three wick trimmers; seven trays of broken jewelers' scales (where was the eighth?); several bent-out-of-shape hose nozzles; a beaten wall-plaque portrait in relief of John C. Calhoun; a scattering of paper clips; a guttering trowel circa 1850 and a five-inch Trylon-and-Perisphere circa 1939; a Union Army bugle with the bell hacked off; a collection of drawer pulls, various; and one snapped-off spring of a mousetrap.

And all of brass.